The
PRODIGAL
TROLL

The
PRODIGAL TROLL

CHARLES COLEMAN FINLAY

an imprint of Prometheus Books
Amherst, NY

Published 2005 by PYR™, an imprint of Prometheus Books

Inquiries should be addressed to
PYR
59 John Glenn Drive
Amherst, New York 14228–2197
VOICE: 716–691–0133, ext. 207
FAX: 716–564–2711
WWW.PYRSF.COM

09 08 07 06 05   5 4 3 2 1

Library of Congress Cataloging-in-Publication Data

Finlay, Charles Coleman.
  The prodigal troll / by Charles Coleman Finlay.
    p. cm.
  ISBN 1–59102–313–0 (hardcover : alk. paper)
  ISBN 1–59102–332–7 (paperback : alk. paper)
  1. Trolls—Fiction. 2. Children—Fiction. I. Title.

PS3606.I553P76 2005
811'.6—dc22

2005005101

Printed in Canada on acid-free paper

For *Cole* and *Fin*,
my own two little trolls.

⇥ THE ⇤
MAN WHO
WALKED AWAY

ran entered the great hall still wearing the stolen wolf costume, battered mask tucked beneath his arm. The curtains were thrust aside from the tall windows, which were open to the last half-hearted revelry of the party outside and the first finger-poking light of dawn.

He dropped the mask on the long table in the center of the hall. A servant set a chalice down and poured chilled wine into it. Bran reached for it without thinking and winced. The first knuckles had been cut from the thumb and forefinger of his sword hand. The fight outside had torn the new calluses. Nor had the nails pulled from his other fingers healed yet as well as he had thought.

Lifting the cup with his left hand, he paused to inhale the sweet fragrance of plums. Then he pressed the cool metal to his bruised forehead.

Ah. Relief.

The relief was short-lived. His lord, still attired in an extravagant lion's costume of gold armor and emerald silk, stepped out of the shadows and paced around the table until he came to rest directly behind Bran's shoulder. The weight of the golden mask pressed on his back.

"Who was he?"

Bran twitched as the deep voice filled the empty room. *Who was he?* Who was the dark-haired man, the giant who had come down out of the mountains and into the castle in disguise with Bran? "I don't know," he replied. "I tell you three times, I truly don't know."

"But he saved your life twice, first from the guards and then a second time by trading his life for yours."

Was he reminding Bran that he might change his mind and not spare Bran's life after all? "That wasn't even the first time. The first time he saved my life, I was a prisoner of the mountain peasants, tied to a stake in a bonfire pile."

That was the night he'd lost his fingers and nails, the night he'd lost all hope, until the stranger appeared. He lowered the cup to his mouth. Swallowed in a single long gulp, the wine was too sweet and too strong, though it brought him a different kind of relief. He thrust out the cup for more wine, but the servant did not refill it.

"So he thought he could do that and just walk away?"

"You saw him," Bran said.

"I did. And that is why you are standing here speaking to me now. Wine."

The servant glided over silently to refill Bran's cup. His head still throbbed—his whole body ached, exhausted by the ordeal of the past few days. He took a small sip. The footsteps around the table were light and deliberate for such a large man wearing over one hundred pounds of costume. Bran lowered the cup and stared into inscrutable eyes peering from a stylized mask, carved from gold and framed by two huge ivory teeth taken from the jaw of a dagger-toothed lion.

"So you know nothing about this man? Nothing of his home, his mother, his obligations?"

"No more than he gave in answer to you," Bran replied.

"Yes, but those answers were mocking."

Bran was not so sure. "Perhaps. He did not speak our language when I first met him, but even after he learned it, he did not explain much."

"How do *you* explain *him?*"

"I do not know," Bran said. "I do not know how to explain him. He went where he wanted, and did what he chose."

"Did he name himself?" Fingers drummed on the table, a deliberate act, signalling impatience.

Bran considered carefully before answering. A man's name was one of the few things he owned, and was his alone to give. But did it matter what he said now? It mattered very much to the man who stood beside him.

"He told me that his name was Claye," he answered at last.

Outside, cheers greeted the sunrise. Light poured into the room, illuminating the shabby, empty-eyed mess of his wolf's mask. Soon, the revelers would begin to make their ways home. Bran already knew that he would not join them. He did not expect to leave the confines of the castle for a very long time.

"Did the name mean anything to him?" The voice was hard now, dangerous, as it had been outside a short time before.

"No."

"That," said the man behind the mask, "explains even less. I have no idea why he chose what he chose."

He lifted one finger casually, and the servant brought him a cup of wine. Perhaps, thought Bran, his head also ached. And he wondered if he should mention the stranger's other name, the difficult one he had given first.

Part 1

A Child in a Basket by the Water's Edge

↠ CHAPTER 1 ↞

Three of them crowded into a corridor* so dark they could barely see where they were going. While Yvon double-checked the rope's knot with his fingers, the nursemaid rocked the drugged infant in her arms, murmuring, "Oh, Claye. My poor baby, my poor, poor baby."

Yvon tugged on the rope to make sure it held fast to the post. Picking up the coiled end, he stepped carefully around woman and child. "Beg your pardon, m'lady Xaragitte."

She cooed to the child, ignoring him.

When he entered the garderobe, a breeze through the seat hole carried with it the stench of waste. He dropped the rope, found the stone slab by touch, and tried unsuccessfully to shove it aside. The siege-enforced fast had weakened him.

"Need a hand?" asked a breathless, high-pitched voice.

Yvon turned his head toward the doorway. A handheld taper illuminated the rounded features of Kepit, Lord Gruethrist's eunuch steward.

"No, ma'am," Yvon said politely. "I can do it."

Gritting his teeth, he shouldered the slab a second time. Stone scraped on stone as it moved aside. He dropped the length of rope through the hole and peered after it. Out of darkness into darkness—that was the way of life, was it not?

He looked up in time to see the eunuch touch three fingers to forehead, chin, and chest, while muttering the names of two gods. "If you survive," Kepit said, "and someday decide to take the dress, our lady will see that you receive my property."

Yvon appreciated the honor, but he did this for other reasons than the comforts of status or property. He glanced at Xaragitte's shape behind the eunuch. "When I tug on the rope, it's safe. Understand?"

The eunuch nodded.

Gripping the rope, Yvon lowered himself into the hole. Lean as he was, he found it a tight squeeze. He emerged from the bottom of the garderobe and braced his feet against the stone. He glanced over his shoulder and saw no sign of the besiegers. Then he craned his neck the other way to see the reason why.

The far end of the castle burned, lion-tongued flames licking the sky. The oak beams of the great hall's roof turned to leaves of black ash, a roiling forest of smoke that obscured the stars. The besiegers had abandoned their posts and crowded around the front gate gaping at the conflagration like moths lured to a candle—just as Lord Gruethrist had predicted they would before he took several skins of oil and climbed high into the rafters to set ablaze the castle that he'd built.

Yvon descended quickly to the small mound ringed by dirty water. He tugged on the rope, and it disappeared above him. He squinted his eyes against the stinging haze and held his breath against the stink of raw sewage.

One man, alone, in the dark, on an island of shit: as a general description it fit every bad moment in Yvon's life, but for the first time it was wholly true.

The sloping mound of old excrement and refuse under his feet was held together by a collection of vines more deeply rooted and intransigent than the mountain peasants. A few bushes grew among the weeds, including an early-blooming crackleberry shrub filled with tiny fruit.

Yvon's siege-hungry stomach rumbled.

Still no movement among the shadows across the moat. His hands did a quick inventory, touching the small knife in his boot, the dagger at his belt, the short sword concealed under his cloak. Fingers brushed the nape of his neck, freshly shorn of its braid. Without it, he had no proof that he was a knight and no right to carry a sword.

A muffled groan sounded above him. Broad feet kicked in the small square hole. Xaragitte was the only person allotted full rations during the siege: she was stuck.

He aged another year with every heartbeat that he waited. At this rate, he would shrivel up like an old man, die, feed the maggots, and become scattered bones before she touched the ground. Feeling like half a skeleton with hunger, he grabbed a handful of the green crackleberries and shoved them in his mouth. They were so bitterly unripe they set his teeth on edge. His stomach knotted, half in satisfaction, half in protest. He gathered another handful and swallowed them without chewing.

Her feet withdrew, then appeared again a second later. Her pale, lovely legs wiggled and kicked until her plump bottom popped free. She dropped suddenly and Yvon braced to catch her, but then the rope jerked short. She tried to smooth her skirt over her knees. The effort set her spinning.

"Don't brush against the filthy stone," he whispered.

She did, despite his warning. The rope slipped, and she made a second abrupt descent. He wrapped his arms around her, breaking the fall. Her soft flesh pressed against him, hurting like an unexpected wound.

He set her down at once and fumbled at the knot in the rope about her waist. "Watch your step, m'lady."

"Don't act like I'm highborn, too fine to get my hands dirty." She smeared her palms clean on her skirts. "I've wiped worse off baby bottoms."

Where—? "Where's the baby?"

She looked up. "We couldn't both fit through."

Another delay! Yvon heard voices on the far side of the castle, mixed with the crackle of the fire. He yanked on the rope as soon as it came loose. It vanished into the hole like a demon sliding under water.

Xaragitte stared up, waiting; Yvon stared at her. She had rare red hair like the goddess Bwnte. Her lover had been a common soldier named Kady, who'd died fighting the Baron's men before the siege started and just after their baby daughter's death from the coughing sickness. Yvon couldn't express his interest in her, not politely. But if only he could spend time with her, he could make his feelings clear. Sure, he was two decades older than her, but Lord Gruethrist was that much older than his new lady, the baby's mother, and they got on well. Yvon would point that out to her. It could work. It'd better. He risked not just his life but everything he'd earned in his life for the chance.

The rope reappeared above them, tied to a basket.

A bell tolled.

Xaragitte dug her fingers into the hard flesh of Yvon's forearm. "They've found us!"

"No," he said, glad she hadn't noticed him jump. "It's for the fire. It's good—if any of the Baron's soldiers are somehow so blind they've overlooked that towering column of flame, they'll hear the bell and go investigate."

If they were somehow both blind and deaf then he would have no problem killing them, even weak from lack of food.

He stretched his hands above his head to catch the basket.

"Be careful," Xaragitte cautioned.

"Oh, I will." He caught and lowered it, peering inside. "He's a very dangerous baby."

She didn't laugh at his joke, but maybe the barb bit too close to the bone of truth. Lord Gruethrist's sudden marriage to Lady Ambit's daughter, the birth of Claye, and Claye's immediate betrothal to Lady Eleuate's infant daughter united all three ruling families in this border province. With Lady Gruethrist childless, Lady Ambit's daughter had been named heir to the Gruethrist title and lands, and would eventually inherit her mother's title and domain as well. The betrothal would give everything to Eleuate's daughter, Portia. The families had counted on inaction from the aged, inattentive Baron Culufre to get away with their grab at united power. But the old Baron had died and been replaced by some young man the Empress favored more. His army had marched on Castle Gruethrist, besieging it. So in a way the siege was the fault of this child.

The baby flipped over, wrinkling his face. He was nine months old, long-limbed but pudgy, with thick blue-black hair. Xaragitte lifted him from the basket and placed him in the sling across her shoulder. "Hush now, darling, you're safe."

Not hardly, Yvon thought. He drew his dagger—hard steel in his hand calmed him—and sawed through the rope. He jerked on it, but nothing happened. He looked up and saw a dark, lumpy shape fall out of the garderobe's opening.

"Crap!"

It was the bag containing supplies for their journey—Yvon batted it away from the nursemaid and cursed the eunuch.

"The poison was already taking effect when Kepit let me down the rope," Xaragitte whispered. Above them, the stone slab slid back into place with a solid thunk.

Yvon picked up the bag and bit back another sharp remark. If they escaped, only Lord Gruethrist himself would know what had truly happened. Even Lady Gruethrist would be told that the child and his nursemaid perished in the fire. The poison Kepit had taken protected their secret. It also prevented the stripping of her dress and the painful execution that awaited her at the Baron's hand when the castle surrendered—eunuchs were assigned by the Empress and were supposed to serve Her first.

Yvon waded into the water's edge and flung the bag to the other side of the moat. "It's too deep for you to cross, m'lady. Best if I carry you."

"I can do it," she said firmly.

He scooped a couple handfuls of the compost into the basket and sank it in the water. "Your skirt'll be mighty heavy if it's wet and we've leagues to go."

She took a step toward the water.

"Hold on tight," he said, lifting her before she could protest. He stepped into the cold water, the surface of it as black as the sky, scattered with clouds of slime. Yvon selected his footing carefully. The Baron's army had been slowly filling the moat with trash and dirt. Now it worked to Yvon's advantage. At the deepest point, the water only reached his waist, and with some strain he held the woman and child clear of the foul liquid. Xaragitte wrapped one arm around his neck, pulling tight and pressing her bosom to his cheek. He concentrated on his next step, aware how easily he might slip. "I was born a commoner, like you," he said without explanation.

"His Lordship told me," she answered equally quick.

"Ah." So she'd made inquiries to the lord about him. Women often did that before pursuing a formal relationship.

"I didn't expect . . ." she began.

"What?"

"M'lady Gruethrist said you were dangerous."

"I am," he said. "To her enemies, and to yours."

He staggered up the bank, setting her down and scanning the shadows for the Baron's soldiers. The constant knell of the temple bell filled the air with noise as thick as smoke.

"He's waking," she said. The baby slurped on the side of his thumb. "We should have given him a stronger draught."

If he cried and brought the Baron's men on them—"Just keep him quiet a few more moments. We're going to walk past those houses, then out across the fields."

His feet squished in his boots as he went ahead to see the way clear. He hadn't taken five strides from the water's edge before the temple bell rang again, much louder than before and lower pitched. The sound was so loud, so sharp, that Yvon stood rooted, unable to move. His bones vibrated like harpstrings, if harpstrings were as long as rivers—his very marrow twanged. By the time he drew breath to protest, his muscles dissolved like meat sliding off bones in a boiling pot, his internal organs melted into a single mass of jelly, invisible red-hot pokers were shoved into his ears, and needles pierced his eyes, while his teeth rattled around loose in his jaw like dice in a gaming cup. Or so it felt. He hurt.

Which is when he realized that it wasn't the temple bell at all. It was magic.

The Baron's wizard had placed a bell ward over the castle, and Yvon'd just hit it like a hammer. His respect for and fear of the Baron increased instantly. He'd seen bell wards set over rooms before, in the Imperial City, and once over a minor palace, after the riots, to hold someone too important to kill, but nothing big enough to ensconce an entire castle.

Reaching his numb fingers inside his shirt collar, Yvon sorted the glass charms hung on silver chains around his throat. He nearly grabbed and broke the hammer charm, which would have put a dent in the Baron's bell but kept it ringing until the gods died. When he found the flame charm, he held it before him and shattered the ampule in his fingers.

Blue fire sprouted in the air and the bell stopped ringing. The pain that gripped Yvon burned suddenly away, though the effects of it lingered.

Wherever the Baron's wizard kept his model of the castle, it and the bell atop it had just gone up in flames. Much like the real castle, probably. Yvon hoped that the Baron was standing close enough to the model to be singed by the heat.

Xaragitte tapped him on the shoulder. "D'oo'eer'at?"

"What?" A ringing in his ears muffled her voice. When she repeated herself, he watched her lips.

"Did you hear that?"

"Yes!" He shouted even though he didn't mean to, his own voice sounded so faint. "I hope no one realizes what it was yet. We must hasten. The Baron's wizard will know that someone has escaped the castle."

The noise had woken Claye despite the sleeping potion. He pulled at his lip with little fingers and his mouth was open, though Yvon didn't hear any crying. It was hard to hear anything but the ringing in his ears. At least the size of the spell stretched it thin. Xaragitte and the baby appeared to have been safe outside the nimbus when he set it off. If he felt this sick, it might have crippled them.

He turned and led them beside the three houses that comprised the whole street. The camp of tents lay just beyond. Something wet dribbled down the back of his leg when he paused. Just as he prepared to run across the open ground past the tents, Xaragitte clutched his arm. He whipped around.

Someone approached from beyond the houses. Darkness obscured his features, but the size and posture belonged to a soldier.

"Stay behind me, stay back," Yvon told Xaragitte.

The man approached them, resting one hand on the pommel of his sword. Not a soldier then, but a knight. A young one, a puppy, without much tail, Yvon saw when he came close. But it wouldn't do to take him lightly. Some puppies bit hard, and this one was big.

"Why didn't you stop when I commanded?" the knight asked.

"Eh?" Yvon ducked his head, like a good, subservient commoner and twirled his little finger in his ear, acting deaf. Not that he needed to act much. "I didn't hear you."

"Why didn't you stop?"

The most believable lie began with an obvious truth. "Because we're leaving the village," Yvon said.

"So you're not loyal to the Baron?" It was an accusation, but an uncertain one. The puppy loosened his sword in its scabbard.

"Of course I'm loyal to the Baron." Yvon jerked his head in the direction of the fiery castle. "But those sparks are going to fall on some roofs soon, and the whole village'll be aflame. You won't catch us in that fire!"

He had a hand on his dagger, ready to grab and stab the knight, but the castle roof caved in, a great crash followed by an upward rush of sparks and ash. They all three jumped, and Yvon missed his chance.

The knight pointed them in the direction of a campfire. "Huh! You may be right. Just come over here first so I can get a better look at both of you."

"Glad to," Yvon said, though it was the last thing he wanted. If his wet pants were noticed, the ruse was up. The damn puppy never turned his back or let down his guard. Fortunately there were no other soldiers around the campfire.

The young knight peered at Yvon's face in the flickering campfire light. "I don't recognize you from the work details. Who'll vouch for you?"

"The temple priestess knows me, she does. She'll be happy to vouch for old Bors," he said, picking a random name. The priestess was the best reference he could give. She'd welcomed Baron Culufre's men and rendered them all kinds of assistance.

The knight indicated Xaragitte. "And who's she?"

"My daughter. Who'd you think she was?"

"I don't like your tone. Or your manners. Grandpa."

"M'lord." The word grated on Yvon's tongue.

"That's better. Let's have a look at her. Sorry, m'lady, but you don't want to go out into the—hey, what's this? You didn't mention any baby."

"What's to mention?" Yvon shouted. "The babe's right in front of your eyes. A fine little girl to carry on her mother's name."

Yvon glanced at Xaragitte, who wrapped her arms protectively around the child. Something in her anxiousness was conveyed to Claye. He fussed, struggling against the sedative to force himself awake.

The young knight took a step back, resting his hands on his hips. "We've got orders about babies. Sorry, m'lady, but you'll have to come with me to see the captain."

So there were orders to look out for Lady Gruethrist's heir. Claye's death would resolve many difficulties, even if he was only a boy.

Yvon dropped the bag from his shoulder, grabbed Xaragitte by the arm, and yanked her forward. "There's no call for that! Look for yourself. You can tell the difference between girls and boys, can't you?"

He tugged at the swaddling with his left hand to hide the dagger that he drew with his right. Xaragitte jerked away from him, and Claye began to bawl.

"Hey there, don't hurt her," the puppy barked, stepping in to disentangle them.

Yvon spun, seized the young knight by his throat, and stabbed. The knight caught Yvon's wrist as it flicked in, deflecting the blade. He clawed at Yvon's choke hold.

The baby howled, a piercing scream.

The two men swayed for a second, deadlocked. Yvon spit in the other man's eye. The puppy shoved him off balance. As they fell, Yvon twisted the dagger around, and drove the iron knob of the hilt into the young man's face. It cracked against the hard bone at the corner of the eye. Yvon lost his grip on the throat, but smashed the hilt down another time.

"Ouch! Stop that, you little nuisance."

Yvon glanced up at the trembling voice. Xaragitte had unlaced her blouse and offered her breast to the baby, who clutched a tiny fistful of her flesh as he sucked. The young knight writhed on the ground, groping at his ruined face. Yvon flipped the dagger in his hand and thrust the sharp end into the smashed socket. The legs kicked out, fell still. Yvon kicked the body but it didn't move again. He quickly scanned their surroundings as he cleaned the dagger on the dead man's shirt and sheathed it.

"Can you walk while he feeds?" he asked Xaragitte.

She looked at him and shuddered. "Yes."

"Let's go then." He located their bag and shouldered it. His whole body ached. "You did good," he said. "Kept calm, quieted the baby."

An acrid haze of smoke settled around them, causing the tears he saw in her eyes. "Whatever I have to do for Claye," she said, "I'll do it."

He nodded once to her, then led her quickly past the ring of tents and into the outer darkness. Twenty leagues of wilderness lay between them and the sanctuary of Lady Ambit's castle. Yvon would have at least two days alone with Xaragitte, something he could never have hoped for while they remained in the castle.

His socks sloshed in soaked boots, his legs chafed in his wet pants, and he stank like sewage. But when they crossed the last of the unplowed fields to the edge of the forest, he looked at Xaragitte, lovely even though night hid all her features from him, and grinned in spite of himself.

He whistled an airy little tune for luck.

The melody fell dull on his deafened ears.

CHAPTER 2

*C*laye *bounced on the nursemaid's arm,* intently trying to catch a beam of morning sunlight as it fell through the branches of the trees. He squealed in frustration as it slipped away between his fingers.

Xaragitte, her mouth wrinkled in a frown, stood too near to Yvon, who was squatting bare-bottomed yet again, this time by a fallen tree.

"You should have delivered me safely to Lady Ambit's by now," she said.

He let his head sag toward his knees, too sick and miserable to answer. It was the third sunrise they'd seen since escaping the castle. Either the sorcerer's magic, or the filthy moat, or the crackleberries— or all three—had turned his guts to slush and wrung out his bowels.

"Claye should be safe in his grandmother's care by now," she said, her comment punctuated by another squeal from the child.

"Soon," Yvon said weakly.

"*Soon?* It's only a two-day journey!"

He groaned, clutching his aching belly as he stood and tugged his pants up. His legs were shaking as much as his stomach. "I'm getting better," he said. "We'll make better time today. Perhaps we can steal a boat and let the river's current carry us quickly to Lord Ambit's castle."

"A boat?" She held the child with one hand, touching three fingers to forehead, chin, and chest, muttering two names, that of god and goddess. "What about the demons?"

"The water's cold with snowmelt, so they'll be sluggish and we'll be safe." He'd risk it for the sake of speed. The river demons weren't always deadly, and in any case Yvon preferred his chances with them over the Baron's men.

Xaragitte shuddered, with a look in her eyes as if she were momentarily transported somewhere else.

Before Yvon could ask her about it, she took a deep breath and steadied herself. "At least the wolves can't reach us on the river," she said.

"The wolves we heard last night were a fair far distance away," he said, shouldering their bag and neglecting to mention that the howls came from the direction they were headed.

Yvon went in front of Xaragitte, threading through the narrow woodland trail. His legs wobbled beneath him—another reason to risk a boat, despite the river demons.

The hills on either side of them flattened as they approached the river. The northern slopes still harbored a few patches of snow in shaded nooks, but the sun warmed the southern faces, and the branches of the trees there were tipped with coal-red buds. Yvon had been with Lord Gruethrist when he first explored this region. Even then, Gruethrist described the land as a woman on her back. Her two long legs were the plump lines of hills on either side of the river valley. Beyond the place where the hills came together, the land rose like the soft mound of a woman's belly. Go beyond that, and you found the mountains. Gruethrist had erected his Lady's castle right in the woman's crotch. Gruethrist was a vulgar man.

Yvon paused to lean for a second against a tree. He thought he could continue walking as long as they headed downhill; he only had to fall forward without falling down. But the journey across the river plain daunted him.

Soon they passed out of the forest and approached great expanses of grassy pasture that shimmered purple with spring's first tiny flowers. Gray smoke spiraled up from a distant house.

Xaragitte walked past him, Claye squirming in his sling, and stopped when she saw the smoke. "Won't we be seen?"

"Yes," Yvon admitted. "But we shouldn't be pursued. It's plowing time. The farmers will be loath to forsake their fields when all they see is a family walking north. They may wonder why we don't stop, but they shouldn't pursue us."

"What if the Baron's soldiers see us?"

He thought about that. "No reason they should notice us either. We're just a family. Always think of us that way."

She cradled Claye to her chest and didn't reply.

Pressing a fist tight into his stomach to still its churning, Yvon set off again. Their new path meandered less as the way became mostly clear and flat. Yvon would have described the valley as sparsely settled until he tried to find a way across it without meeting anyone. He saw more walled farmhouses along the riverbank than he remembered; the land was simply too fertile to pass up, despite the demons. Several farmers waved greetings from behind their teams of shaggy oxen, and Yvon always waved back and walked quickly away. Most, as much as Yvon could help it, never saw them at all. Xaragitte talked constantly to the baby. Yvon enjoyed the sound of her voice. It helped keep his legs moving; he feared that if they stopped, he wouldn't walk again.

He was fighting another mild surge of stomach cramps and light-headedness when he saw, far away, the shapes of two men.

Shading the noon light with his palm, Yvon squinted at them. The men were lean and naked-limbed, bearing long staffs—spears! The

Baron's scouts dressed like that. And they always traveled in pairs. Yvon looked around quickly, picking a grove of trees across the meadow. "This way!"

"What is it?" Xaragitte asked.

He pointed to the men. "The Baron's scouts, may the jealous god rot them. We'll have to run for those trees, lose them. Can you do it?"

Her mouth said "Yes," but her eyes said no.

He realized she was as footsore and weary as he, but he could do nothing about that now. "Good," he said.

Drawing on the very dregs of his strength, he trotted off toward the trees. She tried to follow but faltered after ten steps. Yvon turned back for her, realizing there was no easy way to carry Claye. "Would it help, m'lady, if I took the child?"

She shook her head before he finished asking the question, as if she had considered and dismissed that option before he had asked. "Just let me shift him."

He waited while she positioned the sling with Claye across her back; then they resumed their flight. Claye screamed his complaint, but she did run slightly faster. Yvon looked over his shoulder. The Baron's men had closed the gap between them.

He kept a hand on his short sword. The baby started to cry. Xaragitte's rattled singsong also sounded close to tears.

They reached the trees—a small copse, Yvon saw too late, nothing they could lose their pursuers in. The distance to the next, larger grove was too far.

"We'll have to fight here," Yvon said.

She gulped, in between pants. "Fight?"

Yvon stifled the impulse to clap her on the arm, the way he would a fellow warrior, a young soldier going into his first battle. "Don't worry. They're only scouts."

He chose a spot like a triangle, with a thorn thicket on one side, a line of trees on another, and downed logs on the third. He hurled brush and loose branches between the trees, to impede the scouts if they attacked from that direction. There was a safe place for Xaragitte and Claye in a shallow depression in the middle. Yvon had made do with less before, in battles he'd survived. His heart pounded so hard his ears were ringing again before everything was ready.

Xaragitte had taken Claye off her back to calm him, and he squirmed until she put him down. He started crawling away at once, and giggled in a high pitch when Xaragitte caught him.

"What's he doing?" Yvon asked, in a tone of voice meant to convey *Whatever it is, make him stop.*

She brushed the red hair away from her face, wiped the sweat from her brow. "He's a baby, tired of being bundled up all day, and that's what babies do. They *crawl.*"

Claye clutched a fistful of leaves and shoved them at his mouth. "Ma-ma-ma-ma-ma!"

Xaragitte swept him up and held him. "Aren't you going to answer them?" she asked Yvon.

Now that she mentioned it, he heard the voice, someone shouting for them to come out. He'd lost track of the pursuers while he built the redoubt. He slid his sword free and spotted one of the scouts lurking in the distance. "If they want answers," he said, "let them come looking for them."

"Who're you?"

Yvon whirled at the new voice behind him, lunged at it with all his force, and dropped the point only just in time.

The boy—perhaps twelve summers old—hopped backward off the log, holding his shepherd's staff defensively. Yvon saw his mistake; from a distance, the proportions were the same as a man with a long spear. Yvon was doubly angry: at the boys for chasing them and at himself for not hearing the boy's approach, for thinking they were scouts. His ears still hadn't recovered. "I might ask you to name yourself first."

"I'm Bran, and that's my brother, Pwyl. Hey Pwyl—over here!" The boy looked them all over, but stared mostly at Yvon. "Why'd you run away?"

"We thought you were soldiers."

"Are you one of Lord Gruethrist's knights?"

The boy was too quick. "No."

"Hey, Pwyl, I told you so! He's not a knight."

Pwyl ran up, but stayed behind the brush piled up between the trees. Pwyl was the younger of the two, but not by much. He glanced at Yvon, openly disappointed. "He's got a sword."

Bran held up an empty hand. "Yeah, but he doesn't have a braid."

Yvon didn't like having one in front of him and one at his flank, even if they were boys. "Why did you chase us?"

"For news," Bran said. "You were coming from the south, where the siege is, and we hoped you had news."

"Farmer Rodrey," piped Pwyl, "our neighbor, he said the castle burned down three nights ago and everybody died."

"Farmer Rodrey said it was just five knights dead," Bran corrected him. "That hardly counts."

Yvon wondered which of his comrades had died, and whether they'd sacrificed themselves to protect another secret, just as the eunuch Kepit had. Yvon glanced at Claye, weighing his little life against all those deaths. "This Farmer Rodrey, did he say anything else?"

Bran wrinkled up his face. "That's about all."

"Don't forget Lady Gruethrist," Pwyl said. "She was taken with some illness."

Xaragitte started toward him. "What news of Lady Gruethrist?"

Pwyl stepped back. Bran said, "We don't know any more than that, ma'am. Farmer Rodrey heard she was sickly. Some woman's problem, he said. Why do you want to know?"

"That's just how women are," Yvon answered with a false laugh, before Xaragitte could speak and give them away. "They always want to know one another's matters, even if they don't know one another."

Pwyl smiled at this, but Bran's face didn't change expression. He was much too smart, that one. He hadn't taken his eyes off Yvon's sword once, or come close enough to strike.

Yvon sheathed his blade. "You don't know where we could find a boat?" he asked.

Bran made the warding sign. "No boats around here. The river's cursed with demons." He stepped backward. "Come on, Pwyl, we better be going, before Mother finds out we left her sheep untended."

"Awwww . . ."

"Now!"

"I'm coming." Pwyl walked around to where his brother was standing and waved to Yvon. "Fare you well, whatever path you take. I say it three times. Fare well."

Only saying it twice, the proper way, so he wouldn't draw the third god's jealous eye. "And three times I bid you comfort in your home," Yvon replied. He did not repeat it because his status to theirs did not require it.

As the boys ran off, Yvon sagged against a tree and sunk slowly to the ground, a straw man without his prop. His stomach knotted itself again. Even the news traveled faster than they did. But then, the news didn't eat unripe crackleberries, soak itself in pestilential waters, or have its intestines magicked into knots. The news didn't spend two whole days crouched in the woods, too cramped to walk, crapping its guts out.

Besides, he thought, bad news always travels fast.

Claye scooted over to Yvon, gripped Yvon's cloak, and pulled himself upright. He looked into Yvon's face.

"Ma! Ma!"

Yvon placed his hand on Claye but before he could tickle him, Xaragitte snatched the baby away. She stepped back, resting the child on her hip and rubbing her heart as if it pained her. "Do you think the lady has truly taken ill?"

"Likely, she's fine." Yvon's best guess was that Baron Culufre had put out this rumor to explain away Lady Gruethrist's death should the Empress decide to have her killed. But he didn't wish to worry Xaragitte. "The best thing we can do is deliver her son safely to his grandmother, Lady Ambit."

"Are we close, then?"

Yvon picked up a branch and levered himself upright. He needed a leg more steady than his own. "If we push on hard this evening, we should arrive there tomorrow."

Her face fell, but their only choice was to push on hard. The baby fell asleep in his sling as they trudged on in exhausted silence. The river twisted in the distance, a long blue ribbon slowly changing color as the sun settled on the western hills. They could see it clearly through the trees, when they came to a small tributary. Yvon followed it upstream, looking for swift, shallow water.

"We'll have to wade across," he said.

The nursemaid bit her lip. "Isn't there a bridge?"

"The bridges are the first place the Baron's men will guard. Besides, the river demons prefer deeper water, and they're still sluggish with the spring." He didn't mention the demons' greater hunger after winter.

They found a likely ford with a smooth shale bottom, no more than a foot or two at the deepest. The water was clear and cold as ice. Yvon crossed first. He stood on the far side and beckoned Xaragitte. "See, it's safe."

The water purled through the grasses as she lifted her skirt and splashed into the ripples. Near midstream she faltered, gasped, and suddenly jerked stiff. Yvon staggered toward her, slipping waist-deep in the water. By the time he reached her, she was shivering violently, Claye wailing. Yvon thrashed his walking stick in the water to scare off anything that threatened her. She flinched from his outstretched hand, stumbled across, and climbed up the far bank alone.

He backed toward her, cracking his stick in the water, but he saw nothing—nothing! "What happened?"

She gasped for air. "I think m'lady's dead."

How—? "How do you know that?"

"We were bonded to one another—by m'lady's wizard—during her pregnancy." She staggered off balance, like a drunkard. "For Claye's sake. Just now, I had a sense—" Tears ran down her cheeks. "Something's gone. I can't explain it. I can still feel her, but she's not quite there."

"Can you tell how it happened?"

She shook her head, holding the crying child tight, kissing his face. "No, no, but we *must* reach Lady Ambit's castle and tell her."

Yvon agreed. "It's too late to reach it tonight. We'll make camp and leave at first light."

He went uphill, well away from the water's edge, to a sheltered glen where he built a makeshift barricade of fallen branches. Claye cried inconsolably until he fell asleep. Yvon stretched out on the cold, damp ground at once, but he was too sore to get comfortable, his mind too busy to rest. Xaragitte must have suffered similarly. When the wolves started howling, she gave up the pretense of sleep and sat up. He did the same, breaking branches and feeding them into the flame, and not only for protection. His clothes were still wet, and the air was frosty cold.

"They'll leave us alone," he promised as Xaragitte huddled close to the fire. She shivered, staring off into the dark.

But the wolves came prowling around. Their eyes glinted green beyond the barricade, appearing and disappearing at random. Growls and snarls sounded out in the darkness, and Xaragitte fed more branches into the fire. For the second time that day, Yvon loosened his sword in his sheath. He never did it three times without using it.

Xaragitte began to cry, silent shoulder-racking sobs. She covered her face and stopped as suddenly as she began.

Yvon tried not to notice. "Are you—?"

"Never mind me." She wiped her eyes. "I'm fine. It's only m'lady. I felt her spark again. It's there, and it isn't, at the same time. It hurts, like a pin stuck in my heart."

He wanted to say something, to let her know that he was there to help, but the only words that came to him were the ones that he'd rehearsed. "Lord Gruethrist is much older, and the new Lady Gruethrist much younger. And he came from outside the empire originally, and she was born to it, but—"

"Please. I beg you not to speak of Lady Gruethrist now. It hurts too much."

Breath rushed out of him. "As you wish."

The wolves ran off. Something else out there had disturbed them. Yvon sat, vigilant and silent, until Xaragitte finally lay down again, feigning sleep, and after banking the fire, he did the same. Claye awoke, hungry, as the birds sang their first tentative farewell to night. By the time he had suckled, orange dawn spread over the dark sky like an egg cracked in an iron pan. Everything reminded Yvon of food.

"Today will be the last day of our journey," he told her.

"My feet are blistered," Xaragitte said. "I don't think I can walk much farther."

Claye sat on her arm, tugging at her hair. When Yvon walked by, Claye squealed and stretched out to grab him, spilling out of Xaragitte's grasp. Yvon reached out as Xaragitte caught Claye and pulled him back to her chest.

She smoothed the child's hair. "Thank you," she said.

"I don't want to see him hurt."

"Nothing in the world matters more to me than this baby."

He nodded. "I understand. The sooner we reach Lady Ambit's castle, the safer he'll be."

But the sooner they arrived there, the less opportunity he'd have to speak to her again, and he hadn't yet said any of the things he wanted to say. That pressed like a burr on his thoughts as he led them out of the trees. Below them, wisps of dark, drifting fog obscured the valley along the river's bank.

A low rumble shivered up through Yvon's legs. He shook his head clear and looked closer.

It was no fog below them.

He pointed as he spoke to Xaragitte. "Wild oxen. A huge herd. When we first came into this valley, it took us a whole day to pass from one side of the herd to the other. We killed most of them, to eat, and to make room for farming." A herd this big could ruin a whole year's crop. "I didn't know there were this many left on the southern shore of the river."

"What are those?" She indicated several shaggy giants moving among the oxen.

Yvon hadn't thought there were *any* of those left on this side of the Bealtefot River, not between the water and the mountains. "Tuskers. Mammuts. Have you ever seen one before?"

"Only the ivory." She lifted Claye, face toward the valley. "Do you see them, darling? Big old tuskers, with noses like snakes?" Bouncing him up and down in time with the words, she began to sing.

> *"Climbed up a tree trunk,*
> *it turned into a foot.*
> *Mammut, mammut."*

Yvon watched her, grinning at the old rhyme. She saw his expression and smiled back at him.

Maybe it could be all right between them after all.

"Are they the kind men train?" she asked.

"No," Yvon said, still smiling, looking at her as she lifted Claye toward the herd. "Those are the wood mammuts. Their tusks curve a lot more. Plains tuskers mix with wild oxen, but they're just too dangerous. You can't train them."

"Then why is there a man on the back of that one?"

Yvon spun—there *was* a man. Another climbed up on the back of a second mammut, and another. He gestured Xaragitte into the shelter of the trees. "Follow me. Quick."

"What's wrong?"

"That's no herd of wild beasts. Those are war mammuts. The oxen are food for the Baron's men. This is the supply train for his army."

"What can we do?"

"Pray to two gods they pass by quickly."

As they fled into the woods, the first horn sounded. Others responded, echoing across the valley as they called the order to march. It had been a long time since Yvon had heard that sound. He'd fought some hard battles against war mammuts that he'd rather not remember.

One horn sounded just behind them, on the hillside. Claye squealed at the noise, turning his head.

Long-legged oxen with wide, flaring horns crashed through the trees, driven by an ox-herder with his staff. Before Yvon could draw his sword, the tall man waved greetings to them.

"Blessings, blessings," the herder called to them in a high voice. Yvon took in the skirt, the rounded breasts: a eunuch, like Kepit. A she, not a he. The horn slung over her shoulder was set with emeralds and gold, and she wore a similar jewel-hilted knife. With her sloe-black skin, and height, that made her a chief herder. A member, certainly, of some noble line. "Do not fear," the eunuch called cheerfully. "We shall soon pass out of your lands. Many, many pardons."

"Are you going to join the siege?" asked Yvon.

"The siege?" The eunuch laughed. "There is no more siege. Do you know nothing?"

"Truly, ma'am, we do not," Yvon said, but just one time.

"Two days ago the word came—Gruethrist's keep has fallen—so we crossed the Beautiful Waters at once. The demons fed well, I tell you, but we must allow for that."

"The castle has fallen?"

The herder stopped beside them and smiled, revealing pink gums. "Oh, yes. It burned to the ground, the Baron says. The Baron has ways of knowing."

"What of Lady Gruethrist?" asked Xaragitte.

"One hears sad tidings." She shrugged helplessly, smile all gone. "But her mother, Lady Ambit, gave us sanctuary in her keep, and the lady's consort swore an oath of loyalty to the Baron himself just yesterday. Perhaps all will be well. Ho!" This last she shouted at the oxen, who had started to wander again. "Many pardons, but I must go. You will come to Castle Gruethrist, yes? The Baron is a good lord, and he will need many men to serve him."

Yvon drew a breath. "Wait—if you take your herds across the river, and into the high vales, beware of the lions. They will come in the night and take your calves."

"Lions? Ai! Last night we heard wolves. This land is all a wilderness. How do decent women live here?"

Xaragitte, who'd been rocking Claye, had gone very still.

"My apologies, Lady," the eunuch said at once. "No ill, no ill intended, but it is not what I expected. Ai!"

"It is not so bad as it once was," Yvon said.

"It is bad enough. For your warning, many, many, many thanks!" She said it three times as she walked away, drawing the attention of the gods, who would surely squabble and bring someone trouble. The herder tapped the strays with her staff, driving them toward the main herd. If there was trouble, it didn't seem likely to fall on her.

Yvon leaned on his walking stick, unsure which direction to go next.

⫷ CHAPTER 3 ⫸

Claye puffed his cheeks out until his face grew red. Xaragitte patted his back until he burped up a tiny mouthful of milk. She wiped the curds off her shoulder and smeared her palm on her skirt.

"Why did you warn her of the lions?" she demanded from Yvon. Her voice was cold and distant as the mountaintops.

He rubbed his hand over the empty place where his warrior's braid had hung. Without it, he felt like a mammut without a trunk.

"Lord Ambit would not have sworn loyalty unless the Baron stationed a garrison of men there to enforce it," he said. "So the herder probably saved our lives. She certainly prevented our capture. By the gods of war and justice, I owed her news of equal value."

"May the goddess rot them, may the lions kill them all," she said bitterly, though it was unwise to wish ill in Bwnte's name. Xaragitte sniffled. "Where do we go now?"

"I was just asking myself the same question. We'll have to go to Lady Eleuate's castle."

"That's back in the direction we've just come. Farther!"

"Yes, but there's nowhere else to go. Claye is formally betrothed to her daughter." And it would mean perhaps another week of travel together for the two—or three—of them.

Xaragitte nodded. Slowly, but she nodded. "How will we make our way there, with the Baron's army in the valley?"

Yvon stroked his beard. "We'll join the train of the army, just another family traveling from one part of the valley to another."

"We can't do that."

"Why not? No one knows us; no one should recognize us. And they're marching in the direction we wish to go."

"But they—"

"And they have food and drink down there." She'd eaten the very last of their supplies yesterday: dogmeat, Gruethrist's hounds, butchered at siege's end. Yvon's stomach was a rawhide knot of hunger. "Is this not so?"

"Yes." She hissed the word, like an accusation. "But they would have starved us all."

"Then it's only fitting they should feed us now." Yes, he liked the idea even more. He stared down the slope at the army. They'd have food there, and he might not even need to steal—

A knife pressed into his ribs. He froze. "Wait!"

"Why? You mean to betray us." Her voice trembled, but the knife did not. The tip dug harder into his side.

He said nothing. He remained still. Even the branches of the trees were still. Sunlight trickled through them like water leaking from cupped hands, to disappear as quickly as his best-made plan. Yvon waited, motionless, until he heard her draw breath to speak again.

In that split second, he spun and caught her hand at the base. She held the knife with her thumb and forefinger; the blade was slender, sharp. He buried his thumb in her wrist, and twisted. She gasped, dropping the weapon and wrapping her arm protectively around

Claye, who hung in his sling. But she stood her ground, and stared Yvon in the eye.

"Why'd you do that?" he shouted.

"Lady Gruethrist warned me, she said you were fickle, like every other man, ruled by your emotions. And then all your bellyaching in the woods, and your excuses, and the delays, and being scared by two boys—you would have killed them too—and murdering that—"

"Stop."

"—*murdering* that poor boy of a knight!"

"Stop!"

She fell silent and tried to tug her arm free.

Yvon held tight until his knuckles blanched. He leaned in close as if he meant to kiss her. "I'm bound to serve Lord Gruethrist, as wedding binds him to serve your lady, and he means to defend both her title and claim to the valley against the whims of the Empress and Baron Culufre's forces. When we join Gruethrist in the high country, I'll give him exact numbers of those forces and some intelligence of their intentions. Because we took a slight risk today."

"Assuming he escapes."

"He'll escape."

She pulled her arm away again. This time he let go. "If you betray me," she said, "or bring harm to this child, I'll see Bwnte feast on your festering carcass."

Her distrust slashed deeper than her little knife could ever cut. He pointed to the men and animals milling below them. "The Baron's soldiers don't know who we are—the chief herder just met us and didn't care. We'll be refugees, like all the other landless women—"

"I'm not landless."

Only because she served Lady Gruethrist; only because Lady Gruethrist had promised to reward her with a grant of land for nursemaiding Claye.

They stared grimly at each other.

The baby strained, lifting his head to peer quizzically at Yvon. His tiny fist batted the air. "Ma-ma!"

Yvon looked away first, bending to snatch up her knife. It was well balanced, sharp, easy to conceal. Perfect for close stabbing. He flipped it, so that the blade pointed toward himself, and handed it to her hilt-first. "Lady, I will treat this child as though he were yours, in your own home, until we deliver him safely back to his mother or her family."

She took the knife, holding it toward him for a second, then slipped it back into the sheath concealed in a fold of her dress. She rubbed the back of her hand across dry lips, scowling at him one last time as she started to walk.

He went quickly ahead. Last winter seemed closer and warmer than she did at that moment.

The hills sloped down to a broad flat plain of fertile land that bracketed an unpredictable river. Two bare-limbed scouts jogged away from the main camp. Yvon waved his walking stick at them. They lifted their spears in answer and kept on going. Sometimes it was easiest to hide right out in the open.

Xaragitte did not speak to him, but she sang to Claye. It was the old rhyme.

> *"I felt a snake crawl across my toes,*
> *but it turned into a hairy nose—*
> *the tree became a foot.*
> *Mammut!"*

Yvon led them alongside the army, toward the rear. He counted nearly a hundred braided knights, men like himself, trained in all the arts of war. At least four hundred foot soldiers accompanied them, men like he had been when he first served Lord Gruethrist on the western plains. Another five to six hundred men followed also—servants, baggage carriers, herders, mammut handlers. Half this force, added to the besiegers, could subdue all of Gruethrist's men with ease. There was no choice of meeting them in a direct battle.

> *"A wing flapped in the tree up here,*
> *but it turned into a giant ear.*
> *The snake across my toes became a nose.*
> *The tree became a foot.*
> *Mammut!"*

Twenty mammuts! Yvon's legs wobbled again. Only the Empress's consort fielded more than that. A hundred times that many cattle milled between the hills and the army. Together, the mammuts and cattle would strip the season's infant pastures bare, devouring or crushing every green thing in their path. The Baron could conquer Gruethrist or simply starve him.

> *"I leaned against a big old boulder,*
> *but it turned into a shaggy shoulder.*
> *The wing up here became an ear . . ."*

The usual stragglers chased the rearguard: landless women with children, motherless children with dogs, ragged misfit families herding sheep and goats, gangs of barely adolescent boys who'd left home to join the men—all the types that an army attracted the way dogs drew fleas.

> *"I thought I saw a thresher's flail,*
> *but it turned into a swinging tail.*
> *The boulder was a shoulder.*
> *The wing . . ."*

But it was a good mixed crop, with some faces and clothing that would be at home among the peasant villages, some in the capital of the empire, and some in the western mountains where Yvon came from. Yvon, Xaragitte, and Claye would easily fit in. No one noticed a few more carrots in a stew.

Claye giggled and squealed, and tried to pull himself out of the sling. Xaragitte tickled him. He kicked, and laughed even harder as they fell in behind, neither among the other stragglers nor apart from them. Families usually kept to themselves in an army's train, ashamed of their poverty, hoping to claim land in a new territory and start over. A boy, bone-thin with matted hair, trotted along near Yvon, sizing them up for either handouts or theft. Yvon scowled until he ran off, then cringed at the memory of tagging along the same way, lonely, hungry, and desperate. It was like being trailed by a shadow of his youth.

"Will we walk at this pace all day?" asked Xaragitte, shifting Claye's sling to the other side. Her hair hung limp over her face. Her eyes were dark, and sunken.

Yvon looked at the sky, the sun just showing over the eastern ridge. "Maybe. If so, we'll reach the castle tonight."

"But it took us three days to come this far!"

Fatigue also nipped at his heels. "I know." He thought of the temple priestess. They'd have to find some way across the river without being stopped at the bridge. "We'll have to be very careful."

Claye squirmed and tried to pull himself over Xaragitte's shoulder. She tugged him down again. "We can't let anyone recognize Claye."

"Don't use his name, then! We can't let anyone recognize us either."

From over their shoulders: "You!"

Xaragitte shied at the sound of the high-pitched voice. Yvon continued walking.

"You—old man!" The chief herder ran to intercept them. She couldn't have been a eunuch long, Yvon thought: she still had too much energy. Her grin was broad and genuine. "Greetings, greetings, greetings! I thought it was you, the old man afraid of lions."

Yvon tensed. Did the herder intend a double meaning? Baron Culufre's emblem was the dagger-toothed lion—had she discovered that Yvon was one of Gruethrist's men already? "I'm just a simple farm-husband, fearing for another's livestock."

"Yes, yes, yes. The Baron intended to pasture the herds in that direction, away from the village. But I conveyed to him your timely, welcome warning. Now he will send hunters up there in advance. We did not come prepared for such a wilderness as this, I tell you. We owe you many thanks."

"None at all." Yvon walked faster.

The herder fell in step beside them and politely avoided looking at Xaragitte. "You're here because you've accepted my offer, yes? The Baron generously rewards all those who serve him, and you have served him well already."

"No, we simply happen to be going this way. It was news I was happy to share, as a lady gives water to a stranger who comes knocking at her door."

"Is there anything at all I can do to help you?"

Yvon's footsteps faltered, stopped. He glanced over at Xaragitte. "There is one small favor."

The herder's smile grew wider. "Name yourself, then name your favor!"

"You honor us, to ask our names," Yvon said, politely including Xaragitte. He recalled the shepherd boys from the day before—neither their accents nor appearance would match those names, but Yvon didn't expect a noble eunuch from the Imperial City to catch that. "I am Bran. I accompany my niece, Pwylla."

The herder's expression grew grave and she stopped walking, indicating to Yvon and Xaragitte that they must do the same. "Please, continue."

Yvon swallowed. "We've been afoot these four days, and I have no more food to gift her with, to my great shame. If you would be kind enough to provide my niece with a bite to eat, I will say prayers to Verlogh for you at the festival of justice."

The eunuch lifted the carved horn to her lips and blew several short notes. When she was done, she lowered the horn and thrust out her hands. The intimate gesture surprised Yvon. He hesitated, then tucked his walking stick under his arm, extending his own hands. They gripped each other's wrists.

"Well met, Bran. My name is Sebius. We cannot permit our new but beloved friends to venture so long afoot with neither sustenance nor drink."

Two young, muddy boys, one dark-skinned and the other fair, ran up to Sebius. Others hurried over, but too late. She waved them off. The herder whispered her commands, and the two took off running in different directions.

Xaragitte looked questioningly at Yvon, who made no response at all. She shifted Claye to her other hip and pulled the sweat-damp hair away from her face.

"Aha," Sebius said, noticing the gesture. "The goddess Bwnte herself did not have tresses so red, nor skin as pale and freckled, when she walked disguised across the plains of Maedatup with her newborn son."

A smile quirked across Xaragitte's lips. That resemblance was one of the chief reasons she'd been selected as nursemaid. Yvon felt worse and worse about this chance encounter. Three gods watching them.

"Have you ever seen the mammuts before?" Sebius asked.

"I have, a few times," Yvon answered, leaving off that he hated the beasts. There were only three things in the world he hated and feared, and war mammuts were one.

"And you, m'lady Pwylla—you will not be offended if I address you so familiarly?"

"N-no," Xaragitte answered. "I am honored."

"Ah! Have you ever seen the mammuts before?"

"No, never."

Sebius clapped her hands together. "Today, you shall not only see one, you shall be conveyed like a princess upon one's back. It is my little gift to you, to ease your journey."

"You do us too much honor," Yvon protested.

"Not at all! For all I know, she is the goddess Bwnte, come in disguise once more, and I have a duty to help her."

Xaragitte smiled at her. "Usually, men flatter me with that comparison when they seek the blessings of the goddess herself."

"I am beyond reproach in that regard," the eunuch said, and they both laughed. "So it is agreed, then, yes?"

Yvon wanted her to say no. A short time ago, she'd tried to stab him for suggesting they join the train of the army. Now she was ready to ride one of the Baron's mammuts. But the presence of the eunuch reassured her—she'd worked side by side with Kepit in Lady Gruethrist's service. She glanced at Yvon, her eyes as hard as steel.

"We would love to ride on a mammut," she told Sebius. She tickled Claye beneath his chin. "Wouldn't we, darling?"

Yvon's heart stopped in his throat as he half expected her to call the baby by his true name. Anyone who heard the name Claye would think of Gruethrist.

At that moment, the first of the boys returned leading a mammut, a small beast, only ten feet tall and clearly old, no longer a fighting mammut. The red fur fell off in clumps, the way it always did in spring. Brass knobs covered the sawed-off tusks. Ropes girded about its waist held a bundle on its back. The handler was a slight lad not much older than the errand boys, which meant it was a trusted animal. But the shaggy beasts were too unpredictable, Yvon thought, no matter what their age or use.

Sebius gestured to the handler, who clicked his teeth and gave a command with his feet behind the creature's ears. The mammut knelt to the ground.

"This is Lady Pwylla," Sebius explained. "You will carry her today and ease her journey. Treat her as if she were the goddess herself."

"It is my exquisite privilege, Lady," the handler said. Large ears stood out on either side of his head, twitching like a mammut's. "You may ride up here, seated on the Baron's tent."

"I'll take the child," Yvon said, holding out his hands. At least he could protect the heir.

Sebius tapped her heart. "Oh, no, no, no. No child in swaddling should be separated from his loving mother. The babe shall be perfectly safe."

"Oh, yes," the handler added. "The babe will be perfectly safe up here. Giruma is a very gentle mammut."

"I'll keep him with me," Xaragitte said firmly. "He may soon be hungry again." She turned her back on Yvon.

He went to boost her up and so did Sebius. With one helping her on either side, she climbed onto the kneeling mammut's back and settled on the cushion of the pack it carried. When the animal stood again, she smiled nervously.

"Onward," Sebius told the mammut handler. "We have very far to go today."

"Be careful," Yvon said, walking beside the beast, but Xaragitte did not look at him.

Sebius matched steps with Yvon, speaking in a low voice. "I must see to the strays—the other strays." She laughed, and although he didn't like being referred to as a stray, Yvon smiled in reply. "But later you will walk with me, yes, and tell me all you know about the valley. Yes?"

"My knowledge is a drop of water in a broad river."

"Ah! But a thirsty man is glad for even the smallest drop that wets his tongue. Do you have much experience with cattle?"

"None at all, but for the team that pulls a plow." And that some forty years ago, as a boy. He saw no need to be so specific.

"That is a difficult task," Sebius said, absurdly pleased. "You will talk to me, and perhaps in the weeks and months, nay years, to come we shall labor side by side. I cast divination bones before we departed the Imperial City, and they indicated that my future and fortune would be made by a man named Bran."

Chills shivered through Yvon. "It's not an uncommon name."

"But you are an uncommon man." Sebius continued to grin. "Yes, anyone can see there is something hidden about you. Make my fortune here as the bones foretold, and I shall see you never want for anything again."

The other boy returned, bearing bowls of boiled oats mixed with maple syrup. He gave both to Yvon, to preserve his dignity, and Yvon passed one up to Xaragitte. She murmured thanks.

Sebius grabbed the boy roughly by the shoulder and shook him. "Fetch this lovely woman, the image of Bwnte herself, watered wine to drink. Not a drop for yourself or I'll have you beaten! And when you return, remain in her service throughout the day." The lad darted off, and Sebius turned to Yvon. "I must attend to other duties now, but I've marked the boy and you may order him about as you like."

Yvon nodded acceptance of this around a mouthful of oats. He followed along behind the lumbering tusker, using two fingers to spoon the food into his mouth. He licked the bowl clean when it was empty and stuffed it in his pack.

At the castle, their true identities would certainly be discovered. Yvon knew it. But if they arrived in darkness, and slipped away before the dawn, they had a chance.

The mammut handler talked constantly with Xaragitte as the leagues fell away beneath their feet. Yvon helped her down at the noon halt. "You must watch what you say," he whispered, with a nod at the jug-eared boy. "He'll report everything to the eunuch."

"He'll report that I love my baby and that my baby loves mammuts and silly songs." She changed Claye's position to the other breast. "What kind of name is Pwylla? It sounds like something you'd throw on a rug."

He didn't have anything to say to that.

"You have no honor at all, do you? You didn't have to give our names. But you lie, you break your word without a second thought—"

"Just don't mention *his* name," Yvon said, tilting his head at Claye.

She turned her shoulder against him. Every muscle in her neck looked taut and strained. "I said the baby's name was Kady. Kady, you hear me?"

Her dead lover's name. "Fine. Good."

"And I will say this for the Lady Sebius—unlike you, she has fed me and rested my feet."

Yvon finished eating the food that Sebius's boys had brought them, but it no longer had any flavor. This was not how he had pictured himself and Xaragitte. He didn't know why it had gone so wrong between them or how he could make it better.

Horns sounded, ending the halt almost as soon as it had begun. The Baron meant to push his men, and the men responded. Yvon respected that: battles were won that way. It was one more thing to report to Gruethrist when they met. Some of the mammuts bellowed in reply. Yvon helped Xaragitte back onto Giruma and walked beside the mammut as the march resumed. Xaragitte said something to the handler, and he goaded the old tusker up out of the rearguard.

Yvon stretched his sore legs to keep up with them. "Ho, there!" he cried. "Slow down!"

They didn't. Xaragitte clearly wanted to be away from him. The mammut lingered just at the edge of Yvon's view, Xaragitte's red hair bobbing along above Giruma's dark red fur. Yvon found himself walking among the cattle and the cattle herders. A small group of soldiers back in line considered him suspiciously. Soldiers had a way of recognizing one another, and so he tried, without much success, to carry himself less like a knight and more like a peasant.

A fatalistic mood overtook him, brought on by Xaragitte's treatment and the size of the army. Several times his hand strayed to the hilt of his concealed short sword. He wondered, chance permitting, if he should try to murder Baron Culufre. There'd be no escape afterward. It was a poor alternative to retirement, to taking up house with a young woman, but it might be the best way to help Lord Gruethrist.

With this in mind, he began to scan the army for the Baron; and so he missed the group of mammuts coming together near Xaragitte until he heard their trumpeting.

He twisted at the noise and found he couldn't reach her. The horns of the cattle filled the intervening space like an army's spears as Yvon watched a large tusker approach the mammut which carried Xaragitte and Claye. The smaller Giruma stopped, curling its trunk submissively back on its forehead, but the big tusker still seemed agitated and reared. Its handler shouted, striking his little crook-shaped goad fiercely to no effect. A third mammut approached at a trot.

The big tusker wheeled and attacked the newcomer. Ivory clashed on ivory, heavy feet pounded the ground, and men and beasts alike cried out as they scattered out of the way.

Yvon dodged frightened cattle in his attempt to reach the woman and child he'd sworn to protect. He lost sight of them in the confusion, but he heard the animal screams, the angry voices of several men, and above it all a woman's piercing shriek.

Other mammuts charged in with their beasts. When Yvon arrived at the tumult, one mammut was down on the ground, mouthing mournful sounds, its side slashed wide open. He pushed his way toward it, fearing—

No pack. It wasn't the one that carried Xaragitte.

He didn't see Xaragitte anywhere, couldn't pinpoint her screaming in all the confusion. He ran past a man on the ground, his right leg smashed into a bloody paste, and searched frantically among the milling mammuts and growing circle of soldiers, knights, and herders. Then he spied the huge tusker looming over all the others, and ran toward it.

The handler gripped the monster's neck, fear carved on his face like a totem of the war god. Wetness seeped from the side of the mammut's head: it'd gone into musk, the most dangerous time for tuskers. The other mammuts crowded in to herd the wild tusker away from the wounded animal and the crowd. They formed one surging mass of red and brown fur until a single mammut lurched away in fright, its burden slipping from its back. Xaragitte clung with one hand to a tusk-slashed rope as the animal spun around; her other hand squeezed the baby tight to her bosom. The skinny boy hopped around below her, alternately yelling at her to jump and hold on. The handler couldn't force the beast to kneel. A loose rope tangled in the mammut's legs was panicking it.

Yvon rushed over to catch Xaragitte at the same moment several soldiers did likewise. He shoved them out of the way to take hold of her, barely avoiding the mammut's feet as it bellowed wildly and reeled to one side.

The soldiers, already tense, were ready to rescue Xaragitte from Yvon. But she draped one arm around him, sobbing as Claye wailed with her sympathetically. "It was awful, awful," she cried. "I'm cursed! Everything I do is cursed!"

Several soldiers made the warding sign at her proclamation. Yvon might have echoed the gesture, but Xaragitte's knees sagged and he needed both hands to hold her up. One soldier started toward them. Glancing down, Yvon noticed that his short sword was partly visible. He shrugged his shoulder, shifting his cloak to hide it. The soldier hesitated, uncertain.

Another mammut rumbled just behind Yvon, and a voice spoke, more lordly and commanding than any Yvon had ever known.

"Is the lady injured?"

Xaragitte stopped crying, though one last shudder rolled through her body. She immediately stepped away from Yvon. Yvon turned and froze. Even the baby's eyes widened and his cries suddenly became hiccups.

For young Baron Culufre stood before them, atop a war mammut fit for a king. If not a god.

He looked very much like the Empress, Yvon thought.

⟡ CHAPTER 4 ⟡

*C*laye's tears seemed to dry instantly on his face. He reached out toward the Baron's mammut. "Mahmah!"

It loomed fourteen feet tall, clad from trunk to tail in iron plate and chain mail set with emeralds and lesser gems. Swords too large for any man to wield adorned its tusks. The Baron stood just behind the handler, so sure of his balance that he held onto nothing. His armor matched the mammut's, with jewels set likewise upon his breast and helm, though even the emeralds did not glitter as much as his bright green eyes. His braid was formed of many smaller braids, all bound together, as if he were an army of knights embodied by one man—which, as Baron, he was.

"Is the lady injured?" he repeated in his deep voice.

"She's frightened, that's all," Yvon answered, finding his tongue. His hand twitched toward his hidden sword, but he knew he could never strike and kill the Baron, not here, much less kill him and escape. The back of his neck itched. Remembering that he was braidless, he ducked his bare head and added, "Your Magnificence."

"You served her and the child well to catch them so. How do you serve Us?" The imperial plural.

Yvon now doubted the resemblance to the Empress was chance. But before he could answer, Sebius appeared like a blister after a long march. "This is the man I told you of this morning, Brother. Bran, a farmer of this valley."

Brother?

Yvon looked again and saw the resemblance in the shape of their faces, their stature. It had been too long since he'd been in the Imperial City or followed the brackish currents of its gossip—were these two of the Empress's sons? Perhaps only favored nephews, children of her sisters. But certainly chosen for great things if one this young had been wedded to the aged Lady Culufre. Yvon was willing to bet the Baron's next wife would be some promising younger daughter of a minor house, named heir to the Culufre title. It explained the newness of the eunuch also. A man owned only what he could carry with him to hunt or war, but a eunuch had all the property rights of women, and the Empress's gifts to Sebius would be available to the young Baron Culufre. Sebius might even be the more favored of the two.

This complicated Lord Gruethrist's chances for victory.

"Ah, yes, We recall," Culufre answered. "Whither do you fare, farmer Bran?"

Yvon struggled to recall what he'd told Sebius. "We go to rejoin my niece's family in the mountains."

Culufre permitted himself a small, deliberate smile in Sebius's direction. "We appreciate the importance of families. It is Our great hope that We shall make life at this edge of the realm easier for all families. To that goal, We shall send Our mammuts on to visit Lady Eleuate. You shall travel with them, and tell Our men all you know of the surrounding country."

Claye hiccuped in the silence that followed.

Xaragitte stepped toward Yvon. She shook her head, stroking

Claye's scalp, but whether it was to soothe him or herself, Yvon could not say.

Culufre missed nothing. "Please inform your niece that she should not be dismayed. She shall not be required to ride Our mammuts again if they fill her with trepidation. But We enjoin you to travel with them, on Our behalf, to more quickly speed her to her family's domicile."

He stared at Yvon. At the last moment Yvon remembered to duck his head. "Thank you three times, Your Magnificence, thank you." When he lifted his eyes again, the Baron had already turned to the wounded mammut and gave orders there.

Yvon slowly unclenched his fists. Baron Culufre would be a hard man to dislodge from the valley. But Gruethrist had settled the valley. He was a hard man too and knew the country better, if only he could escape the castle.

The dust rose up Yvon's nose, carrying with it the smell of mammut and cattle, and his ears were filled with the sounds of herders and soldiers and a lone man's keening weep.

"Bran, my friend," Sebius said at his side, "I am very glad that no harm came to your niece. And more than glad that you will help us find our way here. The Baron will certainly reward you, as will I."

Yvon drew a deep breath, and became aware that he'd been holding it. "I am grateful for your aid already. Nothing more is required."

"Perhaps, when the herds are settled, your niece will permit me to visit you and pay her my respects. I owe you compensation for leading her into danger today. It was not my intention."

"And thus requires no forgiveness. It is forgotten as if it never happened. But you will be welcome when you come." Welcomed with a sharp blade perhaps. Although Sebius might prove a useful hostage too, if the chance presented itself.

"We will talk again," Sebius said. "I beg three pardons, but you will excuse me now? I must see to calming the herds. Please excuse me."

Yvon bowed slightly. "A lady comes and goes about her land as she wishes."

Sebius grinned smugly and hurried off.

Yvon turned to Xaragitte. He reached out to her and she withdrew, bouncing Claye against her shoulder to still his hiccups.

"Where is our bag?" she asked. Looking after their possessions, as was her right and duty.

Yvon's head swiveled as if he expected to find the bag nearby. He didn't remember dropping it, but he no longer carried it either. They'd need the blankets to survive the colder nights up in the mountains on their way to Lady Eleuate's. "I beg your pardon, m'lady," he said, mortified.

He ran in search of it at once. Retracing his footsteps proved nearly impossible, but he saw two ragged boys tugging at something where the cattle had been and when he took it from them and chased them off, it proved to be the bag, trampled by cattle and ripped open by their hooves. He peered inside. Their blankets were still there, but the bowl he'd stolen was shattered into a thousand shards. A bad sign, he thought, as he shook the fragments into the churned ground.

His way back through the crowds of animals and people was blocked by the mammut handlers leading their charges toward the river's edge. The Baron's wizard held the hem of his silver-threaded robes out of the mud as he walked along with them to sing the demons at bay. He was a middle-aged man, young for his role, and therefore powerful. No doubt assigned by the Empress herself, another gift to Culufre. Or Sebius.

The eunuch stood with Xaragitte. "The tuskers are heading down to the river," Yvon called out. "Going to bathe?"

"Yes, yes," Sebius replied. "The Baron has decided to call a halt for the night, and so arrive at the castle tomorrow when he'll have the complete day to settle affairs there, instead of at dusk tonight. I came to inquire if you and your niece might join me for the evening meal?"

Yvon felt like a man sinking in quickmud. "We . . ."

Sebius stood formally, right arm across the waist, left arm extended, as a woman did at the threshold of her house. "The campfire is my home tonight. M'lady Pwllya is invited with her child and escort to partake of the best my humble table has to offer."

Xaragitte straightened her shoulders, flipping Claye around in her arms to face the eunuch. "We are honored to accept your invitation, m'lady."

Sebius clapped. "Most, most excellent. Now I beg you, yet again, to excuse me."

Xaragitte glared at the eunuch's back as she hurried away. "I hate her," she said, rocking the child on her arm. "She means to rob Lady Gruethrist."

The experience with the mammut seemed to have changed her attitude. "Let's just eat her food and sleep a bit," Yvon said, "so that we'll have the strength we need when we must escape."

"I'm strong enough now to do whatever must be done," she replied. "Let me know when you are too."

She turned her back on him and carried Claye away.

At sunset, they sat a little apart from the herders on a hillside above the river and ate porridge mixed with strips of meat so salty it was impossible to tell what animal it had once been. Yvon scooped his into his mouth with his fingers and thought it delicious, eating slowly to be gentle on his recovering stomach. Xaragitte set her bowl down to play a clapping game with the baby.

"Mother Bwnte baked the moon,
    And set it out to cool.
Little Sceatha saw it there,
    And bit it like a fool.
He burned his mouth and spit it out!
How big was his bite?"

Claye leaned his head back, his mouth as wide as a nestling bird's. He wagged it from side to side and said "Ahhhhhh!" Xaragitte opened her mouth all the way too and leaned toward him, pulling his hands to the sides and pretending to chomp on his nose. He giggled, and she clapped his pudgy hands again.

"Next night, another bite.
Mother Bwnte baked the moon . . ."

Yvon watched them, thinking about the rhyme. Any story told about two gods in any of their guises was always, really, about the third. The goddess Bwnte might bake the moon, and her son Sceatha, god of war, might spit it out. But in another story, Verlogh, god of justice, gathered up the fallen crumbs and planted them in the ground where they sprouted up as people.

Claye closed his mouth more with each repetition, imitating his nurse. When his lips were tight shut, she kissed his mouth and told him he was a good boy. He tucked his chin into his chest, grinning, but she set him down to rub her chest just above her heart. Claye grabbed a handful of porridge from Xaragitte's bowl and flung it on the ground.

Yvon started up. "Hey! Don't let him waste that!"

A hand fell on his shoulder and he jumped. Sebius's high voice said, "No, no, no, that's fine. With such a lovely child, how can anything be wasteful?"

Xaragitte sucked Claye's hand clean in her mouth and wiped it on her skirt. She stood, lifting the little boy. "I'm glad to see you, m'lady Sebius," she said, without a trace of gladness, "so that I may thank you thrice for your hospitality. But the day has tired us, and we should sleep."

There was a different imperial plural in her voice, thought Yvon: the royal *we* of every mother and her child. It did not include him.

"Of course," the eunuch chirped. "Is there anything additional I may do?"

"You've done too much already," she replied. Taking her blankets from the pack, she went a short distance away. Yvon watched her go, wondering what had happened to the cheerful woman he had once watched from afar in the castle.

Sebius lay her staff on the ground and sat beside Yvon with her own bowl of food. "I see how she looks at you, and how you look at her."

Yvon jumped a second time. "What do you mean?"

Sebius smiled around a mouthful of food. "It is obvious that you are not her uncle, and also that the child is not yours. You stand like a beggar outside her door."

A saying among men, out of place on the lips of a eunuch: *A woman's body is her home—only those that she invites inside should enter.* "It's not like that between us."

Sebius laughed aloud, covering her mouth to prevent spilling the porridge. "Did I tell you? The divination bones foretold that I would meet a man in this valley named Bran, and he would make my fortune for me."

A shiver shot up Yvon's spine. Like most knights, he stayed away from divination. A man could go forward into battle with a clear heart only if he didn't know the outcome.

"So, to bind our friendship," the eunuch continued, "I will give you this advice. A woman outside her home, out in the wilderness, is always anxious. More especially if she has a child with her. You, my friend Bran, should deliver the lady Pwylla to her family. Then return to help me, and I will see that you have new clothes." She gestured at Yvon's filth-encrusted trousers. "The very finest! Also many gifts to give to her and her baby. Then she will see the old jewel set in a new broach."

Yvon grunted noncommittally.

Sebius made a knuckle-rapping gesture. "Knock, knock. Come in!" Laughing, she scooped more food into her mouth.

While they were eating, a small group of soldiers came over and set up camp near the herders. Or near to Yvon and Xaragitte. Even though there was only twilight in the sky now, Yvon thought he recognized the soldier from that afternoon, the one who'd noticed Yvon's concealed sword. Sebius scowled at their proximity, as if it were a slight on the way she controlled the herders, and rose at once to go complain. She was so incensed she forgot to pardon herself from Yvon's presence.

Yvon rose, took his blanket, and went over to sit beside Xaragitte. The move brought him closer to the eunuch and the soldiers, but he couldn't hear the particulars of their argument. The soldiers clearly refused to budge, and though it was already dark, Sebius turned and stomped off toward the Baron's tent down by the riverside.

Yvon gathered up the rest of the eunuch's meal, along with Xaragitte's, and packed it away in their bag.

Xaragitte turned slowly in her blankets so she wouldn't disturb the sleeping Claye. Her face turned toward Yvon, and not even the shadowy light could soften the pain in it.

"What is wrong?" he asked, reaching out his hand.

She lifted her arm to ward him off, then touched her fingers to her chest. "M'lady Gruethrist, she's all twisted up in here. It hurts so bad."

"But she's still alive?"

Xaragitte shook her head. "She's struggling, but whether she's struggling to live or to die, I cannot say."

She appeared to be in so much pain, and her pain ached in him, so he reached out to her again, to soothe her.

"Don't touch me!"

"I only meant to—"

"We're cursed," she said. "The castle burned down because of us, and then the mammut tried to kill me and Claye, and—"

Yvon's hand shot up to indicate silence, and he glanced in the direction of the soldiers nearby. Their faces were lit by the glow of their fire, and their laughter carried across the night air. "Have a care with the things you mention," he said quietly. "The wrong word, wrong name, could see us killed."

Xaragitte shuddered, shrunk in upon herself. "The way you killed that poor boy outside the castle? He would have let us pass if I had done the talking. His face, oh, his poor face, all smashed in."

Yvon peered at her closely. Perhaps she had a fever, more worried about some dead man than him. "He served the Baron—he would have killed us."

"Not all the world is killing," she said, but something softened. She lowered her head onto her arm. "There—they've eased it somehow," she said quietly.

The distant laughter ended. Yvon looked over at the soldiers' camp and saw them spreading their own blankets. One face stared away from the fire into the dark, in their direction. It would be easy enough to murder an old man, a young mother, and her child out here in the wilderness. One could cover up any manner of crime, bury the evidence under the leaves in the forest just over the hill, and then tell the eunuch that her charges had wandered off. Yvon had seen such things done before. He rose up, stretched, and then sat on his haunches.

Claye woke up, lifting his head abruptly. Seeing Xaragitte there, he grinned and giggled, and tugged up a handful of grasses from beside the blanket. Xaragitte yawned, and eyes half-closed, stretched her hand out to him with one finger extended. Claye smiled at her, dropped the blades, and poked his finger toward hers.

"I don't know why we prolong this dance of masks and costumes," she said softly. Her shoulders started shaking. "I've never felt so tired, not even after my daughter died—"

"Listen to me." Yvon leaned forward, talking to her the way he'd talked to too many soldiers on too many campaigns. "We swore to Lord Gruethrist that we would save his lady's son from the Baron, and I can't do it alone. You're tired, and you hurt because something bad has happened to someone you love. But you have to be strong."

Claye's large eyes watched Yvon intently.

"If anything happens to you," Yvon said, "then Claye doesn't eat. So you have to be strong."

Xaragitte stopped crying, exhaled. Absurdly, she laughed at Yvon, then yawned again. Her hand moved to cover her mouth, then sagged to the ground as she fell asleep.

Claye immediately crawled away from her.

"Hold on, now," Yvon whispered, and stuck out his arm to block the child's path. Claye pealed in laughter, twisted, and squirted off in the opposite direction.

Yvon moved to block him again, and Claye turned it into a game. Soon Yvon was crawling around on his hands and knees, constantly herding Claye back toward his slumbering nursemaid. When the child started to grow frustrated, Yvon reached in and tickled him. Shrieks of laughter rose from the hillside, and a mammut pealed back in reply across the nightfall.

Yvon glanced over at Xaragitte. Even that sound failed to wake her.

"Mahmah," Claye shouted, to catch Yvon's attention. When Yvon looked at him, he rolled over onto his pudgy knees again and giggled, looking over his shoulder.

"Oh, you can't escape from me," Yvon whispered, and they started all over again. This was good, Yvon thought. This was what he wanted. They could turn the baby over to Lady Eleuate, wait for Lord Gruethrist to settle things with the Baron, and then he and Xaragitte could start over on their own. He held on tight to that image.

After a while, Claye paused unsteadily on three little limbs, rubbed one tiny fist against his eye, and yawned. Then he scooted over to Xaragitte. He tugged at her bodice strings, shoved them in his mouth, and whined.

Yvon hesitated a moment, then untied the strings himself. He brushed the cloth back with his fingertips, then slowly, gently, cupped her breast to lift it free. Claye pushed past Yvon's hand, rooting around with his nose in the pale flesh until his mouth found her nipple. He sucked happily and soon dozed off cuddled to his nursemaid's bosom.

The sky's deep blue purpled into black. The cool air raised goose-bumps on his skin, so Yvon took his own blanket and covered Xaragitte and Claye with it. Then he sat there, cloak folded around his arms and legs, guarding.

His chin drooped toward his chest and stayed there.

He slept, and in his sleep he dreamed of Xaragitte. She was with him, and he with her, in the way of men and women, and it was good, balm on an old wound. She moaned in pleasure as he thrust against her, but the dream shifted toward something else, some shadow moving in the darkness, the sound of feet through grass, and his eyes snapped open. He was aroused, though he still sat apart, hunched over his knees.

Xaragitte groaned, like she had in his dream, and yet nothing like that either. It was so dark he could scarcely see her. But something was wrong.

"Knew you weren't no uncle," said a voice, fishing for a response that would let him pin their position.

Yvon hunkered motionless and silent. Slowly he slid his knife from its sheath and waited.

"Leave her door open for me when you're done, you dead man," the voice said again, a little louder. He stepped forward from the darkness and paused uncertainly, sword poised before him. *A knight?* No. From his size and the way he moved, Yvon recognized the soldier from this afternoon. Some knight must have lent his approval to the murder along with the sword. That happened sometimes. He took two more cautious steps toward Xaragitte, sword raised. "You hear me?"

Yvon pounced, hitting the man hard just below the ribs, wrapping up his arms, and slamming him to the ground. The air rushed out of the soldier with a "Whoof!" and his sword flew free. Yvon slipped his blade in quick and slit the throat. The man's face froze, and the expression poured right out of it along with the blood.

He stood up and checked to make sure that no one else approached. A few distant snores sounded in the night, but nothing more. He regarded the dead soldier. That was the way he should have handled that puppy of a knight at the castle. He felt angry, frustrated, and tired. He bent again, slashed the man's drawstring, and yanked his pants down to his knees.

He found the man's knife and thrust it into the pelvis, between his legs, so that it stood knob up into the air. "You cowardly little prick," he murmured.

After wiping his blade carefully on the dead man's clothes, he searched the pockets for valuables and found none. He turned to wake Xaragitte. They needed to escape before the Baron's soldiers woke.

She was sitting up, staring at Yvon. She cradled the sleeping baby in one arm, retying her bodice with the other hand. In the darkness, Yvon had no indication of how long she'd been watching or what she'd seen.

"The bond is broken," she said. "Lady Gruethrist's lifespark has been fully extinguished."

⇥ CHAPTER 5 ⇤

Claye dangled like a dead weight at Xaragitte's breast, little mouth agape, one arm dangling toward the ground.

Yvon shoved their blankets into the pack. "We have to go now," he whispered. He said nothing about the soldier he had killed or Lady Gruethrist.

Xaragitte nodded and stood. Her shoulders sagged as soon as she slipped Claye into the sling.

"I could carry him," Yvon offered.

"I'll carry him. You lead us to safety. That's what you promised to do."

"I will." Although he didn't know how. They needed to cross the bridge at the castle to take the trail to Lady Eleuate's keep, but they would surely be stopped there and likely recognized. If they took the longer way around, crossing the river nearer its source in the mountains, by the time they circled back, the Baron's men would already have taken it.

Yvon led them quietly away from the army and followed the trail along the high slope beside the river. He went as quickly as Xaragitte could walk, paying more attention to her than the path, and thinking about how to cross the bridge, so that he didn't see they were surrounded until the first shadowy forms stepped out of the trees around them.

A woman stepped forward, one of the army's camp followers. The other shadows resolved into old men and adolescent boys bearing staffs and short knives. Yvon's hand slipped to his sword. If he hurt one or two, the rest would scatter.

"Hold," the woman said. She approached Xaragitte, stroking Claye's cheek with the back of her hand. "Boy or girl?"

"Boy," Xaragitte replied.

The woman made the kind of murmur that hinted condolences at this misfortune. "What's his name?"

It was a gesture of politeness, acting as though they were two women in one of their homes, already introduced. Xaragitte lifted her chin a little. "Cl-Kady."

Yvon's throat dried and knotted. More than ever, he wanted to be on the move away from the camp and the dead soldier.

"Klady?" the woman asked.

"Kady," Xaragitte corrected.

"You're from this valley?"

Xaragitte hesitated a second. "Yes."

"We're going to reach the castle tonight. Will we be better off claiming land on this side or the far side of the river?"

Yvon understood now. Baron Culufre was bringing the stragglers to be settlers so he could set up a second village of people loyal to himself. This group meant to get a jump on the others and claim the best land for themselves. It meant that Culufre intended to stay in the valley a long time, then. Lord Gruethrist would need to know.

Xaragitte seemed unsure how to answer the question. Yvon couldn't see her features, but her voice came haltingly. "There are lions—"

"Most of the good farming land on this side of the river is claimed already," Yvon said. "There are hills just across the bridge where one may do well enough."

The woman stepped back, her eyes glinting as she looked at Yvon. "That is what we'd already heard. Do you wish to travel with us? You could claim land also, in Sebius's name."

That damned eunuch! Gruethrist would have to deal with Sebius eventually.

Claye stirred uneasily in Xaragitte's arms.

Yvon took a step forward. If he could get them to the bridge before dawn, he and Xaragitte could cross the bridge mixed in with the others. "I know the way here well."

The woman nodded, and Yvon passed through the circle of men.

A bald, old man with stooped shoulders came up and kept pace beside Yvon. "The hills are better for orchards," he said, patting the seed bags slung over his shoulder. "Old fellows like you and I may not live to see them, but our daughters and their children will."

"She's not my daughter," Yvon said.

"They'll still outlive us," the old man replied.

Yvon pushed on as fast as he could go, over trails he had helped to blaze, expecting the families to falter at some point. But the dark-haired woman kept all her people together, badgering the older boys and girls into carrying their younger siblings when they faltered. Still, the stars wheeled in the sky past midnight, edging toward dawn before they neared the castle.

The ruined beams of the castle hall jabbed against the lightening sky like a tree washed up in a flood, with the rooftops of the little town poking up like stepping stones across a dark river. The Baron's soldiers seemed to have word of their coming. A grumpy pair met them and escorted them to the bridge, where they crossed without question. The oak bridge creaked and sagged beneath their combined weight, and then they were across, and Yvon was standing next to Xaragitte and Claye.

"You're welcome to join us," the dark-haired woman said.

"My—my relatives await us in the mountains near Lady Eleuate's keep," Xaragitte said.

The old man stood beside her, running his hand over his bald head. "Orchards," he told Yvon. "I've plenty of seeds."

"May they prosper in the harvest, safe from war," Yvon replied, invoking two gods. He would have to come back with Gruethrist to dislodge these people later, but he didn't wish them any personal harm. "May you prosper."

Already the younger children were spreading on the hillside grass to rest, lying down and falling asleep. Xaragitte looked at Yvon, rocking Claye in her arms trying to keep him asleep.

"Will you give me one of the blankets to sop up the dew and keep us warm?" she asked, with a nod at the bag.

"No," Yvon answered quietly. "We can't sleep. We have to keep going. The soldiers will be along with their mammuts before the morning is gone."

He took a few steps along the shepherd's trail into the hills, but she didn't follow him. Her head was turned toward the other families.

Quietly, he said, "If they pass by us and reach Lady Eleuate first, we'll never deliver Cla—the child to safety. His father will never see him again."

With her head sagging toward her chest, she slouched up the trail toward him.

As she came beside him, he whispered to her. "I'm sorry, m'lady Xaragitte." They trudged in silence up the shepherd's trail, rising into the steep hills above the river.

Xaragitte and Claye napped briefly around midmorning, the nurse-maid falling asleep as soon as she stretched upon the grass on a hilltop beneath some trees. Yvon squatted guard nearby, watching the trail behind them. He knew that fresh scouts could be sent out in pursuit from the castle as soon as Sebius or Baron Culufre had reason to suspect them of murdering the soldier or carrying Gruethrist's child.

When Claye's stirring woke Xaragitte, Yvon fed her a portion of the cold porridge he had saved the night before. His mouth watered and his stomach rumbled, but he suspected she'd need the rest of it before they reached Lady Eleuate's castle.

"How much farther do we have to go?" she asked.

"Wah!" Claye said, slapping at the food cupped in Xaragitte's hand. She pulled it away from him.

"It's a two-day journey," Yvon said. Although a determined force of soldiers could make it in one by marching day and night. "We'll stop tonight and sleep well, then make the ford tomorrow morning and dine well tomorrow night."

She licked her palm when she was done eating. Claye shoved his fingers in his mouth and sucked on them.

Spring had not yet crept this high into the foothills, and the land was bare and still brown. The trail wound through steeper, rocky slopes as it rose toward the high meadows. The mountains surrounding them were not as distant now, and all the peaks had sharper edges.

This was the country of the peasants, the people who had been here before Gruethrist came. Many still lived in their villages farther back in the mountains, pushed there after their revolt. A decade ago, Gruethrist had tried to force the peasants to give up their traditional fields and switch to plows, so they would have more grains to pay in taxes. One of their wizard-priests had proclaimed the sanctity of the old ways and led them in rebellion. There'd been hard fighting, a lot of murders done in darkness against the settlers, before the priest and his followers were slaughtered. But in the end, Gruethrist left the peasants' farming as it was, and collected his extra due in game.

With inferior forces and fewer men, Gruethrist would have to adopt some of their tactics to dislodge the Baron and protect the land he meant his lady's heir to have. Yvon would point that out to him when they met again.

Xaragitte struggled to keep up, using singsongs to the child to measure her pace. When she fell quiet, Yvon looked over and saw her eyes lose focus. Absentmindedly, she almost leaned on him for extra strength. He reached out to brace her, but she caught herself at the last moment.

"It's all right for you to lean on me," he said.

She shook her head dully and staggered on. But her flow of rhymes withered like flowers nipped by frost.

Near dark, they lay down beside the trail, Xaragitte falling asleep with Claye as soon as she had eaten half of the remaining porridge. Yvon made a small ball from the rest of it, rolling it around in his hand, then letting it sit for a long time in his mouth before chewing and swallowing.

He wrapped both their blankets around her and the child, then pulled his cloak tight and leaned against a tree, shivering in the colder mountain air before he dozed off.

He jerked awake before he knew what had startled him. Then he heard a mammut again, from the direction of the trail behind them. Baron Culufre's men meant to make the march in one day and night.

Shaking Xaragitte gently, he said, "They're coming. We must go now."

She nodded grimly and rose. Yvon lifted Claye's limp form and helped slide him into her nursing sling. No sound broke the cool night air again except for their breathing and the soft crunching of their feet over the trail. Xaragitte's head drooped toward her chest and jerked up several times. Before long, she was nearly sleepwalking, eyes all but closed. When Claye woke and wanted to be fed, she became more alert. They stopped a short time later so she could clean the boy's bottom.

"How much farther tonight?" she asked.

"Not much," he replied, but he must have been sleepwalking too. They were on the trail beside the mountain river. A few birds were singing the first notes of morning. Without the faint light in the east Yvon wouldn't have noticed the three tall pines and would have missed the turnoff he meant to take.

He turned. A squat building—the ford wizard's house—sat below the pines, down near the rocky river bank.

Yvon went straight down to it and pounded on the wooden door. "Hey, Banya, wake up!"

Several moments later, the door cracked open. A wrinkled face peered at Yvon through the gap. Finally, the man said, "Are you a ghost? Tell me three times, tell me true."

Yvon wondered what Banya had heard. "Under the sky, I live. Above the ground, I live."

The door swung wide. An older man stepped outside. He wore a woman's sleeveless dress, with big, graceless, copper bracelets on his wrists and an ill-fitting girdle about his waist. He had hard limbs, the same scoured-brown color as weathered trees high up in the mountains. Unkempt hair fell about his wrinkled face and spread across his broad shoulders. His face was stubbled where he'd scraped it clean a couple days before. He stared at Yvon. "You're a dead man."

"You're the second one to call me that in as many days."

"Who was the first?"

"I didn't ask his name before I killed him. One of Culufre's men. Where'd you hear that I was dead?"

"You're missing, that's why." Banya glanced at Xaragitte, and shielded his eyes as he stared at the baby. "They were still digging away at the castle ruins two days ago. It's presumed they'll find your body buried among the stones and ashes, with the nursemaid, the heir, and a few others."

Yvon rubbed his fist inside his other palm. "Let them sift for a month, if it'll help us. We need to lay low until Gruethrist ransoms himself or escapes."

Banya stared off at the morning star, refusing to meet Yvon's eyes. Finally, he said, "If you want to see Gruethrist again, you'll have to do what Sumukan did."

"I'm too tired for riddles," Yvon said. The wild man Sumukan was the friend and companion of the ancient king, Ganmagos. "Do you mean that I must go and cut down the cedar of heaven or that I must slay the god's eight-legged bull?"

"I mean that you must do as Sumukan did when Ganmagos died. You'll have to kill yourself and descend into the underworld to rescue him." Ganmagos returned to the living afterward, and became an immortal, but Sumukan was trapped forever in the land of death. The king wrote a famous lament before he climbed the high mountain and leaped into the heavens to become the wandering red star.

"Speak plainly," Yvon said, still not understanding.

"Gruethrist is dead."

Yvon forced a laugh. "As dead as I am?"

"More dead than you." Banya's expression never changed, but he glanced away again, a way he had when speaking bad news.

Yvon's chest tightened. He'd served Lord Tubat as a common soldier, and stood beside him as a dam against the slaughter of the virgins during the Temple Rebellion of the last succession. When the Empress had offered Tubat his choice of rewards, all he'd asked was that his common soldiers—the handful that survived—be allowed to grow the braid of knights. The Empress granted his wish, and gave his hand to Lady Gruethrist in marriage. Without Lord Gruethrist, Yvon would only be another common soldier. "How did it happen?" he asked.

"The story is that he rushed into the burning hall to succor some of his knights, including you. *You* rushed in to put out the flames, or maybe to rescue his heir—I've heard it both ways—and were trapped when the roof collapsed. The knights were burned beyond recognition, but they found Gruethrist's body under a partly collapsed wall. Crushed, but untouched by fire."

Yvon would have discounted any story of Gruethrist's death but one such as this: he was crude enough to burn his lady's home, but he had always been loyal to his men and would risk his life for them.

The wizard looked directly into Xaragitte's eyes. "After seeing his body, and thinking her child already dead, Lady Gruethrist tried to kill herself with poison. She still lived two days ago."

"She died during the night," Xaragitte said softly. "No, the night before last. They blur so. . . . I felt it because my bond to her was severed."

The wizard paused. "My regrets at her passing."

"This is the babe's nursemaid," explained Yvon. His hands and feet felt numb, like he was outside in the snow. "She was bonded to Lady Gruethrist."

Banya lifted his chin at the baby. "That'd be the heir?"

"He was. Now he's not much more than any other poor orphaned boy. If he was a girl instead . . ." Yvon reached for his missing braid. The enormity of the situation stunned him. The child's mother and father were dead, and Baron Culufre occupied both castle and valley. "Will Eleuate help us?"

"With the lady of the valley dead, and her lord as well?" Banya asked, shaking his head. "No, Eleuate won't hold her daughter Portia to the betrothal. And her husband is the Baron's man now. I say that confidently, as one who served him as a knight once and knows his heart."

Yvon made the warding sign, three fingers touching forehead, mouth, and heart. He hadn't done it in years. "Maybe we are cursed."

"It's war," Banya said. "Hard things happen in war."

Xaragitte kissed the baby's head, though he made a face and twisted his head away. "What path should we follow, wizard?"

Banya glanced at Xaragitte, ducked into the small house, and returned with a small bag. He untied the drawstrings.

Yvon said, "Don't—"

"Please do," Xaragitte interrupted.

Banya whispered into the open mouth of the bag, then shook it with his ear to the opening. The clicking sound made Yvon's skin crawl. Banya shook it again, and held the open mouth to Xaragitte. "Ask your question."

She leaned forward and whispered something into the sack. Yvon strained to hear her but could only make out the sound of the baby's name. Something about *Claye*.

Banya knelt, shaking the bag vigorously, then upending it and spilling the bones. Yvon stood back and stared. The divination sets he'd seen in the Imperial City were more elegant and complex. These were finger bones from a troll's hand, twice as large as a man's, with crude pictures scratched into their sides. Banya peered at them from different angles.

"Mah!" shouted Claye.

Banya frowned. "The voices of the spirits are in a tumult. It's hard for me to find guidance in their chatter. The war bone falls outside the circle when I expected it in the middle. The lesser journey bone obscures the greater journey, here at the top. Both are crossed by the unmarked bone." He poked at the mound of bones. "What did you ask them, ma'am?"

She kissed the baby's head. "What path should we follow."

"Whatever path you choose, it leads away from war and into darkness. This I see for all three of you, though you may not travel there together. Darkness can mean death, but it can also mean sleeping and waking, or change. Those who pass through darkness rather than into it emerge again into the light."

Claye leaned in Xaragitte's arms, trying to grab the bones. "But which path, for his safety?" Xaragitte whispered.

Banya shrugged. Then he pointed toward the mountain range across the river. "If you head into the mountains, you might find a place to hide. It's not good land, but you won't want for shelter—there are abandoned farms up there, left behind by our women when they fled the peasant rebellion."

"Is it safe?" Xaragitte asked.

"Are you safe now?" the wizard snapped back. "Does any creature with two legs or four roam safe upon the earth?"

From down the valley echoed a faint sound, as of mammuts or horns. Claye twisted around in Xaragitte's arm to peer at the noise. "Mahmah," he said. "Mahmah!"

"Will you take us across the river?" Yvon asked Banya. He couldn't think of any other choices.

"Yes. Best do it now, before the daylight comes full. I like it better when I see the demons that I sing to."

Yvon shuddered and touched his sword. There were three things he hated and feared. Mammuts were one and the river demons were another. "Can I lend a hand?"

"Over here," he said. A small flat-bottomed boat leaned against the back wall of the cottage. He gestured to Yvon. "You take that end and we'll carry it down to the river."

It was more awkward than heavy. Yvon's feet slid on the muddy bank, but he stayed upright until they set the boat down. The river flowed out of the mountains, swollen with meltwater, though in the summer it might be only waist-deep.

"I don't see any demons," he said hopefully.

"They sleep along the bottom," explained Banya. "This ford is as high as they swim on the river. You'll see them rise suddenly sometimes, in places where you swear there were none, to snap at the birds. Wait here, while I go fetch my pole."

Xaragitte stood high up on the bank, away from the water's edge. She was no more eager than Yvon to face any demon.

Banya returned, carrying a pole as tall as Baron Culufre's armored mammut and leading a goat by a leash. "What's that for?" Yvon asked him. "Will you feed it to the demon?"

"No, it's for you," he said. "Someone gave it to me as payment for helping with her daughter's wedding. But the damn thing keeps me awake all night. You might use the meat, once you find a spot to stay in for a while."

Yvon's mouth watered at the thought; Xaragitte said, "Oh, thank you!"

Banya hummed his song as they positioned the craft on the river's edge and loaded the goat aboard. It bleated and kicked the side of the craft, rocking it. They coaxed Xaragitte to come down and sit in the middle.

"Have you ever been in a boat before?" Yvon asked her quietly, not daring to interrupt the wizard's song.

She shook her head. Her face had blanched white, pale as the moon; her hair framed it, the color of dawn on the clouds.

"Sit very still then and you'll be fine. There's nothing to worry about with a wizard along." He smiled, and hoped his grin wasn't too ghastly. Then he took his spot in the small boat's bow. "We're ready," he told Banya.

Singing aloud now in an eerie rhythmic chant, the wizard shoved the craft offshore, wading knee-deep before he climbed aboard. The current pushed the boat downstream, so that even while Banya thrust his pole quickly and expertly they did not go straight across.

Halfway to the other side, the goat stamped its feet in complaint. "Maaaa!"

An incandescent glow, as long as the boat, surfaced nearby. Xaragitte gasped as it slithered across the watertop.

"Don't look directly at it," Yvon hissed. "They can bewitch you in a fingersnap."

She squeezed her eyes shut and cowered protectively around the baby. Which showed she had more sense than Yvon, because he couldn't take his eyes off the monster. His hand drifted to his sword. You could kill a demon with a sword—or any other weapon—if your will stayed free long enough to use it. And if you dared the wrath of the gods.

Two more luminous serpentine trails curled toward them. Then the morning sun bloomed suddenly over the ridge, transforming the surface of the water from polished black to liquid light in a blink. Yvon lost all sight of the demons and started scanning the river frantically to find them.

Far away, he heard Banya chanting round in circles; Yvon's thoughts spun in circles too, his hand gripped convulsively on the hilt of his weapon.

Something tapped him on the back.

He found himself staring transfixed over the edge of the boat into the scaly face of a demon. Its hooded head swayed on a thick-muscled neck that protruded well out of the water. The sawtoothed mouth gaped and closed, slit eyes piercing Yvon's soul. As he drew back in revulsion, the flat nostrils flared on either side of the axe-shaped head. Yvon's own nose choked on the demon's sickly sweet scent.

Something hit him hard between the shoulder blades.

He looked up. Banya, still singing, had smacked him with the pole. They had reached the far bank, and the wizard wanted him to leap out and pull the boat ashore. Yvon yanked his gaze away from the demon, crabbed his way around Xaragitte, and splashed ankle-deep into the icy water. Grasping the prow of the boat, he heaved it in close to the shore.

Banya's song wavered for a split second as he lost his balance. But he steadied himself with the staff and continued to sing. His voice was strained.

Yvon noticed the two other demons, heads thrust out of the water like branches from some submerged tree. "Come, come quickly," he called to Xaragitte.

She stood, her face still huddled against the covered baby. Yvon helped her out of the boat and up the steep embankment. She didn't say a word about his hand upon her arm. He was too shaky to feel any reward. The goat tried to butt him as he hefted it onto the bank and handed the leash to Xaragitte. When Banya finally climbed out, Yvon towed the boat completely free of the water.

The song faltered and ceased. The demon shook itself, twisting its head around until it spied them.

"Begone!" Banya shouted. He thrust the butt-end of the pole at the demon, who reared back and barked. Then it sprayed a mist from its hood, snapped at the pole, and disappeared into the river with a splash.

Yvon searched the water, but the other two demons were already gone. He and Banya hid the boat under some brush atop the bank.

Claye sat upright in Xaragitte's arms, a look of intense concentration upon his chubby-cheeked face. "He couldn't stop listening to your song," she told the wizard.

"Well, that's the whole, unblemished purpose now, isn't it?" Banya said, sitting down hard on the grassy slope and rubbing his neck. He leaned backward, closed his eyes, sighed. "May the crows squabble over your meatless bones, Yvon. You let the demon make you dream."

Yvon grunted acknowledgment.

"Nearly fell into the water, where you would have been killed. I had to hit you three times with the pole before you felt it once."

"I've never had good luck with the demons," he admitted.

"Maybe it's your destiny. No man can run away from his destiny. Have you ever seen a rabbit run when it's startled?" He made an arc in the air with his hand. "Runs in a circle, comes right back where it began. Wait there and you can always catch it. The gods do that to men too."

Xaragitte shifted Claye to her other hip, then sat down. The goat grazed at the end of its tether.

Yvon plopped down beside Xaragitte. He could've fallen asleep in an instant, and not just from the lingering effects of the demon. Just as he was letting his eyes drift closed, trumpeting echoed up the valley walls again. A sound like that could carry for miles, but Yvon shook off his torpor and stood.

Banya sat up too. "You need to go."

Xaragitte got to her feet, smoothing her skirt.

"Which way?" Yvon asked.

Banya pointed to some low hills at a right angle to the river. "Head easterly and north along the ridge, around the hollows tucked back in the hills. More than a few old farmhouses you could live in. But the farther you go, the more likely you are to run into cats and dogs, all kinds. Keep that in mind if you sleep outside overnight."

Yvon knew all that. "How dangerous are the peasants?"

Banya looked away from him. "There's more than a few old warriors who took part in the rebellion, but I don't think they'll recognize you without your braid. Most of us westerners look the same to them." He jerked his chin toward the canyon. "I'm going to find someplace to lay low. You two need to go."

"Thank you," said Xaragitte. "Three times I bid you comfort in your home. May it shelter you and bring you comfort."

"Fare you well," Banya said. "Whatever path you choose, fare well." He went back down to the riverbank, humming.

Yvon turned toward the mountains, opening his water bottle for a sip and passing it to Xaragitte. "We should press on until we find some shelter," he said. "By midmorning, if no one's following us, we'll be able to take a short break."

"How will we know that no one's following us?" she asked, pausing to shorten the goat's leash.

"Maaaa!" Claye looked at the goat and grinned.

"We won't unless we see them first," Yvon said, "and if we can see them, it'll be too late."

It hadn't looked like a canyon at all from the riverside, but just over the hill it broadened out into meadows that rose almost above the mountains themselves. Dawn flooded over the dead and winter-trampled grasses, warming Yvon. Xaragitte unwrapped the blanket from her shoulders, and he stuffed it into their bag. They followed deer trails easterly and north, as Banya suggested. Although they saw no peasants, they saw signs of them: distant spirals of smoke, trees blazoned with messages, the foundations of a house destroyed during the rebellion. Halfway to noon, they came upon an abandoned orchard of plum trees. Even the bare branches made Yvon hungry. Eating Sebius's food with the Baron's army had reminded him how good it was to eat.

"Can we stop for a while?" Xaragitte begged.

"I was thinking we should," Yvon admitted. His body screamed for rest. He tied the goat to one of the trees. "You nap first. I'll sit guard in case anyone comes."

Xaragitte sat down and fed the child while Yvon went to refill their water flasks at a brook a hundred feet away. When he returned, she was curled on her side, arms stretched out protectively around Claye. He too slept, a little trail of milk dripping from the corner of his open mouth. Yvon propped himself against a tree beside them and remembered the dream he'd had of her the night before. It would be good if it could be like that between them.

The next thing he noticed was Xaragitte's shriek.

He leapt up, drawing his sword as he awoke. Spinning in a circle, his heart pounding, looking for the soldiers or for peasant warriors and not seeing them, he shouted, "We're fine, we're fine—there's no enemy! We're fine!"

"*We* don't matter," she screamed at him. "*Where's Claye?*"

He was nowhere around. Sword in hand, Yvon rushed frantically through the grove, shouting the child's name. Xaragitte's voice rose from the other direction, and in between their combined cries, Yvon thought he heard a click. Following the sound, he spotted the baby near the brook, pounding two stones, then making a splash in the water.

A little dark-haired, dark-eyed peasant boy crouched beside him.

"Here!" Yvon shouted. "He's over here! Hey!"

The last was directed at the little peasant boy, who'd picked up a stick and raised it over his head. But the sound startled Claye, who flopped over backward and began to wail.

As Yvon leapt forward to grab him before he could roll into the stream, another voice sounded.

"*Sinnglas!*"

A peasant woman, hugely pregnant, wobbled along the stream's bank. She wore a deerskin dress, decorated with glass beads, silver, and pieces of fabric, her lustrous black hair held up with a comb of carved bone. A second boy a few years older ran along beside her. Yvon stopped, lifting his eyes to scan the landscape for any men.

Xaragitte arrived, running to snatch up Claye, crooning soothing words that calmed no one.

The peasant woman frowned at Yvon, and asked Xaragitte something in a sharp tone.

"What's she saying?" Xaragitte asked, rocking Claye.

"I don't know," Yvon said, dropping his sword's point. He saw no one else nearby.

The two little boys were maybe three and five years old. The older one directed the younger one around. The little one still held onto his stick. He looked over at his mother, then hit his brother. The bigger child grabbed the stick away and tried to break it over his knee, but without any luck.

The peasant woman said something else to Xaragitte, then, with both hands resting on her belly, called to her boys again. "*Damaqua, Sinnglas!*"

She toddled off without another glance at either Yvon or Xaragitte, her boys running after her.

Xaragitte jogged Claye in her arms, still trying to cheer him. Yvon paced beside her. He saw no sign of any other peasants. Overhead, black slashes spiralled in slow arcs. Vultures. Seven, eight. "Nothing happened," he said firmly. "We're all fine."

"We need shelter," Xaragitte snapped. Her eyes had dark circles around them, and looked haunted. "You must find us shelter before nightfall."

Yvon met her gaze and nodded.

"You *must*."

"I will," he said, sheathing his sword.

They heard the goat bleating as they returned to the plum grove. Claye stopped crying and twisted his head around curiously at the noise. Yvon didn't mention the vultures. If there was carrion, that likely meant lions or wolves. He hoped that it was wolves.

After gathering their few belongings, they set off again. Meadows that had once been cleared for farming were now overgrown with small trees, still leafless. They startled a small herd of deer in one of the abandoned fields they passed through, and Yvon wished for a bow. Food would be scarce to come by until after the plants bloomed. At least they had the goat. One way or another, that would help them get by.

He expected to find numerous houses, but they had vanished like the families who'd built them. The two of them simply trudged on, forcing one foot past the other league after league, long into the afternoon without a break, until Xaragitte spotted a dark square on the lip of a small hill ahead of them. She raised her hand, and Yvon said, "Maybe."

He walked faster, but as they came close he saw it was only a pile of charred, decaying timber.

Xaragitte stared at it, frowning. Thinking perhaps of the more recent fire at the castle. "It has walls, at least," she suggested. "Perhaps we should stay here tonight."

"No," Yvon said. He had a bad feeling about the place. Those broken walls were no protection from determined man or beast. "We'll head that way, checking the hollows back in the hills, like Banya suggested. There's bound to be something better close by."

Then he led them on a weaving trail, checking every cleft in the hills for some sign of former habitation. But though they passed more orchards, bits of fence, and, once, a plowframe shorn of its blade and perched upon a rock, he found no place that could shelter them. Worse, they'd had little to eat since dinner in the soldiers' camp the night before, and though they drank from clear streams that flowed out of the mountains, the cold water in Yvon's stomach only fed his hunger. Xaragitte did not complain, but she began to lag, shuffling her feet blindly forward. They had come at least ten leagues since Banya's house. Yvon doubted she had ever walked as far in a week as she had the past two days.

Long shadows stretched from the trees like fingers reaching out to grab them. Yvon walked beside Xaragitte, to catch her if she stumbled, wondering at first how much farther she could push herself, then marveling again at how pretty she seemed to him, even footsore and exhausted.

She noticed him staring at her. "Sir?"

He quickly shifted his eyes away. "Yes?"

"Would you mind carrying Claye for a bit?"

His throat tightened. "Not at all."

"I can carry the bag instead."

"It's a feather on my back."

The sling was awkward, and Claye squirmed and squealed, so that

Yvon had a hard time arranging everything to his comfort. The knot in the sling dug into his collarbone every time Claye straightened his legs, so, after a few times of this, Yvon reached in to tickle Claye's ribs. Claye giggled and curled up, making Xaragitte smile, so Yvon tickled him for that reason too. Claye grabbed a fistful of Yvon's beard and tugged.

"Hey," Yvon said, prying the baby's fingers loose and smoothing his beard across his chin.

Xaragitte laughed at him. Then she sang:

> *"Baby, don't grab your papa's hair;*
> *You might find snakes inside of there."*

Yvon glanced at her sideways to see if she meant anything with that innocent old rhyme. But he couldn't tell. The sun squatted low in the western sky and Xaragitte lifted her eyes to it, her smile fading along with the light. "I don't think I can go on much farther."

A wind out of the southwest rustled the treetops. The ragged-toothed edge of a dark cloud chased after it. Rain was coming. Yvon pointed to a cleft between two hills ahead of them, a darker shadow in the gloom. "If we don't find someplace there, I'll build a bower to shelter us for the night."

"I know you'll do your best."

He could go one more night without sleep to sit guard. As they climbed over the last rolling hill, he steeled himself to the work of cutting branches. By Verlogh's justice, he—

"Bwnte's harvest." Xaragitte's hands covered her mouth.

They were both thinking of gods, and by the mercy of two gods, it was a house. Surrounded by trees, set back in the deep shadow at the top of a long slope. They stumbled toward it, Yvon slowly, encumbered by the baby on his chest and the goat, who dug in its heels and refused to go any farther. As Xaragitte surged ahead, he shouted.

"Careful—something may be inside!"

She tripped to a stop. "Oh. I hadn't thought of that."

"Here, you take the boy." He handed over Claye and tethered the goat to a tree—it promptly knelt down, its tongue hanging out its mouth. Then he drew his knife. "I'll have a look around."

The house appeared to have been abandoned but never attacked. It had been a prosperous little dwelling. The door had iron hinges, and rust flaked off, metal squeaking, as he pushed it open. Two dark shapes flew at his head, and he ducked out of the way as they shot off into the trees.

"What's that?" Xaragitte called, panic in her voice.

"Doves," he answered, peering inside. "It appears that's all that's in here. But let me finish searching."

There was just the one large room, with a half loft for sleeping over the rafters. One very rickety table was propped up against a wall in the corner, but there was no other furniture. Thistles sprouted from the piles of bird droppings on the floor, and the ashes in the fireplace had turned to dirt. He looked up and saw dark blue sky through the roof, but when he leaned his shoulders against the walls, they didn't budge. He wrinkled his nose. There was an odd smell, sharp, but he couldn't place it. He went to call Xaragitte and saw her silhouette blocking the doorway.

"Are we going to stay?" she asked.

"There's only a roof over the one corner here, but the walls are sound. It'll do. I'll start fixing the roof tomor—"

"Come back out. Let's do this properly."

He ducked his head to her as she stepped aside. Once outside, he turned to face her. "Lady, I give you this abode, a place to put down roots, a tree to shelter and to comfort you."

She stood at the crooked threshold, right arm across her waist, under Claye, and extended her left hand inside. "Sir," she said. "Welcome to my home. Though it is your nature to roam, know that you are welcome at this hearth and table. May chance often bring you here."

He wanted to kiss her. Instead, he ducked his head a second time. "M'lady."

The wind rushed and shook the trees above them.

As she entered first with Claye, Yvon grabbed loose branches from the ground and tossed them in a pile by the door. They could use them for firewood later. When he found a stout branch the right size, he followed her inside and used it to block the door. Xaragitte had already unpacked their blankets and sat nursing the child. She'd chosen the spot where the intact roof still sheltered her, leaving Yvon partly under the hole if he didn't mean to crowd her. He sniffed the air again. It smelled like coming rain, and he couldn't find the other scent at all.

In the total darkness, she said quietly, "Do you think we'll ever go back?"

"Yes," he answered, spreading his blanket. He removed his sword and knife, placing them beside him; then he pulled off his boots. "Certainly we will."

He lay down and closed his eyes at once.

Xaragitte whispered, "Whatever will we go back to?"

☰ CHAPTER 6 ☰

"Maaa!"

When Yvon first snapped awake, he thought that the sound came from Claye. But when he rolled over, he saw Xaragitte and the baby curled up under their blanket. Claye chuckled, then emitted a laugh, although his eyes were closed. Yvon smiled. What a happy baby he was who giggled when he dreamed.

Yvon rolled over and pressed his head into the crook of his arm. He was poised on the precipice of sleep—

"Maaa!"

The goat. He'd left the goat outside. He listened for it again, but heard nothing for a while. He hadn't believed Banya when the wizard said the creature kept him awake all night, thought that was only an excuse to make them take it. Maybe it'd be fine until morning. He was nearly asleep—

"Maaa!"

He couldn't even open his eyes. The leagues he had walked the past two days chased after him like a pack of wolves. Exhaustion was a predator—he'd seen it kill men before. The only weapon to fight it with was rest, and he needed rest. The goat fell silent. Yvon'd just rest a few more minutes, then—

"*Maaa!*"

He rolled over, his chin slick with drool.

"*Maaa! Maaa!*"

"Yvon?"

"Yes," he mumbled.

"Yvon, is everything aright?" He heard concern in Xaragitte's voice. "I've been talking to you, but you won't answer."

"Too tired." His head felt like a boulder his shoulders were incapable of stirring.

"The goat," she whispered. "Do you think it'll quiet down if I bring it in here with us? It's keeping me awake."

He pushed up on his elbows. "I'll fetch it."

"No, you stay right there," she said, standing up. "You've done enough the past two days."

"Are you sure?"

The goat bleated continuously now. Probably frightened by the storm that was blowing up.

"It will only take a moment," she said.

He flipped over on his side. He heard, as if far away, the branch scrape free of the door, and air stir as the wind blew through the open doorway.

"Maa—!" The goat stopped its noise.

Good. She'd gotten it, then. Yvon let go and sank back into sleep's deeper current.

Xaragitte screamed.

Heart kicking like a rabbit caught in a snare, he rolled over too fast and banged his head into the wall. He twisted the other direction,

got on his feet, and staggered to the door before he realized he'd forgotten to grab his sword.

The blood in his veins turned to ice. His hands braced the door
frame.

Crouching over the dead goat was a dagger-toothed lion.

He'd forgotten the vultures.

Xaragitte stood halfway between the house and the dead nanny.
She took one trembling step backward, and the lion lifted its head to
growl. Raw flesh plopped out of its mouth, fell slap on the ground.

Yvon tried to yell out to her not to turn her back on it, but his
tongue cleaved to his mouth, and she spun around.

The lion leaned back on its squat legs—

Xaragitte took a step and a half toward him, and Yvon's whole
world shrunk to the terror compassed by the pale moon of her face.

—and pounced.

Yvon's hand fastened on a chunk of wood from the stack beside the
door, and with a roar of his own, he hurled himself at the lion, landing
one blow square across its flat snout as it hit Xaragitte between the
shoulders, knocking her to the ground.

The lion crouched on Xaragitte's back—she was screaming—and
barked at Yvon in surprise. He swung again, another blow on the
bridge of the lion's nose. The dry wood cracked and fell to pieces. He
reached down to pull Xaragitte to her feet, back to the safety of the
house, when the lion swiped him with a paw.

Agony knifed through his arm and chest as he smashed into the
ground. The lion leaned over Xaragitte, the twin daggers of its teeth
angled to rip open her back.

Yvon surged to his feet, the shattered club still clutched in his fist,
and charged the lion with a yell.

The lion sat back on its haunches and roared.

Yvon's yell shriveled in his throat, and his charge stumbled to a
dead stop. The roar shivered through him just like the bell ward on

the night they'd escaped the castle, turning his joints to jelly and his will to dust.

For a brief second, absolute silence.

Then the baby cried inside the cabin, Xaragitte sobbed, and Yvon gulped, staring down the cavernous jaws of the beast as its nauseating hot breath washed over his face. Yvon raised the stub of his club and started forward.

The lion turned, snatched the goat with its powerful jaws, and shook it once, snapping the rope that held it to the tree. Then it vaulted away into the shadows.

Rain teardropped out of the clouded sky for a few seconds and then started to fall in earnest.

Yvon sagged, sat down hard. Blood spilled from the slashes in his forearm and side. The pain flashed far away, like lightning from a distant storm, then hit him like a roll of thunder so his whole body trembled.

He groaned and wobbled to his feet.

Xaragitte was flat on her stomach, arms covering her head, sobbing and gasping. Her dress was shredded across the middle of her back, the white cloth cut in strips, tatters so mixed with blood and skin that Yvon could not tell which was which.

"Hold on," he said. "I'll be right back—you hold on!"

Her body convulsed with each panting sob; her legs twitched. It was bad.

He looked at himself. His skin was torn to the rib. If nothing was broken he was lucky. A deep cut on his arm went down through the big muscle, but it was his left arm, luckily, and the blood came out steady, not in little pulsing spurts.

He rushed into the house. Claye wailed, dismayed, alone, afraid. Yvon ignored him, found his knife, and cut off one sleeve, tying it as tight as he could around his arm to stop the bleeding. Claye crawled over and clung to his leg. Yvon shoved him away and grabbed the blanket.

He ran back outside and knelt by Xaragitte in the pelting rain. "I need to sew up those wounds," he whispered. "But I don't have needles or thread."

"I'm thirsty," she said, her voice quivering.

He cupped his hands, trying to catch water from the sky, but it ran through his fingers before he could bring it to her lips. The ground beneath her was quickly turning to mud. "I have to get you inside," he said, pressing the blanket against her back, trying to stanch the flow of blood.

Claye's crying jumped up a pitch, slicing through the rain.

"I need to go calm Claye," she said, the words coming out of her mouth as the barest whisper. "Can't you hear him crying?"

"Easy, easy, now," he said, all his attention focused on taking care of her. "Let me help you."

He raised her gently to her feet, and caught her when her knees buckled. He propped her up and they limped side by side into the house, her feet slipping in the mud.

The rain abated for a moment, and an odd kind of thunder rolled down from the hillside. A humanoid shape stood there, dimly outlined between the trees against the blue-black sky. Yvon's feet stopped moving, and he nearly let go of Xaragitte.

She sagged in his arms, gasping as he caught her. "What?" Her voice was shrill, panicked. "What is it?"

The silhouette reared up, extended its long arms like some grotesque mockery of a man, and then slammed them on the ground. It stood as though listening, then turned, and disappeared over the ridge into the forest beyond.

"Nothing, nothing to worry about," Yvon said, helping her into the house.

But the source of the smell in the house became clear. The creature he had just seen was a troll, and it probably used this space as a den sometimes. Of the three things Yvon feared and hated, he'd rather face a mammut or a demon.

Xaragitte was weeping uncontrollably as they stumbled through the door. Claye lay on the ground, his body arched and rigid, eyes squeezed shut, torrenting a scream.

Yvon restrained Xaragitte as she lurched toward the child, pain knifing through his arm and ribs. "You can't pick him up!"

"Just"—she gasped—"help me sit beside him."

Yvon eased her down beside the wall, kneeling beside her to prop her up. She murmured mollifying words as Claye rolled over, trying at once to climb into her arms. She groaned in agony, flinching, almost blacking out as she fell backward.

"Get away!" Yvon reached around her to push Claye down. His hand formed a half-fist, clenched in pain. He wouldn't let anyone or anything hurt her again, not even the baby.

She inhaled sharply, pulling herself upright. "Don't—hurt—him!"

Her words emerged so quietly they all but disappeared as Claye's cry rose in pitch and volume until it sounded like a river in flood. He scrambled for her arms again. Yvon stretched out his hand, to hold the baby off more gently. But Claye grabbed a fistful of skin and hair, and pulled himself hand over hand up Yvon's arm, like a man scaling a rope, until he grasped Xaragitte by the neck and clung there.

Nothing Xaragitte did comforted Claye. Her singing and her soothing strokes were to no effect, nor would the boy take her breast. He cried like a lost child, forlorn.

The rain poured through the roof, soaking everything. Yvon couldn't tell what was wet with rain and what with blood. He leaned against the wall and Xaragitte, like a buttress holding both of them up. The pain stabbed at him. He wanted to move.

Outside, he heard the troll drum its chest again. It sounded nearer. He looked at the wide-open door, and then over at his sword lying half-sunk in a muddy puddle. His hand jumped to his throat. He still had two charms as well.

"M'lady," he said very softly.

"It's raining," she mumbled, trying to rock Claye. Then she started to sing, in a wheezing off-key voice.

"The silver rain is pouring down.
Pick your coins up off the ground.
Spend them quick before you drown,
my poor baby."

"M'lady, I have to look outside."

"Kady was a soldier," she said softly, eyes unfocused.

"I have to block the door again."

"He would have been a knight. Lord Gruethrist was going to make him a knight." She glanced at Claye, who sucked on his thumb, eyes closed. "You're Lord Gruethrist now. Will you make him a knight? Sir Kady, the barrelwright's handsome boy."

Her voice was weak. A shudder racked her body. Yvon put a hand on her shoulder to steady her, and she flinched away.

"I'm going to stand up now, and step outside, and then I'll be back straight away," he said.

"Death follows me, just like Bwnte," she said. "Bury me deep; let new life sprout up again like a seed."

"No one needs to bury you yet," Yvon said, turning away. He gritted his teeth to bite back the pain when he picked up his sword, pulled it from its sheath, and shook the water off it.

Xaragitte's head leaned sideways in his direction. "We all die. You too, even you." She sang it. *"You too, even you. You too, even you."*

He shook his head, shivering at her voice, and went to the threshold. He stopped to kick aside the branch he had used to block the door. A stick that puny wouldn't last two seconds against a troll. He needed something larger.

The stark shapes of the trees pricked the dark, clouded sky like a hedge of thorns. The rain had tapered off to a few scattered drops.

Holding his sword before him, Yvon stepped outside. He didn't see any sign of the troll on the ridge. One cautious step was followed by another, and then he hurried away from the house, turning in case the troll came out behind the corner—nothing there.

He stopped and tugged on the cords that held the last two magic ampules, letting them rest outside his shirt. He could use them on the troll if it came too close.

With one eye to the ridge, he searched for a fallen branch big enough to block the door. When he found one as thick as a man's forearm and twice as long as a man was tall, he couldn't hold it with his left arm. He had to switch his sword to his left hand, where fingers gripped it numbly, and drag the branch in the crook of his right. Still it kept slipping away. It took a long time to get it all the way back to the cabin's door.

Panting hard, he dropped it outside and stepped through to see that Xaragitte and Claye were safe. He saw Claye lying on the ground in the corner.

"No no no."

Xaragitte's voice made him jump. She stood just inside the door, leaning against the wall. He felt a sharp pain in his heart as he saw her.

"M'lady, you shouldn't be on your feet." He lifted his hand to touch her.

Her eyes narrowed. The pain twisted suddenly sideways.

He teetered forward, sword dropping from his fingers, and looked down. The hilt of Xaragitte's knife protruded from the left side of his chest, between his ribs. He tried to grab it, but his fingers didn't work.

"You're not my Kady," she said. "You tried to hurt my baby. You slapped my baby down."

Her face turned to black dots as Yvon collapsed. Looking up from the floor he saw only her red hair, suddenly bright as flame, like a halo of fire, as if Bwnte herself, the goddess of fertility and death, were in the room.

"No, you'll never hurt my baby again," she said. Her voice sounded far away, like it came from the bottom of a well. Then the walls of the well caved in and everything went black.

Far away, muffled, as if it came through a mound of dirt, he heard Claye crying.

"Mamamamama!"

⊰ Part 2 ⊱
A BOY
INSIDE A CIRCLE
OF WOLVES

CHAPTER 7

"Let go of it."

Windy tugged her shoulder free from Ragweed's grip, cradling the baby protectively between her milk-heavy breasts and the wall of the cave. "No."

"We took a vote and voted you should put the baby down."

"The vote was a tie, so I can do what I want."

Ragweed ground his jaws together until they squeaked. "But the baby's dead—that's why you should let go of it."

"Let's have another vote."

Ragweed smiled broadly, showing off his gray, cracked teeth. "That's a good idea. All those in favor of you putting down the dead baby?" He raised his hand. "And those against?"

Windy raised hers. "It's a tie. So I can do what I want."

"Hey! Wait a moment—"

Before he could protest, she stood up and leaned forward on one long-armed knuckled hand. The sun had finally sunk low enough to go outside again. She left the overhung ledge of the cave, pressing past the tree and through the overgrown shrubs. Leaves wet from a night and day of rain brushed against her, and water ran in little rivulets down her back, filling the cracks in her skin. She lifted her head into the branches to inhale the sharp clean scent of the pine needles. Droplets rolled down over the hard angles of her cheeks in place of the tears she refused to cry.

Windy walked to her favorite open spot on the slope, in the long shadow of the mountain's sheltering spur. From there, she peered over the pines into the meadow below, and, surrounded by shade, watched the last light flow out of the valley. Uncheered by the dying sun, she rocked the baby in the crook of her massive arm.

She glanced up to the mouth of the cave. Ragweed dug in the dirt with his big knobby fingers, then shoved his hands into his mouth. The soil was rich in spots where leaves and needles piled deep enough to decay, and the rain sent worms swimming toward the surface. That had to be what Ragweed ate. Windy stirred the compost with finger-like toes, and a fat red wriggly worm squirmed out. She left it alone. She had no appetite.

Ragweed turned his head in her direction, wrinkled his nose, and snorted. "It's already starting to stink!"

She smelled it too. Her nose was sensitive to the scent of dead things, a main part of her diet. She knew her baby was starting to rot, even though it had been dead less than a day. "I like the way she smells! And I'm not putting her down!"

Ragweed shrugged, then resumed his digging.

Windy stared at the little thing in her arms. She had been such a lively baby, so adventuresome, afraid of nothing. Hardly feared daylight at all. She used to crawl away at the first hint of darkness. So last night when the rain poured down and she'd crawled out of their crowded crack of rock, Windy had listened to her laugh and taken the chance to rub butt with Ragweed. She'd just been getting excited herself when she heard the bigtooth lion's roar and ran out to rescue her daughter.

She'd chased the bigtooth off—it was a cowardly old thing with a limp. But by the time she'd reached her little girl it was too late. Her daughter's skull was crushed, all soft, pulpy, and misshapen. Like a rotten pumpkin. Windy had eaten pumpkins once, near one of the villages of the black-haired people. But now, thinking of her baby, she'd never eat pumpkins again, no matter how tasty they were.

She felt like she'd never do anything again.

The last finger of light lingered on the green face of the meadow. Ragweed strolled over and sat down beside her. He noticed the worm twisting in the leaves, picked it up, and offered it to her. She stuck out her tongue to show she wasn't hungry, to say no. He popped the worm in his mouth, chewed once, and swallowed.

"It's almost dark," he said. "We should go down to that turtle shell again."

The turtle shell is what he called the false cave built by people. "Why?" she asked.

Ragweed shrugged. "Might be something to eat."

"What if those people are still there? The man had a shining leaf." A sword. She had seen it last night when he came outside after the bigtooth ran that way.

Ragweed scratched his head, then probed one of his nostrils with a carrot-sized forefinger. Stirring up his brains in search of an idea, she guessed.

"We could try to scare them away," he offered.

She had guessed right. "You tried to scare them two or three times last night," she reminded him.

"Yeah," he said slowly. His face darkened cheerfully. "They're probably pretty scared by now!"

He didn't seem to notice her answering silence. She sagged on her haunches and studied him thoughtfully. Ragweed was the handsomest troll she'd ever seen—he had a beautifully shaped head that sloped back to a nice point, a brow so thick you could hardly see his eyes beneath its shadow, no neck to speak of, arms like the trunks of trees, and a belly as round and dark as the new moon. Short, bristly hairs ran down between his shoulders and into the crack of his buttocks. Just looking at him used to send shivers up her spine and make her feel all juicy inside. She'd flirted with him, and he'd responded, and she was as happy as any troll could be until she became pregnant and realized that Ragweed was not the sharpest rock in the pile. Of course, she couldn't be that much smarter. When it was time for her baby to be born, she'd let him persuade her to come down out of the mountains to this stupid little valley.

Ragweed grunted. "When I came down here a couple years back, the turtle shell didn't have people in it."

"Well, this year it did!" She'd heard the same statement a thousand times before, and she was tired of it. But more than that, she wanted to blame Ragweed for her baby's death. She wanted to blame somebody, anybody, because if it was somebody else's fault, then it wasn't hers.

Ragweed rooted idly in the dirt. "I'm hungry."

Windy sighed. She'd heard that a thousand times as well. She stood up. Doing anything was better than doing nothing. "Come on. Let's go down to the turtle shell. Maybe they'll be scared off. Maybe we'll find something to eat."

He clapped his hands. The crack echoed off the mountain walls, scattering birds from the trees. "Good," he said. "All you need is some food, then you'll put that baby down."

They walked down the familiar slope. They'd varied the path some every night, looking for new sources of food, but there were only so many ways to go. Ragweed turned over logs and broke off pieces of stumps, but they were the same logs and stumps he'd searched a dozen times before. They hadn't seen the carcass of so much as a dead sparrow in two days; it had been a week since they'd found that deer before the wild dogs got to it. Ragweed grabbed the lower branches of trees and stripped the bark off with his teeth. The rain had moistened them up a bit so they didn't taste so chokingly dry. The scent enticed Windy, but not enough to make her eat.

They arrived at the wide meadow beside the pond, and Ragweed waded into the water to slake his thirst. Windy's throat was terribly parched, despite the drippings she'd licked off the cave roof, so she followed him, holding the baby out of the water as she bent down to take a drink.

Ragweed splashed over and rubbed his hands on her bottom.

"Thhppppt!" Water sprayed out of her mouth. "Stop that!"

"Nothing to interrupt us now," he leered.

She ignored him, bending to take another sip. He reached around and squeezed her breast.

"Yow!" Windy hopped away with a splash, bared her teeth, and smacked him with a backhanded swing.

"Hey!" he hollered. "What did I do?"

"That hurt." She turned away, sloshed out of the pond, and started her three-legged gait through the woods without him. Her breasts ached like a bad tooth. They'd been leaking all evening, and she didn't know what to do. She guessed they'd dry up in a few days, but right now she'd rather step in fire than have him touch them.

Ragweed hurried to catch up. They crested the chestnut ridge where they sat most nights. When the nuts started falling off the trees, this would be a good valley to be in. But that was months away.

The rain-heavy breeze carried new scents. Off in the direction of the sunset, toward the river, she thought she sniffed something dead, maybe drowned in yesterday's flood. Small, but still a good meal, if she'd been hungry enough to go looking for it. She turned her head toward the little hollow of land where the turtle shell stood, smelling the faint scent of the lion, a goat, and something else—

Ragweed caught the same scent. "Hot diggety!" he shouted,

making an enthusiastic scooping motion with his hands before he ran down the hill. "Fresh rotten meat!"

"Be careful!" she cried out. Holding her baby tight to her chest, she ran after Ragweed. He stooped outside the shell, rooting his nose where blood had spilled in the mud. Windy paused beside him, and only then did her ears, which were better than the average troll's, certainly much better than Ragweed's, detect the high-pitched crying.

When Ragweed turned to enter the shell she tripped him, grabbing hold of his wrist so he couldn't break his fall. As he squawked and hit the ground, she rushed inside.

The odors of the dead man and woman hit her first, but the smell of baby poop and urine were also strong. Windy wrinkled her nose, swiveling her head around until she saw the woman's corpse in the corner. A baby was chewing on her long red hair, its eyes shut, so tired it could barely sit up straight as it cried.

Ragweed burst through the doorway behind her. "Ho there! Save some for me!"

He shoved her down and she kicked at him. He dodged her foot, hopping ponderously over her outstretched leg. She dropped her dead daughter, dove under Ragweed's groping arms, and slid across the dirt floor on her tender breasts to grab the crying baby first. She curled around it protectively.

"Go ahead," Ragweed said, clearly disappointed. "It's not much. Won't fill your belly up."

The baby continued to wail as it snuggled into Windy's arms. It rubbed its face around her breast until its tiny mouth closed on the hard pebble of her nipple. It didn't have much of a suck, compared to her little girl, but then it didn't need much of one either.

Ragweed picked up the woman's hand, stuck the fingers in his mouth, and chewed on them. After a couple crunches, he spit them out and dropped her arm. "This one's still warm—the bigtooth killed her. Ought to let her rot for a couple days. She'll taste better with bugs in her."

Windy wrinkled her flat nose again. The dead woman was this baby's mother; she suddenly felt quite protective. "Go chew on that one, then," she said, pointing to the man's body. "He's been dead longer."

"All gristle, no fat, like enough," Ragweed muttered, but he crossed the room.

Windy caressed the baby's head. It had such beautiful black hair, disguising its misshapen skull and lack of a brow. Large—gorgeously large—eyes in the painfully flat face stared right at her before they fluttered shut. The ache in Windy's heart eased as quickly as the soreness in her breast.

"Ack!" Ragweed jumped back so hard he fell on his bottom. He bounced up and retreated across the room to Windy's side.

"What is it?" she asked.

"Go look for yourself! I'm not getting near it, not if it was a rotten mammut on a hot summer night and I hadn't eaten anything in ten days."

Windy carefully cradled the suckling baby to her, took a step forward, and almost turned to stone. The amber-colored ampules strung around the dead man's neck—they were magic, sunlight trapped in warm ice. If either one cracked accidentally it could kill them both, at least according to the stories about similar treasures stolen in the past. She hopped backward so fast the baby lost the nipple. Its eyes flew wide open.

"You'll have to share it now," Ragweed said.

Windy kept one eye on the man's body as if he might leap up and attack her. The baby stretched its neck, trying to get its mouth back on her breast. "Share what?"

"The live meat."

"No!" She dodged his sudden grasp, bolted out the door and into the yard. He chased after her.

"We always share meat," he said.

"This isn't meat—it's a baby!"

He slouched back on his haunches and laughed. "Don't be crazy! You're just sad because you lost your girl. You don't mean to keep that thing."

She hadn't realized that was exactly what she meant to do until she heard him say it. "I can. And I will."

He thumped his knuckles on his chest to frighten her. She wasn't impressed and frowned at him until he gave it up. "If that's how you feel," he said, pacing in a circle around her, "then we'll just have to take a vote. All those in favor of eating the live meat, raise your hand."

He threw his hand up into the air, looking around the way he always did at meetings to see who was voting with him. She ignored him and, gently as she could, switched the baby around, so it could drink from the other sore and swollen breast.

"All right, then, everybody in favor of keeping the meat for a baby, raise your hand."

Windy lifted hers as she looked down, making a kissy mouth at the child. It stopped sucking long enough to laugh and reached up to touch her face.

"That's two against one," she said. "We win."

"It can't vote!"

"Well, it raised its hand." She really just hoped to confuse and distract Ragweed, because even if all the trolls in their band outvoted her, she wasn't about to give up this new baby. She reached down to tickle its belly and saw it was a boy. "He heard you, and he raised his hand. So there."

"But—!" Ragweed sputtered off, then slammed his hands down, splattering mud everywhere.

The baby jerked at the noise, but she made another kissy mouth and a smoochy sound, and he giggled again. His eyelids seemed very heavy as he swallowed gulp after gulp.

"You aren't going to keep that thing, are you? It's an animal."

"Is not." He had eyes just like her darling girl, she decided. Whatever he was—whatever people were—they were more than animals, even if they weren't trolls.

Ragweed circled her. "It's a maggot, that's what it is."

"He's a big strong baby." To be truthful, he wasn't big or strong. But he was a baby, and now he was her baby.

"It's a maggot. It's little, white, and it wouldn't make a mouthful, and you found it crawling on a dead body. Maggot, maggot, maggot!"

"He is not a maggot!" She threw a clump of mud at Ragweed, but it missed and smacked wetly against the side of the turtle shell.

"Well, it ain't a slug." Ragweed hurled a mudball back at her, with better aim. She ducked, blocking it with her free arm. "Slugs have stripes," he said sullenly, flipping over stones. "Least some do. The tasty ones."

Windy rocked her massive forearm until the baby fell asleep. After a while she rose, feeling so relieved she paused to empty her bladder. She looked through the doorway and saw her daughter lying abandoned in the muddy floor. Carefully avoiding the dead man with the dangerous magic, she stepped inside and picked up her daughter. She couldn't just leave her there, where sunlight could reach her. The dead woman was against the wall, under the sagging roof. Windy placed her daughter by the woman, tucking the hand with the missing fingers under the little girl and draping the other arm across her body.

Ragweed looked over the edge of the wall. "Are you sun mad? Get out of there!"

"Not yet," Windy said. Shifting the baby boy away from her arm, she reached up with one hand and jumped, pulling the roof down to seal both the woman and her daughter in darkness. The baby twitched in her arms at the impact of her jumping, and she stopped to coo him back to sleep.

"Hey, that's smart," Ragweed said. "You covered up the man—"

Windy scooped up handfuls of mud and sticks, packing them tightly all around the edges to seal it up tight.

"Hey," Ragweed said. "That's not smart—you're covering up the good meat too!"

She growled at him, startling the baby again.

"What?" he asked.

Rocking the baby in her arm to soothe him, she said very quietly but firmly, "Our daughter is under there too. You won't leave her exposed to sunlight."

Ragweed grunted, but he didn't argue. He dropped down. When Windy squeezed under the fallen roof and crawled out through the big hole, she found him gathering up branches and thorns. She sighed, liking him a little more again. He knew the decent thing every troll did for their dead.

Together they filled in the little hole and the big hole, and heaped mounds around the walls. Windy moved the smaller pieces for fear of disturbing the baby, slight though he felt in her arms. Then they both scooped up clumps of mud, packing it in tight around the holes. When they finished, Ragweed walked around it, lifting his leg and spraying. The scent would scare off scavengers and protect their dead.

Ragweed lifted his nose and sniffed the air. "We have to hurry if we aren't going to get caught out in the sun."

Windy looked up—he was right. They raced across the high ridge, and she could smell dawn in the air. They halted briefly in the meadow to drink from the swollen pond, and she noticed the lion's scent. It too had been here to drink in the night. She decided to blame it for her daughter's death. Then she looked at the child she held.

It's going to be all right, she told herself. *Ragweed will let me keep the baby.*

They would return to the mountains, among the hot springs and the good smell of sulfur, away from all the people. Things would be just like they were before.

"We should leave this valley," she said. She thought about her own mother. "We should go home."

"Not until the pears get ripe," Ragweed said, pushing aside the brush in his hurry to hide. He shoved his huge bulk through the narrow crack into the cave, then rolled over on his back and rubbed his big round belly. "All the trees full of pears and nobody to eat them but us. I don't want to miss that! They won't be eating any pears back home."

"That's a long time from now." She squeezed in after him. It was barely spring; the trees didn't even have their blossoms yet. "What are we going to eat until then?"

He bared his teeth in a half grin. "I don't know about you, but I'm hungry for a little maggot."

She turned her back to him and wrapped her arms around the sleeping child.

CHAPTER 8

"*Y*ou aren't going to keep it, are you?"

"*Him*, not *it*, mother," Windy answered through a mouth stuffed with blueberries. Her large fingers circled the branches, scooping off another bunch of ripe fruit while her mother did the same beside her. The older troll's downy white hair contrasted sharply with her gray skin in the moonlight. "And yes," Windy said, "I am going to keep him."

"We'd heard tales, from Crash, when he went down into the people valleys last year, but I didn't believe him. And then you finally return with it." She frowned.

Windy looked across the bog. Her little boy played in the scrub grass with two little girls his own age—about five winters—but twice his size. Sometimes, she scarcely believed it herself.

"You've been away too many winters," her mother said reproachfully. "Even if you were ashamed."

"I'm not ashamed." She shoved the blueberries in her mouth and chewed. "We were going to come back that first winter, but the baby—"

"Maggot," her mother interrupted.

She swallowed. "That's what Ragweed calls him."

"I know. He's been telling everyone, but we'd already heard it from Crash. So what do you call it?"

Windy had called the baby by her daughter's name for nearly a year, but the boy never answered to it, maybe because she only whispered it to him in his sleep. And then Ragweed called him Maggot so often that it was the only name her boy responded to.

She sighed. "Maggot."

Her mother made a rumbling hum in her throat. She plucked the berries off the branches one by one, filling her cupped hand. "Forty-one, forty-two, forty-three for a handful. I can still count higher than anyone else. And faster too. Heh! So that first winter?"

"Terrible." Windy wanted to explain how she tried to leave Ragweed but couldn't, how there was never a good time to sneak away, not so he wouldn't notice. "It was terrible."

"Why?"

"Before winter even, the baby grew so cold. His skin turned all blue at night and he shivered." She shivered. That winter bloomed into another summer before she found the courage to take her frail child among the icy peaks, and while they hunted food, night to night, and fattened up again, that summer rotted into winter, and before she knew it four years had passed by as swift as midsummer nights. "So we stayed down in the warmer valleys."

"You should have let it die."

"*Him*, Mother."

"No. *It*."

Other trolls hulked through the blueberry patches, eating steadily without talking, filling their bellies while the darkness lasted. The children strayed farther away in their play. Maggot was a delicate child, and the risks he took could stop her heart. His skin was so thin she could practically see through it. She followed after the children, conveniently escaping the prick of her mother's comments.

A rock outcropping capped the slope. Windy waded free of the blueberry patch and went to sit by the stones. "Talking with the stupid dead" they called it, because the stories said that these rocks were trolls who'd let themselves get caught out in the sun. The best thing about the stupid dead, Windy thought, was that their mistake was always worse than yours.

"Hi, stupid," Windy said, patting the rock as she sat.

Distant mountains formed walls on either side of the high plain and the dark sky, close enough to touch, and gave it a comforting cave-like roof. Bringing her son up here for the first time recalled all the memories of her own happy childhood: the bleak beauty of long winter nights—her favorite season before she became a mother—when clusters of the bitter berries on mountain ash gleamed bright against the white skin of windswept snow; the scents of rhododendrons blooming under slivered spring moons, and laurel at midsummer; huckleberries, blueberries, teaberries, and cranberries, each in its season, as many as she could eat; summer fogs so dense she could open her mouth and drink water straight out of the air, with unexpected frosts that cooled her toes while she foraged. She hadn't realized how much she missed the smell of bobcat spray until she'd come up here and caught a whiff of it again tonight.

Maggot played with the girls on the slope below the blueberry bushes, along the edge of the bogs where cranberries grew and the grasses turned shadow-tipped in autumn. Beyond him, a herd of giant elk grazed about a mile away, their wide flat antlers rising and falling silhouetted against the sky. She counted seventeen elk before their heads jerked up in unison and they darted off. Leaning forward, she saw a dyrewolf bolt out of the grasses where the elk had been.

Dyrewolves hunted in packs. Where there was one, there were

more. "Maggot," Windy said. She didn't speak loudly. Her son's ears were as powerful as a troll's eyes.

He stopped playing and waved to her. The two girls looked up the hill, confused by his actions.

"Stay close by," she said, for his ears only. "There are dyrewolves hunting."

He smacked his lips and nodded as if he already knew. Then he put his hands to his mouth. "Awrooooooooo!"

It sounded enough like a dyrewolf's cry to send a chill up her spine. He could mimic almost anything. She saw him turn first, then the girls. When she followed their eyes and concentrated, she heard faintly the dyrewolf howling in return.

"Stay close!" she shouted at the top of her voice.

He waved to her again, and she felt better. After that, the girls pretended that they were scared, running away as he howled like a dyrewolf and chased them. The sight of him, and the sharp shriek of their laughter, made Windy smile. But she remained wary. A pack of dyrewolves could bring down a solitary full-grown troll. And her son was so much smaller and weaker than any troll.

On the steep edge of the slope a stunted grove of red cedars leaned away from the constant wind. When the girls ran in that direction, followed by Maggot, his shoulder-length hair whipped by the hard breeze, Windy was relieved. She could sniff the air and not smell wolves or other dangers in it.

Windy sniffed again, taking in the scent of the trees. Down in the valleys, the red cedars reached great heights, but here the tallest barely overtopped a full-grown troll; although, thinking about it, that still made them the tallest plant around. But they were twisted and deformed by the unrelenting pressure of the constant wind, the west face naked and all their tattered branches stretching east. On stormy nights, the gusts could tumble trolls and send them rolling across the bog.

Windy watched her son, his pale skin luminous in the partial moonlight. Her son was also a creature from the valleys. She wondered what it would do to him to grow up here, in troll country, whether he'd end up deformed in some way like the cedars.

Her mother climbed the rocks, sat down beside her, and pointed to the trees. "Do you know what those look like?"

A trollbird settled on Windy's back and began picking nits off her skin. She stayed still so as not to disturb it. "They smell like the big cedars that grow farther down the slopes. I was just thinking about that."

"No, that's not it." Her mother stretched out a long arm, grabbed the branch of a blueberry bush, and collected more of the juicy blue-black fruit. "They look like the killing leaves."

Windy didn't know what her mother meant. "Killing leaves?"

"Once, there were many more trolls than there are now. Some of us lived in the southern mountains then. When I was a young girl, I did. There were people, blackhairs, also living in the southern mountains then. Too many to count or chase away, but they left us alone and we avoided them."

Windy had heard all this before, and didn't care much for her mother's childhood stories. She shifted her weight. "Maggot has black hair."

Her mother grunted. "Let me finish. Then other people moved in, just like those who moved into the lower valleys here. The two groups gathered together, standing against each other in big packs. Like dyrewolves on one side and little bigtooth lions on the other."

Windy had never heard this story before. The trollbird skittered between her shoulder blades. Her skin twitched.

"The two packs, they had these killing leaves—"

"Sharp leaves of shiny metal?" Windy asked.

"Those too." Her mother made a three-sided shape with her fingers. "But they also had these big ones, one leaf on each branch, in bright colors like the autumn leaves. They carried them on branches. So we crept down out of the mountains to see them. One morning before the sun came up, we heard a sound like the trumpeting of mammuts. We hid in our caves all that day, but we couldn't sleep because we knew something was wrong. When we came back to the field that night, it was littered with carrion. More dead men than there are berries on these bushes, the smell so thick it made your stomach swell like to bursting. And the killing leaves in tatters, shredded, lying this way and that, pieces shaking in the wind." She pointed to the cedars. "They looked just like those trees."

Windy wished she'd never heard this story. "So?"

"People"—her mother aimed her finger at Maggot, rolling around with the girls—"did that. Afterward, the winners—the newcomers—came into the high reaches and hunted us. We moved north, and once again men entered the low valleys, and once again hunt us."

"So?"

Her mother's face tightened into a sharp knot. "So? You bring one to live among us. It should be destroyed."

"No!" Windy rose abruptly with her fists clenched—the trollbird whistled and flew off into the night.

Her mother stared at her, as cold as ice. She was the First of the band, after many votes, its leader. "You listen to me. You need to get rid of that animal. Then you need to have another child, and by darkness and dew, let us hope it's a boy who can breed with those young girls down there as soon as they're big enough."

"Mother—"

"I'm not done yet!" Windy tensed, but her mother kept on speaking. "Our people have few children, and we grow fewer each year. There were fifty-three in our band when you were a baby, and before that there was seventy-one at one time. Seventy-one! How many do you see now?"

Windy couldn't help herself. She lifted her head and counted. Ragweed and seven others, mostly men, down where the blueberries are thickest, another group of ten over on the next hill, and little clusters of two and three scattered in between. Maggot and the two girls. Her and her mother. "Thirty, thirty one, thirty-two. Thirty-three, thirty-four. Thirty-four."

"Thirty-three," her mother corrected. She wasn't counting Maggot.

"That's not a fair question. Frosty took her band and moved away, and—"

"Because the people moved in! They eat all our food and kill us and hunt us away!" The anger faded out of her mother's voice, replaced by weariness. "I see the nights of all trolls drying up like dew beneath a sun that never sets." As Windy watched her mother's face intently, understanding for a moment her sense of loss, the old troll chuckled. "Look! The children are playing catch the snake. You loved that game when you were a little girl."

The two girls were running, tossing a snake back and forth between them. Maggot chased after, grabbing at it, as the girls threw it to each other over his head.

Windy laughed too. It was a good-sized snake—two, maybe three feet long—with its mouth wide open and fangs snapping at the children's arms. Rocky and Blossom were good girls. Windy was so glad Maggot finally had someone his own age to play with.

The snake twined in the air, looping itself in an echo of the criss-cross pattern marking its back—it was the kind that caused sickness if it bit, which made the game more fun. The risk was small because a fast bite couldn't break a troll's skin, and if the snake fastened on an arm and bit slowly, there was always plenty of time to grab the head and pull it off it. Windy remembered one time . . .

Maggot! "No!"

She drummed a short warning on her chest and ran down the slope. All three children froze in fear, and the snake twisted in Blossom's hand, biting down sharply on her arm. "Ow!"

"I've got it," Maggot cried. He grabbed it behind the head and pulled it off.

Windy faltered, then lunged forward. Maggot held the snake up toward her, its long length squirming and twisting around. He kept his grip on it for a second, then let go and hopped out of the way. Its head turned to strike at him just as Windy's foot came down, smashing it into the ground.

Rocky smiled. "I caught it eight times."

"I caught it eleven!" Blossom screamed.

"But you dropped it four times," Maggot said. "And Rocky picked it up again, and she didn't miss any catches."

Windy patted him on the head. "But Blossom caught it more times, so she wins the game." The snake squirmed frantically in the soft ground beneath her foot.

"But if you take away the times she dropped it, then Rocky wins," Maggot insisted.

Windy wrinkled her thick brow and started unfolding her fingers. Eleven catches, then one, two, three, four drops, that was fifteen. The snake struggled harder, so she arched the front part of her foot. When the head squeezed out between her toes, she crossed them and snapped its neck. She lifted the limp snake with her foot to her hand, then offered it to her mother.

"We found it," Rocky complained.

"It's our food," Blossom said.

"You should have eaten it while you had the chance then," Windy's mother said as she took it. She bit off half; the bones crunched in her jaw. With a wink, she tossed the other half to the girls. Maggot snatched it out of the air and led the girls on a chase for it. After she swallowed, she looked up at Windy. "You can't buy my vote with fresh meat, you know."

"I wasn't trying to."

"Leastway, not that little bit." Her eyes grew wistful. "Now a nice bit of rotting carrion—"

"You'll vote however you think best."

"I've already talked with Ragweed, and he's gathering up votes among the men. We'll have enough to exclude it—Maggot—from the band."

"We'll leave then," Windy said.

"Not you, just it."

"Whatever you vote for him, you vote for me. You vote to kill him, you'll have to kill me first. He's my son."

"It could end up carrion," her mother said.

"*He*," Windy insisted.

"Maybe it'll have an accident. Yes, that could happen. Then you could have more children. We have too few children."

Windy didn't say anything. She noticed the men moving off to the east. When the women pounded on the ground, their girls went running. Maggot followed after them, but Windy beat her knuckles into the sod. "Stay," she said.

He sprinted to her side. "What is it, Mom?"

"Stay with me."

"But Mom!"

She bared her teeth and he quieted down, clambering up her outstretched arm to cling around her shoulder. Sometimes she still recalled the way her daughter's fingers and toes had dug into her wrinkles and under the cracks in her skin, but she'd grown accustomed to the way Maggot scooted up the outside. She searched through the blueberries until she found his skin, some strange-smelling thing they had scavenged from valley people to keep him warm. He wrapped it over his back.

Windy's mother looked at her in disgust. "Ughh! Why do you carry that stinking thing?"

"Maggot'd be cold without it."

"Then let it be cold. Let it die."

Before Windy could answer, Maggot laughed. "But Grandma! I don't want to die. You're silly."

She grunted and moved off. They needed to be safely underground before the sun rose to blind and immobilize them. Windy hurried after her.

"Hey, Mom," said Maggot.

"Yes?"

"Hey, Mom."

"Yes?"

"I want to walk."

"No," she said firmly. "We're in a hurry, dear." They had lingered almost too long, lethargic in the summer heat. But trolls moved quickly when the scent of dawn electrified the air, and there was no way Maggot could keep up with the others over this rough terrain for long. She'd learned that the hard way these last few years. Only because of Maggot's recent increase in size and speed had she finally relented and let Ragweed lead her back to troll country.

"But Mom, I want to talk to the other kids."

"I'll catch up with them."

When she did, the girls' mothers scowled at her, their browridges sagging like tree branches covered with ice. Windy tried to find words to ease their disapproval, but they ignored her. She lapsed once more into the canyon of silence that had first appeared between her and Ragweed.

The girls whispered and giggled, refusing to be stifled by the awkwardness of the older women. Rocky ran along at Windy's heels. "Hey there, baby," she taunted Maggot. "Baby riding on your mama's neck."

"Baby, baby, baby," Blossom cried. "Watch out! There's a snake crawling on your back!" She jumped up and tried to snatch away Maggot's skin, but missed, dissolving in laughter.

Windy couldn't see Maggot's expression, but his grip tightened on her and she smelled his uncertainty. "One time, down-down-down," he stammered, talking to the girls, "in the valleys by the big people caves, we'd been out hunting for food all night and we found a nice big dead humpback."

"A whole humpback?" Rocky asked eagerly.

"Yeah, and Ragweed ate *soooo* much, he got really tired, and he fell asleep, and I put my skin over his face, so he wouldn't know that it was getting light out, and then, when the sun came up, he'd turn into stone."

"No you didn't," Blossom said.

"Did too!"

"He's not a bunch of stones," Rocky argued.

"No. Mom took the blanket off his head and woke him up."

Windy smiled. That's exactly what she *did* do, every single time Maggot played that trick on Ragweed. As the children continued to talk, she admired the way Maggot stopped the teasing by distracting the girls. Then, like darkness falling after a flash of light, she realized that Maggot was taunting them back, reminding them that he'd been all sorts of places they never had. For the first time it occurred to her that he was already smarter than she was—if you counted backward from eleven, take away four, that was seven. Less than eight. She sighed. He was at least five or six years old, big enough to live on his own. She'd done everything she could, taught him how to find carrion and other food, how to dig and climb, and all about the history and customs of her people. He sucked all of it in like a lake drinking up a river. But the one thing she couldn't do was make him grow any bigger, any faster.

Reaching up, she took hold of Maggot and swung him down to the ground. "Go on then," she said, picking up the skin as it fell from his shoulders.

"Thanks, Mom!" His face beamed at her like the moon, so bright she almost had to shield her eyes, and then he took off running beside the girls as fast as his little legs could carry him. He looked funny, moving upright on his two feet and swinging his arms even though they didn't touch the ground. The girls slowed down a bit to match his pace.

"It's a freak," hissed her mother, slipping back beside her. "An animal."

Windy's gaze never strayed from him. "Whatever you want to call him, he's still my son."

They trotted steadily downhill for several miles. The trail offered glimpses of the river valley far below and a constant view of the mountains in the distant west. Near the end of the trail, Maggot ran up and tugged at her hand. "Mom, I'm tired."

"Here, I'll carry you." She held out her arm and he tugged on it again, but didn't climb up. If he was too tired to climb, then he *was* exhausted. She lifted him and draped him over her shoulder. He clung to her neck, twining and locking his hands together.

"Where are we going?" he asked.

"To spend the day in caves, at the bottom of these cliffs."

"What cl—"

The word dropped off in midair as they came to the top of a steep wall of rock nine hundred feet high.

"Wow." He said that last so quietly she felt only the air of it stirring against her neck.

A trail wound back and forth down the cliff's face. The older trolls descended quickly, digging their toes and fingers in the rock for vertical shortcuts in the places where the rock allowed. Those who left the blueberry patches earliest were already at the bottom when Windy began her climb, pressed against the wall of stone. "Hold on tight," she told Maggot.

He smacked his lips for yes, rubbing his forehead against the back of her neck as he squeezed tight.

She chose the easiest path down the wall. This place was sacred to the trolls. The story her mother told was that the trolls were born underground, of the earth itself, in the deep caves when all the world was covered with snow, living in the water and eating the fish and bugs that swam there. Most believed that the caves at the bottom of this cliff were the ones that trolls emerged from, like infants from their mother's womb, when they came out into the wider world.

It was still a safe place: the caverns stretched back for miles beneath the mountains, so deep that no people or other predators could ever find them there. All the things that trolls had ever stolen from people were stored there, in hordes cached in such odd corners that some of them had not been counted in a span of lifetimes.

"Hey, Mom?"

"Mmmm?" Windy asked, her face against the stone, her feet reaching out to find the next toehold.

"The girls're daring me to join them. Can I?"

She twisted her head around to see them. The girls were showing off, getting back at him for his adventures by climbing straight down the wall. Every young troll did that at least once, usually around the time they were as big as the girls. But Maggot was not every young troll.

"No," Windy said firmly. "You can't do that."

"Aw, Mom," he whined. But he didn't budge.

"You're a good boy."

"I'm not a boy. I'm almost old enough to be a grown-up, even though I'm as small as a baby. That's why Grandma wants me to die and all the other grown-ups want me to go away."

Something caught in her throat as big as a rock. "What do you think about that?"

"I tell them you won't let anything hurt me." He nuzzled his face against her. "'Cause you don't."

The burden on her shoulders grew heavier as she continued her downward trek. The air around her changed, charged with the tingling feel of daybreak. When she reached the bottom of the slope, she was panting. She looked up and saw the sun shining high on the very top of the cliff face. The wall there had lost the blue-gray tones of night and turned into startling shades of red and orange, streaked with white. It glowed like fire.

Then she noticed the two girls. They'd also seen the light, before she did, and they'd frozen in a spot some fifty or sixty feet up the wall, one above the other.

"Come on down!" she yelled at them. "Hurry!"

"I can't!" Blossom cried out. Rocky just cried.

Their mothers had noticed them missing also, pausing on the trail down to the caves. Blossom's mother, Laurel, shouted to the other trolls, calling for help. Windy didn't know her too well, but she'd been friends as a child with Rocky's mother, Bones. Bones ran to Windy's side and called up at the girls. "Come on down! The mouth of day is chasing you!"

And indeed it did, sunlight trickling down the face of the rock as the night at the bottom grew thin, an insufficient darkness. Windy paced nervously.

Bones tried to scale the cliff, but the lower reaches were climbed over, rocks loose and dusty, a slope of debris that couldn't support the weight of a full-grown troll. She was no more than twenty feet up when the rock gave way underneath her and she slid down in a shower of gravel and stone.

"Don't look up!" Windy yelled to the girls, but it was hopeless. Their eyes were fixed on the sky as the teeth of the sun closed over the uneven upper reaches of rock. Her heart pounded rapidly with worry. She turned to the other trolls and found them arguing.

"Someone needs to go up the trail and climb out across to them," a big troll named Stump said.

"And get caught in the sun?" someone answered. "Not likely!"

"Leave 'em there," someone else offered. "They'll come down before the sun reaches them."

"What if they don't?" Laurel asked. "What'll happen to my Blossom?"

"Let them jump," Ragweed said. He'd been blunting his compassion on Maggot for years.

"We can't leave them." Windy's mother's deep voice overpowered the others. "Those girls are important to the band."

"Let's vote," Stump said. "All those in favor of trying to rescue—"

By the time they decided as a group to get something done, it'd be too late. Windy knew they had to act now, but she didn't know what to do.

Maggot stirred on her shoulder. "What's wrong, Mom?"

"The girls are caught up there. If the sunlight reaches them, they'll fall asleep and drop. Even if they could hold on, the sun would shrivel them up."

Rocky's mother ripped away huge chunks of friant rock in a frantic effort to carve footholds in the stone. Windy stood below her. "If the girls fall," she promised, "I'll catch them. I'm right here with you."

"Thank you," said Bones. Her feet slipped before she'd climbed twice her height.

Windy braced and caught her. It knocked her backward, and she felt Maggot's weight slip from her shoulder and roll free. That was something they'd practiced. If she ever fell on him, he'd be crushed. She extricated herself from Bones and looked around to make sure that he was all right. When she didn't see him, she started turning over rocks. "Maggot! Where are you?"

"He's up there," Bones said.

Windy lifted her head and saw him halfway to the girls, spidering up the cliff. The skin wrapped around his neck gave him a hairy appearance. She jumped after him, but Bones grabbed her. "Don't! You can't make it. You'll fall."

"But he doesn't know how to climb a wall that high!"

"Could fool me."

Windy held her breath. Maggot reached a tough spot and crossed horizontally until he found another handhold above him. He did everything just like she'd trained him, keeping three feet on the wall at all times. If anything happened to him . . .

Along the trail to the cave, the other trolls had finally voted to rescue the girls, but no one volunteered to go get them except Stump. But Windy's mother thought Stump was too heavy and wanted someone else to make the climb. So now they were proceeding to another vote.

Windy shook her head and looked helplessly above her as Maggot overtook Blossom and began talking to her. He put his hand over her face, and it was enough to break the sun spell. She resumed her journey down, keeping her eyes on the ground the whole time.

Bones caught her off the wall and hugged her. "I was so scared!" Blossom said, tears pouring down her face, and then she squirmed away from them to run to her mother.

Higher up on the cliff, Rocky wouldn't budge. Maggot talked to her; Windy could see that much. He pointed down, but Rocky refused to turn her head. He tried to cover her eyes, and she shook her head free.

"She'll come down any moment now," Windy said soothingly, eyeing the slow advance of sunlight down the stone. Most of the trolls had headed off for the caverns without waiting to see if the other girl could be saved.

Bones chewed on her knuckles. "She's so timid, so much more timid. I don't know if she'll make it."

Windy's mother and Stump joined them at the base of the wall. The band must've voted for Stump to make the climb. He paused briefly to look up at the motionless figures of Rocky and Maggot. "Looks like I still have two to rescue after all. I better hurry."

He headed up an older trail—a dead end that Windy had forgotten—that would take him near their position. Windy watched him make his way up, wishing she'd thought to try that way herself, when she heard her friend gasp. She craned her neck around just in time to see Maggot slip. She screamed, but he pressed himself flat and found another foothold some ten feet farther down. "What happened?"

Bones covered her mouth. "She hit him."

"Of course she did," Windy's mother said. "The stupid boy threw that nasty skin over her face!"

Windy noticed her mother's choice of the word *boy*, but didn't comment. "Come down!" she cried up at her son. "Come down now!"

He ignored her and inched his way back up the rock. Stump was at the proper height on the trail, but he had a hundred-foot horizontal climb to reach them. As he began his slow way across, Maggot started yanking on Rocky's feet.

Bones gasped. "He's going to pull her down. Stop! Stop! Wait for Stump!"

"I don't think that's what he's doing," Windy whispered, not quite sure herself what Maggot was attempting. Although the skin covered her eyes, Rocky still wouldn't move.

"Hold on!" Stump shouted. "I'm almost there!"

But he wasn't close at all, having reached a spot where his toes could find no hold. Windy's mother tugged at her arm. The whole eastern sky glowed orange above the rim of the mountains. "Come!" she said, her voice as hard as granite. "We saved one girl and we must go down to the caverns. At once!"

"Wait," Windy implored.

The deep shadows of the canyon barely shaded them, and she too felt the compelling need to run; but then Maggot's plan worked. He took Rocky's foot and put it in a lower toehold for her. She shifted her weight down to it, and the spell was broken.

Slowly at first, then more quickly, they came climbing, sliding, down the rock face. Stump called encouragement on his own speedy descent to the trail. The children were halfway down when a peregrine falcon, flying out of the sun, dived at them curiously. With the day fear on her, Windy expected them to be dislodged by the plummeting bird, but they didn't even notice it before it veered away.

"Come on, you're almost here," Bones called.

Rocky pulled the skin off her face, letting it flutter to the ground as she scampered down the last part of the slope and into her mother's arms. Bones swung her daughter up on her back and hurried off with Windy's mother down the trail for the caves. Windy backed away, under the trees between the cliff and river where night still lingered. "Keep coming, Maggot! I'm right here for you!"

His little spider arms and legs trembled as he moved cautiously from hold to hold. Stump slowed in his dash down the trail. "Your son's a good troll," he said as he passed Windy.

"Thanks," she answered, looking up at the frail little figure clinging two dozen feet up the wall. He fell.

She lunged forward to catch him, cradling him in her arms and hugging him tight to still his shaking. The skin on his chest and under his arms and on his thighs was scraped raw. His fingers and his toes were bleeding, and his teeth chattered. She picked up his skin and covered him as she hurried toward the refuge of darkness.

"We saved them, didn't we?" he said proudly.

"Yes we did," she whispered, in the voice that was just for him. "You're a good troll."

"I'm the best troll. Even Stump's not as good as me."

Her mother waited for them, frowning, just inside the cave. The gray old troll took one look at them and yawned. "I suppose it's too late today to call for any votes. Let's wait and see what sunset brings."

Windy smacked her lips in agreement.

"But you let go of Ragweed. He mates with someone else."

Windy lifted her head, smacking her lips again, relieved. When her mother snorted and moved off into the deeper dark, she rocked Maggot in her arms. "I'm never going to let go of you again, you hear me?" she whispered.

He laughed at her and struggled to get loose.

CHAPTER 9

The roar of the waterfall filled Windy's ears even though she was still too far away to see it. She paused in the bluish night, scratched her broad nose, and inhaled the distant mist. The tang of spruce and hemlock needles mixed with dozens of smaller, nearer fragrances, but she didn't smell the single scent she sought. Somewhere along the way she'd lost track of Maggot.

He'd been gone two whole nights. True, he was old enough to take care of himself now, but she fretted when he disappeared in the daylight. She wanted to stop him and knew that she couldn't.

She continued on toward the Blackwater Falls, her back and shoulders aching. It didn't help that she'd searched for him so long yesternight she'd been forced to dig under the roots of a windblown tree at dayrise. A whole day sleeping hunched up like that was enough to make any troll sore. Her stomach growled as she walked, reminding her that all she'd eaten in more than a night were the few mouthfuls of mushrooms she'd sniffed out among the decaying roots.

It had been a hard season, with a late frost that killed off most of the blossoms followed by a dry summer that withered up the surviving fruit. For the past few years there'd been fewer animals coming through the high passes and precious little carrion. The dyrewolves and lions and great birds all fought over the scraps, so the only way a troll ate a decent bit of meat was to stumble on it first. She'd said as much to Maggot, and he told her he had an idea and would catch up with her. Now he'd been gone for two whole nights. If his plan was stealing something from the wolves, he'd end up carrion himself.

She sniffed the air again.

He had promised to meet her at the falls. Maybe he waited for her there, his scent lost in the mist. She hurried on, passing through a grove of cherry trees that had given up their fruit—what little there was—months ago, in the spring. It was still enough to make her mouth water. There were maples beyond them, the leaves turned crisp with the fall. She found one sprayed with an unfamiliar odor and paused to lick at the stain. Some young male troll marking his territory, eager to prove himself. One more danger for Maggot.

If Frosty's band was around here, then courtesy required her to let them know that she was coming. Windy reared up and pounded out a greeting high on her chest, a sound so deep it made the air tremble a mile or more away. *Bum-ba-da-dum-dum.* "A stranger, but a friend," the rhythm said to those who listened.

Not wholly a stranger, in truth, since she and Maggot had passed this way before. But not part of the band either.

Not part of any band.

For too many years, she and Maggot had been rootless, blown about from place to place like leaves in a storm. But she wouldn't have it any other way if the alternative was losing her son.

She repeated the greeting and sat down. While she waited for an answer, she picked through the long grasses and fallen leaves looking for something to eat. Finding nothing, she continued on her way. With all the thunder from the waterfalls, she doubted anyone heard her.

The gibbous moon sat at zenith, flooding the landscape with pale, colorless light. Not a good night to be out. The panic it caused her was muted by the thick canopy of the trees, subsumed by her worry for Maggot and the hunger in her belly. When she reached the rocky open area around the falls, the light pained her eyes even if it didn't blind her.

In front of her, the water dropped sixty feet, half in a single sudden plunge. Flowers of spray blossomed off the dark black rocks. Halfway down the falls, a triangular ledge jutted out at an angle, broad on the left end and blending into the straight drop on the right. The music of the water changed as it poured over this surface and crashed among the jumble of boulders below.

Unappetizing ferns and vines covered the hillside beneath the tall spruce trees and hemlocks she'd smelled earlier. Mist hung in the air, moistening her dry, cracked skin. Despite the danger of the moonlight and the trolls she hadn't yet seen, Windy ventured right down to the pool and waded out into the cave-cold water below the falls. It eased her aches and took the edge off her torpor. She bent down out among the slick, dark rocks and drank until she didn't feel thirsty.

She noticed a sluggish silver flash deep in the water. Fish. She stepped slowly over to where she saw them, dangling her hand open-palmed with one finger bent, flicking the pink-nailed tip slowly back and forth like a hapless worm.

A large, juicy trout swam almost within her reach, then zipped away. She concentrated on the movement of her finger, hardly daring to breathe as she tried to tempt the fish back again. It slid in for a second look, gliding into reach of her palm, when something splashed in the water beside her and scared it off. She looked up and saw a group of trolls gathered in the meadow beside the pond. Several had stones in their hands.

She waved to them and climbed out of the water. She counted

eleven—four adult females and three adult males with two little ones that made her smile; another male and female appeared to be about twelve winters old, the same age as Maggot. Ready to mate. The oldest female was Frosty, who'd been First of the band for as long as Windy could remember. She also recognized Big Thunder and his son, Little Thunder. The young male was probably Little Thunder's boy, Fart. Although they had started calling him Stinker the last time she and Maggot visited. She didn't remember the girl's name.

"Forgive me for hunting in your pool," she said to Frosty, shouting above the din of falling water. "I didn't see anyone."

"S'alright," Frosty shouted back, looking over Windy's shoulder into the woods. "You still keep that animal around?"

There was no rancor in her voice, so Windy tried to keep it out of her response. "He's my son."

"He was one ugly little monster."

Windy didn't hide the anger in her voice this time. "Not to me."

Most of the others wandered off, turning over logs and rocks as they searched for food. Frosty shrugged, scratched herself, and waddled down to the edge of the pool. "Heard he's traveling by daylight now. Can he really do that?"

"Yes."

The old troll made a strange, noncommittal shape with her mouth. "Well, it's good to see you anyway. Your smell is welcome."

"I like the way you smell also," Windy replied, though it wasn't strictly true—Frosty had a mossy scent, and there was something growing in the cracks of her skin. Windy wondered where the trollbirds were, who plucked out such things. "Where's the rest of your band?"

"This is all of us."

She wouldn't have believed it, except she'd seen other bands dwindle just as fast. "What happened to them?"

"Accidents. Two males caught out in daylight. And then people, blackhairs, are moving through the mountains, heading east. They kill

CHARLES COLEMAN FINLAY ⟶ 133

the game as they go, and sometimes kill us, though we chase them away. After they came through last year, we caught the coughing sickness. Ten of us died. Are you looking for a husband?"

"No."

"Because we have no unmarried males. But, ah, if you were willing to share a husband—"

Windy didn't grab at that fish. "No, I'm not interested."

"Ah, well. We have two children here now; that's more than we've had in many years. It may be getting better soon."

"I hope so."

Another female pushed in between them, Little Thunder's sister, Rose. "If she's not here to mate, then make her go away. There's not enough food as it is."

Rose wanted to be First; that was obvious. Windy stayed silent.

"I don't see her taking food out of your mouth," Frosty said.

Rose slapped her hands on her chest, in the mildest form of challenge. "She's not one of us. She doesn't belong here."

"We'll take a vote, then."

Windy had become accustomed to this ritual. It followed her and Maggot around like a buzzard. She was smacking her lips in acceptance when a flat, familiar drumming sound broke the rhythm of the falls. She turned and saw Maggot striding out of the trees, standing straight despite all her efforts to get him to stoop in a better posture. But her heart leapt up in joy at the sight of him. He was safe. That was all that mattered.

Rose laughed out loud at the sight of him. "He *is* ugly," she said to Frosty. "And a runt."

He was very small for his twelve winters, not even six feet tall although getting close to it. She hoped he wasn't fully grown, though she feared he might be. Most trolls reached their full height by his age. He was undersized in other ways too, all viny muscle with no belly on him at all, and legs so long and slender they looked deformed. His arms couldn't even reach the ground when he bent over, not unless he crouched. His skin was pale and smooth too, so thin it broke at every quick abrasion. And his bristly black hair had grown long and horribly shiny. It hung down his back with ragged ends where she'd chewed it off.

But *ugly?*

Never. Not in her eyes.

Stinker, the young male, loped over toward him, bared his teeth, and pounded his chest in warning rather than greeting. It must have been Stinker's spray she'd smelled. Maggot didn't back down, and though the sound of his little fists on his scrawny chest was as feeble in comparison as the teeth he also flashed in response, something about him made Stinker stop.

"Hey, Fart," Maggot said. "Good to smell you again."

"Hey." The troll's browridge rolled down. "You still stink like milk."

Which was an insult. Windy hurried to her son's side, ready to intervene. "These are our friends, Maggot."

He smiled, a broad and genuine expression that contrasted sharply with the purple moons of sleeplessness puddled beneath his eyes. "Oh, good! I've been trying to catch up with you. I have a surprise."

And then without another word of proper greeting, he sprinted back into the forest. A rock flew through the air behind him—hurled by Rose—but it fell well short. He returned a few moments later dragging a buck deer, one of the furtive whitetails with six points on its antlers. It was lashed with lengths of vine to a pair of long poles. She didn't know where he'd learned such things. A troll never thought of new things like that.

The other members of the band came running. The animal was a couple nights' old, and Maggot had obviously done much to conceal its scent from scavengers. It smelled of mud, and urine, and stinkweed, but underneath all those things, it smelled wonderful.

"Carrion?" Little Thunder asked.

"No," Maggot said, standing upright and staring eye to eye with the comfortably squatting male. Windy had the sudden realization that he stayed in his aggressive posture all the time simply to be as big as the nonaggressive trolls. "I hunted it and killed it like a bigtooth would."

Little Thunder hooted in derision. "How? With your fearsome teeth?" He bared his own and everyone laughed.

Everyone except Windy. And Maggot. He bent down and took something from beside the deer. "With these teeth," he said, and showed off the sharpened sticks he'd played with lately.

Little Thunder flashed his teeth again, rising up on his hind legs to his full eight feet of height, and then retreated. Some of the others banged warnings on their chests.

People used sharp sticks like that to hurt trolls, which was why trolls stole them and hid them deep in caves where people would never find them.

"These are our friends," Windy repeated.

"Then let them eat," Maggot said. He smiled at her again.

Hunger outvoted any lecture she intended to give. She reached down to snap off the vines that bound the deer to the poles. In its side, she noticed the broken-off point of one of Maggot's sticks. He had to get close to the horns to do that, and she looked over him quickly for signs of new wounds. He'd suffered a lot of injuries in his twelve years. But he appeared fine. The other trolls still held back, although she could almost hear their stomachs rumbling.

"What will you eat?" she asked. They had learned long ago that carrion made Maggot ill. He had to eat meat fresh, soon after it was dead, or not eat it at all. He had so many weaknesses, and struggled so hard to overcome them.

"I've eaten," was all he said. She doubted it. He'd never put on the weight he needed or grown the way he should. She opened her mouth to say so, and saw him smiling at her, as if he knew exactly what was coming next. "I killed a striped-tail the same evening, and ate it myself."

Aha, she thought. Trying something small first, then something bigger. Very typical of him. And not waiting long before the second venture either. Also typical.

The other trolls jostled for position, pushing the smaller ones back while they waited for her to take first piece. Windy chomped down on the rear flank, severing the hip joint with her massive jaw, ripping the flesh with her nails, and pulled away a whole leg. The others crowded in as soon as she stepped away, jumping back only when the gas-swollen belly popped. The two children licked those parts up off the ground, while every other part of the animal disappeared within moments. Some of the trolls took more than others while a few had none at all, and those looked to steal any loose scraps.

The meat tasted sweet. Windy gobbled it up quickly, shoving moist chunks of it into her massive cheeks.

Maggot circulated among the trolls. They curled their shoulders against him, ready to run away. They didn't know, as she did, that he wouldn't steal their food because he couldn't stomach it. When he came close to Stinker, the troll rose up and growled at him. Maggot dodged behind him and scampered away. She thought she'd seen one of the sharp sticks in his hand, but when she glimpsed him again, the wooden tooth was gone. Stinker squatted down again.

A second later, in between the sounds of meat being ripped off bones, she heard a pop followed by a howl of pain.

Stinker danced around and around, waving his arms and slapping at his behind. As he spun away from Windy, she saw the stick poking out of his bottom. Maggot must have propped it under him, where his own weight on it punctured his thick skin.

She couldn't help herself; she started to laugh—and so did most of the others. When Stinker dropped the other haunch—that was the piece he'd ripped free—to grab at the stick with both hands, Maggot rushed in. He scooped up the meat and hurried away to the young female, who sat there with nothing to eat.

It was a courtship gift, all very proper. And, coming from Maggot, not proper at all. Windy's laughter died in her throat.

Frosty frowned in open disapproval. It was a glare so very like Windy's mother, it made her feel at home, even though her mother had died during the past winter. The young female appeared stunned, but she made the proper gargling sound in response, grabbed the meat, and ran away to eat it.

Stinker hopped over to Frosty and asked her to remove the splinter. She did, and as soon as it came out, he grabbed some of the ribs from her pile of bones and scooted off. Soon bones crunched by thick teeth, and the sucking out of marrow, were the only sounds in the woods besides the waterfall.

Windy sniffed the air. The mood was mixed. The trolls were glad for the scraps of meat, but Maggot made them nervous. He made her nervous too when he went over and flirted with the girl.

He whispered to her first, drew a laugh, and that wasn't so bad. Then they rubbed faces together, and she bent over abruptly, presenting her sex to him. It was neither swollen nor properly red, and she continued to eat and look around while she did it. Windy suspected that the girl was only trying to make Stinker jealous. But Maggot sniffed at it, stood up, and waved his sex at her face to show he was interested. When he rubbed up against her, the adults were caught between horror and humor. But since neither Maggot nor the girl gave off the proper musk, and since the girl was so much larger than he was, they treated it like an uncomfortable joke.

Windy sighed miserably.

She'd always hoped that Maggot would find a nice girl to mate with and settle down. She didn't care for grandchildren so much, but his happiness mattered to her. She knew that she and Ragweed had been happy, even if only for a short time. She wanted that for her son.

So Maggot's earnestness worried her. However much the other trolls considered the pantomime a joke, Windy knew that he was serious about mating with the girl. The girl noticed it too, at about the same moment, because she squealed and jumped away. When Maggot stood there confused, Stinker growled and charged, shoving him to the ground.

"Wrestle him!" Little Thunder shouted.

The others in the little band took up the chant at once. "Wrestle, wrestle!"

Stinker's face wrinkled happily at the suggestion. He reared up on his hind legs, almost eight feet tall and over two hundred fifty pounds, battering his chest with the danger-death warning. "I challenge you!"

Maggot sat on the ground. He looked at Windy, his eyes cold and certain. There were times when she wished he were not so completely fearless or that he would not take such risks. But what could she do?

She smacked her lips: yes.

He stood up—two feet and a hundred pounds shy of Stinker's size—pounding death on his chest, using cupped hands instead of knuckles to make a sharper, cracking sound in place of the deep resonant bass.

The adults formed a rough circle around the edge of the glade. Or, rather, a half circle spread out behind Stinker. Windy sat alone in the other half of the circle. The girl hovered on the edge between the two, knuckle-walking toward Windy then back again toward her band.

"You're a baby bird in a nest," Maggot said, snapping his fingers in Stinker's face. "I'm going to crush you like that!"

"You're a worm!" Stinker screamed. "And I'm going to squish you like a, uh, like a, like a worm!"

Maggot fell forward to stand on his hands, and waved his foot at Stinker's face. "You're a snake in the grass—I'm going to break your skinny little snake-neck between my toes."

Some of the other trolls laughed at this. It was a good trick, something none of them could do. Besides, the insults were a big part of the fun of wrestling, and Maggot was good at them. Telling a troll he had a neck was like telling a twelve-year-old he smelled like milk.

Stinker was not so good at insults. He grabbed at Maggot's foot like a fish going for a fingernail. Maggot flipped backward and landed upright. Stinker rushed him, but Frosty thrust her long arms between them.

"Are you done talking already?" she asked.

"Just let me at him!" Stinker said.

Frosty looked to Maggot, who bounced up and down a little nervously. He lifted his chin. "Just have him bend over," he said, "so I can fart in his ear to see if he knows his name."

"Let me at him!"

"Not until I say ready," Frosty commanded. "Do you both agree to this?"

They did.

"Does anyone vote against it?" She looked at Windy.

Windy refused to raise her hand. Sooner or later, Maggot had to learn what was going to happen to him if he picked fights with other males over a girl.

"Let them wrestle already," Big Thunder hollered.

Frosty turned back to the boys. "There's to be no eye poking, or nose gouging, and no killing, but everything else is fair. Do you both agree to that?"

"What if I smash him by accident?" asked Stinker. "What if I fall on him? He'll squish like a berry."

"What if I rip his head off?" Maggot spit back. "What if I rip his head off and drink his brains out of his skull? Oh, wait, I can't—he doesn't have any."

"No killing!" Frosty told Stinker. "You'll fight until I say stop." She stepped back with her arm outstretched, dropped it suddenly, and cried, "Go!"

The first exchange happened quickly. Stinker charged with his arms upraised to strike; Maggot dropped to the ground and kicked Stinker's ankles out from under him. As Stinker crashed into the dirt,

Maggot attempted to leap past him for the poles he carried the deer carcass in on—going for his sharpened sticks, Windy realized—but Stinker lurched to his feet and thrust his hand out wildly. Maggot smacked into the giant forearm and flopped on his back with a sharp cry of pain.

Stinker took a running leap high into the air so he could crush Maggot. Windy gasped aloud; but her son rolled out of the way, and Stinker slammed hard into the ground. Maggot came up with a handful of dirt and flung it into Stinker's face.

When Maggot made another dash for his sticks, Little Thunder moved to intercept him. The delay allowed Stinker, howling and blind, to lurch after Maggot's scent. His flailing hand caught her son's ankle and tripped him. Maggot fell down, and Stinker fell on top.

Her son's pale skin glistened in the bright moonlight as he wriggled half-free. He and Stinker rolled over several times in their struggle. The lopsided little circle of hooting spectators moved with the pair as they tumbled down the slope to the side of the pool below the waterfall. Stinker ended up on top, spit flying out of his mouth as he pounded his hands at her twisting, dodging son. Windy's fingers kneaded her breast anxiously. Maggot groped in the mud, then smashed his fist into Stinker's nose. She assumed he had picked up a rock as a weapon, but he hadn't. Instead, he shoved a big ball of mud up Stinker's nostrils, choking him. As the troll curled away gagging, Maggot squirmed free.

Or almost free. Stinker grabbed Maggot's foot with one hand while the other clawed at his clogged nose. Maggot whipped around, and she heard a snap followed by a howl of pain—he'd broken Stinker's finger to break his grip.

"Run," she whispered, hoping he would hear her. "Run, run far away, run fast, and I'll come find you when it's safe."

But he didn't run. He pounced on Stinker's back, slipping his arm under the troll's and pressing his forearm down on the back of

Stinker's neck. Windy's eyes went wide. This was a practical joke that Maggot played on her often, holding her arm out of the way so he could tickle her.

"Run," she pleaded.

Then Maggot did the same with his other arm, something he'd never done to her. Stinker spun in a circle, unable to reach Maggot, who perched on his back like a trollbird.

"Rip the maggot's head off!" Little Thunder screamed to his son, and the other trolls screamed with him, slapping their hands on the ground. The uproar made Windy tremble.

"Bite him!" Rose cried. "Bite him really hard!"

"Fall on him!" Big Thunder yelled.

The last suggestion made the most sense, and someone had just suggested that they vote on it when Stinker took the initiative into his own hands—or rather legs, as his hands flapped uselessly over his head—and flopped backward. Windy plunged her fingers into the loam and groped for bedrock to root herself to. She wanted to run to Maggot's aid, but knew she could not. Not yet. But as soon as the two hit the ground, she would rush in—

They didn't hit the ground.

Maggot had anticipated Stinker's move. As the troll fell back, Maggot kicked his legs out and landed upright. With his feet planted firmly, he bent Stinker's chin into his chest. Then, with a heart-wrenching cry, he folded the troll over double.

Stinker's skin turned a darker shade of gray. He couldn't breathe. The veins stood out on Maggot's head, like ridges in the moonlight. Windy held her place. All fell silent except for the rush of the waterfall as they watched her son strain his long legs to snap Stinker in half and grind him into the dirt.

Surely, Windy thought, looking at her son, *his heart will burst*. If his didn't, hers would.

That's when the girl shrieked and rushed forward. She leapt on

Maggot's back, slapping and clawing him. "You beast! You, you *animal*!"

Maggot let go instantly and fled across the glade for one of the trees. He dashed in among the branches and climbed above the height of the trolls. "Hey, Fart," he taunted, between loud, ragged breaths. "Your mama had to run and save you!"

It was all the more effective as an insult because Windy sat there and did nothing. The other trolls howled with laughter, even Little Thunder, as the girl cradled a sulking, weary Stinker in her arms.

"Look at mama troll with her baby!"

"Better clean his nose, Mama, it's a mess!"

Windy let go of the dirt, brushed it off her fingers, and relaxed. They'd ridicule Stinker for years for losing a wrestling match to her boy.

Frosty lumbered over and sat down beside Windy. Neither one said a word. Then Frosty reached out and started grooming her, picking off loose scales of skin and crawling bugs. Windy sighed in contentment.

"That was good fun," Frosty said, crunching a big tick between her molars. "Your son, he fights like a troll."

"He's a good troll," Windy said.

Little Thunder overheard and grunted his approval. "He brought us some fresh rotten meat. That was good. You and your son, you can come visit our band any time you want."

"Visit, but not stay," Frosty said firmly, with a glance at Rose. "We can take a vote, and you and he can argue otherwise, if you insist. But I won't support it."

Windy didn't insist. She'd heard the same thing many times before, from Sulfur Springs down south to Deep Hole Gorge in the east. "We're just glad for your hospitality. Maybe I could come to your den to sleep for the day, and tomorrow night I can tell you what I've seen in the seven bands."

"That smells good. And your son? Where will he spend the day?"

Even Frosty knew that it would not be safe for Maggot to stay there, not until Stinker got over his anger. "He can take care of himself," she said loudly. "He's a grown troll."

She glanced over. Maggot smacked his lips at her, and descended from the tree. His skin looked like dropped fruit in the moonlight, covered with dark bruises and deep cuts. As he ran off into the woods, she worried less than she had only two nights before. He'd proven that he could take care of himself. She was proud of him, prouder than ever.

So why did she feel so sad?

⇥ CHAPTER 10 ⇤

The air outside the cave blew wonderfully cold in the short daylight. In the summertime, cool air inside the cave refreshed her; now it felt warm compared to the winter wind, almost enough to make her feel sluggish. Windy longed to run out and roll in the snow to wake up, but the last wings of daylight still feathered the cave's entrance.

Some of the other trolls walked up from the deeper recesses of the caverns, rubbing their eyes. "Is he back yet?"

Windy opened her mouth and thrust out her tongue.

The trolls frowned, but not much. One of them chewed on a big-eared bat that had fallen from its perch high up in the cave. Sometimes the trolls threw stones at the bats to knock them down. Thousands hung upside down on the tall ceilings of the caverns, night creatures like the trolls and hard to catch in the summer when they flitted around too fast for the eye to follow. But they seemed to sleep all winter long and were easy to capture. One in the mouth melted away to nothing like snow. A whole pile of them didn't add up to a decent meal, though it was something crunchy to snack on.

Windy sighed. Winter was the best time of year for a troll. It was easier for her to stay active in the cold, and the nights were so long that there was enough time to eat and play. Best of all, it was the season of meat: weaker animals succumbed to the harsh temperatures and foundered in the deep drifts, leaving plenty of carrion for the trolls. She scratched the back of her neck, then her elbow. Scales of gray skin floated through the air like snow. That was the only problem—their thick skin dried up and came off in big flakes that left the skin beneath pink and raw.

She thought of Maggot's thin skin, no longer so white, scorched brown by the sun, rubbed raw by the wind, with so little fat beneath it that she wondered how he stayed warm at all. In comparison, her own itchiness didn't seem like such a big problem.

The last trolls straggled up from their day's sleep. There were no children in this band—the last had been killed by a cave bear during the summer—and none of the females were pregnant. Yet these seventeen individuals constituted the largest remaining band of trolls in all the eastern mountains. Windy knew of nine at Blackwater Falls, and seven each in the bands at Deep River Gorge and Sulfur Springs. There were some farther north, in the Black Rock country, some said, or toward the Big Deep Water. The Piebald Mountain remnant from way down south had moved north a few winters before, looking for a place without people. It was believed that there were many far to the west, in the mountains beyond the sunset, but no one living had ever seen them.

A shadow fell across the cave's entrance. As the trolls surged toward the promise of darkness, a thin, almost skeletal figure entered.

One of the girls gasped. "What an ugly troll!"

"He's beautiful!" Windy snapped. The girls dissolved in giggles, and she realized she'd been had.

Maggot was still short, not even six and a half feet tall, and painfully thin at a little over two hundred twenty pounds, but he had grown as big as could be expected. He was eighteen or nineteen winters old now—Windy had lost count of the years. His pale skin was covered with more scars than she could count or remember. The new and fading marks overlapped each other, from the numerous deep scratches left by the nails of other trolls to two long purple worms across one thigh left by a bigtooth lion. Some of them he'd never explained to her, nor had she asked him to.

Ragweed snorted. He was the biggest male in the band, grown boulder-bellied with age and presumably wise. He stood next to his current mate, a pretty young girl named Cliff, and glared balefully at Maggot. His nose wrinkled, and he shouldered his way forward.

Windy sniffed and smelled the same odor, of many people, but no one stood there except her son. "Maggot?"

He stepped out of the light into the dark, and she saw him clearly then. He wore something on his feet, not just wrapped animal skins but things shaped from the forelegs of deer. They had the people scent on them, as did the skin across his shoulders.

"Showing his true odors," Ragweed said, looking over to Windy. "And this is the troll—I use the term loosely—you want to be First?"

Before she could answer, one of the younger trolls called out, "Got any ripe meat, Maggot?"

Her son inclined his head toward the cave entrance. "Part of a humpback."

The other trolls looked expectantly to Windy. She lifted her lips, like someone with her mouth full, to say "go on," and they all shoved past her to pour out of the cave. Exclamations and the sounds of small squabbles followed as they divided the carcass of the humpback.

Windy looked at Maggot, brushing his new skins with her fingertips. "Where did you get those?"

"I scavenged them, how else?" He held out the old metal knife he'd used for the past three years—something else he'd scavenged. "You take it."

He had a new one in a sheath, hung on a string about his neck.

"Thank you," she said. Her fist enclosed it.

"Keep this one with you," he said.

"This time I will." He'd given her such gifts before, but in truth it wasn't as sharp or as effective as her own clawlike nails. And it was always hard to remember where she'd left such things when she went outside. If she could hold onto it through the night, she'd take it deep into the cavern when she went to sleep at dayrise. There she'd add it to the piles of similar baubles the trolls had accumulated over tens of lifetimes, counted beyond memory. She gestured to his covering skins. "Why tonight?"

He crinkled his nose, signifying uncertainty. "Because," he said. Then, "I was cold. These were warm."

"But tonight you're supposed to challenge Ragweed for First of the band! You've worked so hard to make the others accept you as one of them. This just reminds them of the differences."

He ran his hands over her skin, as if picking for parasites. There weren't any in this cold. She did the same for him. They sat like that a long while, touching each other without speaking another word.

"I *am* different," he said finally. "If they accept me, it'll be because of who I really am."

She didn't know what to say to that, so she rose. "We should go. The vote will be at midnight."

"I'm ready."

"Aren't you thirsty? Don't you need to go down to the lake inside the cavern and get a drink?"

"No, I'm fine."

They stepped outside. A waning thorn of moon pricked the horizon. Nothing remained of the humpback except the poles Maggot had carried it in on and a few stray bits of fur and bone. A new pole, with a pointed leaf of metal on one end like those stored in the deep caves, lay propped against the stone. Maggot picked it up to carry with him. A tramped-down trail led across the deep snow to the vale. It passed through several miles of forest filled with pinecones and acorns for anyone willing to dig them up.

"Let's cut over the hills to join the others," Windy said. She'd eat something later, when her stomach settled.

"That smells good," Maggot replied.

Fluffy flakes of snow swirled in the air. There was no trail to follow this way. Windy's broad flat feet buoyed her up across the deep drifts, and her wide hands helped support her weight. She moved along quickly on all fours. She still expected Maggot, as thin and small as he was, to glide across the surface, but his narrow feet continually broke through the crust of snow. As they crossed the naked ridge, Windy heard wolves howling.

Maggot looked over his shoulder. "I should've brought my snowfeet," he said.

Windy paused for him to catch up. "Are they something else you scavenged, with all the rest of this?"

He smiled at her. "I scavenged the first ones years ago. I've been hiding these things from you, and the others, for years. Mostly caching them in the trees, like carrion."

She didn't know what to say except, "Good. That's smart."

The wolves howled again, much nearer. Windy sniffed the air, but scented nothing upwind. She hoped they were timberwolves—she'd never learned to tell one wolf's howl from another. Dyrewolves could be deadly. "They sound hungry."

Maggot grunted. "The winter's been long and hard. Much of the meat I've taken for you would've fallen to them."

Windy glimpsed the pack gliding through the distant trees like wisps of brown-gray fog. A canny old female led three, no, four males. Another handful-plus-two trailed behind. They had the blunt snouts and broad shoulders of dyrewolves, just as she'd feared. A pack could easily bring down a single troll or even a pair. It had happened to Bones and her mate a few winters past.

The snow cracked, and Maggot sunk to his knees. Windy went back to help pull him free.

"They're slow," he told her. "They tire quickly. You should run ahead and join the others. You'll be safe."

"I can't do that!"

He stopped in his tracks and turned toward the trees. "I can climb; they can't. Neither can you—you're too heavy for those branches. Eventually they'll go away."

"I've always stood beside you."

He snorted, troll fashion. "Now's a good time to change your habits."

Before she could run or Maggot could bolt for the trees, the baying dyrewolves bounded across the snow. They almost appeared to be swimming, the way they paddled their paws to stay afloat on this cold white lake.

She shoved her son toward the trees. "Run! Save yourself!"

Maggot laughed and placed his back against hers, his knife in one hand, spear in the other. "It's always been the two of us against the world, huh, Mom?"

A smile shadowed her mouth. Before it faded away, the dyrewolves closed in, spreading out in a circle. She smelled uncertainty on them, and hunger, but no fear, neither from them nor Maggot. The only fear she smelled was her own.

The wolves scented it too. Two of them dashed in and snapped at her, but stopped short when she bared her own teeth and snarled back.

She'd never been this close to a dyrewolf. Their bodies were stocky, with short, powerful legs. They had thick ruffs around their necks, and fur streaked gray, white, and brown. But it was their massive heads, all out of proportion to the rest of their bodies, that made her most afraid. They had shorter snouts than the timber wolves or wild dogs, with teeth like sharp stones in their bone-crushing jaws, and wild, intelligent eyes.

As the two wolves stopped short of her, three others attacked Maggot. The old female lunged at him first, but it was a feint. He swung his knife at her in counterfeint, and when the old male made the real attack, Maggot thrust the spear through his neck. Blood gushed out, turning the snow pink. Maggot twisted the spear and pulled it free to jab it at the third beast while the wounded one yelped and crawled away.

The dyrewolves withdrew a short distance. "Let's go," Maggot said. "Down this way, toward the vale."

Windy smacked her lips in assent, and one of the males dived in to fasten on her arm. "Aiieee!"

Others leapt in at Maggot. She heard him shout as he drove them back, but all she felt was pain as the dyrewolf's teeth sank right through her flesh. She drove her fist down onto the soft snout. The wolf snarled, and its yellow eyes squeezed shut, but it didn't let go, so she pounded again and again as the wolf shook its head, dodging the blows, and when that failed to free her arm she thrust one of her long sharp fingers deep into a yellow eye. It popped like a grape under her nail, squirting its warm juice across her hand, so she thrust farther into its brain. The dyrewolf shuddered and died, but still it didn't let go.

She pried with her fingers until the dead animal's jaws cracked. She stopped screaming as she dropped it to the ground and swiveled around to answer the next attack.

If any of the other wolves had charged in, they could have pulled her down and killed her. She saw now that they hadn't only because Maggot had held them away. His footprints formed a protective circle around her, and he stood poised with his spear raised. Half a dozen animals bled from cuts to their necks and faces.

"Step away from the dead one slowly," said Maggot, his voice as sharp as his weapon.

She did exactly as he told her. They were scarcely out of arm's reach when the dyrewolves surrounded their dead companion, licking at the bloody snow and baying.

"Keep moving, faster now," Maggot said tersely. "If you pack snow on the wound as you go, it'll help."

She noticed the blood pouring down her arm. Something felt wrong with the bone. Numbness stiffened her fingertips. Without slowing down, she scooped up handfuls of snow and packed it as Maggot told her, clamping her good hand down tight on top of the wound. It eased the burning and stanched the bleeding. She found it difficult to walk on two feet, but she shuffled along until she found and followed the deep trails in the snow made earlier by the other trolls.

She'd never felt so close to her own death before. She trembled from it, and yet, as they left the dyrewolves behind and climbed the low rise between two peaks to descend into the larger valley, it all seemed unreal, something that had already happened in the distant past. She was changed, but she did not know how or why.

"Have you fought them before?" she asked her son. "Alone?"

Maggot smacked his lips once. *Yes, but it was a small meal, nothing.*

Her son was covered by many scars. How had he been changed? She felt faint-headed, apart from herself, as though she floated over the snow.

They entered the sacred glade with its circle marked out by thirteen boulders. The other trolls saw Windy's wound and crowded around to hear how it had happened. While she told them about the dyrewolves, Maggot circulated and spoke to Rocky and her mate, and to Blossom and Scabpicker and all the other trolls whose votes he hoped to win.

"Let's start," Ragweed shouted.

"I'm ready whenever you are," Maggot said. "You want to be First, so you should go first."

Ragweed scowled, unsure if he had just been insulted. Windy sat down as he trotted around inside the circle of stones, trying to impress the other trolls. He was still handsome, she reluctantly admitted to herself. His gray skin looked exceptionally rocklike against the white snow.

"Look!" Maggot pointed. "He's running in circles! And that's who you want for a leader?"

Ragweed swerved, rushing at Maggot, rising up to his eight and a half feet of height and pounding his chest. Maggot straightened up as tall as he could stand and stretched out his arms as if to pound on his chest. While Ragweed paused for the challenge, Maggot dropped without warning to four legs and ran around the circle. He didn't go more than a quarter of the way before he stopped to scratch his ass. It was a perfect imitation of Ragweed. Windy wasn't the only one to burst out laughing.

Ragweed laughed along with them, until his brow drooped with belated recognition. "Hey!"

Maggot stood up straight again. "Are we here to vote or wrestle? I can't tell by the way you're acting so far."

"That's enough," Laurel said. She was now the oldest female in the band, and a former First. "Both of you have ideas for what we should do about our problems. Ragweed, maybe you should begin. Tell us why we should vote for you to be First of the band."

Windy shook her head, squeezing fresh snow on her arm to ease the pain. *Maggot* had ideas for the good of the band—not Ragweed—and he had talked about them often while Berry, the previous First, died of the yellow water. Ragweed opposed everything Maggot said, more out of habit than for any other reason. Somehow they'd ended up as the two candidates for First.

Ragweed paced, then paused, then squatted and looked each troll in the eyes. "You all know me," he told them. "I was born in this band and I've lived here all my life among you."

How conveniently he'd forgotten their six years of wandering, thought Windy. But he smelled earnest. He'd always had a charismatic fragrance.

"We've faced a lot of problems," Ragweed continued. "Some of you are as old as me. You remember back when we were little trollings, there were fifty, sixty trolls in this band. The mountains were ours. We found every bit of carrion, every calf and fawn that went unprotected. Vote for me and I'll bring those days back. We'll make things like it used to be, when the caves were safe for children and the land was ours to scavenge."

He paced again. "Now, if you don't want to vote for me, you can vote for Maggot. I'd say that he's as ugly as a possum, but that'd insult the possum." Laughter, to that. "The worst thing is that he's the size of a trolling, and he still follows his mother around like one, and she covers him up funny."

More laughter at that.

Ragweed glanced over as if expecting Maggot to attack him for these insults, but her son stayed motionless. What was wrong with him? He ought to be roaring his disagreement. She swallowed a handful of snow to wet her parched throat.

"Vote for me," her former mate concluded. "Because I'm the real troll. Thank you."

Three or four of his strongest supporters cheered madly and pounded their chests in challenges directed at Maggot.

Windy sniffed worriedly. To her, Maggot smelled wonderful, unique. But to the others he would smell foreign, not like himself but like a strange band of people because of the things he carried. Seemingly oblivious to this, Maggot bounded over to one of the boulders and climbed on it to make himself taller.

"Vote not with your eyes, but with your bellies," he began, and Windy's spine shivered like a reed. Maggot had trained his voice to make it deep and resonant like Ragweed's. "Ask not who looks more like you, but who has done more for you. Ragweed is a handsome troll, and I admit that I am skinny, frail, and small. But you're not looking for a mate, with the beauty of a mate, but for your First, and I have been the first to serve you all. Who brings you more mea—"

He jumped as a ball of dung sailed by the spot where he stood. Cliff and Ragweed's other supporters hooted and waved their bottoms at him. Laurel sprinted over on her knuckles. "We'll have none of that now!"

"No muck-slinging!" old Stump shouted, and it was taken up as a general cry. One more ball of dung was hurled halfheartedly, but no more was needed to ruin the rhythm of Maggot's speech. Windy could cry. It would be a close vote under the best circumstances, but now . . .

Maggot pointed to her. "Ragweed says that I stand beside my mother, and that is true! I'll never deny it. Tonight as I came to this place, dyrewolves attacked my mother—you see the teeth marks on her arms. But I stood by her to protect her and I will also stand by all of y—"

"Aw, he bit her arm himself," cried Ragweed.

Maggot turned and bared his teeth at him, then mocked his own small mouth. They'd seen her wound, so a few trolls laughed. But inside, Windy cringed. Her son's unimpressive mouth would lose him votes. Trolls voted for big teeth. He was emphasizing all the wrong things!

But Maggot continued. "Ragweed says he's going to give you more food, more fruit. How? People come into the high valleys, eating everything and destroying the caves where we sleep. I've walked across these mountains, from the head up north to the southern tail, and I've seen whole bands vanish in the space of a few years. Who last heard word from the Blue Peaks band? Or the Sinking River band? If we don't want to disappear like the others, without a trace, we need a plan."

The trolls looked around, like someone seeking better-tasting food.

Windy shifted fretfully. It was the truth! Maggot told the truth, but the trolls didn't want to hear it. He was losing them.

"What is Ragweed's plan?" Maggot asked. "He promises you that everything will be like it was. If he promised to grab the sun in his fist and move it backward across the sky, would you believe him?"

He'd lost them! Windy groaned aloud, and when the others looked at the noise she grimaced and held her injured arm. But you couldn't mention the sun before an election, you just couldn't! She'd thought her son was smarter than that.

"If you elect me First, I will not lead you back but forward. I will take us and join up with the remaining trolls at Blackwater and Sulfur Springs. Together, we can make one large band again and there will be mates for everyone and children will be born. I will teach you to make weapons, to hunt down the food we all must have. And I will lead you against the people who trespass—"

"Can we vote now?" one of the trolls asked. Others took up the call. Truthfully, thought Windy, most had probably made up their minds beforehand. Laurel called for the vote. Hope soared in Windy's breast when she counted the hands. Ragweed only got seven votes. Then Laurel called Maggot's name and four arms went up—hers, Rocky's and her mate Skeeter's, and Stump's. The vast majority of trolls had lost interest long before and when the vote was called they wandered away to roll in the snow or dig in it for things to eat. Maggot saw the number of hands up and didn't even vote for himself. Instead he jumped up on one of the boulders, drumming the death tattoo on his chest.

No one paid him any attention.

Laurel declared Ragweed the winner. Three or four of his supporters hollered and cheered. Cliff danced wildly around the circle. Windy rose and went over to thank Rocky and Skeeter.

"If anyone could think past tomorrow's darkness," Rocky said, "they'd know that everything Maggot says is true."

Her husband was the last known survivor of the Blue Peaks band. He shaped his lips in agreement. "I'd say we should go elsewhere, but this is still the best band and our best hope."

"These are hard years," Windy told him. "But daylight is always followed again by darkness. Things will get better."

Stump came over and started to groom her. "How's the arm?"

"It hurts."

"We'll take care of you," he rumbled. "Your son's a good troll. I've always said that."

"I'm very proud of him."

Stump exuded a sprit of musk, testing the air to see if she'd respond. His interest surprised her. He examined her arm. The worst bleeding had stopped, but the numbness reached way down into the bone. "Yep," he told her. "We'll have to keep you fed, take good care of that."

"It'll be fine." She pulled her arm back and hid it behind her. She musked a bit into the air as well. Not because she was really interested—because she wasn't, she was too old for that foolishness and had spent too many years alone with her son. But she didn't want Stump to feel bad. When he started grooming her again, Rocky giggled and Skeeter shushed her. Feeling embarrassed, Windy looked around helplessly for Maggot and saw Ragweed's supporters chasing him away.

"You weren't baiting him again?" she asked when Maggot came and squatted down with them.

"I wanted to wish him good luck," Maggot said. "But he doesn't want it."

Rocky sensed his agitation and picked considerately through his hair. "In the spring," she said, "people will see how bad their decision was. We'll have another vote."

"Perhaps," Maggot answered. His face was wistful, sad. He wore a smile that was less his than the skins that covered him. "Listen, I didn't say anything earlier because I was saving it for the feast when I won. If I won. But it's better this way, because there's more for the four of you."

Skeeter licked his lips. "What is it? Another humpback?"

"People," Maggot said plainly. "A small group crossing from the southern pass. I don't know if they got lost, or what, but the blizzard trapped them, made it hard for them to move. I buried the bodies under their stuff and pissed all over it."

Stump grinned from ear to ear. "Where are they? Let's go!"

"Follow the wind, down the rocky river, where it passes between the tall stones. There's a glade of chestnut trees there." He smiled at Stump. "If you can't find the meat, you can always eat the chestnuts."

"I know that spot," Rocky added enthusiastically. "There's a deep rock ledge down there, along the river. We can spend the day sleeping there and eat again tomorrow night."

The other three stood up and left at once. Windy rose also, and black dots swam suddenly before her eyes. When they cleared, she noticed Maggot sitting still. "Come on," she said.

He stuck out his tongue. "Would you ever eat the flesh of another troll?"

"No!" Something was wrong with him, to make him so stupid. Trolls buried their dead away from light, so that they could pass through the hot day of death and enter again into the long sweet night of life.

Maggot came over and sat beside her. "So will I never eat people flesh." He paused, picked at her skin one more time. "I'm people, Mother. I'm not a troll."

"You're a good troll!"

"I've tried hard. You saw that tonight. I'm a better troll than Ragweed in every respect, but one. I'm not a troll."

Sharp pain shot all the way up her arm into her chest. "What will you do?"

"Go down to the western valley where I was born. I've studied people for years now, as they passed through the mountains. Maybe I can learn to be like them. Maybe find a band that I can join."

Ah, so that's it, she thought. *Maybe it's for the best.* She took his hand in hers, and walked up out of the stone circle. "We'll go downstream with the others," she told him. "We'll sleep overday under the rock ledge, and tomorrow we'll continue on our way."

He tried to pull his hand free; she gripped it as tight as an old root wound round a rock.

"Mom?"

"Yes."

"Mom?"

"Yes."

"Mom, this is something I have to do alone. You need to stay here. This is where you belong."

Stump reappeared on the edge of the hill. He spritzed an odor of worry for her. He was very kind. When he saw she was all right, he gave off another musk.

Maggot had never once given off the proper musk, had never once said that he loved her. And yet she knew that he did, that he always would.

"Go with them, Mom," he said softly. "I'll be fine."

He pulled his hand again, very gently. And she did the hardest thing she had ever done in her life.

She let go.

Part 3

A Troll Abroad in the Wars of Men

⇥ CHAPTER 11 ⇤

Slashes of bright color, a ragged line of them, stomping and shouting, penetrated the forest's net of browns and greens.

Maggot shifted his position in the tree for a better view. Pine needles pricked his bare back. The bough swayed slightly under his callused feet. Blue and yellow and white, closer, closer still, and then, leaning forward, Maggot—

Yes, the flat chest and beard were those of a man. Maggot flared his nostrils, frowned, rocked back on his haunches.

He had come down from the mountains in search of a mate. So far he'd seen nothing but men.

The man in blue stomped and shouted within a few yards of Maggot's tree. He carried a large section of log on a sash across his bare shoulder, so he must be very strong. Maggot picked his nose and flicked snot at the man's head, but the man didn't notice anything.

People were stupid. Compared to trolls.

The man passed under the tree and into open sunlight. He wore strips of white skin wrapped around his feet and tied in a knot at top. Another skin skirted his waist, with blocks of green divided by cracks of sharp blue.

Maggot peered off into the deep, unexplored forest. He'd like to find the creature that had that skin.

Maybe he should steal this man's skin and wear it to make himself stink more like people, and that would help him find a woman. Maggot had been stealing things from people for the last five or six winters, whenever people crossed the mountain passes. So he'd seen a few human women. At least he thought they were women, although who could know for certain when they were covered with extra skins and the stink of dead things.

But he had discarded his people items, the skins and blankets, because it was too hot down here in the valleys with winter's snow already melted. He'd kept only the knife and spear—the small hard leaf, the hard leaf on the branch.

As he descended the tree to follow the man, Maggot heard shouts. He pressed aside the branches just in time to see the man pound his fists on the log he carried. Birds erupted from the trees and fled away to the sky. The log resonated with a deep, full sound, a troll greeting sound, like fists on a chest. For a second, Maggot's heart leapt into his throat, a loneliness too hard to swallow.

Retrieving his spear from the pile of needles, he eased out from the evergreen's sheltering cape. He sniffed experimentally, trying to smell something besides the scent of pine. Not for the first time, he wished for the broad flat nose of a troll.

He ran to a thick stand of brush and hid. The man with the log knuckled out a rhythm more complicated than any message used by the trolls while the others chanted words in a beat that matched their step. They repeated it over and over until it almost made Maggot crazy.

"*Lion, lion*," he repeated with them, not knowing the word. "Ugh ugh ugh ugh ugh ugh ugh!"

People talked stupid.

He mumbled it again and rapped his knuckles against his chest, shaking the knife sheath that hung on a string about his neck. But for once his mimicking skills failed him. The pounding made no more sense as a message than did the words.

A quick scuttle to another cluster of trees upslope and he saw the next person in line—another man! By the time he reached the peak of the ridge, Maggot had counted four handfuls and two fingers of people, all men. Two more carried the big logs. Every fifth man, or thumb, held a large, flat disc of metal—the troll word described the taste of it—shaped like certain mushrooms. When the men tapped the mushrooms with sticks, they made a chilling ring. All the other men thrashed the brush with long branches.

Stupid men were scaring all the animals away and not just the birds. Maggot's stomach rumbled. There was little to eat here. The trees were just unfolding their leaves, sending forth seedlings that spun down to the ground like wounded butterflies, and only the smallest flowers bloomed, little white stars and tiny blue-and-pink blossoms that hung upside down.

The man beating the brush nearest to Maggot stepped cautiously, careful not to tramp on any flowers. Maybe people scared winter off this way, Maggot thought. These lands were more fertile than the high mountains and earlier in the season too. Maybe this was magic, the false-flavored nature his mother had warned him to avoid.

He decided to run ahead of the men to see if there were any women farther down the valley. He crossed the ridge, but near the bottom of the slope he saw a flash of light and dove instinctively into the cover of a thicket. Thorny branches scratched at his skin as he peered out.

A second line of silent people in drab clothes carried spears with the points thrust out in front of them. They stood closer together, angled toward the noisy log-and-mushroom men.

Maggot crouched his way along behind them, counting. There

were more people here than in the largest troll band! And they were all men. Picking up a pinecone, he winged it at the back of the last man in line. The man's head snapped forward. He reached over and shoved his neighbor while Maggot grinned and backed away.

His stomach gurgled a second time. He escaped the closing jaws of these two lines of men and went off to find something to drink, maybe even something to eat, before he continued his search for a mate.

He jogged through the woods until the noise of the thrashers was faint, far behind him. He found a trickle of water and followed it down the hillside where it joined a stony brook that soon dropped over a steep incline. Maggot paused on a jutting rock at the hill's lip and looked at the stream's low, looping crawl toward a pond in the meadow. One dot of dark blue flitted across the sunlight, chased by another toward some distant nest. Maybe he would find fresh eggs here.

At the edge of the woods, beside the stream, he noticed scat. Bigtooth scat, from the size and shape of it. Dusty white—several days old at least. He bent and sniffed. It didn't smell fresh. Still, with a bigtooth in the area he would have to be much more careful about where he denned up. Though he might get a chance to steal fresh carrion.

He bent on hands and knees by the cool, clear pond. In his head, Maggot had always seen himself as a version of his mother, as a troll. The twig-nosed, nut-mouthed, shaggy-headed face in the water still surprised him. He brushed his hair over his embarrassing high forehead before a woman saw it.

Maybe if he spent more time among people, he'd start to see himself like them but find a troll in his reflection instead.

Before he could kiss his image to sip the water, he heard voices—people coming. He snatched up his spear and hid in the undergrowth while three people entered the meadow.

His breath caught in his mouth. His knees wobbled.

One of the people was a woman!

He straightened, inhaled, and leaned forward uncertainly.

She had saggy breasts, somewhat like a woman, and a round, smooth-skinned face like a woman. But her hips narrowed like a man's. Sunbright loops around her neck and similar bands around her arms echoed those the men wore. Her skin was as black as polished rock and her hair was fog-colored like an old troll's bristle.

Maggot puffed out his cheeks and exhaled. He'd hoped women would be, well, he didn't know. More attractive.

The two other people were men. The younger had skin a soft brown color, with hair as black and thick as Maggot's. He was tall and lean, like Maggot, and had even less hair on his chin. The third man was bearded, pale like Maggot, his brown hair pulled back and twined like vines. Though not as tall as Foghair or the boy, his shoulders were broader and he looked stronger. Other men, carrying spears, joined them.

The bearded man studied the meadow carefully, following the edge of the pond over to the stream. When he found the bigtooth scat, he motioned the others over to investigate. He must be the First, Maggot decided. Even Ragweed, who was not an especially good First, looked at things and brought them to the notice of other members of the band.

They were very excited by the smell, or sight, of the scat. They talked very quickly, gesticulating and pointing in the direction of the noise made by the log-and-mushroom men. The men with the spears made jabbing motions at the scat. So even people were wary of bigtooths. That showed some intelligence.

Foghair lifted the horn to her mouth and blew a series of short, clear notes. A few moments later, the clamor on the hillside shifted direction.

Then they filled their water bladders and spoke quietly among each other until they were interrupted by a crashing noise on the hillside. A whitetailed deer burst from the woods and froze, looking back toward the din of the log-and-mushroom men. Three more deer emerged from the trees and traipsed to a halt.

The boy tapped his chest. The bearded man, First, gestured to one of the spear carriers, who passed his spear to Boy. Boy skipped forward and flung his spear into the air—

Maggot blinked, having never used one as more than a long arm with a claw on the end!

—which fell into the flank of the nearest deer. It bleated pain, collapsing as the other three scattered. The deer staggered up and dragged its rear legs in a circle, the spear bouncing wildly. One of the spear carriers rushed forward and put the animal down with a second thrust through the throat.

Maggot felt a dead-end cave crack open into a wide new cavern— *you could throw spears.*

Maybe people weren't so stupid after all.

As the spear carriers emptied the guts out of the beast, Foghair blew her horn again. The drumming and ringing and thrashing stopped, and all the others came in.

Two men tied the animal to a long pole. Maybe they were taking the meat to their women. Maggot had already decided to follow them to find out when he saw the mammut.

The shaggy red giant ambled into the meadow. Sun blazoned off metal knobs that adorned the ends of its tusks. A small man perched on its head behind the flapping ears. Stranger yet, a tent—a cave made out of sticks and skins, striped blue and yellow—sat astride its back. There were two people in it.

Boy presented the deer to the mammut riders, one of whom said something—the higher voice sounded like a woman's—before they turned away toward the lower valley, with the men carrying the deer and the others chasing after. Maggot followed them, like a shadow stretched out far and behind by a low sun.

Their trail paralleled a stream to where it met a river gushing over a rocky bed. The men approached a village of tents—a cluster of caves made of skins like the one on the back of the elephant—at the river's edge. Fires burned there, making Maggot wary. That magic eluded him. The only time he had ever tried to take hold of fire, he'd burned his hand.

Maggot hid in a large copse of trees that occupied a slight rise at the river's edge, downstream from the camp where too many men moved about constantly, like bees at a hive, making them impossible to count. Though he watched for a time, he saw no more women, and he began to despair that Foghair was the only one after all.

Exhausted, Maggot sipped from the river, then crawled under a fallen log and covered himself with leaves for a brief nap. He awoke refreshed, with the moon only half itself and dropping out of the sky. Though he moved about in the day now and had for many years, despite his mother's fears, some part of him still felt more comfortable at night. When he crept forth for a closer look, he left his spear behind so he could have both hands free for scavenging. His knife still dangled from the string around his neck.

He approached the darkened camp slowly, anxious at the smell of fire and burned meat, wondering how he'd find the women here if there were any. A big animal coughed at the edge of the tents, and Maggot dropped into a crouch.

Three lean, long-legged, spotted cats—unlike any big cats Maggot had ever seen—padded through the darkness. Their eyes glinted green. One paced back and forth, pausing to bat at one of the tents. So he was not the only one to prey on these people tonight.

Staying low, Maggot crawled off to the opposite side of the camp. While the men were distracted by the cats, he'd go in and take what he wanted. He was creeping inside for a closer look when one of the tents moved.

Maggot froze.

The huge bulk of the tent budged again, then lifted a snakelike appendage into the air.

The mammut! It swayed like an old tree in a strong wind. Maggot had known mammuts before, especially on the morning side of the mountain range. Trolls and mammuts fed side by side sometimes during the summer nights. Maggot had always been fond of the creatures because they were bigger than trolls. Even Ragweed looked diminutive next to one.

The little cave was no longer on its back. Maggot approached it gently, reaching out to pat its side. Big clumps of winter fur came loose at his touch. The trunk turned around, snaking over his shoulders, his head. All the while, the mammut rocked, lifting its back leg, dropping it, repeating the motion, until Maggot noticed the iron band affixed to its ankle. The mammut was chained to a stake driven deep in the ground.

That just smells wrong, Maggot thought as he hunkered down to examine the stake. It was the size of a small stump and buried deep. Gripping it with both hands, he braced his shoulders and tugged. The soil was soft. He wiggled the stake from side to side, pulling until it came free.

Shoving the animal's hard, unyielding side with his hand, Maggot whispered, "Go on, go away."

The shaggy creature shuffled in place.

A buzzing snore droned out from one of the nearby tents. Maggot spun around—he had forgotten to watch the tents. Leaving the mammut, he slouched toward the new noise, alert for signs of movement, his heart pounding at his own stupid distraction. He spotted one of the logs that the men carried through the woods propped at an entrance flap to one of the tents. He hefted it, expecting a heavy weight, but found it remarkably light. He saw at once that it was hollow, with the ends covered by some stretched skin. People did a lot with skins. Maybe because theirs were so thin. He tapped the end with his fingertips, and the sound made him jump.

Maggot felt suddenly nervous around all these people and their things. Carrying the log under one arm, he hurried back to the nearby copse.

Sitting down at the base of a tree, he propped the log between his legs. He tapped at it again with the tips of his fingers, and it made a light noise.

It reminded him of woodpeckers drilling dead trees. He smiled, wishing he'd had something like this among the trolls. He could have sounded almost like them then. With his fists, he pounded out the danger-death warning. The log resonated just like Ragweed's chest. He repeated it a couple times, adding a shrill scream at the end. He grinned, imagining the reaction of other trolls.

Looking back in wonder at the camp of men who made such things, he noticed some of them clearly outlined against a big fire that hadn't been burning as brightly a short while before.

First stood there, with Foghair by his side. Maggot recognized them by their posture, as surely as he would recognize a member of another band.

Maggot prepared to flee into the farther darkness, to retrieve his spear, when the mammut trumpeted somewhere far beyond the camp. It *had* wandered away after all.

He laughed. "Run, mammut, run."

And that's when he saw her. A woman. The Woman.

She came out of a tent and stood between Foghair and First beside the fire. She was taller than First, almost as tall as Foghair, with fire-light glinting on her dark hair and tanned skin. Her long robe gapped open at the neck to reveal the curve of her breasts. Many of the men showed fear in their posture—even Maggot, with his puny nose, could smell it on them—but she stood there with her fists on her hips and stared curiously into the dark.

A second woman, whom Maggot scarcely noticed, snatched at her sleeve like a small bird plucking straws, but she shrugged it off. First said something, and she grinned. He said something else, and her laughter rang through the night, splashing over Maggot like cold water.

Maggot had felt the need to mate many times. The feeling that surged through him now had as little in common with that urge as a flower did with the giant poplar trees. He had no name for it. It threatened to drown him, like a mountain stream after a sudden cloudburst.

Still holding onto the skin-log, he crawled backward, then ran as far as he could, away from the tents and into the night.

Chapter 12

With daylight stalking the hills above the valley, Maggot finally found what he sought: a crack between two rocks beneath an overhanging stone. He pawed in the mud, enlarging the opening. When he crawled inside he found a good den, ripe with the old, faint stench of skunk.

From the inside Maggot dug the hole bigger until he could pull the hollow log in with him. It was a good den, though not big enough for him to stretch his legs out full-length. He rolled one way, then the other, then flopped over and over, trying to get comfortable enough to sleep. Once, he nearly dozed off, only to be startled awake when his leg twitched, kicking the log.

Awake, he couldn't stop the thoughts. He'd been afraid. He didn't understand it. Yes, he'd been afraid many times before when wrestling trolls much larger than himself or hunting down creatures whose horns were sharper than his sticks. Venturing into daylight the first time despite his mother's warning. This didn't feel anything like those. Why should he be afraid of this woman? Had he not wrestled

Little Thunder's son, Stinker, and won? Had he not killed stags in the mountains with sharp sticks and his own bare strength? Had he not turned his face toward the sun and not been turned to stone?

He had to go back to the skin-caves to see the woman again. To give her an interest gift. To show her his intentions.

Wrapping his arm around the log-drum, he held it tight, thinking of her until he fell into a restless sleep.

Maggot awoke with darkness rising, went outside, and pissed on the stones to mark the cave as his. Leaving the log behind, he ran bare-handed down to the river in the moonlight.

He hadn't eaten much for two or three nights, so when he spotted the conspicuous purple-globed flowers of wild onions, he stopped to dig up several mouthfuls. The bulbs were small, so he satisfied his hunger by chewing on the pungent green stems.

Twice, on his way, he surprised deer and chased after them. Neither time did he catch one, and he thought again about that spear-throwing trick. Yes, that could be a very useful skill.

The moon was crawling into its cave when he reached the camp, but the light from it was still enough to illuminate a transformed landscape. The copse of trees that had sheltered him was nearly gone; all that remained were the few largest trees, some deadwood, and piles of branches. A rough palisade of upright logs now surrounded the tents.

Higher up in the mountains, people lived in bark caves surrounded by similar walls of sharpened stakes. Maggot had only seen them a few times. In the late winter, those people abandoned their village for wilderness hunts, and it was these smaller groups Maggot stole from. He'd thought that those people and these were two different bands, but they both built similar walls, so now he didn't know.

Maggot skulked through the remains of the copse until he found the fallen, rotting tree where he'd hidden before. He thrust his hand into the leaf-filled pit beneath it, fishing around until he found his spear. Resting the shaft across his thighs, he squatted down behind the log to watch the camp for some glimpse of the woman—the Woman.

Above his head, a red-breasted bird began to trill at the dawn. Its song sounded uncertain, confused at the sudden absence of trees and shelter that had been there only a day before, or perhaps calling for a mate or nestlings that were no longer there. Maggot listened to it, wondering what would be the proper gift to show the woman his interest, and caught himself in a sigh. Nothing ordinary would do.

People began to stir in the camp, shadows among shadows. Maggot crawled down for a closer look. Twigs tangled in his hair as he squirmed through a wallow and peered over a rugged lip of dirt.

A man much larger than the others walked forth from the camp leading the three spotted cats that Maggot had seen the other night. This giant rubbed their haunches vigorously, each in turn, then shoved their hindquarters, shouting. The cats took off running, their rear legs overreaching their bent heads as they blurred across the floodplain.

Maggot had never witnessed an animal move so fast on the ground. Falcons attacking out of the sky, yes, but this took his breath away. When they looped out in a big circle toward Maggot's hiding place, he held that lost breath and pretended to be one of the stupid dead. Because if he did move or do anything else stupid, they were likely to see him and he could end up dead. He glanced back to the camp—

And saw the woman.

He craned his neck, straining to see her clearly above the lip of ground, through the web of branches. She came out and stood next to the giant. The other, birdlike woman accompanied her and a bearded man with a trollbelly, but Maggot scarcely noticed them. She wore tight-fitting pants and a loose, open breasted shirt like many of the men, but the curves of her body were distinctly feminine.

When she clapped her hands and shouted something to the cats, laughing, Maggot's heart pounded and a shiver coursed up his spine and down again just as it had the other night.

He followed the arc of her eyes and saw that the cats had turned in his direction. The one in front aimed its head at him like the point of an arrow, digging its legs into the turf.

Maggot squeezed his spear tightly, touched the knife at his throat, and did not move again, even to blink.

Then the second cat overtook the leader and swung out a paw to trip it. They balled up as they tumbled, rolling across the grass, snapping at each other. The third cat's legs slipped out from under it as it turned while passing them, and then it too pounced onto the pile. The big man clapped his hands and called to them, and one popped up and zipped off in his direction, followed by the other two.

Maggot exhaled and let his head sink to the ground. When he gazed up again, the woman and the others were returning to the camp. The log-and-mushroom men gathered outside the palisade, along with the spear carriers. Shortly afterward, the mammut came striding forth—so they'd recaptured it. Too bad. The little cave was perched upon its back with the man riding just behind its head again. The mammut rider shouted something, and the creature bent on its front legs!

This was certainly magic, the wrong-tasting nature that his mother—

The woman and her female companion climbed up on top and sat inside the little stick cave. Then, with much shouting and noise, the people set out all at once, like a great band of trolls going to feed at dusk. The mammut lumbered among them, carrying away the woman.

Maggot rose to his feet and followed them at a distance as they traced the river toward its source in the mountains. Pairs of spear carriers ranged outside the main group. With his newfound respect for the way they threw their weapons, Maggot could not come close enough to see the woman's features. But the blue-and-yellow tent atop the mammut bobbled along at the edge of his vision, always in view.

She was looking for something from her perch; all these people were looking for something. The deer perhaps, like the one they had killed yesterday. He'd have to get it first and bring it to her.

Miles upstream from the camp, the procession turned aside from the river plain and spread out along the edge of the forest. Maggot ran up to the first ridgeline to get above the people and observe them.

As he slipped between the trees in a hurry to find some position where he might see the woman again, he topped a steep rise and saw three men running from the opposite direction. Maggot dropped to his hands and knees, sidling into a hiding place behind a tree.

The three men were mountain people, with bright red skins covering their heads. Maggot realized that they, like him, were tracking the other group.

Maggot crabbed his way down the edge of the slope. The three men changed direction, fading back into the trees where Maggot couldn't see them. He hurried downhill instead until he found the group he sought—First and Foghair, with the Boy and several others, including the big man who'd had the cats. They knelt by something and grew excited, then hurried on. Maggot ran to the spot as they left it.

Scat. Bigtooth scat. He squatted on his haunches and poked his finger at the scat, breaking it into big chunks. He crumbled a piece between his fingers, sniffed it. Fresh, no more than a day old.

So they hunted the solitary bigtooth cat the way that packs of little bigtooths hunted deer or bison, with some lying in wait while others chased the prey into their clutches.

Maggot looked at the scars on his thigh and traced a finger over the hard ridge of the scar that crossed the back of his neck into his hair. He had surprised a bigtooth once before, in a cave in the lower mountains by the southern pass. Or rather the bigtooth had surprised him. He'd woken from his sleep one day with the cat's mouth closed around his head. He'd had his knife at hand and his mother nearby, or he wouldn't have escaped. It had taken a long time for his skin to knit together and heal, and he had been sick with a fever for many days. His nostrils flared at the memory. He had never killed a cat before.

Lifting his head, he looked downslope where the woman rode on the back of the mammut. And sighed. He hefted the spear in his hand and mimed throwing it. Maybe he wouldn't have to get too close to the bigtooth.

Or—maybe—he'd let the people kill the bigtooth. He could steal it from them and then give it to the woman.

With that thought, he retreated into the trees. But although the stupid people made their big noise all day, over a series of forested ridges and through several long ravines, they didn't flush the bigtooth once. By the end of the hunt, Maggot was checking to see if they had tails—they chattered as noisily as squirrels and seemed about as dangerous.

As the mob began its disordered ramble back toward their newly palisaded camp, he ventured close for one last glimpse of the woman. All he saw was the striped tent bobbing on the mammut's back, until that too finally dipped below the horizon. So it had been wishing for snow in summer's heat to think he could steal the bigtooth. He'd have to go find it.

A single bigtooth would range over land occupied by several troll bands, days and days of walking. But they tended to stay in one area as long as they found easy prey, and they always stayed near the watercourses. He stared out across the floodplain, watching the river come down from its source in the mountains. Deer moved up to the higher slopes in the spring. The bigtooth had to be following them.

Twilight cast its uncertain mist across the landscape. Maggot raised his head to the sky and saw the evening star—what the trolls called One-Eyed Mouth. It beckoned to them from their caves in the evening, calling them out to feed.

He lifted the spear another time as if to throw it.

Heading upriver in the fading light, he followed the trail from ravine to creek to ravine, until hungry and thirsty, he paused at the mouth of a larger tributary stream for a drink. The perch was too steep to sip from, so cupping his hand in the current, he splashed water into his mouth.

A few large shadows slipped silently into the woods on the other side of the water. Deer. Maggot snatched up his spear and followed their movement into the hills.

The stream babbled over a wide bed of rocks, making frequent and sudden falls. The mountain walls were steep on either side, thick with trees, and marked by sudden sprays of water that gushed out of narrow defiles. Maggot climbed upward over this rough terrain until the land opened out at last on marshy flats.

Vague shapes moved across a gray landscape of soft-edged growth and smooth, dark planes of water—a herd of several dozen grazing deer. Maggot skirted them slowly.

A bigtooth roared somewhere over the hills—the deer lifted their heads toward the sound and scattered.

Maggot ran, his feet splashing, toward the hilltop nearest the source of the roar. He practiced throwing motions with the spear as he went.

The moon was a little fuller tonight, and still in the sky, casting a pale light among the trees. When he reached the higher, drier land he circled through the woods, looking for any sign of movement, listening for any sound.

Off to his right, across flatter ground, he heard the snarling and snapping of wolves. He took a few hesitant steps that way.

The bigtooth growled from the same direction.

Maggot sniffed the air, looked at the clouds above the trees, and then angled through the forest to come at the noise from downwind. He saw the timber wolves first, counted five of them. They stalked the bigtooth, who sat in a little clearing in a puddle of moonlight, crouched over a large doe, with an arm cast across the body like a mother protecting its child. It had chewed off the doe's head.

The two dagger-shaped teeth jutting from the upper jaw were

longer and wider than Maggot's knife. The short bobbed tail twitched at the back of the cat's massive, stocky body.

One wolf lunged at the bigtooth's flank, and the cat surged up to bat it with its massive paw. But as soon as the bigtooth moved, two other wolves darted in and tore at the carrion. One grabbed hold of the front leg and dragged it several feet before the bigtooth turned, snarling, and drove them away.

The wolves could take the meat—Maggot wanted the bigtooth. He chose a tree he could climb easily, and then, visualizing the way the boy had killed the deer, he lifted the spear, aimed it at the bigtooth's heart, and threw it.

It sailed wide of his target, and over it, to crash sideways into some bushes.

He grabbed his head in dismay—stupid people! Why did they throw their spears like that?

As the cat whirled to meet the new threat intimated by the sound of the spear hitting the brush, the wolves seized the chance and the meat. Two snapped at the bigtooth to hold it at bay while two others lunged in and dragged off part of the doe. The wolves retreated a short ways with their trophy, and the bigtooth turned to eat the rest before it was all gone.

The fifth wolf trotted curiously in Maggot's direction, and he scrambled up the tree to escape it. Sitting fifteen feet up, Maggot hurled insults at it because he didn't have any rocks.

Maggot watched the wolf turn aside for its portion of the meat, and he spit after it. He'd been stupid with the spear for thinking that being people would be so easy. He would have to try to find it later, or steal a new one.

When the wolves began to harass the bigtooth again, the cat decided that it had eaten enough and abandoned the remainder to them. It set off with a slow, arrogant stride on a trail that led around the hill and down to the streamside.

The woman wanted the bigtooth. Was she worth the danger?

With the carrion distracting the wolves, Maggot decided to chance it. He dropped from his branch, sprinted over the hilltop, climbed another tree by the trail, and waited, hoping.

Trolls rarely attacked living creatures, but when they did, it was like this: they hung on the face of a steep rockwall, or cliff, and dropped on their prey as it passed below. They wrapped it up in their long arms and bit its neck, or clawed open the stomach with one of their hands. Maggot had perfected the technique when he was small by dropping from trees on Ragweed's neck. Ragweed never looked up at the trees. At least not at first.

Neither did the bigtooth cat—Maggot hoped it didn't get a second chance to learn from its mistake.

The big cat swaggered along the deer trail, shifting its head from side to side, its tongue lapping the long teeth. As it passed beneath the limb on which Maggot sat, he leapt onto its back. He snaked one arm around its throat and braced his legs to stop its first attempt to roll over on its side. It turned its head, slashing its jaws at Maggot as he plunged his knife between its ribs, deep. The cat roared, twisted, and Maggot kicked his feet, fending off its rear legs as the claws came up to gut him. He wrenched the knife free, stabbing the cat's breast again and again.

The bigtooth growled, ripped its head from Maggot's grasp, and rolled the other direction. Maggot dropped his knife and jumped for the tree. He pulled himself up onto a branch as the big cat slammed into the trunk. Maggot slipped, caught himself, looped a leg over the next branch, and heaved himself higher. The bigtooth paced at the base of the trunk, its side glistening slick with blood.

Maggot dripped sweat. He couldn't catch his breath. The bigtooth's blood mixed with his own—he'd been slashed on his side and the back of his calf, and he'd scraped his leg climbing the tree.

"If you aren't going to die"—he gasped—"then go away."

The bigtooth seemed to like this advice, because it suddenly started running down the trail. Before it passed out of sight, it staggered and collapsed face first.

Though it lay there motionless, Maggot hesitated to drop from the tree until he considered that the wolves might come investigate and then he'd have to fight them off. He didn't have the strength for that, so he climbed down, retrieved his knife, and picked up a long stick.

He poked the bigtooth with the stick. It didn't move. He cracked the stick over its side. It still didn't move. He inched closer and shoved it with his toe—it was like kicking a warm rock, but it didn't kick back.

Then, placing one foot on its side, Maggot pounded the danger-death warning on his chest, laughing.

"Too late," he told the bigtooth. "Sorry."

When he nudged it with a toe, his grin turned to a frown.

He couldn't carry the whole beast back down the valley to give to the woman. Maybe he could just show her part of it. The skin, since people seemed to use so many skins.

Looking at it again, he wanted the claws too so he could show how brave he was. And the teeth.

Maggot knelt and took the front paw in his hand—it still had a deadly weight to it. He sawed with his knife, breaking the joints at the ankle to remove the big clawed feet but leave them attached to the pelt. Then he sliced up the belly, and the legs, and hacking, pulling, finally removed the skin in one piece, leaving it connected to the head, which he also cut off. He ate the liver as he worked, and strips of the meat, which were strong-tasting and stringy, but satisfied his empty stomach.

When he finished and looked up, vultures circled in the dawn-pale sky. They could have the rest.

Rolling up his trophy, Maggot slung it over his shoulder and took the long way around the stream so he wouldn't wash off any of his by now impressive scent.

He grew tired like any troll in the morning. Before he returned to the woman's camp, he climbed into the crook of an elm tree and settled down to nap in the notch where its trunk divided into three.

Ants crawling across his skin to get at the bigtooth jerked him awake. He squinted at the sky, turning his head to find the sun. He'd slept straight through the warm part of the day.

He brushed the ants off the bigtooth's tongue and eyes, off the long yellow teeth, licking them off his fingers for a snack as he climbed down and resumed his journey. The cuts on his calf and side throbbed, and a bark scrape on his thigh hurt, but it was nothing bad. When he looked away from them, he forgot that his wounds were there.

The mammut, spear carriers, log-and-mushroom men, and others left trampled grasses, broken limbs, and other signs of their passing along the riverside, an easy trail for Maggot to follow. They had returned for a second day of beating brush in the hills, not knowing their quarry was already dead. Maggot smiled as he went, imagining the woman's surprise when he brought her his gift.

The sun was low behind the mountains, the sky as red as blueberry leaves in autumn, when their camp came into view. Fires burned inside the palisade. Maggot circled around to the hill beside the river, above the camp where he could see over the wall. He concealed himself in the remaining trees to look for the woman again.

He saw her for only a heartbeat, taking long strides through the firelight between tents. She entered one with blue-and-yellow stripes, like the covering on the mammut's back. He counted carefully—it stood in the second arc, third from the end.

When hardly anyone moved about the camp, Maggot took the bigtooth's skin and approached the palisade. Not seeing anyone or anything moving through the cracks, he slung the pelt over his shoulder and vaulted the wall.

He tried counting the tents, orienting himself, but the smoky, meaty stink of all these people made him jumpy. He started walking fast, then running, in what he thought was the right direction. He was rounding the second arc when he came face-to-face with one of the spearmen.

The man looked at Maggot, looked at the bigtooth's pelt, looked at Maggot, and opened his mouth to scream.

Maggot panicked. He grabbed the man by the throat, twisting his head hard as he dragged him to the ground the way he would wrestle a troll. The man went limp when Maggot landed on him. Maggot rolled away, hand still covering the mouth for silence, when he realized that he'd broken the man's neck.

His heart thumped in his chest—other voices sounded nearby, coming closer. He'd dropped the pelt when he lunged. He scooped it up and spotted the woman's striped tent, third from the end, just as he had counted. Dashing to it, he pulled aside the flap and plunged inside.

A fire burned in a polished dish, illuminating the interior to day-like brightness. Maggot blinked.

The woman sat on something beside the fire. She started to move, then stopped when Maggot stopped.

He gaped. Her hair had become suddenly long, longer than Maggot's. The other, older woman held it—pausing in midstroke as she ran something like a knife across it. Maybe she was cutting it—

"You st-stink," Maggot stuttered quickly, in proper troll fashion, before he lost his courage. "You stink a lot."

The older woman's mouth opened and closed like a fish surfacing to eat.

Afraid that she would scream, Maggot quickly made a vigorous "No" expression by thrusting his tongue and shaking his head from side to side.

The woman reached out a restraining hand to her companion. Never taking her eyes off the bigtooth's skin, she said something that Maggot couldn't understand.

But what was there to understand? She was even more beautiful than he'd imagined her, with sharp lines to her face and a broad, flat nose. She had blue eyes matched in color by a gem that dangled on a golden vine around her neck. Her yellow robe opened at her throat and was slit up the side so that her legs stretched free. She smelled like lavender and lilac.

He fumbled with the skin, holding it out for her.

She raised her eyebrows, said something again.

"It's for y-you," he said, thrusting it out again for her to take.

She glanced up at the older woman, shrugged, and gestured to a spot at her feet.

Yes! He dropped to his knees and spread the pelt out on the floor, tilting the head up to her, making sure she could see the claws. When he stood up, his heart was galloping.

She bent forward to look at it, said something again.

Maggot took this as a hopeful sign of her interest, and, just to make his intentions clear, stepped close to her, spread his legs apart, and waved his painfully swollen sex at her face.

She leaned back in her seat . . . then sprang forward and kicked him hard in the crotch.

He toppled like a tree in a storm, slamming into the dirt so hard that it knocked all the air out of him. He tried to inhale, but couldn't catch his breath at all. Probably because his sex was lodged in his throat.

She grabbed a long knife and held it toward him, prodding him with the toe of her foot much as he had done to the bigtooth. When he didn't move, she stepped away and examined the pelt, flipping over the paws, looking at the teeth. She spoke to him the whole time.

He didn't understand the words, but her tone was clearly admonishing. Somehow he propped himself upright on knees and elbows, gulping air, looking at her, trying to fathom what he'd done wrong.

There was a shout outside the tent, and the woman stood and turned sharply toward it. When she moved, Maggot could see her sex through the part in her robe. Though it was obscured by a patch of curly hair, it was clearly not swollen or red. She wasn't interested in him after all. Glancing down at him, she followed his eyes and pulled her robe closed and stepped away from him. A second shout came from outside, more frantic than the first. The older woman ran to the entrance of the tent and shouted out a reply.

Maggot realized that they'd discovered the body of the man he'd killed. And there was no reason for him to stay now. He stumbled to his feet and lurched past the older woman to leave the tent. He paused a second to orient himself.

The flap flew open behind him. The woman stood at the entrance, her hand reaching toward him as she said something else he couldn't understand. The long knife was lowered. Probably she was asking if he wanted the bigtooth's skin back.

Another tent flap snapped opened opposite her, revealing the outline of the boy who'd cast the spear. His eyes widened; then he shouted and began waving his arms.

Quickly, Maggot stared into her eyes, stuck out his tongue, and shook his head from side to side. She could keep the pelt. Then, cupping his crotch, he ran despite the pain, heading for the main gate because he knew he couldn't climb the palisade. Separated by the wall of tents, and the confusion of darkness, men sprinted past him in the other direction.

Only one guard watched the entrance. Grimacing in pain, Maggot lifted his fist to force his way past. The guard took one look at him, threw down his spear, and fled screaming into the night.

Maggot followed. When he overtook the guard, the man covered his face with his hands, shrieked, and fell down.

Enveloped in darkness, Maggot ran until the pain in his groin faded compared to the ache in his legs and in his chest. He kept on running into the hills, toward the tree-covered slopes of the mountains. Water streamed from his eyes.

The moon followed him as he ran, a sliver more than half full ensconced within a bright sphere of hazy light.

The rains were coming.

⊰ CHAPTER 13 ⊱

Maggot kept on running into the hills, toward the tree-
covered slopes of the mountains. Finally, exhausted, he reeled
from tree to tree, looking for someplace to hide from the rising sun.
The hillside was pierced by out-thrusts of massive lichened stones,
thick with nut trees and berry bushes. Smells of redolent spring earth
and verdant damp pervaded the air. It was a very trollish place. He'd
fled the life of a troll to become a man. Now he returned to trollish
habits, following the natural shelter of the hills in search of a safe location, hoping to find the hole where he'd hidden the hollow log.

He was scouring a hillside when he saw, in a dell below, a den-
shaped mound covered with thick vines and shrubs. Hickory trees
towered protectively around it. He went to explore.

Taking hold of the vines, Maggot pulled himself atop the mound.
It was constructed of logs, like the palisade but stacked atop one
another. A wall and part of the sheltering roof had collapsed at one
end, but a fallen tree canopied the hole—its dead branches sustained a

mass of fallen limbs and brown leaves. Some of the logs pulled away in Maggot's hands, revealing a spacious den. He crawled inside. The hollow extended nearly the full length of the mound. In parts of it he could stand straight up. It was a good place to hide for the day. To decide where he should go, what he should do next.

He sagged against the darkest corner and squeezed his eyes shut, trying to forget the woman. But an ache in his heart worse than the pain in his groin made him toss and stay awake.

Daylight cracked open the sky.

Maggot rolled over and stretched his tired limbs. Dusty sunlight penetrated the room, illuminating the scattered bones of maybe two people. And a tiny, cracked skull that clearly belonged to a troll. Maggot jerked upright.

The bones were partly hidden by a beam where the roof had fallen in. He braced his shoulder under the rotting wood and heaved it aside—leaves and dust showered over him. A little stripe-back ground squirrel scampered across Maggot's foot, then zagged back into the safe cover of the collapsed wall.

A baby troll's bones were nested against a human skeleton. A troll and a man, together.

It disturbed him that light should fall on this child's bones and prevent the soul that once wore them from finding its way back into the comforting darkness. He looked up—this was a poor imitation of a cave. Eventually it must collapse, and that might leave the bones completely exposed.

He probed the dirt with his fingers, loosening a thin layer of decaying leaves and dead vines. Beneath that he found it packed hard. He saw stones in one of the corners. He pried several up out of the ground until he found a large, flat one with a sharp edge. If he scraped a hole and buried the bones then they should stay in darkness long after the logs all fell and rotted.

Raising the stone high above his head, he plunged it into the dirt. The edge bit the soil. He worked mindlessly, forgetting himself in the good pain of muscle and bone bent to a purpose, until he'd finished a shallow pit.

He picked up the skull, his thumb fitting in the bony ridge of the brow. His other hand took the tiny lower jaw.

"Who are you?" he asked aloud. He was thinking how Windy had found him, adopted him—here a human mother must have found and adopted this baby troll. "How did you get here?"

He held the skull and jaw together, opening and closing the mouth. The teeth clicked against each other, but his little counterpart said nothing to him.

Gently placing the skull in the pit, Maggot turned to gather the long bones of the arms and legs, glad that no big scavengers had cracked them open for their marrow. The knobby backbones were easy to scoop up, but the ribs and the small bones of the hands and feet were scattered either by smaller vermin or the vagaries of time. Maggot dug through the humus and roots, determined to gather them all if he could. Strands of long red hair were tangled in some of the bones. No troll had hair that long or that color, so he plucked them free before placing the bones in the pit.

The longer he worked, the longer he avoided any thought of the woman. He didn't know what to do. He still desired her. But he didn't understand people, didn't know how to be one, didn't know why he'd expected it to be so easy to get her to show interest in him.

He kicked the dirt into the trench, nudged the flat stone over it with his toe to cover the bones, and sighed.

He let himself look at the other skeletons. Being creatures of the day, perhaps they wanted their souls to bask in sunlight. He didn't know. He decided to leave them as they were, not knowing the proper way to show respect.

Something glinted inside one rib cage. He bent to look. Two tiny gemlike shapes, as smooth as pebbles from a stream but shining with some inner light, were strung on tarnished strands of silver about the neck. Maggot thought at once of the woman and the blue gem that dangled from her throat. He palmed the skull, snapping it to one side so that he could lift the two strands out of the body. Untangling them from the ribs, he draped them around his own neck, slipping them under the sheath that held his knife. The chains felt cold around his skin, but the lucent stones pulsed with faint heat against his naked chest. Now he had something that made him more like the woman and connected him to her.

He squeezed the stones in his fist. He could never go back to being a troll or even to living among them. Just because he hadn't impressed the first woman he met didn't mean he would never find his mate. He would have to learn their ways.

Sunlight no longer drifted into the den, but it was too soon to be night again already. He crawled out through the hole, looking up and sniffing the air. Dark clouds scudded across the sky. Trees shook in a wind that smelled like thunderstorms.

Branches fell from the treetops. Maggot spied one lying on the ground that was mostly straight and about the length of a spear. He lifted it, aimed it at a distant trunk, and threw. It sailed wide in the wind.

As the first fat drops of water slapped his shoulders, Maggot ran to pick up the stick and try again.

The sky broke open, releasing a sudden downpour. Lightning veined the skies like pulses of pain, chased by stampedes of thunder that started far away, galloped overhead, and faded many heartbeats later in the distance. It grew darker than night, impossible to see, even the air squeezing him. He turned toward the den for shelter, thought of the little troll he'd just buried. He felt too sad to stay here tonight.

He climbed the hillside and gazed across the dim, gray shapes of the sodden landscape. He had been on the right track the night before. The cave where he had stashed the skin-covered log was nearby. The entrance, when he found it, had filled with water. He lay on his belly in the puddle and peered inside. Drops of water teared down the stone walls, but it was dry compared to the world outside, and it was his alone. He cast the log out into the rain to make more room for himself, crawled inside, and curled up to nap.

He awoke in total dark, dizzy and light-headed—the hole had collapsed, thick with mud. He dug in the mud with his fingers, scooping out handfuls and flinging them aside. One hand groped naked air, and he almost cried out, expecting his mother to grip it and pull him free the way she had whenever he had become trapped in some tight passage of a cave. But she wasn't there for him, nor was anyone else, so his hand flailed around until it gripped the rough stone, while he kicked his legs hard, shoving, swimming through the muck.

Curled on his side, slick with mud, Maggot lifted his head to the sky, swallowed a gulp of air, and stared into the glaucous eye of the clouded moon.

He staggered upright, wanting to pound out a "happy" tattoo on his chest. He grabbed the log, but soaked, cracked, and half-full of mud, it made a poor noise. No matter—he was people now, and people did not pound their chests like trolls.

As he started down the hill for the valley, a new rain began to pour like gravel coming down a steep slope. Maggot's skin felt bruised and sore from the constant pelting, but there was no place to hide. The wind whipped the rain around the backs of trees. By the time he reached the narrow river, the plain alongside it resembled a marsh. The water churned brown and muddy, thrashing at its banks like a bison wallowing in a mudhole. The palisade stood half-submerged beside the river's curve—

The tents had disappeared. The camp was gone.

His feet kicked up sprays of water as he ran across the rain-soaked meadow. Inside the log wall he found nothing—no sign of the people, no trail. The rain had washed away all marks of their passage. Emptiness shot through him—he had no idea which direction they'd gone or where the woman came from!

He walked toward the rise with the trees. Water swirled around their roots, ripping at the bank, but he could climb them for a quick view.

A sudden rich scent of wet soil filled his nose.

Behind him, a roar shook the air, above the din of the rain, as though a bigtooth as large as a mountain pounced upon the valley.

Looking over his shoulder, Maggot saw a cliff face of water, dark as scabbing blood, appear behind him, rushing down the river's course. He sprinted up the slope for the trees.

The wall of water hit the palisade and shattered it in a shower of splinters, slamming into him just before he reached the grove. The wave lifted him up and knocked him into one of the new-hewn stumps, then dragged him under the water before he could snatch a breath.

He banged into another trunk, swallowed a throatful of muddy water, and burst to the surface, gagging and spewing, gasping for air and grasping at branches. His hand closed on one, and it snapped as he swept past. Just before the water washed him away from the trees he flung an arm around a trunk.

Troll-sized boulders trundled through the flood. Maggot wrapped his arms around the trunk and held on tight as several slammed in quick succession into the roots of the tree, shaking it and Maggot to the tip of their limbs before rounding the bend and disappearing downstream.

Still choking out the water he'd swallowed, he pulled himself up onto a limb that sagged beneath his weight. He leaned there, panting, his face against the rough bark.

With the passing of the first wall of flood came a steady and bewildering array of debris. Every fallen branch and dead tree in the forest flowed past him. He saw the damp brown body of some animal gone too quickly to identify. It might have been him.

The tree listed slightly, like a tooth loose in a jaw after being punched, as the water gnawed away the bank that held its roots. Maggot shifted position, preparing to leap to another refuge. He scarcely noticed the uprooted tree flowing swiftly toward him until he heard the voice.

An arm crooked over the trunk, and a head tilted back just barely above the surface of the water.

Maggot forgot escape. He clambered quickly out on the branch until it dipped toward the water. It swayed under the burden of his weight, creaking. He'd have maybe one chance to grab the man. He edged out farther, wrapping his legs tightly around the limb and holding on with one arm to hang as low as he possibly could.

The drifting tree must have been nearly sixty feet long, wider than the river had been before it flooded. It appeared to speed up as it came close, and the nearly submerged ball of roots smashed into the base of Maggot's sanctuary, throwing loose a hail of dirt and stones that splattered in the water. With a loud pop, the branch cracked under his weight, plunging him headfirst into the river.

He held on tight with his left hand as he fell, hoping for something to keep him afloat, but he bobbed to the surface in the same spot. The branch remained half-attached to the tree.

The other man's fingertips fell short of Maggot's grasp. Cold water sluiced around him. The current shoved and thrust, pivoting the top of the tree downstream and dragging the root-ball free. Maggot kicked his legs, lunged out a second time, and caught the other man's outstretched hand.

The tree drifted into the current, pulling the man away. Maggot held on, but his other hand slid down the rain-slicked branch, tearing him from safety.

The other man struggled to disentangle himself. The tree bucked in the water as it rolled over other debris and shoved both men under. Bark scraped Maggot's side and then the protruding roots buffeted his face, but he held on. The great battering ram finally drifted past, and both men splashed to the surface, their mouths gaping. Maggot still gripped both the branch and the other man.

A sharp crack shot through the air—the trunk split and the branch jumped out farther into the stream. The force of the water threatened to rip them loose, but the current pushed the branch around, swinging them behind the tree, where they were sheltered from the fury of the flood.

Maggot shifted his grip to the man's wrist and dragged him forward until he also clutched the branch.

With his arm around the other man's waist, Maggot pulled them both up the branch with one hand. He could not reach his original perch, but they oscillated near another, and when the current brought them close enough, Maggot reached out and grabbed the new branch and lifted them onto it.

They hung there, arms over the limb, legs trailing behind them in the water. If the flood uprooted this tree, they'd simply have to float with it or drown. Maggot couldn't get the man—or himself—into another tree.

"Are you hungry?" he asked, in the manner one troll greeted another.

The man responded with words that Maggot didn't understand, but Maggot gathered that he was fine. The man looked much like he did—raw red scratches and scrapes covered half his body, mud the rest. His black hair was slick against his head like Maggot's, only much shorter.

Having rested a few moments, Maggot helped the other man climb out of the water into the vee of the tree. Then he pulled himself up, and they scrunched together back to back, each hugging the branch in front of them. Their small cluster of trees was an island—a submerged island, but still a recognizable landmark—in a broad lake of brown water that appeared to fill the valley from one set of hills to the other. It was hard to tell in the darkness.

The man spoke again.

"We'll see our way clear in the morning," Maggot said, thinking morning might comfort a man the way night comforted trolls. The man grunted something that didn't sound comforted.

The sky drizzled.

Vague, shadowy shapes slid by, carried by the river out of darkness, briefly to be glimpsed, and then into darkness once again. One of them bleated mournfully and was gone. Maggot watched for other men to rescue, but as it grew darker he couldn't see much farther than the broken branch. It lashed in the vortex of the current like the tail of some agitated creature.

Sore and drained, Maggot finally locked his hands around the trunk like a child around a mother's neck, and leaned against the rough skin of the tree, closing his eyes.

A hand tapped his shoulder hard.

He looked back. The other man mimed falling asleep, leaning his head sideways, eyes closed.

"I know," Maggot said. "Good idea. We can't do anything else, huh." He leaned against the trunk again.

The man hit him harder this time, the knuckle hitting a nerve that jerked Maggot awake.

"Hey!"

The man mimed sleep again, and then falling off the tree into the water. Maggot thought about explaining that this wouldn't happen, but changed his mind.

They shared a strange intimacy, crushed together, their backs resting against each other, skin wet and cold. Yet they were able to see each other only by the most difficult contortions. Maggot had never been so long in the presence of another person before.

He pushed himself up and adjusted his position to face the man as well as he could. "Not much of a cave, is it?"

196 ~ THE PRODIGAL TROLL

Gesturing with one hand, the stranger repeated a phrase several times. Maggot didn't understand, so he stuck out his tongue. The other man laughed, shaking his head from side to side, then spoke the phrase again.

"No," Maggot murmured, sticking out his tongue.

The stranger, clearly frustrated, shook his head and enunciated the phrase carefully.

Maggot shook his head from side to side.

The man raised his eyebrows. So Maggot raised his. The man shook his head. *No.* Shaking the head meant *no.* Maggot didn't know why *no.* But now he knew *no.*

He touched his knuckles right below his mouth, to say, *This is what sustains me,* and spoke his name. "Maggot," he said.

"Maw-kit," the stranger answered hesitantly.

Maggot repeated the gesture. "Maggot, Maggot."

"Maqwet," the stranger said more carefully.

"Maggot!" He repeated the gesture emphatically.

"Maqwet." The stranger put his knuckles in the same place. "*Chin,*" he said.

"*Chin,*" Maggot repeated.

"*Chin!*" The other man smiled broadly.

"You have a good stink, *Chin,*" Maggot said.

Now that they knew each other's names, the learning went more quickly. Maggot could make a better variety of sounds, and soon they quit practicing the troll words and spoke only the language of people. He savored each sweet syllable as if it were a berry in his mouth. *Hand. Eyes. Water. Tree.*

Those were the words he would use to talk to the woman.

The broken branch quit lashing in the water. The other man pointed up at the sky. Three, four, many handfuls of stars twinkled through breaks in the clouds.

Maggot smiled, looked up again, and saw one less star. Dawn already ate them out of the sky. It was a silent morning.

The waters swirled away like an exhausted fit of temper, transforming the green meadows Maggot recalled into a flat of mud and devastation broken by innumerable pools and unrecognizable debris. High clouds browed the sky, and carrion birds dropped like dark hailstones to feast among the refuse.

"We walk," the man Maggot called Chin suggested, and Maggot understood him. It felt like such a triumph.

"We walk," he agreed.

Maggot wrapped his arms around the trunk, swung under the branch, dug his toes into the bark, and climbed to the ground. Chin fell. They stood and stretched their stiff limbs.

The mud sucked at their feet as they waded across the swampy bottoms to the higher, drier hills. Chin lifted his head and thrust out his lips. "Brothers."

Maggot followed Chin's eyes. Coming toward them, between the trees beside the riverbank, he saw two men with bright red cloth wrapped around their heads.

"Brothers," he said, relishing the word. He gestured to himself and Chin. "Brothers?"

Chin looked at him and nodded. "Brothers."

"We brothers." Maggot quickened his stride to meet the others.

⇥ CHAPTER 14 ⇤

"**H**e is saying what?" *Maggot asked.*

In the moons since he had rescued Sinnglas—that was his friend's name, he knew now, not *Chin*; *chin* was their word for the food-slipping-in-place—Maggot had made great strides in learning people talk. But the newcomer's accent was just different enough that Maggot could not understand him. Nor did it help that he and Sinnglas sat on the far side of the council, in the place of least favor.

"Wait." Sinnglas leaned forward. "I'm listening."

Maggot waited. And listened. Mostly he watched.

The newcomer was only the latest visitor to come to the council cave of Sinnglas's people. Council *lodge*, he tried to think the word, though the space, shaped of cut and bent branches, and dark inside, resembled a stuffy cave, especially when crowded by several dozen men and the pungent aroma of their medicine weed.

Strangers had been coming for weeks to the council lodge, but this newcomer impressed Maggot more than the others. He was older, with shoulders as broad as a troll's and arms as long. His nose bent like a hawk's beak, and he talked through it more than through his mouth, making raspy, indistinct words Maggot could not follow. The newcomer's clothes were less like those of the men around him, and more like those Maggot had seen among the lion-hunting men. He carried many weapons, and two men followed him wherever he went, like a pair of trollbirds.

Everyone in the council lodge listened to the newcomer with great seriousness, as if he were the sound of dawn.

They sat cross-legged on the ground, frowning and sighing somberly, while the newcomer droned. Maggot had tried sitting the same way and didn't like it, so he continued to squat troll-fashion on his haunches. It also raised him slightly above the others and made it easier for him to watch their reactions. The newcomer sat in the center at the council's place of honor, beside Damaqua. Damaqua was the First of this band. He was also Sinnglas's brother.

One of Sinnglas's brothers. The other two sat behind Maggot, at the farthest end of the hall, squeezed back against the wall. Their names were Keekyu and Pisqueto. Their eyes gleamed as happily as the morning they had found their brother Sinnglas safe from the flood.

The newcomer finished speaking. He unfolded a cloth lying across his lap and raised a broad belt of beads, mostly black and white. Maggot couldn't quite read the picture—it looked like several men hunting an animal.

Several of the older men shouted, then fell quiet. The newcomer handed the belt to Damaqua. Keekyu and Pisqueto traded half-smiles and nods.

Sinnglas pretended to relax, but his eyes stayed focused on his older brother. Maggot felt like he had the first time he could remember watching trolls vote on something.

Damaqua held the belt up, inspected it, then turned it around, lifted it high, and presented it again to all the men gathered in the lodge. Now Maggot saw the picture clearly. Four men hunted a bigtooth lion. One of the men had bright red beads atop his head, the color of Damaqua's turban. Damaqua spread the belt on his lap, folded it, and handed it to the silent man who sat on the other side of him. Tanaghri, his advisor.

Sinnglas didn't like Tanaghri; therefore Maggot hated him.

Tanaghri held the belt with open distaste. Damaqua stretched out his hands for the pipe, placed the long thin stem to his lips, and puffed meditatively, sending little blue clouds of smoke into the air. The longer he waited before speaking, the more important his words would be. Finally, he laid the pipe upon his lap, leaving his hands upon it, and spoke in his strong clear voice.

"We are honored," Damaqua said, "to have so famous a First Man as Squandral come among us."

Maggot didn't understand the mountain range of differences that divided Sinnglas from his brother, but he liked the slow, rolling rhythms of Damaqua's voice. Squandral was the newcomer's name; Maggot taloned on to that.

"His exploits," Damaqua continued, "are known from the mother-water, River Wyndas, to the northern seas and over the mountains to the ocean. Who else among us besides Squandral has killed giants, has wrestled with the Old Ones, or defeated the invaders in so many battles? He was a friend of my father, when my father was First, and together the two of them turned their paths to peace, forging alliances with the invaders. For many years now we have traded with the invaders and lived peacefully beside them. When a man so renowned in war leads his people away from war, men follow."

Damaqua puffed on the pipe again. Maggot had understood the words, but only half the meaning. Later he would have to ask Sinnglas the meaning of *giants, Old Ones, invaders, war.*

No one else spoke or showed any expression. Damaqua placed the pipe to his lap, and gestured for Tanaghri to leave. The older man placed the belt down. Sunlight and the buzz of insects slipped in when he moved the skin at the door aside. Keekyu and Pisqueto shifted uncomfortably, scowling. But Sinnglas stayed fixed in his position, so Maggot did not move.

"Now Squandral has come down all the way from the place where three rivers meet to share his counsel with us," Damaqua said. "His words have led not only his own people, but all of our bands since the time of our fathers, and our fathers' fathers. If we are wise, we will listen to his words as young bucks look to the stag to see which way to run."

The door-flap opened again, and Tanaghri returned with a long bundle wrapped in cloth, which he handed to Damaqua, who said, "These are a sign of our respect for the gift of Squandral's wisdom."

A murmur of approval here. Damaqua unfolded the bundle and presented the gifts—a blanket of some fabric divided in squares such as Maggot had seen among the hunters; strings of glass beads, glittering like gems; an elegant dagger wrapped in snakeskin.

Maggot mulled this over. The newcomer, Squandral, gave them a belt; they gave him other items. Not that different from the trolls, he supposed, who shared whatever they had. If you found two bats on the floor of a cave, you gave one to a friend, and she did the same for you. That way everyone always had a bat to eat.

Sharing was a simple rule among trolls, but with people it was much more complicated. When Maggot had first arrived with Sinnglas, he'd had nothing but the things he carried—his knife, the two lucent stones strung around his neck—and he'd received gifts from many people. Damaqua had presented him with a blanket like the one given to Squandral. One evening Maggot went with Sinnglas and his two brothers into a house to talk to a man—Sinnglas had many people to talk to, all the time—and the old woman there gave Maggot a bowl of hominy. He was tired of carrying the blanket and gave it to her in exchange. Damaqua heard about it and was furious. He ceased speaking to Maggot afterward and no longer invited him to meals.

Sinnglas, strangely, was not displeased. So Maggot thought that he had done something right, but he still had no idea what it was.

Squandral said things through his nose about each gift, but Maggot couldn't understand him or read his expression. He wondered if Squandral would keep his blanket or give it away for something to eat.

Damaqua puffed on the pipe before he spoke again. "Now the honorable Squandral asks us to put aside all our years of peace like a bad harvest, to set aside our relationships with the invaders like crops ruined by insects. This is a hard thing for us to do. If we thrust aside all our crops, what will we eat and where will we get the seedcorn to plant when next year comes? Look around us here. What man among us does not carry something taken in trade from the invaders?"

Maggot had a belt now, a breechcloth that he liked, and a fine hatchet that he kept waiting to find a use for—most of the other men also carried them. He wore no shoes upon his feet nor any of the other adornments preferred by Sinnglas's people, having too many things to carry about already. When he leaned over the shoulders of the other men for a closer look at the gifts, Squandral stared at him. He was a hard man, made of granite. Maggot met his scrutiny without flinching.

Damaqua continued speaking, emphasizing his words with his hands. "The honorable Squandral says that a time has come for war, that the invaders push into the higher valleys, killing our game and squeezing us against the wall of the mountains. This is true. He says that they move onto our land with no respect for our use of it and build their farms and houses. This is also true. He says that we must rebel against them, as we did thirty years ago when he and my father were young men." He slapped the back of one hand against the other palm. "That if we strike the hand that steals from our plate, it will be less likely to steal from us again."

His gaze rested on Sinnglas, challenging him.

"I do not say yes or no to Squandral's proposal," Damaqua said.

"Let us have our feast and consult with one another, and then reach our consensus."

He handed the pipe over to Squandral, who sucked at it like a baby at its mother's breast. Throughout the room, men bent to trade counsel with one another.

"How will they vote?" Maggot whispered in Sinnglas's ear.

"We will not be unified in this. Damaqua cannot win a vote for peace, but my followers cannot win the vote for war."

War. That word he did not yet understand. Sinnglas's language baffled him. It had one word that meant *to dig*. There was no way to say, as a troll could, to-dig-with-the-fingertips-in-soft-soil, to-probe-with-toes-in-dirt, to-scoop-handfuls, to-overturn-with-the-feet, to-open-new-passageways-underground. The words for food and for the finding of it also seemed greatly impoverished to Maggot. And it had words like *war* that described nothing tangible, nothing he could imagine. Whenever he asked Sinnglas to describe the meaning of war, his friend embarked on a long series of stories about the invaders, their abuses and injustices.

But these abuses drove Sinnglas; Maggot understood that much. Sinnglas had been following the men in the camp of tents to watch against them when the flood struck, separating him from his brothers. He had been preparing for this war then. So if Maggot had not saved him, there might not be a war at all. The war was very important to Sinnglas. Maggot was glad that he had saved Sinnglas.

Squandral, the newcomer, spoke again, and Damaqua repeated his words about feasting and careful thought and agreement, and then the men rose to leave.

Maggot followed Sinnglas outside. The weight of all his tools and weapons still felt odd to him, bouncing against him as he walked. As did his clean skin and hair. He had scrubbed himself raw in imitation of the other men.

Sinnglas and his two brothers carried their bows and quivers.

Maggot followed them outside the village palisade, larger and sturdier than the one by the river, as they crossed the fields and meadows toward the forest. No one spoke for a long time, until they were far away from anyone else.

Maggot lost hold of his tongue first. "The man, he nose, like a hawk—"

"Squandral," Sinnglas said. "A great man. First among his people, a friend of my father's when he was First among ours."

"Squandral," Maggot repeated. "He wants we do what?"

Sinnglas meditated on this, wearing the same expression on his face that Damaqua had when smoking the pipe. The two brothers looked very much like one another.

The four men followed a path through the woods and over a ridge. Another person waited for them down in the glade—one of the two trollbirds so recently perched upon Squandral's shoulders.

"That," Sinnglas said, "is what we have come to find out."

Away from craggy-faced Squandral, this man made a stronger impression. He was lean, with a long axe-shaped head. He and Sinnglas exchanged nods, and then they both squatted down, troll-style, resting arms on their knees. Maggot hunkered down beside them, but Keekyu and Pisqueto waited at a short distance.

"Greetings, Menato," Sinnglas said.

"And greetings to you." He lifted his chin in Maggot's direction. "So this is your foreign wizard. Is it true that Gelapa has put a curse on him?"

Because of the charms about his neck, and because of things that Sinnglas had said about him, these people believed that Maggot was a wizard. This made men hesitant around him and the women afraid. The women avoided Maggot, even though he told them he was no wizard. The only other wizard in the village was Gelapa, an old man who rattled turtle shells at Maggot whenever he came close. People feared him too. Another thing Maggot didn't understand.

Sinnglas merely shrugged. "Gelapa is weak. He drinks too much of the medicine water. He could not heal a bullfrog its croak, and his curses couldn't make a rabbit jump."

"Heh." Menato lifted his chin again at Maggot.

"His name is Maqwet." Sinnglas was unable to give Maggot's name the deep throaty inflection of a troll. "He comes from over the mountains."

Menato smiled. "Squandral calls him the Vulture, because of the way he hovered over the council meeting. There is a hungry look in his eyes."

"Heh," Sinnglas said. "Vulture. That's good."

Off to the side, Pisqueto chuckled. He was very young, with no hair on his chin and hardly any flesh on his bones. Keekyu, who was older than Damaqua, smiled, rubbed his nose, and stared at the ground. He had an unfamiliar sick smell about him sometimes.

"We have heard rumors of him," Menato said. "We have heard that he is one of the southerners, come from over the mountain to pledge their men in joining our war. Now that we have seen him with our own eyes, Squandral doesn't know what to believe."

Sinnglas answered with a small, tight shake of his head. "He is not one of the southerners. We have seen them, you and I, when we went raiding among them. Maqwet does not look like them, does he?"

"No."

"Also, he knew no more of their language than he did of ours. And yet he can describe all the passes through the mountains, and the paths of the rivers and the ways they flow."

Maggot had tried hard to explain himself to Sinnglas, and he had wearied of it. All he wanted to do was learn enough to follow the woman where she went. He would help Sinnglas as a favor for that knowledge, and then he would go find her.

"So where is he from then?" Menato asked.

"Maybe he is like First Man," Sinnglas answered. He glanced sideways at Maggot and explained. "When the animals stole the secret of speech from Earth Spirit, they began to mock Earth. Mammut said, 'Look how weak Earth is: I can tear it up.' Flathorn Stag said, 'Look how ugly Earth's plants are, I will mark them with my antlers.' Crow tried to warn them that Earth was angry, but they wouldn't listen. So Earth Spirit let loose a great flood that drowned all the animals. Those that survived crowded together on the high mountaintop, and Earth Spirit opened a crack in the ground and out came First Man."

Maggot craned his neck and concentrated. He knew almost all these words, but had never heard this history before.

"So," said Sinnglas, "Earth Spirit took the power of speech away from the animals, all except for Crow, and gave it to First Man. Then Earth said to him, 'You may take one thing from each of the beasts and keep it for yourself.' From the lion, First Man took a tooth and fashioned it into his knife. From the mammut, he took the long tusk and made a spear. From the stag, he took the flathorn and made it into a shovel, and so on. The animals remember their loss, and so continue to tear up the earth, but Earth Spirit pays them no heed. From Crow, First Man took nothing, and Crow, in gratitude used his speech to teach him wizardry."

"Heh," Menato said thoughtfully.

Sinnglas stared at Maggot, seeming to measure his response. "So I say you are like First Man. You appear after a flood, coming out of the mountains, born, as you tell us, of no woman. You came unadorned, naked as a newborn, but with tools, as First Man did; and like First Man, you are also a wizard."

Maggot sank back on his haunches. "No. When they raised hands for First, I lost the hands to my father," he said, the words he had repeated many times now coming to him more easily. He looked at Menato. "I have never speaked to a crow, but now I speak with happy-bird-that-visits-in-the-night." There was no word for trollbird: that was the best translation Maggot could manage.

"Heh," the lean-faced man repeated. He didn't move for several long seconds. "He talks like a wizard."

Sinnglas laughed. "Yes. And he saved my life, when I was swept away in the floods. You may believe that also."

"Ah, the floods."

"My life was saved, but others died, and we did not find their bodies. Now their spirits haunt us. We lost all our spring planting and much of our remaining seed, and many animals were destroyed. Plants we collected from the forest have been swept away. This will be a hard year for us."

Menato shifted his legs, placed his fingertips on the ground. "It is the invaders who do the damage to us. Our village was spared the worst, but the floods swept away the tame cattle of the invaders, whole herds of them. Now the invaders come and trample our fields, hunting the deer and bison we would eat. They tell us that we will have to pay a heavy tax in crops this year. The Lion will devour us all."

Maggot frowned. He supposed that a lion could eat several handfuls of people, but no lion he had ever seen could eat all the people in this village.

Sinnglas nodded. "Their emissaries have said the same to us, though our second crop is late planted and less than it should be. They already planned to bring their herds up here to pasture, and so they came to kill the lion and the wolves that live up here. But the floods drowned their herds and so they do not come. Damaqua says it is a sign that we should continue to accommodate them. But I say they will come next year, when they are stronger and we are weaker. It is better if we strike now, while there is still strength behind our fist."

Menato pursed his lips. "This is what Squandral thinks also. He respects and fears the Lion. But we are too weak to act alone, so Squandral will not go to war without Damaqua."

"Without Damaqua or without our village? Damaqua will be for peace, but we are divided. He cannot get consensus."

"But neither can you."

Sinnglas shook his head. "No, I cannot."

Maggot shook his too, practicing the gesture so that he would not stick his tongue out when he meant *no*. Pisqueto looked at Maggot, stuck out his tongue, and bugged his eyes. Keekyu smiled, briefly, and Maggot laughed aloud.

They all sat silently for a time. The warm sun on Maggot's back made his skin itch for shade.

"We must do something," Menato said finally. "If we do not stop the invaders here, we will have to flee south across the mountains and fight for land within the country of our enemy."

"Some already flee," Sinnglas said. "They went that way last winter but never arrived."

"We must do *something*. This is what Squandral says."

Sinnglas's mouth tightened. "I will raise a raiding party, such as one that we would take across the mountains into the land of our enemy. But I will lead it down into the valleys stolen by the invaders. Damaqua cannot stop that."

"That is good."

"I will call for the dance tonight, as the old men gather in the council lodge. But it will only be my venture, not the will of our village."

"It will be a start," Menato said. "I will tell this to Squandral." He rose to leave.

As he slipped off into the woods, Maggot and the other brothers stood around Sinnglas.

"That went well," Pisqueto said, his grin as bright as a half-moon. "The famous Squandral will be with us when we fight! How can we lose?"

"I did not hear Menato promise that," Keekyu said.

"Nor did I," Sinnglas admitted. "Likely we will make this raid alone." Then he smiled too, an expression somewhere between the grim face of Keekyu and the boyish joy of Pisqueto. "Perhaps it will just be the three of us then." He glanced at Maggot. "Perhaps even four."

"Four," Maggot said firmly. "What is, we go do?"

"To hunt and kill the Lion of the valley," said Keekyu. "If we can, and if the Lion does not kill us first."

Pisqueto stopped smiling and bounced less.

"He speaks truly," Sinnglas said. "But without the Lion to protect them, the invaders will be afraid."

"Four of us not are needed to kill lion," said Maggot, swinging his arm to show how he had choked and stabbed one. "I kill lion, one time, all me. From out of tree, I felled, I stabbed lion in heart. Take me to valley where this lion is, and I will kill him."

The three men waited quietly for a moment. "You will come with us and have your chance," Sinnglas said.

Keekyu took steps along the trail. "We must go with the news, and prepare the men of the village for the dance, and for the expedition that is coming."

"It's war!" Pisqueto said. Sinnglas nodded.

Maggot shared their happiness. "It's war!" he said cheerfully.

✂ CHAPTER 15 ✂

group of women, ranging from old and stoop-shouldered to young and grinning, was gathered just outside the palisade gate. They shied away from Maggot as he passed by, but he was too busy thinking about the other woman to care. He was going to war with Sinnglas, and while he didn't know what *war* meant, he knew there was a lion to kill. The woman had looked at the lion's skin. He could kill Sinnglas's lion too, if it was bigger, and present her with that skin to show her his intentions.

Sinnglas led the other three through the village. It contained thirty-nine lodges—Maggot had counted them twice—although some contained only a few fire pits and some contained many. They came to Sinnglas's wife's lodge and entered. People looked up as the four men walked past the other fires to the room where Sinnglas lived.

His wife turned her round face questioningly toward them, but Sinnglas said nothing to her. When Maggot, Keekyu, and Pisqueto sat beside the fire pit, she placed bowls of ground corn before them.

212 ← THE PRODIGAL TROLL

Keekyu picked up his bowl, took one bite, and grunted. "I don't dare eat this."

Sinnglas's wife stopped what she was doing, but didn't look over at him. Pisqueto, bent over his bowl, said around a mouth of food, "Why not?"

Keekyu sighed, his older face sagging sadly. "When we have no corn to eat next winter, I'll remember this bowl and die of heartbreak."

Pisqueto grinned. Sinnglas's wife smiled very slightly and went back to work. Maggot scooped his food into his mouth, but everything tasted like smoke to him, stifling his appetite.

Sinnglas didn't eat. Instead, he retrieved his hatchet and sat apart to mark it with red paint, tie red feathers to it, and bind it with strings of black beads. His wife walked toward him, then away. She pulled first at one braid, then the other, plucking at the quill-work flowers that outlined her dress.

"Will it be tonight then?" she asked finally.

"Yes," Sinnglas said, without looking up.

Her shoulders slumped as she turned away.

Maggot was not sure what had just happened between them. People were not demonstrative in the same way that trolls were. While living in their lodge, he had seen Sinnglas and his wife couple several times, but he had never seen them groom one another—women did that only with other women, men with men. He had not been introduced to Sinnglas's wife, or told her name; and when he had tried to speak to her, she always turned away from him. Perhaps that was what he had done wrong with the woman in her tent. He should have just given her the lion's skin and not mentioned the good way she stank.

Sinnglas's wife placed a second serving in front of Keekyu. Pisqueto made a pleading gesture, but she took away his and Maggot's empty bowls to clean them. Keekyu smacked his lips noisily, taunting them both as he ate.

When Sinnglas completed his preparations, he rose to leave.

Maggot and the two brothers followed him to the clearing outside the council lodge.

A tree trunk, stripped of bark and branches, rose out of the ground. It stood half again taller than a man, as straight as a ray of light. Skins of snakes, some of them longer than Maggot had ever seen, looped around and around the post in great flimsy coils, slowly shredded by time and weather. The wizard Gelapa tended the snake-skins, collecting them from the lower valleys. When the wind blew, he crouched by the post, listening to the skins as they scuffed and whis-pered. Later, he made announcements according to what the skins had told him. Although Maggot had tried listening to the skins, they said no more to him than grasses rustled by the breeze.

Gelapa sat beside the pole now, with his head canted to one side, listening though no wind stirred the skins. He wore his hair in two short braids, like the women. His eyes were deep-set, wrinkled at the corners and resting on thick folds of skin. He squinted at the four men, scowled at Sinnglas and Maggot. Then he shook his head, saying, "Young men will always be young men."

"If only leaders would always lead us," Sinnglas replied.

He raised his hatchet and made to strike it against the post, but the wizard coughed. "Does the wind carry the future to you"—he turned his head to Maggot—"or to your friend, that you know the future and the vote of the council before the council votes?"

"I raise a raiding party, Grandfather," Sinnglas answered. All the men called Gelapa Grandfather. "Those who wish to follow me may do so."

"Who do you make your raid against?" Gelapa asked.

People gathered to watch, including many of the women from the gate, alerted perhaps by Sinnglas's wife, who hovered nearby. Sinnglas held his blow and spoke loudly, so that they might hear him. "Against those who take the meat from our mouths. Against those who steal the harvest from our fields."

The wizard rose slowly. He stood stiffly, with his back bent, glaring at Sinnglas. "So you say, Grandson. But will you return from your raid with meat and corn and gourds, or only with news to make the mothers mourn?"

"I will come like the sun, rising high above the mountains, bringing another season in which our people may grow—"

"No," Maggot blurted. "Like the sun, not."

Sinnglas stared at the ground, caressing his hatchet. "And what should I say instead, Maqwet, my friend?"

Maggot inhaled, thinking of the things he wished he might have said when he'd campaigned against Ragweed to be First. "You say instead: the sun, when you return, will fear your coming. It will not to rise unless first you give it your speak. The sun, when you speak, will hunt down the lion. Like a pack of dyrewolves, it will tear the lion to pieces."

Sinnglas's hand paused in its stroke. A smile twitched at the corner of his mouth. "You will have to say it for me; otherwise I would be bragging."

"I will say it for you."

Gelapa teetered unsteadily away from Maggot. His face was marked by loathing. "So that's how it is?"

Sinnglas nodded. "Yes, Grandfather."

Gelapa looked to the crowd, encompassed them with a sweep of his arm. "Do well, then. We have a distinguished guest among us. It will be good to show Squandral the spirit of our young men, and also the wisdom of our elders."

Sinnglas raised the hatchet and thunked it into the post. A strip of snakeskin broke loose and fluttered to the ground.

Keekyu shook his fist at the crowd. Some cheered and shouted Sinnglas's name, while others rushed off among the narrow paths between the houses to tell the rest of the village.

Gelapa bent to the ground and gathered up the snakeskin, saying, "Ah ah ah, *that's* how it will be. Very well, let some mother prepare to weep." Before he shuffled away, his sunken eyes glanced off Maggot once last time.

Sinnglas had many friends—the men he visited frequently. One showed up at the post, then another, their arms full of items Maggot had never seen them wear before. Pisqueto and Keekyu went and collected similar things. In a short time nine men had joined Sinnglas and his brothers. The youngest was a slight lad who barely had hair about his groin; Sinnglas was the oldest but for Keekyu, and the only man among them who was married. Keekyu had no mate. Most were around the ages of Pisqueto and Maggot, between fifteen and twenty winters. They entered the building beside the council lodge.

A few men stopped, pointing with their chins at Maggot's long hair and smiling. Mostly they ignored him. They put on skirts that hung to their knees, beautiful things with fringes like hair and covered with tiny beaded patterns. Some were made of deerskin, and some of a soft, plush fabric marked with colors like Maggot had seen among the lion hunters. They fastened elaborate belts about their waists and slipped soft boots upon their feet, some tying bright red leggings about their knees, pausing often to praise one another.

Maggot wandered around the lodge watching them dress. When he heard voices outside, he went to the entrance and pushed aside the skin.

The villagers had gathered in a big circle centered on the council lodge next door. Mostly women and children—he saw none of the older men who formed the council. The wizard paraded around in front of them, speaking on the sacredness of the ancient ways of their people.

The crowd murmured and parted from behind. Damaqua strode through them, ducking his head as he entered the council hall.

Behind Maggot, a young man shouted, "*Ai-yi-yi-yi-yi-yi-Yi!*"

Some of the small children ran over to the lodge to peek into the door. When they saw Maggot they stopped short, eyes wide. He dropped the skin and chose a place against the wall where he could crouch.

All of the men wore their black hair cropped short, although Sinn-glas and his brothers had been letting theirs go uncut since the spring. Sinnglas had told him that the invaders prohibited men from wearing warrior's braids: when they came to trade or collect their taxes, they cut off the hair of men who wore it too long or killed the men instead. Inside the lodge, men covered their hair with caps, some red and some white, one man's a yellow like buttercup flowers. Sinnglas's cap had a silver band around the base, as did several others. All were adorned with clusters of white feathers and a single eagle's plume projecting upward from the top. Many had a short braid of black hair affixed in the back. More and more of the men broke out in trilling screams as they painted each other's faces with stripes and dots.

Caught up in the spirit at the preparations, Maggot imitated their shout. *"Ai-yi-yi-yi-yi-yi-Yi!"*

The men fell silent, glancing at Maggot and then to Sinnglas. Perhaps he had not done it right. His voice, schooled to deepness by life among the trolls, did not always hit the highest notes.

Then Pisqueto laughed and answered with a call of his own. Several men echoed it, and they all returned their attention to grooming one another. When Sinnglas finished painting Keekyu's face, he came over to Maggot.

"Stand," he said, and Maggot did. "Turn around."

Maggot turned around, feeling Sinnglas's hands in his hair, sorting it into three long strands.

"You will not dance with us," Sinnglas said, looping one strand over another. "You are not of our village, nor did you come to us bearing the black-beaded warclub. But this will give my brother Damaqua and his followers something to think about. Perhaps, this will also make Squandral see the necessity of war even without my brother's support."

"Would that be good?" Maggot asked.

"It is our only hope as a people. Our fires grow cold. Where once we had villages all along these foothills, from the great sea in the north to the plains in the south, there now remain but a few: three in this region—my brother's, Squandral's, and Custalo's—plus several more farther to the south. The game in our hunting grounds diminish, and the soil of our fields grows thin because the invaders occupy the land where we would have once planted new crops."

Maggot's throat grew choked as Sinnglas spoke. He had witnessed the same thing among the trolls.

Sinnglas finished the braid and tied it at the base with a ribbon. "Now you look like a warrior, as we did in the days of honor before the invaders came."

Maggot tugged at his braid. It pulled his scalp tight. It was just like the one worn by the bearded man, the one he called First, who had led the lion hunters.

"The path of peace pursued by my father and my brother leads us only into the invaders' trap," Sinnglas said. "We cannot move over the mountains: our enemies prosper there and outnumber us, but they do not pursue us here because of the giants living in the high places and because they do not wish to anger the Lion. So this is where we must stand and fight."

Maggot thought that he would like fighting. From what Sinnglas told him, it was a kind of wrestling like his old bouts against Fart and other trolls. "I will fight with you."

Sinnglas squeezed Maggot's forearm. "This dance will let us see if all of my people feel as you do, or if they would rather hide in the woods like deer, a few here, a few there, always frightened of the Lion's roar."

Drums sounded outside, a rhythm tapped and cut short. The wave of voices rose and fell. The wizard had ceased speaking.

The men inside the lodge stamped their feet impatiently and flexed their arms. Naked from the waist up, each man carried a war-club, bow, or other weapon. Some wore no more than the basic cloths, and a little paint. Others wore decorated bands about their arms and thighs, and several had rattles tied in bundles about their calves.

They were all ready except Sinnglas, whom Maggot had delayed. Sinnglas tied a set of copper bells, tarnished green with age, below his knees. He jingled when he stood and walked to the head of the line waiting at the entrance. Then he ran through the entrance. The others followed him, screaming.

Maggot exited last, walking, silent. The dark blue of evening bruised the eastern sky.

Sinnglas's shrill cry continued as he led the runners outside the circle of people. Over a hundred people gathered, the whole village, until the elder men of the council came out of the lodge and stood in the circle. Squandral joined them, gazing down the beak of his nose like an eagle perched on the mountainside. The trollbirds hovered at his shoulders. Narrow-faced Menato scanned the crowd until his eyes lit on Maggot, paused, and moved on. When Damaqua finally emerged last, he stood there solemnly, lids half-closed like an old troll asleep on his feet. Tanaghri, his advisor, slipped away.

Sinnglas led the dancers around the outside one last time, stopping when he reached Damaqua. The jingling and the rattles fell silent. They stood there, the two brothers facing one another. The crowd murmured and shifted. Sinnglas opened his mouth to say something.

Damaqua stepped aside first.

Sinnglas gave a frightening whoop, which was answered by the others as they poured into the open circle. There was a collective exclamation from the audience to which Maggot added his voice. The drummers were seated off to one side next to Gelapa. Four men sat at two drums, like the one Maggot had stolen, only shorter and squatter. They began to pound and sing as the feet of the dancers resounded upon the ground.

"Heh," someone said behind Maggot.

He jumped, spinning to see Damaqua's advisor, Tanaghri.

"Tell Sinnglas that he should enjoy his dance tonight," Tanaghri said. "Let the young men feel good. But the council will send a messenger down to the Lion's men to warn them of his coming. It will be best if he turns them elseway, over the passes, to attack the farms of our ancient enemy."

"I to tell him should go now?" Maggot asked, so flustered he couldn't put his words in proper order.

Tanaghri snorted. "Only a fool needs close instruction. No, tell him alone, later, when the dance is done."

He turned away and passed through the crowd again.

The rapid song paused—Maggot spun to see the drummers and dancers waiting. Just as he drew breath to ask someone about this, the music and dance resumed at a faster pace, building to a crescendo. When it ended the dancers paced, heads down, in a tight knot until Sinnglas whooped, the others answered, and the drummers began a new song.

The dancers pounded their heels upon the ground in time with the music and struck exaggerated poses with their weapons. One man listened and another watched, one man struck with his club while another cut with his knife and others drew their bows. Kinnicut, the blacksmith, wielded his iron-headed war hammer as though he stood at his pounding stone. Sometimes they attacked and sometimes defended.

It was not the way that Maggot would hunt a lion.

But then his way, dropping from a tree, was the troll way, and he wanted to learn to be like people so he could find the woman again and show his interest to her.

The dancers continued until their bodies glistened with sweat. Maggot had never hunted animals or wrestled another troll where the action continued as long as this. Sinnglas extended the time between songs when the men stalked menacingly within the circle. But again and again he raised his voice, the dancers answered, and the drummers played.

As the seventh or eighth song—a rapt Maggot had forgotten to count—built toward its culmination, a tapping sound came from the circle of observers. The drummers stopped instantly, mallets poised in the air. The dancers paused too and stood relaxed, breathing deeply.

The interruption was made by Kagesh, one of the council members. "All my friends and relatives," Kagesh said. "This dance pleases me, and I hope it will continue unabated. I give thanks to the war-dancers for the spirit with which they perform their duty to our people. When I was a young man, I was the greatest dancer in the village. No one could surpass me. So I know that it is thirsty work. To the dancers I give this flask of medicine waters, to allay their thirst when they are done."

Some of the people laughed or clapped, and some of the dancers smiled. But not Sinnglas, who had many times decried the invaders' medicine waters. Keekyu, often the brunt of his brother's complaints, stepped forward and politely accepted the gift on behalf of the dancers.

The drum sounded, Sinnglas whooped, and the dancers responded. The performance resumed. During the next dance, there was another tap and another lapse into silence.

Tanaghri stood at the left hand of Damaqua again. "All my friends and relatives," he said. "It is fitting that the dancers should perform tonight, for we have among us the eminent Squandral, who has gone to war in his own day. I want to recognize the women who assisted in the preparation of the feast that honored Squandral. We did not eat so much food, or so well, when I was a young man. Since I cannot give presents to them all, I ask that one comes forward, she who was greediest and ate most from the pot."

The crowd laughed at this, and one bent old woman was pushed forward by the others, shuffling over to Tanaghri to accept his gift of a silver coin. She held it up and grinned with gap-toothed goodwill. The people applauded. When the old woman stepped away, the drummers resumed, the dancers cried out, and the cycle repeated.

More interruptions followed, many of them barbs exchanged between the older men or comments honoring the singers and dancers.

The speakers gave away medicine weed and silver coins and other items, some to the singers, some to the dancers, some to one another, as twilight fell. Maggot soon realized that the speeches gave the dancers a chance to rest, and encouraged them, so that they could keep up their performance. When they danced, Maggot found himself pounding out the rhythm with his own feet.

Then Damaqua tapped, and the drummers and dancers fell silent. Sinnglas froze in midmotion, forgetting to relax.

"All my friends and relatives," Damaqua said in his fluid, resonant voice. "I would like to recognize my brother Sinnglas, the leader of this dance. Maybe you remember our father, who was wise and had long vision so that for many years he served as our First." The word he used was not *First*, but that's how Maggot understood it. "I would like to present Sinnglas with this medal, on which the Empress's face is printed, to remind him of what our father wore all those years he lived in peace with the invaders."

The medal hung on a ribbon around Damaqua's neck. He lifted it over his head and offered it to Sinnglas, who stood motionless with his warclub raised above his head. Damaqua walked into the circle, medal dangling from his fist.

For several seconds, the only sounds to be heard were the rapid chirps of the crickets and the distant burps of frogs.

Sinnglas covered his brother's fist with his hand. One of the drummers started pounding again, and after missing several beats, the others joined in. But Sinnglas did not let go of his brother's hand, or else his brother would not let go of the medal. And because Sinnglas made no sound, the other dancers stood still amid the drumming.

Maggot shifted, fidgeted, until his eyes met those of Sinnglas's wife, and he saw her worry and fear for her husband, her embarrassment by this thing done wrong, and then Maggot found himself pushing through the silent throng of watchers until he ran into the circle, raising the war whoop in Sinnglas's place.

As he started pounding his heels in imitation of the dancers he had watched so carefully, one voice took up the cry with him—Pisqueto. Then Keekyu, then the others. They all commenced dancing. When he completed the circle, Maggot saw Sinnglas take the medal from his brother, hang it about his neck, and join the dancing, and he felt glad.

He slashed with his knife, reliving his struggle with the lion, showing them all his skill and fearlessness before they went to hunt another lion. He dropped to his knees, nearly tripping the man behind him, wrapped his arm around an invisible throat, and plunged the knife between its ribs.

The dance went by more quickly when one participated. The tempo increased sooner than Maggot expected, but before the song concluded Sinnglas jumped to the side of the drummers and tapped wood for silence.

"All my friends and relatives," he said, panting, bending to untie the bells from his legs. "My wise brother Damaqua recalls our history for us. He reminds us that the long period of peace we had with the invaders began with a period of war. To show him that we must be like our father, and move through war to peace again, I give him these copper rattles. If he has not forgotten the ways of our people, perhaps he will come back into the circle and show us how to dance."

Laughter, and even applause, answered this turnabout, some of it from Squandral's two men. Damaqua accepted the rattles with an expression as blank and ominous as the sun. He did not put them on.

The drummers resumed. Sinnglas whooped, and this time Maggot fell in with the others. While he danced, he felt larger than Ragweed, or Big Thunder, capable of anything. His glance caught Pisqueto's coal-dark eyes, and he saw the same thing reflected there. Caught up in emotion, he missed Squandral tapping for silence and stopped only when he heard his voice.

"All my friends, all my relatives," he said, speaking loudly, through his mouth, so that Maggot understood his words. "In all my years, I have never seen a war dance as memorable as this one. My praise goes out to all the dancers. Like one of those within the circle, I am a visitor here in your village. I speak of the one called Maqwet, who came out of the mountains, I am told, in the same way that First Man did."

Maggot stood straighter. He didn't know why the story of First Man had come up again. He'd told the trollbird, Menato, that it was untrue.

"While I do not have any tooth or tusk to give him," Squandral said, "if he plans to stay among us, he must learn to put something on his head. So I give him this cloth and ask him to wear it when he goes down among the invaders."

He unwrapped the red length of fabric from around his head, and a single braid dropped loose. A warrior's braid.

Sinnglas whooped immediately, before the drummers struck a single beat or Maggot could accept the proffered cloth. First Gelapa, the wizard, and then Damaqua, and then most of the other council members withdrew into the lodge. The drummers refused to continue without their leaders present. Pisqueto and some of the others danced without the drummers, singing the war songs themselves. Others stood there, confused.

Sinnglas ran over and embraced Squandral. "You are with us then? You will join us in this war?"

"Though it breaks my heart in two to do so," Squandral said loudly enough for others to overhear. "I thought I had seen enough of war, but the invaders treat us badly. Some of their men burned with the fire water, and set upon a group from our village. They killed my niece and her husband, and their little child. We asked for justice, but Baron Culufre says he can do nothing. I will join you until my family is revenged and the invaders know that they cannot treat us so."

"With you by my side, the enemy will fall before us."

Squandral grunted noncommittally. "Our chances were not good the last time, and that was thirty years ago, when I was a young man. Our losses were great, and we were weaker when the war was done than when it began. We have not grown greater since, but the invaders spread like locusts in the summer. Yet, if we do nothing, I fear our people will disappear completely."

"It is what I have been saying. Damaqua will change his mind now. He will join us."

"I will carry the hatchet into our village," Squandral said loudly. "And I will send Menato south with it to Custalo. Together we shall have at least fifty warriors. We had many more than that the last time we fought the invaders, and their numbers were much less."

Sinnglas made a sharp cutting gesture with his hand. "The wolverine feeding at the carcass of a deer has many fewer teeth than the pack of wolves around him, yet holds onto his own. It is not our size that matters, but the strength of our attack."

"Still, our women and children should prepare to flee into the mountains."

"That will be wise," Sinnglas admitted. "We should strike quickly, with surprise."

"That will be wise also." Squandral said something through his nose that Maggot didn't quite catch.

"I did see the snakeskin fall," Sinnglas answered. "Did the wizard say whose death it presages?"

Squandral shrugged. "All men die. Let us hope it is a good death, whoever's it is."

They said their farewells then, and Sinnglas and Maggot returned to the lodge of his wife's family. She put out two bowls of food. Maggot ate while Sinnglas removed his regalia. Their children, a little boy and a little girl, peered at him with awestruck eyes from behind their mother's skirts while she presented Maggot with a bearskin bag. He peered inside and found more food. He scooped some out with his fingers. It tasted like parched corn, but it was sweet like the maple syrup. He shoved several fingerfuls into his mouth. Her mouth dropped open aghast, but Sinnglas laughed out loud.

"No, my friend," he said. "That is to sustain us on our journey. Save it for tomorrow. We must take the warclub to Custalo's village and dance there next."

Maggot closed the bag reluctantly. He was not used to the idea of saving food for tomorrow, but he could learn, just as he meant to learn what *war* was.

Outside in the central plaza, Sinnglas and Maggot joined the other dancers gathered around the post. They dressed plainly, carrying weapons and bearskin bags of food. A light wind rustled the dead snakeskins.

"We must strike quickly, take them by surprise," Sinnglas told them.

Maggot recalled Tanaghri speaking to him before the dance. He was supposed to remember something, but it was a stem lost in the swirling waters of the past day.

Perhaps he would remember later.

— CHAPTER 16 —

Maggot stood in the central plaza of Custalo's village when the dancing was over. He stared at the stars, letting the sweat evaporate from his skin. A crowd of people stirred around him.

"War is good," he said, grinning.

Sinnglas grinned too. "This war is very good."

So far *war* involved only dancing. Menato had come ahead to prepare the way for them, so Sinnglas's men were welcomed enthusiastically in Custalo's village. It was two villages, actually, on a high plain that straddled the mountain ranges; one was a little smaller than Damaqua's village and the other a bit larger, situated within a morning's walk of one another. They had danced in both villages over the course of two nights. Maggot liked the dancing. It was exciting in a different way than wrestling—when it was over, no one was injured and all the dancers felt good.

"That is a very great honor, my friend," Sinnglas said, indicating three eagle feathers in Maggot's hand. Custalo, hearing the story of Squandral's gift of his turban to Maggot, had presented the feathers to Maggot during the dance.

"What do I do with them?" Maggot asked. The sweat ran down his hand, making the feathers damp.

"You wear them in your cap," Sinnglas said.

Maggot did not like having his head covered, but he was trying hard to be like people. "You to show me how. I am glad to war with you, my friend."

"Good," Sinnglas said, turning to talk to the men from Custalo's village. About four handfuls had already changed out of their dancing costumes and were prepared to go.

Maggot spun in a circle and regarded this village that was at once both familiar and strange. This was troll country. He looked over the palisade and wondered if his mother or any of the other trolls were out there watching him the way he had sat through the nights looking over the walls at people. With his eyes closed in a thick fog, he could find his way from here down to the hot stinking springs, and from there, even with his nose squeezed shut, he could trace the trails rock by rock down to the safety of the caves. Now he had crossed over the wall and was on the inside. He was closer to the woman he wanted.

Keekyu screamed and flung his arms about, laughing. Maggot watched him share a bottle with some of the other young men, who grew also increasingly boisterous. Noticing his attention, Keekyu walked over and thrust the bottle at Maggot.

"Go on, take a drink!"

The noise of conversation around Sinnglas fell suddenly hushed. Maggot saw his friend glaring, his face as angry as it grew during the dance.

Custalo stood beside Sinnglas. The old warrior had a gentle face like a baby's, until one read the harsh shape of his mouth or felt the cutting manner of his eyes or listened to the stories of his raids against their enemies across the mountains. People and their things could be so different on the inside than on the outside. Trolls were not like that. Custalo stared at the eagle feathers crushed in Maggot's fist.

Keekyu gave him a sloppy smile. "Go on!"

"No," Maggot said. He turned away. If he had to choose between Sinnglas and anyone else, he would choose his friend. He held the feathers more gently as he joined the others.

Sinnglas's followers and the men from Custalo's village walked north for several days. On the third night, they camped on a bluff overlooking a river much wider than any Maggot had ever seen in the high mountains.

Despite a slight breeze, pungent grease smeared over their bodies, and smudge bundles burning in the fires, the biting insects swarmed to devour them the way crawling bugs consumed the final shreds of meat off the bones of a corpse. A few men slept despite the insects. Sinnglas, Keekyu, Custalo, and the few other older men crowded around a fire, planning strategies. Maggot sat with Pisqueto on the edge of the bluff, trying to escape the stifling heat.

Below them, groups of deer rested in the river water among the long grasses. Nothing but their noses and antlers showed above the water's surface.

"Smart," Maggot said, slapping another insect as it landed on his neck. "Perhaps we go down to the water with them."

Pisqueto chuckled. "Heh."

"When will we come to Squandral's village?"

"Tomorrow. It sits between the hills, at the place where three rivers come together."

"Three rivers? Are they all as big as this?"

"The one that flows west is larger, but it leads down to the River Wyndas, and the sea." He lifted his chin. "Look."

A faint, phosphorescent light as long as a small tree drifted in a serpentine path downstream toward the deer. At first Maggot took it for the reflection of the moon, or perhaps the milky band of light that crossed the sky.

"Is it a snake?" he asked, thinking that now he understood the source of the snakeskins on the pole in Damaqua's village.

"No."

The light vanished below the surface of the water, reappearing in front of one deer slightly apart from the herd. Only the glowing head of the creature appeared, a beacon of light wavering in front of the transfixed deer while a few animals turned to climb out of the river. The head darted forward, the deer bleated, and all the herd splashed up the bank to scatter into the woods. The snake—or whatever it was—coiled around its victim, dragging it under. The river churned like water boiling in a pot, and then the splashing stopped.

Pisqueto slapped more bugs. "The Old Ones."

"Old Ones?"

"If you come near one, you mustn't speak to it or look into its eyes— the Old Ones will take you to the other side." Pisqueto tugged on the gorget at his throat. It was carved in the shape of a snake circled on itself. "Have you not seen the images of the Old Ones among us?"

"I see," Maggot said. He lifted the colored amulets around his own neck. "I thought they things like this. To say we are people."

"No." Pisqueto glared angrily. "The soulless made those."

Frowning, Maggot smacked his nose as an insect landed on it, and then he winced at the blow.

"The soulless, the invaders," Pisqueto explained. "In the wintertime, when the Old Ones grow sluggish, they seek them out on the riverbanks or dig their burrows in the mud and kill them. That is why our people grow few. The spirits of the Old Ones do not protect us anymore because we do not protect them. Now, Banya, their wizard, he shows respect but . . ."

Pisqueto's voice trailed off. Maggot lifted his necklaces, the light-filled stones clicking as they bounced against each other. "These not like yours?"

"No. Has Sinnglas not talked to you about them?"

"No."

"Heh. Why do you wear them?"

Maggot recalled the woman with the blue gem against the skin of her throat. "They remind me of one."

Pisqueto's grunt did not say anything that Maggot understood. They sat quietly, stirring only to slap at the bugs. Much later, the Old One, glowing faintly now, dragged its distorted and distended form upon a mud bank in the middle of the river. One by one the deer timidly returned to cool off in the water at another place farther upstream.

"Why do they go back, when they know it is dangerous for them?" Maggot asked.

Pisqueto crushed yet another fat mosquito on his arm, leaving a tiny streak of blood. "Because they must. Because where else can they go?"

After a while, Maggot said, "Tomorrow we will go to Squandral's village. Then we will make your war."

The post in Squandral's central plaza was covered with more skins than Damaqua's village and many more than Custalo's. But it sat at the junction of several rivers, all of them containing Old Ones. The dancing that night included men from all three villages and some outlying places. During one of the dances, Maggot became so wrought that he stabbed the air repeatedly and screamed. "Show me the lion," he shouted. "I to kill him!"

Squandral's men chuckled. "Look at the vulture," they said.

Afterward, Sinnglas came over to Maggot and smiled. "You will have your chance, my friend. We will go avenge the deaths tonight. Now you will see what war is really like."

"Good!" Maggot panted.

He was ready to chase down any lion they wanted and destroy it.

They set out in the darkness for a settlement of farms downstream, where Squandral's niece and her family had gone to trade the day they were murdered.

They ran hard, heading south and west, crossing the rivers at fords. Before dawn they came to a clearing surrounded by pines in the shadow of a mountain's steep slope. The men from the different villages kept mostly to themselves, but Sinnglas, Squandral, and Custalo met together with a few others. Sinnglas took Keekyu with him.

Some of the older men slept or rested. Maggot had the wakefulness of night and newness both upon him. So he joined those who prepared themselves. "This cap," he told Pisqueto. "It I cannot wear to war." It distracted him.

Pisqueto shoved the red cloth in the back of Maggot's belt. "But you will have to stay out in front so that we can see it," he said, laughing to himself. Then he tied the eagle feathers into Maggot's braid. They tickled his shoulder when he moved his head at first, but soon he no longer noticed them.

Sinnglas and Keekyu returned. Keekyu made a bow-drawing motion to Maggot. "The invaders asked us to give you a bow before we attack them."

Some of the other men chuckled.

"What?" Maggot had practiced with Keekyu's bow until his thumb was rubbed raw. Though he could shoot far, he had not yet gotten the knack of hitting the target.

Keekyu laughed, then looked at Sinnglas. "I'll tell the others the plan?"

Sinnglas shrugged, and then squatted down beside Maggot and Pisqueto. "Squandral has made a good plan."

"What is it?" Pisqueto asked.

"We'll attack them just after sunrise. A few men from each village will be our reserve. They will stay downstream from the settlement, in case the invaders try to escape that way. I want you with the reserve, Pisqueto. You too, my friend, Maqwet."

"I to be with you," Maggot said firmly. Then thinking of the red cloth in his belt, he added, "Out in front."

"Nor will I stay with the crippled old men and boys," Pisqueto complained.

"It is not just old men and boys," Sinnglas answered. "It is for those who have never fought before, to stay with those who have fought the most to give them wisdom and guidance."

"Will you or Squandral or Custalo be with the reserve?" Pisqueto asked.

"No."

"Heh," Pisqueto said. "But you three have fought the most, haven't you?" He grinned in triumph when Sinnglas looked away.

Maggot stood up, drawing his knife. "I will be with you, my friend, out in front."

The group of reserves took cover alongside the river trail behind mounds of debris—dead branches, uprooted trees. Maggot and Pisqueto went with the main force of men upstream. They passed around a settlement, or small village, its rooflines distinguishable against the sky.

"When will we start to seek the lion's tracks?" Maggot asked, doubting any bigtooth lion would hunt so close to a cluster of houses.

Sinnglas angrily gestured him to silence, while some of the other men glared at him. Pisqueto came up beside Maggot and whispered, "We just passed his dung heap."

Maggot had seen no sign of scat, but he studied the ground closely as they walked on.

With the birds singing for the morning, they divided into two columns. Squandral and Custalo led the main group of more than forty warriors back toward the cluster of fortified farmhouses.

Sinnglas took his eleven men and proceeded down to a stream, to approach from the flank. They hurried silently through the shadows under the woods, the dark shapes reminding Maggot of trolls running back to their caves at sunrise after a night of too much feeding.

Just ahead of them on the trail, a loud crash in the brush was followed by *gobblegobblegobble*.

Three huge birds burst from the trees, an arrow flying out of the darkness to hit one of the straggling turkeys and pin it to the ground. Its shrill cry accompanied vigorous flapping in a circle as two men ran out of the woods after it. The men dressed like the hunters in the skin caves, their clothes bright blocks of color in the gray light.

Sinnglas whooped, just like he did in the dance, as Keekyu lifted his bow, drew, and shot. His arrow sailed through empty air: the men had already reversed direction and bolted away.

"But—" cried Maggot.

Half a dozen bows twanged as Sinnglas shouted at the men, "Catch them! Quick! Quick!"

Keekyu ran ahead, always looking, with Pisqueto and Maggot at his side. Pisqueto's eyes were wide with excitement. Sinnglas and the other men spread out through the woods. Maggot listened to the crashing footsteps of the men ahead and noticed when the noise stopped. Before he realized what this meant, a bowstring vibrated.

Maggot hurled himself behind a tree, but he saw a silver flash in the air. Keekyu screamed and crumpled over backward, his scalp laid open bare to the white bone of the skull. Blood streamed everywhere, covering his pale, still face.

Pisqueto froze. He took one look at his brother and gulped. Then he spun around and ran away.

Before Maggot could run after him, Sinnglas was screaming. "Attack, attack! Don't let them reach the houses!"

Maggot obeyed.

Branches slapped at his face and arms as Maggot plunged through the trees after the men. The strangers stopped long enough to draw and shoot, then ran again. The shafts flew wild, sailing over Maggot's head to crash in the leaves.

The two men broke into the open, one ahead of the other. Maggot emerged from the woods just behind them. Dawn cast its pale light across the lush grass as they all ran over the meadow beside the stream toward the settlement. Kinnicut, the blacksmith in Damaqua's village, ran past Maggot and flung his warclub. It spun through the air and knocked down the trailing stranger. Kinnicut jumped in the air, trilling his triumph, as the tripped man crawled away on all fours like a beast. Then Sinnglas came up and smashed his warclub into the stranger's head, once, twice. On the second strike, the skull splattered like a fruit.

Maggot stopped.

"Kill him!" Sinnglas shouted, pointing toward the second man. Several men drew their bows, but their comrades who continued the chase were in the way, so they didn't shoot.

Sinnglas dashed after the man. Maggot raced at Sinnglas's heels.

The stranger entered a second, narrower band of trees. Someone shot at him, but the arrow struck wood as he dodged behind the trunks. Maggot realized that the man still ran for the houses, so he angled through the trees and clambered over the small ridge to reach the man first.

Maggot came out of the trees on the edge of fields dug in straight lines like the patterns on the stranger's clothes. A group of houses sat across the fields.

The man rounded the hilltop not twenty feet away, shouting words that Maggot didn't understand. Maggot covered the distance in a few short steps, took the man by the hair, and jerked his head back. The man squirmed, batting at Maggot with the bow in his left hand while his right hand slipped off Maggot's greased body. He looked straight into Maggot's eyes, and said, in Sinnglas's language, "You *Wyndan* piece of shit."

Maggot plunged his knife into the man's heart and twisted. The man dropped his bow and sagged, but Maggot held him up by the hair. Blood bubbled at his mouth, a single crimson sphere that swelled like the moon and popped.

Sinnglas arrived at Maggot's side. "Over the wall!"

There was no time to think or feel. Maggot dropped the body and joined seven or eight men sprinting in a ragged line across the fields. Someone twisted an ankle and fell down.

Maggot outdistanced them all.

His eyes encompassed everything at once. The strangers had fortified their houses, surrounding them with a fence and filling the spaces in between with a rough wall of logs and wagons. Someone must have warned them of the attack. Flames leapt from a rooftop, lighting the situation. Their shaggy cattle clustered inside, jostling away from the fire, lowing in distress. Squandral's men and Custalo's engaged the strangers on the far side, trading screams and arrows. The bulk of the defenders, a handful of men, were on the far side of the structure; Maggot glimpsed their backs in the flickering light. One—no, two—defended the wall nearest Sinnglas's men.

Maggot hit the wall at a full run and vaulted over it.

He rolled on his shoulder and landed upright on his feet, the way his mother had taught him. His momentum carried him straight into the larger archer, and he struck repeatedly with his fist until the man fell.

Something cut across his back, and he twisted, slashing with his knife, feeling it bite, pulling through. The attacker fell backward, which is when Maggot noticed she was the woman.

He stood paralyzed, like the deer transfixed by the demon.

No, not *the* woman, but a woman. This woman was smaller, like a boy, and her hair was a lighter shade of brown. But she had the same nose, the same sharp-angled face. She sat propped up where she'd fallen against the wall, grimacing, trying to push a blue wad of intestines back into her stomach. One leg kept kicking hard against the ground while blood spurted out between her legs.

Someone screamed.

Maggot spun. A man charged around the corner of a house aiming a spear at him. Maggot dodged the thrust, blocking the shaft with his knife hand and shoving the man down.

He stood there, dumb, confused, as Sinnglas and the other warriors came over the wall. One of them silenced the woman as others killed the two men. They attacked the defenders from behind, and Squandral and Custalo and all their men came over the barricade on the other side.

Something inside Maggot became the shell of a tortoise or a snail, something very hard. He seemed to himself to be moving slug-slow while everyone around him darted like bats in the sky.

In a matter of moments, the warriors murdered every man, woman, and child. Maggot watched them drag a small child out from under a bed before they killed him. Then they knocked down the fence, driving the cattle into the fields, plundered the bodies, and began to rob the houses.

Maggot staggered back to the wall, tried to climb over it, and fell, weak, on the other side. He stood up, wiping his arm against his mouth to take away the bitter taste of bile that suddenly filled it.

As flames leapt from the remaining rooftops, Maggot ran out across the fields. He wasn't running away. He was only running to find Pisqueto, only running to find himself.

⇥ CHAPTER 17 ⇤

Sinnglas and Pisqueto sat cross-legged by a cold fire, apart from the other men. Maggot squatted troll-like near them. He scratched under his arm, scratched his crotch, sniffing the night air for carrion or other scents. The dusk soothed him with its promise of night.

"This time I will prove myself," Pisqueto was saying to Sinnglas.

"You've proved your courage many times now," Sinnglas replied. "No one doubts you."

In the weeks since that first dawn raid, their band of warriors had attacked several more settlements. The new settlements were well defended, and though the two sides had traded insults like trolls before wrestling, little had come of it. Because the raids had gone badly, the other warriors blamed the men from Damaqua's village, especially Sinnglas, for starting talk of war and sat apart from them. Maggot had not missed the killing when the new raids failed, but Pisqueto had risked his life in each confrontation, getting in harm's way of the invaders' arrows to taunt them.

When Sinnglas and Pisqueto finished eating their small meal, they scrubbed their teeth with green, ribbed reeds collected from the stream. Maggot picked up a reed and followed their example.

"I've shown that I don't fear the Lion's men," Pisqueto said. "But I have yet to prove that I can do any harm to them."

Sinnglas sighed. "Already I must go and tell our mother that one of her sons has left his bones in a foreign land. Do not make me take twice that news to her, little brother."

Pisqueto turned his head away and rubbed the palm of his hand against his eyes. The iron arrowhead had pierced Keekyu's skull, making him the sole death in that first raid. At least, Maggot thought, among Sinnglas's people. Everyone in the settlement had died.

He flared his nostrils, sniffing again.

With another sigh, Sinnglas turned his head toward Maggot. "There are two worlds, one seen and one that is unseen. Which one do you walk in, my friend?"

"What do you mean?" Maggot asked.

"There is the world of the seen—you, me, the tree, the stones. I walk through it. Then there is the world of the unseen." He made an exaggerated sniffing noise, mimicking Maggot. "Your spirit, mine, the spirit of the tree, the stone. Sometimes our body is in one place, but our spirit another, seeing things of the spirit. Gelapa, the wizard of our village, spends most of his time in the unseen world. He says the medicine water of the invaders takes him there. While there, he is able to see the unseen—"

"Hmmm?" Maggot asked.

"The spirits of the dead. The weather before it comes."

Maggot continued to scrub his teeth. "No, I smell the weather more than I see it. Today the air smells wrong. Sharp, like rain, but no clouds in the sky."

"Heh. Gelapa is a wizard of the unseen world." Sinnglas pursed his lips and raised his chin in the direction of the ampules on Maggot's chest. "Those are the weapons of a wizard of the world of the seen. Is that what you are?"

"No." Maggot shook his head emphatically. He found himself saying no frequently, though his skill with the language continued to improve. "These remind me of someone."

"This is why I ask," Sinnglas said. "Our situation does not look good to me. I am left out of the war councils, which are ruled by old men. They think in old ways."

"And that is bad?"

"It will be very bad."

A piece of the reed had broken off and stuck in Maggot's back teeth. He fished for it with his tongue. "But more warriors, they come to join us."

They had trickled in since that first attack, from other far-flung villages and from the ranks of those who had not joined the dancing at first. Their numbers were now higher than Maggot could count. Many fistfuls of fists, though Damaqua had not been among the late arrivals.

Sinnglas looked out over the encampment of warriors. "When the invaders attack us tomorrow morning, they will come in great numbers, more than ours. They have two and three men to our one, and war mammuts with them."

Maggot had been out to see them too. The army of the invaders carried banners with a golden lion on a field of green. The Lion. No wonder Sinnglas's people feared it so. "If it so bad, why do they come to join us?"

"What else can we do?" He indicated the charms around Maggot's neck a second time. "Maqwet, my friend, are you sure you do not know how to use those to help us?"

The reed came loose from Maggot's teeth, and he spit it out. Once he had not known how to clean his teeth either. Someday he might know how to use them. "No."

Pisqueto snapped the reed in his hand. "We will show the invaders how real men fight."

Sinnglas looked away. "We will certainly meet the Lion with the weapons we have."

At sunrise, they heard the mammuts trumpeting as the invaders' army marched up the valley.

Squandral, Custalo, and the other old warriors had chosen a spot where the valley rose gradually into thick forests. They created natural-looking breastworks of fallen trees and branches, cunningly rearranged to provide dead ends and shifts in cover all along the trail. Their men concealed themselves in small groups through the woods, while Squandral and some of the others built a fire on the hilltop.

Sinnglas gathered the men of his village, the warriors who had danced that first night, and spoke privately to them.

"Those of you who wish to stay back with the old men are welcome to. No one will call you cowards. But someone must go forward, to be the point of the spear. The war mammuts will come first, and unless someone hamstrings them, they will destroy our breastworks and our defenses."

Pisqueto thumped his fist on his chest. "They will say that those who faced the mammuts showed great courage."

The men nodded at this, some reluctantly, but one by one, they agreed to follow Sinnglas. He led them down the trail to a place of thick underbrush, with spaces scooped out beneath. Maggot thought it might have been a giant skunkbear's den, or maybe even something made long ago by a group of trolls. There was no scent or scat about the place to tell him, nothing but the dusty scent of old leaves, but it had that feel.

"We'll hide here," Sinnglas told them. "And under those thickets there. But hold your blow until the vanguard is nearly past us. Then strike quickly and hard."

Maggot lay on his stomach and crawled into the big hole under the brush, choosing it for its familiarity. He settled into the dark shade with several other men, and covered himself with leaves as if he were going to hide from the sun to sleep.

He had no chance to rest, though. They heard the invaders coming from far away, shouts and branches breaking and metal rattling, and then they saw a cloud of dust along the trail. Two armored mammuts came into view, each one with a man perched just behind its ears. Pikemen surround the mammuts, bristling like an angry porcupine.

There was a gap between this group and the main army on foot behind them. Maggot's position made it impossible to count their numbers precisely, but he saw there were many more than the twelve of them waiting to attack. His grip on his hatchet felt too tight, so he let go and rubbed his fingertips against his leg to loosen them.

The mammuts came close, showing the shorter, cleaner fur of summer. Sun glinted on their armor. Maggot counted feet as the pikemen went by: twenty-three feet—he was sure he had missed one. One man passed close enough that Maggot could see the white knob of a bunion on his inside toe. They were in no formation. Some carried their pikes over their shoulders and others carried pikes at their sides.

As the last feet passed by, Sinnglas gave a shrill whoop.

The men screamed with him as they burst from their hiding places, and the scream had the same effect on the soldiers that a lion's roar had on its prey. Half froze where they stood, and a couple went down with arrows in them. Maggot saw one fall under Sinnglas's war-club, and Pisqueto flung himself on the stunned pikemen with fury.

Maggot charged for the nearest mammut, intending to drive his hatchet into its leg to cripple it, when a man turned to block his way. Maggot knocked aside the half-raised pike and struck at the man's head with his hatchet, knocking him down. A braided man attacked him with a sword. Maggot deflected the blow with his hatchet, but the impact knocked the weapon from his hand. Maggot grabbed the other man's wrist, drawing his knife and stabbing. The blade chinged off his iron shirt. Maggot stabbed again, this time at the throat, his cut partially deflected by a collar.

Sudden bellowing raised hackles on Maggot's neck.

Kinnicut, the wide-shouldered smith, had driven a long-handled axe under the knee of one of the mammuts. The shaggy beast dragged the bad leg, screaming in fury, lashing out with its trunk.

"Go, go!" Sinnglas shouted.

Kinnicut ran for the woods, with other men leaping into the thickets. The soldier crawled away clutching his bleeding throat, trying to regain his feet. Maggot spun—

Pisqueto grappled with one of the pikemen.

Screaming, Maggot slashed at the back of Pisqueto's attacker. The blow staggered him enough for Pisqueto to jerk free. Then Maggot saw reinforcements running to the aid of the invaders, and the remaining pikemen clustering together to charge them, and Sinnglas was screaming at them to run, run; so he grabbed Pisqueto by the arm and dragged him off the trail, and they fled.

They hurdled the breastworks when they reached them, and turned to see what they had done. Two, maybe three bodies lay in the open glade. The rest of the invaders had taken up a defensive formation around the other mammut. The injured mammut, blind with panic, tried to escape, dragging its crippled leg behind it. The rider behind its head had lost his goad and did all he could just to hold on.

Two of Sinnglas's men were too injured to fight any more. One suffered a deep sword cut that had shattered his collarbone. The other had lost fingers from his right hand. He wrapped a cloth in knots around it, his face pale and sweaty.

"The mammuts," Sinnglas directed. A few bowstrings sung immediately around Maggot, but he left his bow over his shoulder—his aim had improved but was still not that good.

One or two of the arrows landed in the mammuts' hides just as the

Lion's archers started shooting back at Sinnglas and his men. At the sound of the twanging bows beside it, the injured mammut lost control, grabbing the rider from its back with its trunk. The small man's shriek cut short when he smashed into the ground, was lifted, and smashed again. The hobbled mammut then attacked the invaders. Their line broke, but re-formed after the animal ran past them down the trail.

Some of Squandral's men charged in a brief counterattack that achieved little or nothing before they ran back uphill and resumed their defensive positions.

The rest of the enemy forces came up. After taking a long time to organize themselves, they began a slow advance behind a wall of shields. The invaders' archers poured a steady volley of carefully aimed arrows at the warriors. Their attention focused on Squandral's part of the barricade across the main trail. Maggot took his bow—it had been Keekyu's, the one he'd tried to train Maggot with—and stuck up his head, shooting blindly before he ducked again. The invaders were packed so tightly it seemed impossible to miss. But he never saw what happened to his arrow. His stomach bubbled like a sulfur spring. He wanted to stay at Sinnglas's side and help him, but he wished they were both elsewhere.

One of the men in their line grunted as an enemy arrow came straight through the pile of branches, deflected in such a way that it lodged in his thigh. By this point, the enemy were less than two hundred feet away.

"Back to the next set of trees," Sinnglas said.

Maggot helped the man with the broken collarbone, not carrying him, but propping him up and pushing him along. Pisqueto was the last to leave, firing arrow after deliberate arrow. The enemy archers noticed him, and half a dozen bolts protruded from the trunk of the tree he hid behind. Only when the last of the men were behind the next bunch of trees did he come running back to join them.

The enemy paused at the edge of the woods, reorganizing. They were very slow, very deliberate in everything they did. Maggot peered through the green treetops at the sky. Somehow, the morning was already half passed.

Pisqueto crouched next to Maggot. "This is not good."

"How many arrows do you have left?" Maggot asked, fitting one to his bow.

"None." He said it simply. Maggot divided his partial quiver in half and passed a bunch of them over.

"Keep them," Pisqueto said. "Watch my bow while I go find some. Keep it for me if we have to run."

Maggot nodded understanding.

Pisqueto crawled back in the direction he'd just come from. In the light that fell through the trees, Maggot marked the indistinct shapes of the enemy soldiers. Sounds of heavy fighting came from the right flank, where Squandral had withdrawn his men to a ridge. Bellows thundered through the woods closer by—the second mammut had broken through Custalo's lines and now roamed somewhere behind them, smashing their breastworks. Sinnglas's group was left of the center. On the far left flank a few southerners guarded a ravine.

Pisqueto was out on his belly sifting through the leaves when an arrow bolted into the ground beside him.

"Look out," Maggot shouted.

A handful of enemy archers had taken up positions behind the trees that Sinnglas's men had just abandoned. Pisqueto pulled the arrow from the ground, rolling for cover as Maggot and a few others shouted and shot back. But Sinnglas regarded his brother and did not raise his own weapon.

"It's going to be a long day," he said. "We'll need arrows more than we need men to pull the bowstrings before it's over."

Maggot counted things the same way.

Pisqueto zigzagged back to the breastworks and vaulted over the logs. He came back up beside Maggot and retrieved his bow.

"How many?" Maggot asked.

Pisqueto held up the quarrels. "Five."

They'd shot off at least four at the enemy, but Maggot would count the small gains where he found them.

The two sides traded shots for a short time, shooting whenever an enemy stuck his head up over the fallen trees or stepped into the open. Then whoops sounded from the far left flank, and the southerners flooded through the woods behind Maggot, retreating for the center of the line.

Without knowing what had happened, Sinnglas gathered the men from his village and fell back to defend a new position, but everything was confusion. Some of the men became lost. Maggot could no longer find the man whose fingers were cut off, and someone else was missing too. Sinnglas grabbed some of the southerners as they ran past, shouting at them, calling shame on them for fleeing, commanding them to stay. Some kept running, but some stopped. A group of six, led by a man who knew Sinnglas, joined them. And then their group, swollen to fifteen, was in the front of the battle as three times that many invaders pressed through the trees.

The exchange of arrows went quickly, as if everyone on both sides was in a hurry to expend them and close hand-to-hand.

A dozen pikemen advanced behind others holding shields. Their weapons were long enough to thrust through the barricade of logs and brush, but they were walking upslope. Maggot crouched, squeezing his arms under a fallen tree. At the last moment, when they charged, he screamed, thrust upward with his legs, and hurled the tree at them. It shattered their line of pikes as it rolled down the incline. The invaders broke and scattered, except for a shield carrier pinned beneath the log and quickly stabbed to death by one of the southerners.

The invaders quickly organized another charge. Maggot hacked away at a shaft thrust at him through the branches, but the end was sheathed in metal and turned aside his knife. One man came over the barricade and went down in a pile with Pisqueto. Sinnglas's men broke and ran, retreating again.

They were being crowded together with Squandral's men and Custalo's, all toward the center, but there was no longer any center, and Maggot and some of the others, in their mad dash for cover, ran through the enemy's broken line, scattering in half a dozen directions downhill.

Leaping over fallen trees, branches whipping his skin as he crashed through the brush, the charms leaping at his throat, Maggot stumbled to a stop when he entered a clearing that contained the fallen mammut. One of the invaders lay dead on the ground nearby, within the circle of trampled grasses.

A group of invaders, four footmen without armor, ran into the clearing on the other side. Maggot took cover behind the arrow-pricked corpse of the mammut, the only barrier between him and their spears. They glanced at him and ran on through the clearing without attacking.

Maggot sheathed his knife. Gripping a handful of red fur, Maggot pulled himself up onto the dead animal's flank to retrieve some arrows. He tore three of them free before he realized he'd lost his bow and quiver. He must have thrown them down when he started to run, but he couldn't remember.

From his high perch, looking off through the woods, he thought he saw Sinnglas alone against some invaders. Throwing down the arrows, he jumped to the ground and ran to help.

Instead he found a solitary warrior, one of the southerners, beset by an armored knight and two spearmen. The southerner spun, swinging his warclub in huge arcs, to deflect the weapons thrust at him. Blood streamed from several wounds. Maggot lowered his head and charged like a bull bison into the spearman who attacked from the rear. The man bounced off the ground as Maggot grabbed a jagged-edged stone and swung it at the man's head. The man rolled aside, and the blow missed.

Maggot lifted the primitive weapon to strike again, but the second spearman rushed him. Maggot threw the rock. It hit his attacker below the chin, snapping him backward. Maggot picked up the fallen spear and aimed it at the armored knight, who stepped forward with his bloodstained sword. They were both screaming at each other.

The roar in Maggot's throat choked off in midbirth.

The knight lowered his sword to a defensive position as his cry also broke.

It was the man Maggot had seen in the camp by the river, the one he called First. His head was covered by a helmet, but the braid showed, and the beard was cropped shorter, but there was no mistaking him. The green cloth of his shirt was embroidered with a golden lion.

They exchanged a small nod of recognition.

A cluster of knights and spear carriers appeared out of the trees, raising an exultant cry. The warrior Maggot had rescued tugged on his arm, and they ran, fleeing through the pine trees, upslope around the ravine.

How had First recognized him?

How had he not known the woman he wanted was one of the invaders? He should have guessed earlier, when he saw the mammuts.

At the top of the hill, the warrior leaned against a beech tree and slid down to a sitting position. He left a red streak of blood on the smooth white bark. Lifting his water flask to his lips and drinking, he offered the same to Maggot, who gulped thirstily.

"Heh!" the man said. "Rescued by the giant."

Maggot had heard the word before, but Sinnglas was reluctant to speak of it. "Giant?"

The man stared at him oddly. "In the mountains, the giants who walk in the darkness, leaving no shadow behind them. Who hurl stones on men and play the war drums."

"Trolls!" Maggot said.

The man wrinkled his brow at the unfamiliar word. "Giants," he repeated slowly. "You are as large as one, and you throw men and stones around like they do. You fight like a giant."

Maggot thought about the man's description. The scent of wrongness that he had not named became clear to him. "No, the giants never fight like this," he said. "Not among themselves. They would talk and vote, and then follow the First or go their separate ways. This fighting, is a wrongness to it."

The man laughed and then winced. He held out his palm, whispering, "Wait . . . wait . . . there!"

Maggot followed his gesture. Only a few hundred feet away, a large group of the enemy approached, having followed the wide, concealed path offered by the ravine. When Maggot looked back, the other man's chin rested limp against his chest, eyes open.

He ran off alone through the trees, headed for the high ground. The sun sat directly overhead, shining down piteously through every break in the canopy. The air had become stiflingly hot, and thick with silence, pierced only by the occasional scream or distant trumpet of a mammut. He saw movement atop a flat ridge that thrust out from the mountainside.

Maggot climbed up the steep slope, through tulip trees that rose a hundred feet or more into the sky. One huge tree had blown down lengthwise across the ridge's edge; its uppermost branches tangled among other trees and kept it from slipping away. Maggot heard arrows zip over his head at attackers behind him. When he climbed over the fallen log, he nodded to the archers. He saw Squandral and Custalo with maybe sixty or seventy men. Squandral glanced at Maggot's bare head and turned his face away.

Sinnglas sat with Pisqueto and five other men from their village, including the man who'd lost his fingers, but not the one with the broken collarbone. Maggot joined them. The men were binding their wounds, except for Pisqueto, who, uninjured, sat repairing the fletching on an odd assortment of arrows.

Sinnglas acknowledged Maggot, then pointed with his chin to several places over the ridge. Maggot observed the invaders forming into organized groups in the cover below. The shaggy red mammut moved between distant trees.

"Do you have food in your bag?" Sinnglas asked. "Eat if you do. If not we shall find some for you."

Maggot checked. He did. He showed Sinnglas a ball of the cornmeal and molasses before he put it in his mouth. "I have some to share if others need it," he said as he chewed. "How did the fight go?"

Sinnglas shrugged noncommittally. "Women in at least eleven lodges across the villages will rend their clothes and scream when the news reaches them. Perhaps more. Most men will have scars to show they were here today. The invaders have lost more men than we have. But then they have so many more men to lose." He stopped, and stared off into the sky. When he spoke again, his voice dropped. "Truly, I did not think they would come in such numbers nor prove themselves so brave."

Maggot swallowed, then sucked on his fingertips. "This fighting cannot go on, Brother."

Pisqueto looked up from his work. A faint smile played briefly on his lips before evaporating like a drop of water on a warm rock.

"Truly today you have been my brother," Sinnglas said. "But your words strike as hard as any weapon. We cannot go on fighting. Even the old men know this."

This admission relieved Maggot. "What do we do now?"

"Squandral argues that we should sue for peace, much as he and my father did thirty years ago. He argues that we have proven ourselves as men, and the invaders will show us the respect due to brave men."

"Heh," Maggot said. "That would be good."

"I do not think that is the direction this river runs." Sinnglas indicated the charms around Maggot's neck. "I ask you one last time: will you not use the invader's magic against him, to help us?"

Maggot covered the forgotten ampules with his hand. "I do not know how."

Sinnglas tapped the ground with his knuckles. "Then we must flee for a safe place. The men we fight today move like a storm coming over the hills. We are helpless to stop it. Once we cross over the ridge behind us, we can follow the wall of the mountains north. We can cross through the high gap, into the next valley, and return south to our families. It is a longer way, but safer, and with luck and the blessings of the spirits we can return before the Lion's army comes. We will have to pack up our village and move. Perhaps over the mountains, toward the sea."

He did not sound hopeful as he said this. Maggot considered it for a few moments. "I do not want to go in that direction."

"I had hoped you would come with us, my friend."

Pisqueto set down his arrow and his feathers. "No, Maqwet is right. I, too, will stay with Squandral and fight."

"Brother!" Sinnglas's eyebrows drew up in alarm. "Think of our mother—come, flee with us, and plant your anger as a crop you will harvest next year and the year after that." He twisted his head back to Maggot. "Will you also stay with Squandral? Have you no mother? Will she not weep to see you throw your life needlessly away?"

"My mother—" Maggot stopped.

Sinnglas and Pisqueto watched him closely.

"My mother was to me like rain to growing things or darkness is to roots. She sent me in this direction, to join men like myself. I think she would"—he couldn't think of the word in Sinnglas's language, not even the equivalent, so he used the troll word—"*roll-over-and-over-in-the-odor-of-grief* to see what I have seen today. To see what I have done. I will not war anymore."

"I will stay and fight at Squandral's side," Pisqueto said. "Until the last invader is killed or they let us live in peace."

Sinnglas's lips thinned. "Very well, then. Every man must follow his own path as he sees it laid before him, whether it leads to war or away from the lodge of his mother."

Maggot gazed upon the army gathering in the woods below, searching the faces for First. The air had the dry, sharp fragrance of summer, filled with the buzz of flies and the whir of insects.

"I will go part of the way with you," he said. The woman he wanted was not in either of these armies. Nor was there any lion here for him to slay to give her. "But when you cross the mountains, I will turn back and go west."

"That will take you into the heartland of the invaders."

"Good," Maggot said. He sat cross-legged, rubbing his tired hands together. Pisqueto picked up his arrow, and resumed tying feathers to its shaft. Sinnglas stirred, and then let himself settle down to the same absolute stillness as Maggot.

"Heh," he said finally.

CHAPTER 18

Late in the afternoon, the invaders made one concerted charge up the hillside, with the pikemen behind the shields pushing as far as the fallen tulip tree that blocked the ridge.

Maggot stood between Sinnglas and Pisqueto, batting aside the pikes and thrusting back the shields with a long branch to create openings for their spear and arrows. His exhilaration slowly exhausted itself until he was leaning on his branch during the increasingly longer periods between assaults. When the attackers slid down the slope again near sunset, Maggot palmed the sweat off his forehead and body. Only a very few warriors yipped in celebration.

Maggot turned to Sinnglas. "Will they go away now?"

"No, that was just to pin us here," Sinnglas said, rolling his shoulders. "The knights and the mammut will attack us up the long trail tomorrow morning while those below cut off our escape."

The mountain loomed behind Maggot.

"So we will leave tonight," Sinnglas said quietly. "As soon as the moon is gone down."

"Heh," Pisqueto muttered nearby. Picking up his remaining arrows, he met Maggot's eyes and lifted his chin toward Squandral's men.

When Maggot thrust out his tongue, a smile flickered over Pisqueto's face and disappeared—all the youthfulness had gone out of his expression. Catching himself, Maggot shook his head, and Pisqueto ran off to join Squandral's men without saying any farewells. Leaning on the tree and studying the woods below, Sinnglas didn't see his brother's departure.

Maggot massaged his sore neck and looked at the sky, wishing for darkness.

Sinnglas, with Maggot and nine other men, offered to guard the breastwork against any night attacks. In the full dark, while most of the warriors snatched fitful sleep, the eleven men slipped over the side and ran down toward the enemy camp where the slope widened into a rolling meadow below the trees.

Gathering speed as they ran, Sinnglas's men vaulted a thin line of guards at the bottom of the hill and ran through the camp, screaming and striking random blows at sleeping men. Maggot's heel landed in someone's stomach, producing an audible exclamation, but otherwise he did no one any harm. As the invaders raised a cry and rushed to defend themselves, Maggot and the others dashed across the meadow and were free.

The running figures rejoined each other. As Sinnglas led them north, along a narrow, tree-covered trail in the shadow of the mountain, Maggot counted everyone and hurried up to Sinnglas's side.

"There are only nine of us now," he whispered.

Sinnglas grunted. "Like Pisqueto, others have chosen their own paths again."

He led them north through the chilling night, along narrow, tree-crowded trails in the shadow of the mountain, ever higher until they reached a flat knob above the trees that Maggot would not have recognized as a gap. Sinnglas, however, picked out a treacherous, curving route to the cold summit. From the top, a mist-filled valley opened below, and beyond it, looming like a wall against the dawn, another long ridge of mountains.

Across that second ridge of mountains lay the way back to the Deep Cave band of trolls. Breathing that familiar air, Maggot's footsteps faltered. He stopped.

The other men passed him, until Sinnglas paused, no more than a dark shape farther down the barren trail. "Will you not choose differently, and come with us?" Sinnglas asked.

Maggot's hand went to his chest to grasp the charms that hung there on their silver threads. He did not know which way to find the woman. But he knew he must go back and try.

"I did not come this far to go back," he said with a little half shrug, rolling his shoulders forward and then forgetting to relax them again.

Sinnglas lifted his chin. "The spirits will bring us together again. There will always be food for you in my home."

"And for you in mine," Maggot answered as he had heard others say.

Sinnglas's face widened into a grin. "Send word when you have found that home, Maqwet. My brother."

The two men walked to each other and gripped forearms. Letting go, Sinnglas turned and rejoined the others. They ran down the mountainside until they disappeared like shadows slipping into deep water.

Maggot shivered. He was alone again. He shook himself to dispel the cold like a coat of dust, and turned back, slouching forward as he ran.

Sleepy shreds of fog, too weary yet to rise with the sun, obscured the mountainside down among the trees. Maggot ghosted his way through this distanceless world, unsure which path he followed across the steep slopes. He went downhill, taking vertical paths when he came to dead ends, leaping out onto the branches of trees, then shin-nying down the trunks when he could find no other way.

The fog burned away toward noon, but a great weariness settled on Maggot. He found a hollow spot on the slope, halfway above one trail, halfway below another, where something had once been washed away. He buried himself beneath a pile of leaves and branches, plummeting into heavy, thoughtless sleep.

Hushed voices woke him. He rolled over, still blanketed in lethargy, not knowing how long he'd slept, and wondered if he should investigate.

He heard the voices again—they were speaking Sinnglas's tongue. He could make out the word *invaders*.

Slowly poking his head up through the leaves, Maggot heard the voices come from the trail above him. He glimpsed a few heads passing between the trees. The men were moving toward the fighting, or where the fighting had been.

He eased out of his hiding spot, climbing up the hill for a closer look. Bits of light penetrated into the gauzy air between the high treetops. The men—no, boys: they appeared to be as young as Pisqueto or younger—stood uncertainly on the trail, discussing whether they should go on. At first Maggot took them for stragglers, warriors separated from their vil-lage leaders. But as he crept along the hillside, he saw two quivers on most backs and no sign of bandages. They were latecomers, probably from the villages south of Custalo's, boys just arriving to join the war.

Stupid people, not knowing the war was over.

Maggot crouched across the trail and pulled himself up the slope, crossing over until he found a rotted log above them. He put a foot on it to see if it would rock—it did—and then he kicked it over the edge. As it crashed down, he drummed out a troll's warning on his chest.

Below him, the boys ran back the way they had come. Maggot hurled stones through the trees at them, stopping only to pound his chest and holler again.

When they had retreated out of sight, he hunkered down and slouched forward, resting on his hands. The war was over.

He sniffed the air for something to eat. Remembering, as if from a dream, the bag at his belt, he scooped all the remaining food into his mouth and swallowed it in a gulp. He threw down the bag and went searching for something to drink.

Sinnglas had traversed the distance from the scene of the fighting to the gap in the mountains in a single night, but then he knew where he was going and ran with a purpose. Maggot meandered on the way back, on and off the trails, stopping again to nap beneath a log when he felt tired.

He moved more purposefully when the sun hunted over the western horizon, until he sniffed faint smoke and followed it to a small clearing nested in the hillsides.

Maybe thirty warriors were gathered around a small fire. They passed a pipe around the circle, the smell of it staining the air. Maggot looked for Pisqueto, but many of the younger men were gone. Perhaps they were dead, and perhaps they only lured the invaders in another direction.

"—we must gather our families, and flee across the mountains," Custalo was saying, loud enough for all the men to hear. "There is no shame in the wolf, when he runs away from the lion and its dagger teeth."

Squandral took the pipe and puffed at it deliberately before speaking. The flickering firelight exaggerated the sharpness of his features.

A tightness cramped in Maggot's belly. He crept close to the circle, and squatted, suppressing the sound of his grunt.

Passing the pipe to the man beside him, Squandral gestured sharply with his hands. "They have insulted us again. This time we must hunt the Lion down and kill it. Let us go back now and attack the invaders, striking them in the night—"

Maggot's ball of steaming dung hit the side of Squandral's head and splattered on the trollbird, Menato, who sat beside him. Men scattered, jumping up and grabbing their weapons.

Stupid people. Maggot drummed a rude tattoo upon his chest and keened mockingly before crouching down and running off to a new location. The men froze where they stood, wrapped in the fire's honey-golden glow like flies trapped in amber.

"It is one of the giants," Custalo said. "For the last four or five years, they have been an affliction on my people, coming in the night to steal our clothes and weapons."

"That does not sound like the giants," Squandral said. Or at least that's what Maggot thought he said; his nasally voice was hard to understand.

"We fear you not!" Menato shouted, still scrubbing furiously at his face.

Squandral waved him to silence. The broad-shouldered, craggy-faced old man lifted a hand to shield his eyes. It held an arrow. He stared into the darkness with the bow in his other hand. Maggot, now almost behind them, pounded his chest again and watched them spin. Squandral's arrow came first, followed by several others, but Maggot had moved away instantly. The missiles shot through the brush or sailed above his head and into the night.

After several moments of silence, one man asked, "Do you think we hit it?"

"Perhaps it was only up to mischief and we have driven it off," Custalo suggested. "That happens also sometimes."

Squandral hushed them all to silence, then gestured to Menato, who kicked the small fire. The sparks scattered, spinning upward as they cooled to cinders and the light of the fire sputtered out.

After that they whispered quietly.

A group of three crept out away from the camp, in Maggot's direction, but he withdrew, avoiding them. When they were well out from the camp, he crawled between them, raised his head, and screeched laughter. He scampered out of the way as the two groups unleashed arrows at one another. One of the men in the camp was struck. Squandral shouted at the other men to return.

Maggot crouched behind a tree where they would not see him, and choked down his laughter until his chest ached.

One group argued loudly with Custalo, and then slipped away, six or seven of them. Soon another group split off and ran away into the darkness, and then another departed, and another, until all had gone in the same direction as Sinnglas.

Maggot sat in the dark and scratched himself. He considered following them, but they no longer interested him. Wiping his hand clean on the grass, he grabbed hold of the glass jewels on his necklace. He had two of them. He would find the woman again, and give her one to show his interest.

By morning, he'd become distracted by his search for something more to drink than the dew he licked off rocks and leaves. He found a pool of murky water in a gully filled with rotting logs. The few sips he took didn't taste so good, but when he broke open the wood he discovered grubs. He was chewing a mouthful of them when the smell of smoke and roasting flesh reached his nose. Hurrying after it, he found himself in the empty battlefield beneath the tall poplars.

The remains of a huge bonfire smoldered in a clearing. Maggot proceeded carefully in order to avoid the invaders, but found none, only dead warriors, both invader and Wyndan, piled up about the slaughtered mammut and set aflame. All the ground around the mound of flesh had been cleared of brush, and a trench dug, so that the fire would not spread.

The mammut's fat puddled inside its corpse, sending up a smokeless blue flame that made the air twitch and shiver. Though the night was nearly over, insects came from far away to hurl themselves into the fire.

It was much the same way that his friend, Sinnglas, and the other warriors had hurled themselves into war.

Tiny bats dipped and spun out of the sky, screeching as they ate. Maggot remembered his own hunger, and the taste of meat, so he left the pile of blackened, smoldering bones.

He noticed a squirrel's nest, a hive-shaped mass of leaves and twigs, in the crook of a branch, so he climbed up. He thrust his hand into the nest and grabbed hold of anything he could reach. The leaves thrashed wildly, and then teeth sunk into his thumb. He jerked his hand out—a squirming ball of reddish-gray fur covered his fist.

The tree swayed as he tried to tighten his grip. Wriggling free of his clutch, the squirrel ran up Maggot's arm, the tiny claws digging into his skin, and leapt to the branch, and then to another tree, and disappeared.

Maggot dropped back to the ground and sucked his bleeding thumb. The taste was sharp and bitter in his mouth. He was very hungry.

Somewhere nearby, snarls answered the screech of carrion birds. He followed the sound just as his mother had taught him. Trolls did not kill one another for food, but perhaps people killed each other to feed the beasts.

Dew sheened metal lying in the brush, weapons scattered like fruit from a murderous tree. Maggot still had the knife in the sheath around his neck and needed nothing more, so he passed by them.

He made his way toward the sound of crows and nearly stumbled over wild dogs. They gazed at him with yellow eyes and sated bellies as he circled their rending of some warrior's headless corpse. One pink-headed, turkey-necked vulture perched on something in the crook of a tree. Crows rocked on the branch above it, flying off as Maggot approached. The vulture flapped its wings at him, screeching its anger, then tried to fly away with his trophy, but dropped it.

Maggot ran and picked it up—a severed head with its eyes pecked out and a half-eaten tongue hanging out of its mouth. He thought it might be the man who'd called him a giant, but death changed a man's features beyond easy recognition.

Voices cracked the stillness. The wild dogs lifted their heads at the sound and slunk away.

Maggot bit down on a lock of the dead man's hair and, carrying the head in his mouth, wrapped his hands around the trunk and braced his feet against the bark to climb into one of the trees. Men never looked up high in the trees.

Five, then six men came out of the woods, one of them clinking as he carried an armload of weapons. They were gathering anything that had been missed before.

Forty feet up in the air, Maggot lay flat on one of the tulip's wide branches. He held the head in his fist, swinging it until he'd judged the weight and distance. Then he let go.

The dead man's head sailed through the air. As it began its downward arc, Maggot threw his voice after it.

"Yaaaaah!"

The men looked up at the moment the head bounced off the man carrying the weapons. He screamed, and the collection of pikes and arrows clattered to the ground. When he ran, the others followed him. Two, who were braver, paused a short distance away, but their friends continued running, and so they did too.

Maggot wrapped his hands around the trunk and quickly lowered himself to the ground. He picked up the head and stuffed it down a groundhog hole so they wouldn't be able to find it. Then he ran on, following the old faint tug in his heart toward the lower valleys.

The invaders left a trail of trampled grass and stinking mounds of mammut manure that even a stone could track. But by following them, Maggot went hungry. The game scattered ahead of them, while a pack of wolves and groups of wild dogs followed warily behind, eating any carrion or scraps and scaring all the rodents and small animals into hiding. Maggot caught grasshoppers, climbed trees for eggs, and gathered pods of seeds—little meals here and there.

When the trail led to the banks of an unfamiliar river that curved between rough hills, it turned upstream toward the headwaters. One morning he came to the river's source and found the cold ashes of the invaders' camp. He was less than a day behind them now. He wasn't following the army for any special purpose, but they seemed to be headed the same direction as he was. Crossing over the watershed, he traced their path until it joined a similar stream on the other side.

He followed it all day and ran on into the twilight, chasing his hunger. By the first full measure of darkness he came to a cluster of buildings like the ones he had attacked with Sinnglas. It seemed like a place to find something to eat. He approached cautiously, crouching toward a blank wall iced over by moonlight—

And he remembered the woman he had sliced open, the way she'd sat against the wall when she fell, the sound of her voice as she grunted. A hard knot of bile swirled in his throat.

He held onto his hunger and fled.

He passed several similar buildings in quick succession, sitting beside the trail or on the hills above it. Most were lit within by fires. Then suddenly the trail opened onto a wider valley flanked by tree-covered slopes and overlooked by a bare, bedrock hill. A stone lodge many times larger than any he'd seen in Damaqua's village or elsewhere occupied the heights. He ran under the trees, stirring the old pine needles with his feet, smelling nothing more than their scent, until the cries of animals and men rose up into the night.

A camp of tents—like the very first one he'd seen, beside the river —was spread on the cleared land below the stony bluff of the lodge. Huge bonfires licked the night with tongues of flame, and the scent of cooking meat filled the air. Maggot slipped through the trees until he was within a few hundred feet, close enough to hear voices without words. A group crossed in front of the fire, and Maggot saw that one of them had a vaguely familiar bulk. Trollbelly. One of the men who'd been hunting the lion.

A thinner figure the same height followed Trollbelly, stopped, put fists on hips. Laughter arrowed through the darkness straight at Maggot.

The woman!

It wasn't possible. But it was true. There she was.

His hand clasped the dangling pair of necklaces. How was he supposed to go and give her one? She was only a silhouette in the shadows, beyond his reach or understanding.

He felt stupid. He didn't know how to be people at all. He looked at himself, dirty, nearly unclothed, more like a troll than a man.

She passed beyond the fire and was gone.

An itch began between Maggot's shoulders, shooting down his back to his feet. Retreating through the trees, Maggot wheeled away from the soldiers and the camp and the woman, walking at first, then jogging, until he came to a deeply rutted track that followed the high bank of a stream, where he broke into a run. The stream wound through a yellow-green valley, like a long, brown snake slithering through the grass, all the colors muted in the moonlight. It twisted through a cluster of hills, doubling back on itself like a small animal fleeing a predator, growing into a river as it went.

The river babbled as it dropped sharply, flowing precipitously over rocks. Maggot jumped down the hills, from stone to stone. With the last drops in elevation, the river widened even more, and the surface smoothed out into deeper waters, and Maggot knelt at the water's edge to drink. When he rose, he forced himself to keep walking so he wouldn't tighten up. As he rounded another curve, he saw a yellow light flickering in the distance on the far side of the water.

He approached slowly. The light came from a small building at the river's edge. Maggot would have circled around it, but a dark and regular shape stretched across the water.

Maggot's stride shortened, faltered.

This was a *bridge*. Like a log across a ravine or a slab of stone across a fissure inside a cave. But to where? Where did he want to go?

A man came around the corner of the small building, carrying a torch in one hand and some kind of sack in the other. His long hair was yellowed by the flame. Something inside the sack he carried squirmed and mewed. He walked with the cautious, stiff steps of the old down to the water's edge, placed the torch in a holder, and began to sing.

> *"There was a ripple on the river*
> *Gleaming in the starlight,*
> *As it flowed across the rocky ford*
> *Against the current in the dark night."*

The old man's voice wavered like a palsied hand, but still the slow, lilting chant hooked Maggot's attention and pulled him closer: the words were in the language of trolls.

Or close, if not quite the same tongue. They sounded foreign but familiar to Maggot, like the words used by trolls in the Raven Rock band far to the north. He did not understand some of the words at all.

Directly across from the old man, he slipped down the muddy bank to listen. As the words flowed over the water, the melody changed to something sharper, more stochastic.

"On this side, we're only guests,
We beg our meals and a place to rest.
When it's time to journey home,
Let the river demons come."

A shimmering rose beneath the bridge, a luminescence Maggot first took for a liquid reflection of the Milky Way. Then he remembered sitting on the hillside near Squandral's town, and he leaned forward.

An Old One!

The river here was small in comparison to that one, no more than fifty feet across, and shallow enough to see the bottom. It didn't seem nearly big enough to contain the twenty-foot-long beast that swam slowly to the surface.

"When the demon calls we answer,
And carry it an offering;
Where the demon goes we soon abandon,
And leave the others to their suffering."

The old man waded knee-deep into the water, rocking back and forth as he chanted, his voice growing stronger. The shape glided toward him and stopped. A pale, glimmering head rose out of the water on a reticulated neck, almost level with the old man's face. It swayed back and forth to the rhythm of the song and the old man's motion.

Maggot recalled the way the deer had been bewitched.

"Silent rows the loaded ferry,
Afterward no bones to bury;
Ripple, ripple, running red,
Blanketing the demon's bed."

As he sang this last verse, the old man lifted the squirming bag by its topstrings and the Old One flared its head, leaning back as if to strike.

268 ⁀ THE PRODIGAL TROLL

Maggot jumped up, pounded out the danger warning on his chest, and cupped his hands to his mouth.

"Don't answer it! Run away!"

The song wavered and broke as the old man staggered back toward the bank. The demon curled its head at the sound, and then faster than one would think something that size could move, it twisted, coiling and uncoiling, across the water.

Maggot's feet slipped in the muddy bank, and his hunger- and travel-racked reflexes were too slow to recover. The scaly face shot up from the water, flaring its head.

A mist enveloped Maggot, stinging his eyes and nose, burning his throat like the naked sun. He clutched his face, sliding down the concave bank toward the water. His limbs began to go slack. Something smooth and wet encircled his legs—he would have screamed, or kicked, if he could, but his body felt as it did when he woke suddenly from a dream, paralyzed and unable to move.

Far away, he heard the voice of the old man. The words were like fish under ice: Maggot saw their shape, but he couldn't reach them. Even with his eyes squeezed shut, the world took on a silver sheen shot with coruscating color.

The coils tightened around his legs and bent them against each other awkwardly, painfully. Maggot slid slowly backward, his numb fingers gouging thick clay. The tightening reached his chest. He inhaled and could not exhale.

Then the world turned from silver to black and the fires were extinguished. Maggot thought it might be a relief—desire sank into deep water and released all dreams.

— Part 4 —
HOMECOMING

CHAPTER 19

I t is the deepest cave he has ever known, perfectly, comfortingly dark at the bottom. His spirit, cut loose from his body, floats. He ascends the large, coal-black tunnel toward the surface, and when he grasps at the walls to slow his passage, his hands slip like bare feet on wet boulders.

At the end of the tunnel the noontime sun awaits, a faint spark at first, growing into a radiant circle of heat. Maggot sees it and he is afraid. The sun is death, the light is death, and he longs to go back down into the safety of the darkness. He wails, like a child again, like a frightened baby, noise pounding in his ears like a waterfall on the rocks. He calls out for someone, anyone, to grab him, to pull him back, but he has left all the trolls behind. Even his mother can come only partway up the tunnel, and she shouts at him, but her voice grows cold like stone in the winter, filled with crystals of ice, until it cracks, and falls apart in shards and splinters.

The sun fills everything except the very lip of the cave. Maggot twists, thrusts out his hands to clutch at this dark circle that lingers at the very edge of his vision, sticks out his feet to brace against the wall of the tunnel. His limbs are too heavy to budge, immobile as though they're confined in ropes or vines.

Somehow he stops his motion.

And he sees that the cave is no cave, but a mouth and a throat and he is on the inside. The sun is no sun, but an egg, as yellow as yolk, with cracks running through it. Inside the egg he hears a voice. Then suddenly something snaps and he falls, dropping like a spider when its thread is severed. He plummets down the throat until it widens like a vast cavern, and the cavern becomes the night and fills with stars. He rushes toward the earth, twisting over and over as he falls, and the ground rushes up to meet him, with the silver turtle egg of the full moon laughing at him, and then he hits the ground, slams into the ground and slides right through it, until the dirt falls in all around him and smothers him like a root.

So he lies there like a root, and patiently waits to flower. Water trickles in through the dirt and reaches his hard throat, and he drinks. The hard thing inside him cracks like a nut in its season. It is enough for him to send out a single thread, a searching tendril of thought shaped like a sentence.

"Where am I?"

In the land of the dead, comes the reply.

But Maggot knows that already. He exhausted himself to find out nothing new, and for a long time he lies in the thick, heavy miasmal dark, gulping the water that trickles down to his inanimate throat. What he wants to find is a way out, to the land where other spirits reside. He sends out new shoots of thought, but before they break free of the rough-packed ground, something reaches down to him with a voice like liquid light.

Who are you? it asks.

Maggot has to think about this question, for a time that stretches out like seasons full of frost and the first soft warmth of spring, through the dew and fog of summer, across crystals frozen on the tips of grass. The answer begins like another searching shoot, a pale white hair that wriggles slowly upward, crawling through the humus to the surface.

"I am me," he answers.

The great disappointment at this response penetrates all the layers that separate them, confusing Maggot. His failure to communicate smothers him, and finally he ceases struggling to break free. The moment he ceases, he unknits all the potential locked up in the inert vegetable knob he has become, transforming it into a host of roots and fronds, bursting forth in every direction at once, down farther into the darkness and up toward the light. The tendrils become fingers, and with one green hand he takes hold of the darkness deep underground and with the other he reaches up and clutches the round leather ball of the sun. And though it burns his palm he does not let go.

He opens his eyes for the very first time, and the rays of the sun stab at them like daggers, but he does not flinch or draw away. There is a difference between fearlessness and courage, between stalking the demon and facing the demon's maw, and he has crossed the watershed that divides these two rivers of experience.

The sun sees it also. It sheathes its blades.

He lay under blankets on the floor in the corner of a small, clean room illuminated by large windows. When he tried to speak, he heard his voice break like a dry branch. A man came across the room to stare at him. It was the old man, the one he saw by the riverside. His silver hair hung in long clumps down his side. Bronze and copper flames danced around his head, like lights in the northern sky.

The old man poured a sour water into Maggot's mouth, the merest trickle. It spilled from the corner of his lips. Something small and warm curled against him, rumbling.

"Too much life in you for death to swallow whole," the old man said, in the language of the trolls.

"How long?" Maggot asked.

"Nights," muttered the man. "Two, three. Count the first, don't count the first."

"It was not yet dawn, when I saw you."

"Yes. True." It was the same word in the language of the trolls, but he repeated it twice. He seems unhappy at this admission. "Three nights."

"Three."

Maggot closed his eyes and slept, as both men and trolls did when they arrived safely home at a long journey's end. He felt that he had not slept in a long time, if ever.

He awoke again in sunlight to the sound of hammering, screaming, and cruel laughter. Cries of anger and defiance came from voices he almost recognized. He listened a long time, taking it for a fever dream. Surely the pack of tiny cats—orange, black, gray, and white—running in and out of the house, basking in the sunlight, were part of a fever dream. The scent of their urine and spray was too intense to be real, and the pregnant orange one that curled up next to him in the blankets made a purring noise unlike anything he'd ever heard.

He poked that little cat experimentally. The scratch along his thumb felt real enough, so he was pulling the lips back to look at its teeth when the old man entered the house.

"What is that noise?" Maggot asked, looking to the window.

"*Wyndans*," he said, a word that Maggot remembered on another man's lips. The old man looked out the small window that faced the river, and the corners of his mouth speared down. "They came to scavenge peace. I told him not to come. Before. When he came for the demon's skin. No good-smell is to come."

He used the words haltingly, as Maggot did when speaking Sinn-glas's tongue. Maggot pushed back his layers of blankets and attempted to rise to see out the window also. "Who?"

The old man came and pushed him back down into the covers firmly, irresistibly but without violence. Without answers either. Maggot was too weak to resist and let the coverlets form a cocoon about him. The small orange cat curled up in the hollow by his stomach.

The old man boiled a pot of water, making tea as Sinnglas's wife had sometimes done. Outside, someone screamed.

Maggot stared at the old man. The old man stared into his cup at the leaves. The cat closed its eyes and slept.

The screaming lasted a long time.

Maggot woke in the dark, feeling hot and sluggish, dry and empty. The cat was asleep on his face, and it made his face itch, so he pushed it away.

The old man sat by the hearth, with his back to Maggot, chanting. The teapot fire had burned down to coals, but his shadows twitched and leapt across the walls as if they were cast more by the faint, shim-mery lights that danced about his head. Sometimes Maggot saw those lights, and sometimes they blinked out of his view.

Without turning or looking up, the old man stopped his song. "Are you hungry, yes, true?"

"Yes," croaked Maggot.

He tapped his head. "Beside you."

Maggot rolled to his side and saw the cup and bowl. He wet his throat first with the tepid tea, then began to scoop the food into his mouth. Boiled oats mixed with sticky syrup. The cat came back, leaned its head down to sniff at the bowl, thrust out a pink tongue.

In the corner opposite him, beside the old man, Maggot saw the head of the Old One that had attacked him.

"Eat with slowly," said the old man.

"Thank you," answered Maggot. "Where—"

The man grunted, then put his hands on the floor and turned himself around, holding one hand across his waist, the other extended. "Name yourself; then name your favor. My name is Banya, and welcome to my home."

"I will remember your stink, Banya. My name is Maggot. Where—"

"Maggot? Not Claye?"

"Maggot. Little, white, crawls on dead things." He wiggled his finger like a worm.

The old man leaned forward, face grimacing in concentration, clearly puzzled. "Maggot is not a name for men. Your name is Claye."

"Claye?" He thought that perhaps the old man—Banya—was using the wrong words or not understanding him. "Sinnglas called me Maqwet."

"Sinnglas? That's not a name to be spoken aloud here," he said suddenly in Sinnglas's tongue, leaning back and glancing toward the door. "You speak his tongue?"

"Yes."

"I should not mention that name again, were I you. The tongue, where did you learn it?"

"From Sinnglas." Maggot felt very confused now. He put down the bowl, full and sleepy.

Banya scowled. The flames that licked about his head flickered as if in agitation. "No. The tongue of the *Collegis*."

"I know only the tongue my mother taught me," Maggot said in the trolls' language again.

"Yes, true! That tongue. Too long since with Collegis I, too short with." Banya started rocking, and the shimmering flames cooled, calmed. He shifted back to Sinnglas's tongue. "I know your mother. She taught you not."

"You know Windy?" Maggot pushed himself upright off his elbow, too quickly. Black dots spun before his eyes, and he sunk dizzily back among the bearskins and blankets. The cat jumped to get out from under him.

"Windy?"

Maggot whistled like a breeze through rocks. "Windy."

Banya resumed his rocking, staring at Maggot instead of the fire. He did this for a long time, saying nothing. He shook his head. "No, that is not her name. The resemblance to what she looked like then, and to her consort, is uncanny."

"Where?" Maggot asked. "Where did you learn to speak like trolls?" He switched to the word Sinnglas used. "Like giants? Was your mother also a giant?"

"Giants?" His eyes lit up, and he stopped moving. "Windy was a giant?"

"Yes."

"Say it three times, speak it true!"

"My mother was a giant. Yes, yes, yes."

"No!" He looked up fearfully, the fires like dancing spears. "You must only say it twice!"

"But you said—"

"Fool! Now you've drawn the attention of the jealous god!"

He rose, his knees cracking like ice in the spring sun. He took a bundle of herbs and set them alight, smudging a sweet smoke around the corner of the rooms, chanting quietly as if unwilling to let Maggot overhear him. He collected something else from a pot, grabbed a staff, and went outside. Maggot heard him at the four corners of the house, tapping.

When he returned, he would not speak to Maggot but sat by the fire instead, talking quietly to the dead face of the Old One. The cats rubbed against him, but he paid them no mind.

Maggot thought he napped briefly. He wasn't sure—he closed his eyes, he opened his eyes, nothing changed. Eventually he had to rise to relieve himself.

Seeing him struggle, Banya helped pull him to his feet, holding him up with a viny arm. The copper bracelets were cold on Maggot's skin. Together they hobbled out the door.

They faced away from the river. Maggot wanted to look across to see the source of the screaming, but Banya propped him up against a bush right by the door. As his stream splattered over the leaves and ran down the wall, Maggot began to laugh.

"What?" the old man asked.

"Heh—marking it as my cave."

Bracelets jingled, followed by a sharp sting as Banya slapped Maggot's bottom. A black cat started rubbing against his ankles, and he had a hard time finishing.

When they staggered back inside, Maggot propped himself up surrounded by the blankets. The small coals had gone out. The flames surrounding Banya's head had also cooled and faded away.

Banya shook his head and muttered. "Gruethrist took Lord Eleuate hunting for giants, once, when he first settled this valley. I hope Verlogh found no pleasure from it."

"What?" Maggot asked.

"I'm just thinking aloud," Banya said. "It is a habit of the old, bringing our thoughts into the air with the hope that they'll survive us."

The night was warm, but Maggot shivered. He thought he had a fever again.

"In the Collegis, some say that men stole language from the giants. The giants were created first and ruled all the land, but then men came; and though we were brute, speechless creatures we knew the secret of fire, and with fire we drove back the giants."

Maggot closed his eyes to listen to Banya's voice, and found an afterimage of the old man's radiant silhouette patinaed on the inside of his eyelids. He jerked upright, eyes open.

"Pramantha, beloved son of the goddess Bwnte and a mortal man, went out hunting in the mountains with other men and was attacked by the giants. He was very clever, however, and by means of gestures, he promised to show the giants how to extinguish fire if they would give him the secret of language. And then he showed them how to use water to quench flame."

"Heh," Maggot said. Trolls would like that.

"The giants gloated. They shattered the ice caps that covered the mountains. They grabbed the edges of the oceans and pulled them over the land. They deluged the world, intending to drown the sun and bring an end to daylight forever. But they kept Pramantha with them, teaching him the language as they had promised. And that night, after he had learned the language, Pramantha rekindled fire from a spark that he had hidden and cast it back into the sky, where the moon carried it to the sun and lit the fire anew."

"Ah," Maggot said. So the moon carried the sun's fire. That seemed true. "What happened then?"

"Pramantha gave language to all the people that survived, but each man shaped it to his own use, and soon none could speak to each other. Pramantha's heir founded the Collegis to preserve the true tongue and all the secrets of the earth Pramantha knew."

"No, what happened to the giants?"

Banya shrugged, and his voice grew lighter. "People prospered and the giants declined. Some say it is also because Pramantha stole magic from them, and made them less by it." In the tongue of the trolls he added, *"I haven't tasted it myself."*

Constantly rearranging the blankets as a barricade to the assaults of the cats that surrounded him, vying for attention, Maggot asked, "What is magic?"

After a moment's pause, Banya grasped one end of Maggot's blanket and held it up. "The world is a single continuous skin of invisible power. Things that happen in one place, change things in another. Something small causes a big change somewhere else. A butterfly flaps its wings in a field and all the way across the mountains, a wind stirs that knocks down trees. Magic is the way of finding those connections, and bending them to the use of people."

Maggot laughed. "That's not possible."

The old man reached under the blankets and pinched the sole of Maggot's foot. Maggot's leg kicked, scattering his covers and all the cats but the gray one.

"It isn't?" The old man snapped his fingers. "Something this small caused something that big."

"But that wasn't magic!"

"Heh." His mouth twitched down at the corners. "I do not have much talent except for singing and seeing. But you shine with the power like a beacon on a hilltop."

He paused, and Maggot said, *"The false-flavored nature."*

"Yes, true. They call it that also at the Collegis: *the false-flavored nature.* Magic, sorcery. The invisible power. The gods speak to one another with this invisible power. Like lightning in the sky. And just as lightning can be drawn down to the earth to a tall tree or an iron pole, the power of the gods can be drawn down also."

Maggot's head ached. He gave up fighting the cats, and the gray one settled in comfortably around him, its body warm, vibrating against his skin as it purred. "How—?"

Banya rose and went over to the head of the Old One. From the base of it, he gathered several items and returned to Maggot's side. He held up the two necklaces. Maggot's hand touched his chest, realizing they were gone.

"This hammer charm is the sigil of Verlogh," Banya said. "Verlogh is the god of justice and of revenge. This other is a waterdrop, swollen like Bwnte's pregnant belly. Bwnte is the goddess of fertility and death, of water and flood. These sigils were fashioned to smash the spell of an enemy." He placed them over Maggot's neck. "I return them to you now."

Looking at them, Maggot realized that the glow he thought he saw in them was really an inner light like the flames that flickered around Banya's head. He pressed his fingertips against them, wondering if the warmth he felt was the same.

"Used in the absence of a spell, these charms will react with the magic inherent in the earth itself, but how so, who can say. I beg you to take care of them and not to break them." He pushed the cats aside impatiently and pulled the covers back over. "You are weary—you must still rest. Here is your knife; I return it to you now. I'll place it here beside your bed."

His gestures, left hand under the right, seemed formal, required, but Maggot didn't know what it meant. He yawned and rolled over, feeling depleted. "Will you tell me this again?"

The wizard nodded. "I will. You are a man who has walked among the giants and in the land of the dead; you speak the wizard's tongue and carry magic items. When you are better, in another day or two, we will set out for the Collegis. I will take you as far as Lady Culufre's castle and her wizard. Perhaps I will go farther. I must seek absolution for slaying the demon to save you. We will have much time yet for your instruction."

He rose from Maggot's side, walked over to the window, and pulled back the cloth that covered it.

Pale dawn peeked in like a curious child.

"Stay awake a moment longer," Banya said. He picked up a small bag that clicked when it shook. He tugged on the drawstring. "Now that sunrise is upon us, will you ask the bones one question for me?

Maggot burrowed deep into the covers, pulling them up over his head so that only his eyes looked out. He shivered hard. The cat crawled up and sat on his neck. "What is it?"

The door burst open.

The first man through the door slammed his forearm into Banya's chest—the old man grunted as he fell—and the second man swung his warclub at the wizard's upraised arm. The club cracked against his wrist, and he cried out as the bones spilled out of the bag and clattered over the floor.

The cat turned its head, ears peaked. Maggot tried to lift his head, and the cat slipped, sinking its claws through the cover into Maggot's throat. He froze. He wanted to say *stop* but his throat was a dry riverbed over which no words flowed. He knew these men. Kinnicut, the smith from Sinnglas's village, and another whose name fluttered at the edge of his tongue.

Kinnicut's warclub fell again with another sharp crack, and again with a wetter thud. The first man lifted Banya's smashed head by its silver hair—his jaw hung broke and loose, a disconnected block of sagging flesh that drooped down to the chest—and took out his braid-cutting knife.

Kinnicut put a hand up to stop him. "Not the wizard's," he said. "It will bring evil spirits to the other side."

But the other man had already stopped. He tossed the head aside and pointed at the Old One sitting in the corner, emitting a wail of grief. "Aiieeeee!"

Kinnicut lifted the scaled visage reverently from its post. "It will make a fitting offering for our grandfather."

"Yes," the first man said. "Let it accompany him."

He kicked the door open. Kinnicut went first, carrying the Old One's head, and then they were gone.

Maggot shivered himself to stillness over a long time, like boiling water in a pot left on the fire while the stones grew cold. His body felt as numb and cold as stone, and as empty as a pot when he was done.

The cat jumped off the pile of skins and went over to sniff at Banya. A white cat had slipped in through the door, then a mix, and others, to gather at his body also.

"Meeeeeeew."

Maggot pushed off the blankets and rose. He put on the breech-cloth and belt, then the knife. He held the two charms around his neck, and stepped over to Banya's corpse. Too many cats swirled around it to count.

He bent to look at the spilled bones. They looked like the finger and hand bones of a troll, a big one. They were marked with symbols Maggot couldn't decipher, except for the two on top—a blank bone under one marked with a skull.

The door hung sideways, broken from its hinges. Leaving everything behind him undisturbed, Maggot stepped outside into the daylight and walked around the corner of the building.

On the hill across the river, past the bridge, three tall poles rose straight from the ground. Three bodies topped the poles.

Maggot walked slowly toward them.

CHAPTER 20

The stones of the bridge were smooth under Maggot's feet. They vibrated slightly, or pulsed, a warmth much like that of the charms around his throat. He looked down.

His gaze rolled off the bridge and into the rippling water. In the clear water beneath the central arch, he saw the headless body of the Old One filling the trench where it must have once lurked. Hundreds of silver shapes darted around it, picking at the flesh. Bones poked through the flesh, gleaming white, smooth and knobby, like stones polished by the flow of water. A new Old One, three or four feet long, settled along the spine, ready to take the other's place.

A crow shrieked three times in quick succession. Maggot lifted his head and continued across the bridge.

He saw the muddy bank covered with footprints where the Old One had attacked him. The road along that shore led upstream toward the big stone lodge where he'd seen the woman. A second stream entered the river just below the bridge. It flowed out of a gap between steep stone walls. Flood debris was tangled among the rocks. Maggot would have called it a river once, before he saw the rivers near Squandral's town. A path led from the bridge beside this stream, up to the hilltop where the three poles stood.

Maggot mounted the hillside. Purple-black grackles and bluejays hopped from branch to branch, making shrill warnings at his approach. Most of the birds perched in the trees were deciding if it was yet safe enough to feed on the feared shapes of the men. Even the vultures in the sky seemed wary.

Three poles, three bodies.

Piles of gifts were heaped up around the base of the first two poles: bowls of corn, offerings of weapons, fresh scalps with red hair and blonde and curly black among the bits of fingers, thumbs. At the bottom of the third post, the head of the Old One leaned backward with its mouth gaping at the sky. Offerings, according to the customs of Sinnglas's people, meant to carry the souls of the dead men down death's river to the eternally fertile land of heaven's valley.

The smell of blood mixed with filth, knotting Maggot's empty stomach.

All three men were naked, hands bound in front, with the sharpened stakes shoved between their buttocks and up through their bodies. The first man was Tanaghri; his face was distorted almost beyond recognition. Damaqua's face, beside him, appeared calm, but sad. There was, in dying, thought Maggot, an erasing of all lost votes and unshared meals. The bound hands of the two men were different; Tanaghri's clutched fistlike, Damaqua's open in supplication.

The thumbs of the third man twitched.

Gelapa. The wizard.

His face was empty, slack. Little beak-shaped bits of flesh were torn away from his cheeks and shoulder, tiny triangular gouges filled with crusts of blood. The point of the pole pressed against the skin of his right shoulder, caught at an odd angle beneath the bone.

The bound hand twitched once again.

Spirits could be willful; this one had lingered here for a purpose. "Grandfather," Maggot said softly. "They should not have done this thing. Do you wish to descend into the good night?"

Gelapa's eyelids fluttered.

"It is over then." Maggot drew his knife and stretched up to press it into Gelapa's heart—a short trickle of thin blood, almost none at all, perhaps none, then nothing.

Two black birds swooped in to peck at Tanaghri's face, screaming shrilly at Maggot, fearing his competition.

Ignoring them, Maggot went behind Gelapa's pole, moved the legs aside, and bent his shoulder against it. It tilted slowly, then stuck in the soil and stopped. He dragged it down far enough to slide the corpse off. It was amazingly light, a mere shell of a man, like the ones left by cicadas after the bug had crawled out and away.

He wasn't sure what to do.

Recalling the skins draped about the village pole, he carried the naked body down to the bridge and dropped it in the water. It sunk, surprisingly to Maggot for such a shell, and the current tugged it into the deep trench alongside the Old One's corpse. The fish scattered, like ripples from a splash, and slowly returned in odd numbers. The smaller Old One slithered across the body and covered it. If their skins had spoken to him, perhaps his skin would speak to them.

He saw three roads: upriver, toward the woman he wanted but did not know how to speak to; downriver, toward the light but ever-present tug in his chest; or through the gap marked by the shells of Damaqua and Tanaghri. That way lay Sinnglas. Sinnglas needed to know what had happened here.

Knowing he might follow all three paths eventually, Maggot chose the middle path, crossing the bridge and ascending the hill beyond the corpses.

The birds screamed at him, rising into the air as he approached and falling into the trees again as he passed. As the leagues fell away beneath his feet, he found his appetite again. Wild grapes dangled from vines that spiraled up the trees beside the little river. Some of the fruit lay shriveled and black on the vine, but some was still ripe. Maggot grabbed the vines, ripping them free of the leaves. He stripped away one cluster of grapes after another, shoving the dark, damp fruit into his mouth until his belly filled. Then he went down to the bank of the stream to wash the stringent aftertaste from his mouth and drink to quench his thirst.

Late in the day, he came to a wide meadow where the water curved around a small tree-covered rise with downed trees and a few boulders piled up among the roots. One branch dangled like a broken wing from a split trunk.

It was the same place he had been before, where he had first seen the woman and rescued Sinnglas, but it had been transformed, and so had he. Not full circle, then, but more like a grapevine climbing a branch or a tree, spiraling upward to reach a height where it might bear fruit.

Clouds of mosquitoes rose like fog at his presence, and he hurried on to escape them.

A vast, tense quiet filled the valley as he went on. Few animals were out, and all of them bolted at the scent of him. Sleeping when he grew tired and scavenging wild fruit when he was hungry, Maggot passed the night and another day before he neared Sinnglas's village.

Night fell again, but it did not bring comfort to Maggot. The moon hung like a pale lid in the sky. The stars—the eyes of trolls, the band of all the dead ones—came out to stare into the darkness at him.

As he came to the hill where the village sat, he saw that its walls had been knocked down. Young men whooped, but it didn't sound like the dancing Maggot had once joined there. Then a solitary mewl of pain winged across the night like a screech owl's mournful cry.

Maggot slowed his footsteps, drinking in the cool air as he walked up the slope to the place the gate had been.

The walls were tumbled and charred, but the damage extended far beyond that. The council lodge had been knocked down, all the lodges scattered, and the sacred post of the Old Ones where Gelapa had once sat no longer rose above the heads of the warriors gathered in a crowd.

Maggot turned his shoulders sideways to pass through the circle of men—there were exclamations of recognition—only to find Sinnglas in the middle. There were two men—

"Sinnglas, my brother," he said.

Sinnglas spun, his angry, contorted expression changing to a smile of joy. "Maqwet, my brother! How fitting that you join us now." He extended his arms, inviting Maggot to grip them. One hand held a knife.

Maggot took a half step forward and stopped.

There were two men tied to a pair of short stakes with kindling heaped about their feet. Small fires crackled amid the twigs and branches. One man was dead. The hair had been sawed off his head and hot coals heaped on the raw bone of his skull, and there was an odor of burnt and burning flesh. He had no shine about him at all. But one man still lived. Strips of skin had been cut from his chest and arms, but he breathed. Weak flames of green and yellow light spiked out from his head.

"You will stop," Maggot said simply.

With a puzzled frown, Sinnglas dropped his arms. The fire shimmered on his bloody blade.

Maggot pursed his lips toward the living prisoner. "You will cut him free and let me take him away from here."

Sinnglas laughed. "You were there when Keekyu died!"

"Nothing you do here will gather his bones."

"Do you know what they did to Damaqua?"

"I saw Damaqua—"

"He went to the invaders to sue for peace, to find out what he must do to protect the women and children of the village."

"—and I came here to tell you that his suffering is done."

Sinnglas's face twisted. "But our suffering goes on. Our fields have been destroyed. The voices of the Old Ones are stolen from us. Our women have no roofs to cover their heads or shelter their children—they hide in the mountains like wild beasts and expect us to give them peace and safety, to bring comfort to the spirits of the dead." He jabbed the knife at the prisoner. "This is how we give it to them."

Maggot finished his step forward, but two men moved to block his way. The glowering Kinnicut swung his long-handled warhammer. Pisqueto stood beside him—Maggot recognized him now, though he had not at the wizard's lodge. He was no longer a young man. Weeks of war had aged him years.

The rest of the men crowded in behind Maggot.

"Over the mountains," Sinnglas said, "where you come from, they may have other ways, but this is our way. You have been a friend to me, Maqwet. Do not make me your enemy here."

Some of the young men trilled, shrill cries that had a more anguished tone than they had before the war began.

The fire crackled. The prisoner let out a sigh.

"The war is done," Maggot answered finally. The charms weighed at his neck as he remembered what the wizard had told him of their power. "Cut him free."

Sinnglas shook his head no. Kinnicut yelled and raised his war-club, but Pisqueto blocked his arm. "Stop."

Kinnicut pulled his hand away and stepped back.

Sinnglas's face fell. "You too, Pisqueto? Will I have no brothers left to stand beside me?"

Pisqueto jerked his chin in Maggot's direction. "He fought beside us at the farm, chasing down the man outside, and he was also the first over the wall. He attacked the mammut with us—"

"But *I* brought it down!" Kinnicut said.

"Yet Maqwet shared the danger." Pisqueto looked at Sinnglas. "He saved your life from the flood and gave you back to us." He looked to the other men, an equal among them, speaking as a leader. "My friends, my relatives, we owe him one life in return."

Sinnglas turned his back to Maggot and Pisqueto, his head bowed, facing the darkness. "Take him, then."

Maggot ignored the roar of protest from the crowd and rushed forward to kick the coals and kindling away from the man's feet. Drawing his knife, he severed the ropes that bound the man's legs to the pole and those that held his arms behind his back. The man's clenched hands were covered with caked blood—either his fingers had been cut off or his fingernails removed. Maggot couldn't tell. When the last rope parted, the man groaned and pitched face first into the ground. He immediately attempted to push himself up with his hands, gasped in pain, and slumped again.

Maggot sheathed his knife. He lifted the man by his elbow, propping his shoulder to help him stand. The man said something Maggot didn't comprehend.

The warriors argued like trolls before a vote.

Sinnglas stood aside, arms crossed, refusing to look at the scene. "Leave him there, Maqwet, and you will still be my brother. If you keep walking, never show your braid to me again or I will cut it off."

"I am sorry, Sinnglas, my friend. It was good to have a brother. You will still be a brother to me. But war is done." Maggot helped the man limp toward the gate.

The warriors blocked his way, Kinnicut at their head. "Vulture," he said, "leave that carcass for us, or your body will feed the wild dogs with his."

Pisqueto stepped forward to intercede again, but Maggot grabbed the hammer charm around his neck and snapped the silver thread. "Step back or I will break the magic."

Pisqueto's face paled and he fell back.

Sinnglas spun around. "You would not use it to help me, but you'll use it against me?"

Kinnicut growled and lifted his hammer.

The glass snapped between Maggot's thumb and finger, drawing blood and a brief flash of light in shades of rust and crimson. The men faltered at the burst of fire.

A sound came like thunder from below them. It faded, then came again. The ground began to shake. The prisoner staggered on his unsteady feet, lurching off balance, and Maggot had to grasp him with both hands.

The first rumble became a roar, and the ground swayed from side to side. The damaged lodges bent like trees in a high wind, pieces falling off, the last posts toppling. Kinnicut dropped his warclub and covered his head, while others threw themselves into the dirt.

There was a short pause—

—then a sudden up-and-down bucking, like a bull ox with a wildcat on its back. It scattered people like seeds off a tree in the wind. Maggot fell one way, and the prisoner fell another. Then the earth was still.

Maggot climbed to his feet, pulling the injured man after him. Sinnglas stared lividly at him, his hands empty, the tone of his voice hurt instead of angry. "You had *this* power, but you would not use it to help me?"

"I did not know how to use it then." He hooked his arm around the other man's waist. "But I am using it to help you now. I will scavenge peace for you if I can."

The fire crackled. Wood cracked as another lodge fell over. Those sounded faint and far away to the deafening roar of Sinnglas's silence. Finally, he said, "Go then."

The other man wrapped an injured hand over Maggot's shoulder and shuffled his feet forward. Maggot led him toward the old gate and the path away from the dead village. Maggot's body groaned for rest, but he knew that Kinnicut and some of the others might choose a different path, whatever Sinnglas wanted, and hunt him and the prisoner down.

The prisoner seemed to sense the same thing. He walked on with grim determination, stumbling but staying upright. He cradled his right hand protectively against his body. They passed over wrecked fields to reach the meadows.

They needed distance and a safe place to hide.

"There is a den," Maggot said in Sinnglas's language, in case the other man understood it. "A troll and some people once lived together there."

Hills thick with trees disappeared behind them, and they crossed lush meadows. An owl swooped overhead but did not call to them. The man babbled low under his breath, lapsing into silences that stretched out for longer periods of time until he fell into a steady quiet, punctuated by his regular breathing and irregular exclamations. He stumbled several times, letting Maggot catch him, but each time he marched on.

They came to a low bank by the river, where they stooped to drink. The man scrubbed at his hands, weeping silently at the pain of the cold water.

"We must walk," Maggot said, repeating the phrase in the language of the trolls. The man seemed to understand, rising to walk again. They turned away from the river, toward a north-south range of hills and the den of bones. Pale, splintered moonlight sifted through the leaves and branches.

The man's eyes fluttered closed as he stomped steadily on. Just when Maggot was sure his companion had fallen asleep on his feet, the ground shook again, lightly, just enough to shake the leaves on the trees. The man's eyes jumped wide open in fear.

"Stay awake," Maggot told him. "We're almost there."

The man nodded, strongly, took two or three more steps, and his lids drooped shut again. He pitched forward, out of Maggot's grasp, and crashed into the ground. He got up, shaking. As he stumbled on, he spoke to Maggot, putting his crippled hands together and leaning his head sideways against them.

Maggot indicated the dark uneven line of hills before them. "Can you go a little farther?"

The man nodded, moving in the directions Maggot indicated, and didn't ask to stop again. Maggot put a hand on his elbow and guided him, pushing him as fast as he could stagger. When they were within a rock's throw of the hill, the man simply collapsed.

Maggot looked at the brightening sky. He saw the rounded shape of the mound at the top of the rise. Bending down, he lifted the man and tossed him over his shoulder. His body trembled under a weight more substantial than Gelapa's corpse. He dug his feet into the soil and trudged upward.

It felt as though he were pushing a boulder up a hill. Somehow, he reached the top. New vines and brush had overgrown the mound, but Maggot dragged the stranger through the hole in the wall. Morning light fell through the broken roof. Though his braid had been cut off, and he was naked, and pain had changed the shape of his face, there was no mistaking the man.

It was the one he'd called First, the soldier Maggot had seen in the valley all those months before, the one that had spared him in the battle beneath the tulip poplars.

As injured as he was, he could no longer be a First. But he would still know the woman that Maggot had given the lion's pelt to.

CHAPTER 21

While he was sleeping, Maggot's muscles had tightened like the strings on Keekyu's bow. When he awoke, he crawled on his knees and elbows, trying to stand, gave up, rolled over on his back, and slowly tried to stretch. Bad as he felt, the other man looked worse. He sat propped up against the wall like a man who'd drowsed off guarding something.

Years before, on the way south to visit Scoop Rock band, Windy had denned up for the day. This was at the time when Maggot had first begun to venture out by himself in the daylight, and he had gone out to a glade, where he hid behind a tree and watched a rabbit. A panther pounced out of the tall grass and caught it. The rabbit screeched, the panther chewed on it a bit, then let it go, only to swat it down when it tried to run.

Trap, release, swat, repeated over and over again.

Four bloody lines soaked the gray fur as the rabbit shrieked, rolled, and bolted. Maggot, upset, chucked sticks at the sleek and tawny cat, distracting it long enough for the rabbit to escape. That was before Maggot knew that, unlike the stocky bigtooth cats, panthers could climb trees. He was small enough then that he ascended out of its reach, swinging sticks at it until night fell and his mother came looking for him.

The man across from Maggot was no rabbit, but he had the same bloody lines across his chest: four long raw scabs, seeping a pink and yellowish fluid. His hands were balled up, cradled against his body. Maggot leaned forward—the man's feet were red like nearly ripe cherries, and covered with blisters that had torn during the long trek overland.

The stranger's eyes popped open. He straightened, back thumping hard against the wall.

Maggot didn't move, giving no sign of threat.

Seeing this, the man took a deep breath and let his hands relax. His right hand was missing fingers. He looked at the unburied skeletons, then met Maggot's eyes.

Maggot shrugged.

The man relaxed. He touched the three remaining fingers on his right hand to his lower lip and spoke a word.

His name! He was trying to give his name. The word had hard sounds, mixed together, that were difficult to reproduce. Nonetheless, Maggot touched his knuckles to his own jaw by way of introduction. "Maggot."

The man wrinkled his forehead. His injured hand shook as it tapped his mouth again and repeated his name emphatically.

Maggot tried to get his mouth around the word, but it was too much to swallow in the first bite. He put his knuckles on his chin again, as he tried to say it, and recalled his mistake when he met Sinnglas. He smiled at the memory—what a very short word to mean the *place-where-food-slips-in*.

"Chin," he said.

The man touched his lip a third time, repeating the word slowly and loudly like Windy talking to a deaf old troll.

Like a star showing up suddenly in the sky, Maggot realized: the *place-where-food-slips-in.* The man wanted water and food. "Thirsty?" he asked in Sinnglas's tongue, in case the other man understood it. He tapped his mouth with his fingers and beckoned him to follow. "Thirsty this way. Water is at bottom of hill. Drink for thirsty at bottom of hill. Thirsty, come this way."

The man dug his feet into the floor and tried to lever himself upright against the wall, but grimaced and stopped halfway. Maggot pointed to the hole and started crawling toward it. The man sank to his knees and elbows, dragging himself across the floor after Maggot. When they were outside, neither man could stand. The man crouched there with his shorn head leaning in the dirt, panting, chest heaving.

Maggot slowly moved around until his face was pressed against the wooden wall. Gripping the logs, he pulled himself upright, hand over hand, stretching his legs and back until he felt like he could stand again.

Helping the other man stand took considerably longer. With branches for crutches, they gimped down to the spring like a pair of three-legged herons. They collapsed by the little pool of water, lying on the soft grass to drink their fill. Maggot, having learned the habit of bathing from Sinnglas, scrubbed his face and limbs. While he finished, the other man cleaned and examined his own wounds, brows knit in intense concentration, a muscle knotted in his jaw. He soaked his feet and fingers for a long time in the icy cold water.

He talked to Maggot the whole time. Maggot listened, grunting encouragement from time to time, trying to catch the sounds of the words. The troll language rumbled and cracked, while the tongue of Sinnglas's people rolled on sibilantly like a stream over rocks. The stranger's words all fell short. They were sharp, barking and ringing like Kinnicut's hammer pounding iron against stone.

Above them the sky began to darken. The clouds over the western sky reflected the sunset in hues of pink and purple, shot with streaks of yellow.

Finally the man looked right at Maggot, stared him in the eyes, placing his injured right hand over his heart. Fresh blood flowed from the wounds. "Bran," he said. He tapped his heart for emphasis. "Bran."

Then he directed his knuckles at Maggot's chest.

Maggot repeated the gesture. "Maggot."

"Mhagha?" Bran leaned forward.

"Maggot," he repeated slowly.

"Mhuuuu-ghuuu . . ."

Remembering what Banya had told him, and too tired to work at anything more difficult, Maggot placed his hand over his own heart. "Claye," he said.

Bran smiled and nodded. "Claye."

Bran's feet became infected, swelling and leaking stinky pus. Sharp red lines shot up his legs, and a fever took his whole body, lasting on and off for days.

Maggot brought him water—not in a skull as he'd originally planned but in a hollow piece of wood he found in the dwelling. Beans and squash grew wild nearby, and there were berries on the hillsides and nuts not yet ripened on the trees. He found eggs, and caught a snake, and they had enough to eat.

They talked when Bran was coherent, and Maggot learned the names of the foods they ate and body parts and pieces of the landscape. By enacting a few motions, Maggot also learned the words for eating, drinking, walking. At other times Bran raved, swinging his stick, and then Maggot would retreat outside, waiting until he calmed again.

"I have to get out of this crypt," Bran said when the fever finally broke. He was so wasted, weak, and depleted that Maggot had to help him crawl outside and limp down to the spring.

A near-full moon filled the clearing with its pale light. They sat by the water and watched the sky. Maggot was hungry for meat, even carrion, if he could find it fresh. "Bran," he said. "What is—?" and he emitted a coughing bark.

Bran smiled. "That's very good. A deer, right?"

"Deer? Yes, deer. I am hunger for—"

"Hungry. Hungry for."

"I am hungry for deer. Or, what is—" and he lowed.

"Bison. That would be good to eat too. Here." Bran tilted his head back at the moon, cupped his scabbed-over hands to his mouth, and howled.

Maggot grinned and howled back, and soon the two of them were howling at the moon. Far away, over the distant ridge, they heard a querulous wolf howl back in response.

"Heh," Maggot said. He put his open hands atop his head and used the trollish word. "*Flathorned elk*. Now you speak *flathorned elk*."

"No," Bran answered. His smile was sad. "The wolf is the only animal I can imitate. I had to listen to too many of them when I was a young shepherd on my mother's farm. They'd come right down to the flock after the sheep. But I sat awake fearing their silence more than their howling."

"Is"—Maggot cupped his hands to his chest like breasts, and borrowed another trollish word—"*female* down you come from?"

"Women?" He smirked, turned his head. "There are women."

"Women, good," Maggot said seriously. "You take me. You speak me women." In his head, the noun was singular.

Perhaps Bran caught the earnestness in his tone of voice. "If you want. I will take you and *introduce* you *to* some women."

He turned his head toward the pool of water. He knew one woman in particular who would want to meet this strange man.

Portia, Lady Eleuate, had carried the dagger-toothed lion's pelt around their camp by the river, pointing out the stab wounds in it. "One man did this, and he did it with a *knife*."

300 ⟶ The Prodigal Troll

"It could be a spear," Bran had argued.

Portia was not beautiful in the manner most men desired women. Her features were too strong, and not especially feminine. But when her eyes flashed, the way they had at that comment, some men could not help but fall hopelessly in love with her. Bran had seen it happen, from far too close a vantage point.

She poked her finger through the holes. "Four stabs, close together, into the heart. Could you do that with a spear?"

He said nothing, because he could not.

"Perhaps it was sick," offered Sebius, the eunuch. "Or injured."

She flung the skin to the floor and snorted. "We bring a war mammut, half a dozen knights, soldiers, two dozen beaters, and we can't even *find* the lion. One man tracks it down, kills it with a knife, and brings the pelt to me." She grinned at that. "To *me*."

Her father knelt by the skin, examining the teeth and claws. "This animal was not sick or injured."

That's when her betrothed spoke. "You're lucky the wildman didn't stick his knife in you the same way."

"Lucky?" She had sneered at him. "Do you think you could stick your knife in me? Would any of you dare try? You'd get a broken blade for your trouble."

"Lady," Sebius said, trying to take her aside. "Lady, do not speak so vulgarly in the presence of men. You know how excitable they are, how ruled by their temper and emotion. And there is this to consider: the wildman *is* a killer."

"Captain Bran?" she said, pulling away.

"Yes, m'lady."

"Have you ever killed another man?"

He hesitated before answering. "You know I have, in service to the Baron."

She threw her arms up in the air. "Oh, no, Sebius! There's a killer present! I'm in horrible danger! Bran?"

"Yes, m'lady?"

"Baron Culufre could use the services of a man who can hunt down and kill a dagger-toothed lion without any help. It would free up his war mammut, his knights, his soldiers, and other men for more important tasks, like, oh, cutting down trees and building walls and staying close to the safety of their campfires. On his behalf, I charge you with finding this man."

"Yes, m'lady. As you wish."

Sebius had glared at him as if betrayed, while the other men grumbled. Portia had only smiled. "Or one just like him, as you prefer. If you think any one of you could do the same, then the search is done. No? I thought not."

And now he'd found him. Or been found.

The wild man cupped his hand at his crotch, trying to indicate something about the way men and women fit together. "Women, big there, smell?" he asked.

Bran thought about it. "No, that's not where women have their noses."

After a second, they both laughed, and after laughing, fell silent, each to his own thoughts. The wolf's howl sounded lonely as it ranged farther away.

Maggot was digging a hole. Inside their den, Bran carefully gathered the bones of the two people just as Maggot had gathered those of the infant troll. He was scraping a shallow trench in the dirt with a sharp-edged stone when he saw the gleam of metal. Brushing away the thin layer of leaves and dirt, he found a long knife like the one Bran had carried in the battle. His fingernails picked at the rust-flaked blade; the leather or fabric that clung to the hilt fell off in his grip.

"Here," he said, offering it to Bran.

"I can't take it," said Bran. Maggot thrust it at him, but he didn't take it. "Three times I tell you, I cannot take it."

"Take it," Maggot said.

"I am unworthy of the honor," Bran answered. "But since you asked three times, I will not insult you."

He received it on the palms of his ruined hands, holding the blade toward himself until Maggot released it. After considering the missing fingers on his right hand, he gripped the hilt of the sword and swung it lightly. The weapon toppled from his grasp, and both men jumped out of its way.

Maggot bent to retrieve the weapon, but Bran snatched it up in his left hand first, wincing as his fingers closed around it. He swung it more confidently, bending his knees to make a short stab. "It's not a bad weapon. I can clean the blade and restore it somewhat."

"You call that—?"

"A sword."

"Ass-hoard?"

"Sword."

"Sword. You will show me how to sword?"

"How to *wield* a sword. Yes, it will be my pleasure."

Maggot loved the way that Bran constantly corrected his language until he could sense the improvement. He did the same with the new weapon. Weeks passed in which Bran taught Maggot, sometimes with the sword, sometimes with branches. "No, no," he'd say. "Use your height, your reach. Every parry must be followed by a blow. Attack, always attack, at least until you are better."

While Maggot's skills improved, Bran's health did the same. Nails grew back in his remaining fingertips, frail, thin things that cracked and flaked, but nails. Where the fingertips were missing, he developed blisters, let them burst, and began the long slow process of developing calluses.

"How did you kill that lion?" Bran asked one evening, as they ate meat that Maggot had caught and Bran cooked. He mimed the daggerteeth.

Maggot pointed over the ridge, where it curved away north into the higher mountains. "The lion over there? I found the lion, I killed the lion. With this knife." He drew it from the sheath at his neck and handed it to Bran.

"It was sharper then, I hope."

"Yes," Maggot said. "Sinnglas show me how to"—he made a whetting motion—"stone to sharp knife. Maybe he not a good show-er. I think is time to find new knife."

"I will teach you how to keep it sharp," Bran said.

"Good," Maggot said, but he was not thinking about the knife. He rubbed the back of his hand over his mouth, sighing. "The woman, with the lion?"

"In the tent?" Bran asked. His eyes took on a distant look, as if he were seeing something beyond his reach. Maggot wasn't sure what it meant. "You mean Portia, Lady Eleuate."

"Huh?" Maggot said, not understanding. "Hair, long. Nose like—" He made a shape with his fingers.

"Portia."

Maggot repeated the name. "Speak me her."

"Speak to you of her?" Bran said, and smiled, and then he too sighed. "Do you know the story of Talandra, the daughter of Sceatha, the god of war, and a mortal woman, Lynceme, Queen of Terce? Ashamed that she had been seduced by war, Lynceme delivered her daughter Talandra in the forest and abandoned her there. But a mother bear found Talandra, suckling her—"

"No." Maggot fidgeted. "Speak me Portia-the-lady-Eleuate."

"I'm trying to say that Portia is like Talandra."

Maggot sat upright. "She was mothered by a bear?"

"No, no," Bran said. "But when Talandra grew up and returned to

304 ~ THE PRODIGAL TROLL

her mother's country, no man was good enough for her. She was stronger than any man, could run faster, hunt better, and she spurned all arrangements her mother made for her to marry."

"Slow," Maggot said, not understanding one word in three.

Bran tried to shape the words with his hands so Maggot could comprehend them. "Lady Culufre has no daughters, but she has a son, Acrysy, and she has betrothed Acrysy to Portia, so that Portia becomes her heir. Acrysy is young, and they are not yet joined, so many men have vied for Portia's attention." His voice dropped and he licked his lips. "Including a few much older than her, and altogether unsuitable."

When Bran glanced up, Maggot shook his head. "Portia—?"

"Portia's mother died when she was a small girl. So she was raised by her father and his soldiers. Like Talandra, she spurns all suitors, even though she runs and hunts with them."

"She runs and hunts?"

"Yes."

"Good!" Maggot also liked to run and hunt. He understood that much at least.

"She was the first to spear the boar when we hunted him last fall. She would have hunted the lion once we flushed him. Those of us who know her better think she will make a good Baroness, though. If you could see the way she hunts, you'd know that she approaches every task with a purpose. She knows her duty and would never shirk from it."

"It is good," Maggot repeated, feeling a happiness within. "You speak me her. We go to find her."

"Not yet," Bran said, staring at his hands and feet.

"Yet!" Maggot snapped. "I want we go find her."

"Not yet, Claye, my friend, not this soon." Bran's head hung low, and his voice dropped. "I would not have them see me this way. If I return too crippled to walk, too crippled to defend myself, they will see me always as a cripple and never as a whole man."

Maggot rose, stretching his legs. "Yet, soon."

Cool weather came, and the two men roamed the abandoned valley like lords of the harvest. Apples and pears piled up in huge brown mounds beneath untended trees, accompanied by the constant buzz of bees drunk on the sweet nectar of rot. And still they had all they could eat fresh from the branches. With the lion dead, Sinnglas and his hunters gone, and the wolves gone off to chase the Baron's army, there was meat as well. The deer were in rut, aggressive and careless, giddy with freedom from their usual foes, and Maggot had little problem chasing them down. Bran grew stronger; Maggot grew restless.

They were foraging far from their den when Maggot saw the smoke from campfires over the horizon. He pulled Bran in that direction. "Your people. We will go to them."

"No," Bran said.

"Why? Is good, your people. Is Portia."

"No Portia," Bran said. "That'll be the army, marching on Custalo's village to destroy their winter supplies. They're going opposite the direction that we wish to travel. There will be no women with them."

"It is time for us to go soon," Maggot said.

"Soon," Bran said, but he hurried them back to their den.

The next morning the dew crisped into frost. When they crawled out of their den, the wind was shaking the red and yellow leaves from the trees.

"It is time for us to go," Maggot said. "Today."

"Not yet," Bran said. "I cannot let them see me wearing only these rough clothes fashioned from the hides of deer. If I go down into the city as a beggar, they will always see me—"

Maggot barked out his disgust. With the dead leaves drifting in the air around him, he walked down the hillside alone, toward the valley, in search of the woman, Portia.

⤐ CHAPTER 22 ⤏

*A*s *he sprinted over the hills* toward the river, Maggot thought the wind was running ahead of a storm like a herd of deer before a bigtooth cat. He sniffed the air, trying to catch the scent of it, and watched the sky out of the south to see if it carried any clouds. He didn't want it sneaking up on him. By the time he reached the river, his temper had cooled.

Bran was his friend. Bran knew Portia. Bran had needed time to heal, and he had healed. Now he wanted people clothes, the same way a troll would want to wear his own scent when returning to his band.

So Maggot would find him people clothes.

Retracing their steps from the day before, Maggot spotted the trail of the army and followed them south. He caught up with them before nightfall and, climbing the trees on the hillsides above their route, tried to count them. He thought there were maybe a fistful, times two fists, times four. Many men, more than lived in both of Custalo's villages.

They didn't pause until twilight, when they put up a few quick

tents or threw down blankets. After many quiet indistinct conversa-
tions, a few peals of laughter, and some labored grunts, the whole
camp settled down to sleep. Maggot was crouching around the
perimeter, picking out the locations of the guards, when he saw a solitary figure scurry away from the camp.

Maggot followed the figure cautiously until he disappeared in the
shadows under some trees. Crawling cautiously on his belly, a lump in
the darkness beneath a tree resolved into a man curled up in a blanket.

Checking twice to see that no one else came out from the camp,
Maggot crept closer and pounced—straddling the man and clapping a
hand over his mouth in one quick motion.

When the man began to struggle, Maggot pressed the knife to his
throat and he stopped.

"Take off clothes," Maggot said in Bran's language. When the man
tried to move, Maggot squeezed his legs, pinning the man's arms more
tightly. He found a knife around the man's neck and took it. "If you
speak, I kill you."

The man nodded, so Maggot slipped his fingers off the man's
mouth. The man took a deep breath, then whispered, "I can't take
them off if you're holding me down."

Maggot moved aside, keeping his knife at the man's throat.

Still lying on his stomach, the man kicked off the blanket and
started shucking his pants. "I told you all, one time only, one time," he
mumbled. "And I didn't want to do it no more, which is why I came out
here to sleep. But you can't leave me alone, can you?" He stuck his
bottom up in the air. "Go on, get it done, because I want to go to sleep."

"Take off your shirt," Maggot said.

"It's cold!"

Maggot pushed the knife into flesh.

The man pulled the shirt over his head. "Yes, yes, but no pinching.
I don't like the pinching."

With the man's knife already stuck in his belt, Maggot gathered up shirt, pants, and blanket in his arm. He didn't know what *pinching* was, but he grabbed some of the man's skin between his thumb and finger and twisted hard.

The cry of protest covered the sound of his own dash through the trees and away from the camp.

Frost formed on the grass again before he returned to the cabin late the next morning. He found Bran outside under the cloudy sky, lifting, lowering, and lifting a log.

Striding into the open area, he said, "Bran, my friend, I can to move that log for you."

Bran started, dropping the log with a thud. "Claye! I can *move* that log for you." His head drooped, and then he lifted it. "I was just testing my strength."

"I saw many, many men on their way to Custalo's village." He thrust out his burden. "Here are the clothes you need."

"Ah," Bran said, taking them and holding them up. He laughed. "These will fit well enough. I should have mentioned to you that I also wanted new boots and a mount—"

"Boots?"

"Boots, to cover my feet."

"I will go find you boots," Maggot said. "Just let me sleep a little while, and I shall—"

Bran laughed, then fell serious. "Thank you for coming back. I did not expect it."

"I didn't think to look for boots."

"It's all right, my friend. No man can walk in another man's boots. I spent my whole life until I became a soldier barefoot, and went barefoot some time then too, until I became a knight. My feet have healed well enough. I'll have the cobbler fit me for new boots when we return to the city." He discarded the skin garment he had fashioned and pulled on the clothes Maggot had brought him. "But for these, I am indebted to you again. Even plain clothes make me feel like a man and not a beast. Though you made quite an impression on Lady Eleuate without them."

"Impression?" Maggot asked.

"I did not tell you the whole story of Portia," Bran said. Then he sighed. "After you left her the lion's pelt, she wanted to search for you. She told everyone she had finally seen a man who might be worthy of her."

Maggot made a little rumbling growl in his throat.

"This angered Acrysy and also her father, Eleuate, the dowager consort, and they called an end to the hunt, retreating ahead of the rains. But she made me promise to bring her back up to the valleys to search for you later."

"And did you?" Maggot asked. All weariness had fled from him, and then, when he thought he understood Bran's reluctance to take him to meet Portia, his legs went weak. His hands squeezed his head. "You did! And she was with you when Sinnglas's warriors—"

"No," Bran said.

"No?"

"No, I speak it true three times."

Maggot sunk to his knees, leaning on one hand and covering his face. "What—?"

Bran knelt in the long, damp grass and fallen leaves beside him. "I fell out of favor after the spring hunt. And then I also took some blame for our losses against Squandral at the Battle among the Poplars, and I lost my captaincy."

"But Portia?"

"I never had the chance to keep my promise to her. After I was disgraced, my enemies—enemy, in truth, for it was Acrysy—arranged to have me posted at a poorly defended settlement, one the peasants were likely to attack. As they did. They killed all the men there but me and . . . and . . . the one other knight." He paused and swallowed. "They took us back to—"

He rubbed at the naked spot on the back of his head, where new pink skin grew over the raw bone where his braid had been.

"I am glad that nothing happened to Portia-the-Lady-Eleuate," Maggot said, exhaling. Two knives and the wizard's charm swayed from his neck as he bent over. He sorted through the strings and lifted one from his head. "Here, this knife is for you also."

"My debt to you becomes a flood." Bran accepted it in the manner he always took weapons from Maggot, point first, inspected it briefly, and hung it around his neck. "That reminds me," he said, and ducked into their den.

Maggot was bending down to the entrance when Bran crawled out again, holding a small leather bag on a cord. He pointed to the ampule at Maggot's throat.

"You'll have to hide that," he said as he handed Maggot the bag. "Wear it about your neck in this."

Maggot's hand went to the charm, and he thought of the blue gem on the gold strand around Portia's neck. He had meant to keep this for her interest gift. "Why?"

"That's wizard's work. If you're seen in the city with it, they'll assume it's stolen and might kill you to recover it."

He showed Maggot how to work the simple drawstring he'd created for the little bag. As Maggot followed his instructions, Bran continued talking.

"The braid could mean trouble also. You must take the sword back because of it. At least you have some notion of how to use it now and you carry yourself like a knight. It's too bad I didn't think to wish you might steal clothes for yourself as well."

"Is there a problem with these?" Maggot tugged at his breech-cloth.

"Those are the clothes of a mountain peasant. But you don't look like one, not much. You'll be fine with me."

"Let's go now, Bran."

"It is time." He exhaled hard again, then bent to pick up the shirt he had discarded for the new clothes. They crawled back into the den to take up the dried meat and fruit they had collected and stored. Bran set aside a third and arranged it in a careful pile just inside the hole they used as a door.

"Why do you do that?" Maggot asked.

"We used this house without the lady's permission," Bran said. "Even if she's dead, Bwnte watches over her possessions. So we leave a gift and a sign that we visited here."

When they stood up outside, Maggot pointed to the hole in the roof. "I wonder who visited here that time," he said. "And what they left for a gift."

Bran looked up silently and frowned. An ominous cloud loomed over the sky.

As they descended into the valley, the wind took the world in its mouth and shook it with bone-snapping strength. Branches whipped back and forth, snapping as they fell from the trees.

Maggot fell into the watchful silence of a troll on the move, but Bran talked above the wind, displaying his hands and pointing to the fourth finger on the right one. "Still no nail here, but I'm getting a callus. The rest are sorry-looking, but they've toughened up enough that I can hold a sword. Might even be able to pull a bowstring for a shot or two. Once we're back, I'll have new gloves made."

Farther on, he said, "All will be well once I talk to m'lady Sebius. She has been my mentor, my provider, since I was a young man come to serve the Baron."

All day they expected the sky to crack open, but they were still dry when they reached the hill above the bridge. It was near sunset, and clouds covered the land with a thicker darkness than night. The bones that had once been Damaqua and Tanaghri were gone, and the gifts scattered. Only the three stained poles remained on the ground. Bran ignored them, pointing to the house across the river. "We'd best go see Banya."

"The man who lived there is dead," Maggot said.

"You know this?"

"I saw it happen. The same men who did that to you."

"Ah," Bran said, in much the same way Sinnglas said "Heh," as if it explained everything. He led them down to the bridge and paused in the middle. The water was as clear as a sheet of ice under the dark, swirling sky; the little Old One stirred among the bones, while smaller ones slithered searchingly among the rocks. Bran shook his head. "The demons are restless because a new wizard has not yet been summoned for them."

"Demons?" Maggot asked.

Bran swept his hand toward the water.

"*Old Ones*, demons," Maggot said. "Demons are always restless until they are fed."

"We'll stay here tonight," Bran said, crossing the bridge. "But well up the bank, away from the water's edge."

Bran would not sleep in the dead wizard's house. When Maggot asked him why, he would say only that it belonged to Bwnte now. Maggot did not understand how it was different from the den they had stayed in—someone had died there too. But Bran grew reticent and would not explain.

They stretched out sheltered by the wall of the house, but the cats swarmed over them, mewing and poking and brushing their cool noses against bare skin. Both men flipped and tossed, unable to rest. The first drops splattered out of the sky sometime before the middle of the night, sending the cats indoors as the two men leaned with their backs to the wall beneath the eaves. Before morning the water was whipping sideways through the air.

Bran shielded his eyes against the sky. "There are only two times you can leave for a journey in the rain: too early and too late."

"Which is this?" Maggot shouted back.

"Don't know yet. But we should go on as far as we can."

"We used to play in rains like this when I was a child."

"We did too, my brother and I," Bran said, suddenly smiling. He stood, and gestured for Maggot to do the same. "The sooner we reach the city, the better. There's an old shepherd's path leading out of these meadows down to the lower valley. Sure footing even for weather like this."

Maggot stepped onto the path that would take them upstream, toward the great stone lodge where he'd seen Portia, but Bran stopped him.

"Portia, she is this way," Maggot said.

"No, we must go this way first, before we see Portia."

Maggot did not question him. Bran led them on a path along a ridge beneath the trees. The wind didn't blow steady, but slammed its fist down here and there, sometimes knocking them off balance. Stunned birds sheltered on the lowest limbs, close to the ground, bedraggled, motionless. Passing within a few feet of them, Maggot could not distinguish a dove from a finch, a bunting from a redbird, except by general size.

That night, they sheltered under a rock ledge that had been used by the shepherds Bran mentioned. He could not get a fire started in the charred pit of stones, but Maggot did not notice the cold. The rain finally let up.

"This is bad," Bran said. "Spring floods destroyed the early planting. The valley won't have had its first frost yet, but now these storms could keep the farmers from getting the harvest in."

"Why does it happen?" Maggot asked.

"Some years are like that. Others, the fields overflow with gold. You have to take the bad with the good."

The sun glowed weakly through the clouds the next morning, one coal surviving a doused fire. It seemed like it might flicker out at any moment.

A cold drizzle began to fall as they continued on their way and the coal of the sun expired behind the gray clouds. At times the drizzle turned to sleet. Maggot spied houses and farms in the hollows below the trail. Once they spied a bald, old man with stooped shoulders moving through an orchard, wrapping the bases of the trees, but aside from that, nothing stirred across the landscape all day but the two of them.

So Maggot, rapt in his stride across the slick, rock-strewn path, was not prepared when they came to the top of a hill and the city spread out below them through the dismal, gray haze. But then nothing in his experience could have prepared him for the size of it. A great stone bridge arched over a broad and turbulent river. A stone wall enclosed the length of the far shore, and beyond it a massive edifice rose whose top was round and smooth like a gourd, but glossed gold like the back of a giant beetle. Another building bulked behind that, surrounded by a round lake of water as dark as the sky. Jumbled around these two structures were other buildings, stretching as far as Maggot could see, upstream and down, too many to count. They were grouped around narrow paths like islands in a marsh, their browns and reds and tans all dulled by damp.

On this side of the river, partially obscured by the hills, Maggot saw fewer buildings. They were set back on higher ground much farther from the river's unwalled bank. One large building without a roof rose above the others, surrounded by a spider's web of wooden frames that bent and swayed in the wind. The few people that he saw moving were as small as ants in an anthill.

Maggot forgot to breathe until he said very quietly, "I had no idea there were so many people in all the world."

"Only fifteen thousand or so here," Bran said. "Maybe forty thousand in the province. It's grown quickly in the last decade, with the Baron's reputation and the Baroness's prosperity. A disastrous crop this year will set things back."

"Is this the Imperial City?" Maggot asked, recalling Bran's descriptions of the great city.

Bran laughed at him. "Not hardly. I've been there, to take my oath as a knight in the Empress's service. This is to the Imperial City what Damaqua's village is to this."

That village seemed a small and paltry thing to Maggot now, and he'd thought it huge. "A range of mountains, as to a single mountain, as to a hill."

"Yes," said Bran. "There's no one place you can stand to see the whole Imperial City, at least approaching it as I did from the east. The Baron has modeled this city on the Imperial City; m'lady Sebius more so as she builds the new official structures and her personal palace on this near bank."

Maggot squinted into the rain, drops running down his cheeks and dripping from his forehead. Lightning flickered, rippling through the clouds. Thunder clapped and chased it across the sky.

"Come," Bran said. "Let's go see the city at hand's length and find a decent roof."

He took them along a narrow, twisting path that descended quickly through steep walls on either side, making abrupt turns. The sky, dark all day, grew darker by the second, and the wind kicked up again, whistling in the passages around them. Bran picked up his pace until they were nearly jogging forward.

They rounded a sheer-faced hillside into the midst of a copse of trees and found themselves surrounded by a dozen startled soldiers who nevertheless had the wits to raise a hedge of spears around them. Bran reached out his hand, telling Maggot to stay calm.

"Two gods, I don't believe it," one man said.

A tall, lean boy, with soft brown skin and hair as black and thick as Maggot's, strutted outside the circle of spears—the boy that Maggot remembered from the hunt, the one who'd thrown the spear. "See!" he said, grinning. "The peasants do know this way into—wait!" He folded his hands behind his back. "Why this is the estimable Bran, come back from the dead."

Bran bent his head. "It is good to see you again also, Acrysy, m'lord."

"Did I give you permission to speak?"

Bran opened his mouth to answer, then slowly closed it.

"Of course, a traitor never asks permission," Acrysy said, swaggering over to Bran. "And here we have proof of your treason, sneaking back into the city with a peasant warrior."

Maggot's nostrils flared.

Acrysy paused in front of Maggot, his eyes widening. He stepped back, gripped the shaft of a spear, and jerked it toward Maggot's throat. "And *this* is the murderer who visited our hunting camp! This is the murderer who assaulted m'lady Eleuate, my bride-to-be! So the two of you were working together, even then. Now you reveal yourself truly, Bran, sneaking into the city to do murder again. This is even greater proof. Who did you come to murder this time? My mother? M'lady Sebius? Did you come to kill me this time?"

"I came to kill no—"

His hand shot out and slapped Bran's face. "Quiet! Traitors may not speak!" His breath came very quickly. He slapped Bran again.

Only Bran's lack of reaction prevented Maggot from striking back, despite the ring of spears.

318 THE PRODIGAL TROLL

"It is good you cut off your braid," Acrysy said. "It saves me the trouble of having it done. A base-born shepherd's son like you should never have been a knight."

One of the men lifted his knife to cut off Maggot's braid, and Maggot spun on him.

Acrysy let go of the spear shaft and jumped back. "Wait! Wait until we display them in public. I warned Sebius that an attack might come from this direction. Now she'll have to listen to me. Bind them!"

Maggot looked at Bran, puzzled. Bran thrust his hands out in front of him. A guard stepped forward and started wrapping them with rope. Overhead, lightning split the sky. The rain, only briefly in abeyance, resumed its slow fall.

"That's a nice knot there, Romy," Bran said. "Who taught you how to tie knots like that?"

"Enough of that," the guard said. He tied off the knot and flicked his eyes nervously toward Maggot. "Tell your friend to stick his hands out too."

"Hurry up," Acrysy said. He had a small, mushroom-shaped tent that he raised above his head to keep off the rain.

"Be careful—he won't like it, Romy," Bran said quietly. He looked over to Maggot. "Just stick out your hands. It'll be fine. Sebius will set things aright."

His half-smile and voice both gave away the lie. Or at least his uncertainty.

Maggot stuck out his hands, knotted into fists. When Romy stepped up to wrap the rope around them, Maggot rammed his fists into Romy's chin. As Romy flipped backward, Maggot ran.

He dodged the first butt-end of a spear, but the second slammed into the side of his head, and the next swept his feet out from under him. After that he lost track, curling up in a ball, with his elbows in front of his face while spear-butts and boots fell upon his ribs and back and head like hailstones. Someone tied his hands together between the kicks, and Maggot did his best to keep his wrists flexed, bent out, against the pressure of the ropes. Someone twisted the rope, so that the fibers bit into his skin, yanking Maggot to his feet. They took his knife and sword. Rain and wind lashed at them. Romy reached out to take the sack strung around Maggot's neck.

"I wouldn't do that," Bran said. "And I did warn you he wouldn't like being tied."

"Why not?" Romy said.

"It holds his father's foreskin. The lining of the bag is made from his grandfather's scrotum."

Romy's hand twitched back. "Gods of war and justice. Does that really do—"

"What did he say?" Acrysy shouted above the storm.

His words were cut off by two ferocious bolts of lightning, striking so close that the thunder sounded at once, shaking the air around them. The clouds ruptured, spilling a deluge so thick it was hard to see through.

"Forget it! Let's go!" Romy shouted.

The soldiers, heads down against the storm, prodded Bran and Maggot with their spears. The sharp tips did not annoy Maggot as much as the restraints, and the cold rain rolling off his skin did nothing to steal away the heat of his temper.

CHAPTER 23

Maggot's feet dragged in the mud as the soldiers shoved them down to the building covered by the spider's web of scaffolding.

"Put them in the cells," Acrysy said at the stone arch of the entrance. The rain drummed its fingertips on the toadstool that covered his head.

"We can't," Romy replied. "We still haven't repaired the damage the earthquake did to that wing."

"Earthquake?" Bran asked.

A shaft swung out and struck the side of his head. As he staggered, Maggot growled and lurched toward the guard who'd hit his friend. Several hands grabbed him, fists pounding his stomach and kidneys. The scaffolding began to sway in the wind, its upper frame knocking at the stone wall.

"Use one of the locked storerooms then," Acrysy shouted. He passed under the arch and disappeared into a doorway.

The soldiers grabbed Bran and Maggot roughly by their arms,

dragging them through the slop into a small yard with walls on three sides. They entered a stone corridor lit by greasy torchlight. The air smelled of smoke, and people, but underlying it all Maggot tasted the cold and damp. As a group they stumbled down narrow steps, one of the men going ahead to open a heavy oak door. As Bran entered the room, Maggot glimpsed a low roof and bare walls. A hand in the middle of his back shoved him after Bran.

"It's nothing personal, m'lord Bran," Romy said.

The door slammed shut, ensconcing the two men in darkness.

As if he were in any other deep cave, Maggot explored the boundaries of their space, trailing his bound hands along the wall, feeling the joins at the corners, the seams at floor and ceiling. He went slowly, as if there might be hidden crevasses, but he found none. The walls were rough and the ceiling propped up by curving arches.

"What happened?" Maggot asked as he explored. "Why would they treat us this way? They are your people, your *band*."

"It's more complicated than that."

The voice came from right beside Maggot, down low. Bran sat against the base of the wall. Had Maggot taken another step, he would have tripped over him.

"Baron Culufre has ruled here for"—he paused—"seventeen years now. Yes, I was twelve then. But he comes originally from the Imperial City and so do almost all of his knights and soldiers, at least the core group. Only I ever rose to any position among his men."

Maggot completed the full circuit of the room, returning to the door. A thin line of dim light squeezed around the frame, but not enough to illuminate his bonds.

"I grew up in this valley," Bran said. "My mother's farm—well, she's given it to my brother Pwyl's wife now—is less than a day's journey from here. So I'm an outsider to many of them."

The ropes binding Maggot's wrists were too tight to pull loose, so he nipped at them with his teeth.

"The Baron's half-brother, m'lady Sebius, the eunuch—"

Maggot looked toward Bran's voice. "What is eunuch?"

"A man made like unto a woman, to have the rights of women." Bran's feet scuffed the floor as if he were uncomfortable. "Like a wizard taking the robes. But eunuchs can own property, own land, pass it on to their chosen heirs."

The answer created more questions than it solved. Finding the rope too rough and hard, Maggot gave up chewing at it.

"Sebius was made a eunuch to hold land for the Baron, since the skills and loyalty of the Baroness were not known at that time. But she's proven to be a strong lady, wise with her wealth, and though Sebius has grown rich—this is her palace—she's not the ruler she had hoped to be, I think."

Maggot inched his way along the wall, palms skimming the surface, seeking any sharp nib of rock. Finding one, he rubbed the rope against it.

"Sebius was the chief herder when the Baron arrived." Bran fell silent a moment. The only sound was that of stone abrading rope. "I still remember the sight of that army marching across the river plain, all the mammuts—most of them were sent back to the Imperial City eventually. I said good-bye to my mother and ran after the army, promising to be back within a week. But Sebius took me into her service. There must have been a dozen of us: old men, women, boys. And as Sebius prospered, so did we. I was promoted many times."

Maggot gave up on the first stone and moved along the wall seeking something sharper to work with.

"The Baron has never done anything similar, surrounding himself always with those he trusts from the empire's heart. And yet . . ."

"What?" Maggot found another and rubbed with better luck, fraying a thread or two.

"It's hard to say. The Baron has put down roots here. Sebius, who should naturally have put down roots, remains much more attached to the empire. The Baron has never traveled back to the Imperial City except for the last Empress's funeral, but Sebius returns every other year or so. Her intervention there raised me to a knight, despite my birth. I think she wanted to show that she had the power, the connections, to do that."

Bran fell silent.

Maggot worried at the ropes, certain that water could wear away bedrock faster than he could break them. The angle was bad, and the stone had quickly lost its edge.

"She owes me a great deal too, though," Bran said. "If Acrysy does this alone, then as soon as Sebius finds out the truth we are saved."

"And if Sebius raises a hand with Acrysy?"

Bran shuffled his feet again and sighed. "She has the power to do whatever she wishes."

Maggot was unsure how much time passed—it was always hard for him to tell in a deep cave. Based on his thirst, it seemed like a long time. When he became tired, he curled up on the flagstone floor and drowsed. Bran's dry voice woke him, but whether it was a short or long time later, he had no idea. The light lining the door had disappeared.

"They mean for us to be afraid, friend Claye."

"Afraid?"

"Of the darkness. It is like a tomb in here."

"It is dark like an old cave. If you crawl through a new cave in darkness, that causes fear. A sudden drop-off can trap you in a deep crack where no one can reach you and you cry until you die. That happened with a girl I knew"—to Blossom—"and nothing the whole band could do in a week could save her. But this is like an old cave. Here we have solid ground, solid walls." He smacked his feet against the floor, pounded his fists on the stone. "What can happen to us here?"

Bran's laughter bounced around like a pebble dropped down a deep shaft. "Perhaps."

"There is no danger in the dark," Maggot said. "Unless the dark holds enemies."

The smell in the small room was changing, but Maggot was hard-pressed to say how. Bran's sweat was strong, and his own, but something else tickled his nose.

"Mother Bwnte," Bran said. "May she curse Romy for paying such attention when I trained him. My hands have gone completely numb, they are bound so tight." Shuffles across the floor were followed by fists hammering on the thick door. "Open up! Sebius! Sebius! Open this door! Come here right now!"

Maggot searched again for a sharper-edged stone. He found one close to the floor. By kneeling, he could scrape hard against it. After a while he touched the rope to his leg. It was warm in the cool room. His shoulder pressed against the damp wall while he worked.

Bran pounded for a long time, alternately begging and threatening, until finally he wearied of it and plopped down against the far wall. "I can almost feel my fingers again," he said. Then muttered, "The ones that remain." And added louder, "Can you hear my belly thunder? That's not the worst of it. I'm so thirsty I could drink the mother water itself."

"Here's some water flowing from the wall," Maggot said, turning to lick the trickle at his shoulder. It tasted a bit moldy, which was the odor he'd smelled. He was hungry too. If he got the ropes off, he might eat them. "Enough to wet your lips, and maybe your throat, but it won't fill your belly."

Bran scrambled over, bumping into Maggot and kneeing his head. "Sorry about that. Where is it?"

"It's about the height of your waist. No, lean toward me. It's near that sharp edge in the stone."

"Found it." Bran lapped at the rock like a wildcat drinking from a pool of water. When he finally stopped, he sighed. "How could anything taste so terrible and so sweet at the same time?"

Maggot rubbed his head against his arm, soothing the spot that Bran had kneed. "About the women?"

There was a pause. "Yes."

"Bran, how would I find the women?"

There was a longer pause. "Go to any dwelling and knock on the door. Women live in every house."

"No. The women. The one in the camp, in the tent, the one I gave the lion's skin to."

"Ah, the *woman*."

"Woman?"

"Woman, when there's only one."

"That's right! There's only one. Only Portia."

Bran paused again. The *tap-tap-tap* of dripping water sounded somewhere in their cell. "My lady Portia is betrothed to Acrysy, the man who captured us. Things have not been amicable between them, so I don't think you'll find her here."

"Oh." The darkness seemed thicker to Maggot. "Then I will just have to go where he is not."

Maggot slept, woke, slept, and woke again, but the intervals of time were meaningless—they could have been short naps or long periods of sleep, but either way he did not feel rested. Though he satisfied his thirst with the dripping water, hunger consumed him. The rope continued to fray under his patient sawing.

Voices and footsteps echoed unexpectedly down the stairwell. Bran, who was leaning against the door, jumped aside just as thick oak slammed open. Light flooded the room. Maggot squinted, blinking like a bat tossed into daylight.

"Greetings, greetings, greetings." The voice was as smooth as polished stone and just as hard. "So you're still here, are you? I extend my ample gratitude that you could await the occasion of my visit."

"Sebius, m'lady," Bran said, his voice light with hope.

As Maggot's eyes adjusted to the glare, Sebius—the womanly one that Maggot had called Foghair—stepped into the cell.

Acrysy followed behind her, sneering.

One guard with a short spear in his hand went to stand in the corner by the door, another filled the doorway, and at least one more waited out in the hall. Even if his hands were free, Maggot doubted his chance of fighting free.

Sebius had a scent like urine in a bed of flowers, Maggot thought. He—was Sebius a he or a she, man or woman? Not a woman. Sebius, Maggot decided, was a he. Sebius walked over and lifted Bran's damaged hands. He patted the knuckles where fingers once had been. "Is this all those murderous untrustworthy heathens cut off?"

"Isn't it enough?"

The eunuch sighed, his voice rising a pitch. "Well, a woman always hopes for a daughter. I promised you once that if you took up the dress, I would make you my heir. You earned my fortune for me."

"M'lady is generous with her praises." Bran pulled his hands free. "May she be as generous with her mercies."

Sebius smiled and laid his palm affectionately against Bran's face. "Oh, Bran, Bran, Bran, why did you have to come back? You make things very difficult for me, give me very difficult choices."

"How?" He pulled his face away from Sebius's hand.

"Because Lady Culufre's son identified a dangerous path into the city and guarded it in fierce weather, apprehending a known traitor in the company of a recognized enemy."

Acrysy smirked, as if he had accomplished all this single-handed. Maggot wanted to knock him down.

Bran bristled. "Known traitor? I've served you, m'lady, since I was a boy. When did I become a traitor?"

"To be honest, only after I thought you were dead. It seemed most appropriate to use you then, as I have in life. Now I find it hard to reverse statements I have publicly made."

"That's not true," Acrysy shouted. "He *is* a traitor. He turned my betrothed against me."

"Yes," Sebius admitted, slowly raising an open palm that silenced the youth. "There is that. Though admittedly, Lady Eleuate's wild daughter has never been fully reconciled to the thought of taking you as her consort—"

"That's not true!"

Sebius drew a deep breath. "As I recall, her exact words were 'You may have my hand in marriage, but no more of me than that; you may roam all of my mother's estates, but you will never have my bed.'" He looked to Bran. "Do I have that correctly, my protégé? Speak truly to me, as you have always done."

"She added disparaging remarks about his youth and poor character," Bran said.

"Ah, yes." Sebius grinned sadly.

"Liars," Acrysy hissed. "She *will* marry me, and I will be the next Baron here. She wouldn't deny me if that stupid hunt hadn't ruined everything. You ruined it on purpose!"

Everyone stood there silently after this outburst, until finally Sebius spoke to Bran. "But the fact remains that she only openly defied the arrangements after the lion hunt. Which was your idea, Bran."

"It was your goal to bring the two of them together," Bran replied quietly. "Without mothers around, so that they might get to know one another. I merely suggested the means. I have always served your goals, m'lady."

"But my goal is a smooth succession of power and the unification of this province to the glory of the Empress."

Bran straightened. "I accepted blame for the bad end of that venture and sacrificed my captaincy on the altar of Lord Eleuate's wounded pride. But we had other purposes there as well, to rid the valley of the lion who endangered our flocks, and to scout out the numbers of the peasants and begin their removal. Surely we accomplished both those things, to your glory, m'lady, and the advancement of the realm."

Sebius made a small humming sound. "Since you received the blame for something you did not do, you now wish to steal credit for the work of others?"

With everyone's attention focused on this conversation, Maggot made a sudden lunge toward Acrysy, who jumped back. He was too far away to reach the boy, and stopped short as the guard in the corner and the one at the door leapt toward him with raised spears.

Neither Sebius nor Bran had moved.

"I don't know what you mean," Bran said.

"You didn't drive away the peasants, nor did you kill the lion—your friend accomplished that feat." Sebius waved a hand casually in Maggot's direction. "He is your friend, isn't he?"

Bran's mouth turned into a thin line. "He saved my life."

"As you spared his, in battle?"

Maggot lifted his foot, and the guard jabbed the spear at him again, saying, "None of that, now, or you'll hurt for it."

"Is that what they say?" Bran asked.

"I saw it," Romy said from the doorway. "I had to speak the truth, Captain Bran. I saw you spare his life."

"The truth is that the two of you worked together during the hunt," Acrysy interjected. "You gave this peasant access to the camp—you posted the guards after all, and how else could he get past the walls without your help?—so that he could assault Lady Portia, and commit his vile affront upon her."

330 — THE PRODIGAL TROLL

"I did no such thing," Bran said.

Sebius reached out to caress the side of Bran's face. "But it was so convenient to blame you for everything when we thought you dead. You sabotaged the hunting party and ruined the wedding. You betrayed our war plans to the peasants, giving them their brief victory and escape."

Bran's chin hit his chest.

"If I could have blamed the floods on you," Sebius's voice said softly, "my darling boy, I would have done that also."

"The spring floods or the fall flood coming?" Bran asked, trying to pull his head away and bumping into the wall.

Sebius laughed. "Both. It will be a very hard winter, and the people will need someone to blame, some distraction."

"Blame them both on me, then," Bran said. "Call it the consequence of some sacrilege I performed to the demon gods of the peasants. I'll take credit for it all. You will have your scapegoat and your spectacle to appease the hungry crowds."

"You'd do that?"

"If you set free my friend, yes."

Maggot shook his head. He would not leave without Bran. But Bran didn't notice.

"You see, Acrysy!" Sebius stepped back and raised his hand up in the air, smiling, his teeth shining. "You see what kind of loyalty he has? He serves me still, gives me exactly what I wish and seeks to benefit his friend as well. It takes years to reap a crop like that; a length of time measured out in strings of pearls would not be worth as much."

Acrysy crossed his arms.

Sebius laughed at him, and embraced Bran, who stood there limply. "The crops cannot be harvested with the ground like this, and everyone is gathered in the city already for fear of the uprising. Conveniently, I have convinced my beloved brother to move up the Dance of Masks and Costumes for the Feast of Bwnte, and this has diverted their attention from the double disaster. When I see him, I shall essay to discover his reaction to the possibility that you are alive and well."

"And my friend? He is not one of the peasants. He saved my life when they would have burned me."

Sebius smiled again. "Your friend may not be a peasant, but he dresses like one and fought with them. Too many saw him in battle and heard his weirdling cry. It put fear in their hearts. No, your friend will fight his last battle against the splitting pole. His cry shall have a different keen on it then, and the soldiers will forget their fears as they cheer his death."

"But Portia, Lady Eleuate—"

"Exactly. And then Portia. All the more reason to kill him quickly. I shall apologize deeply for the error, after."

Maggot flexed on the balls of his feet, tugging his wrists against his bonds. He would die fighting before he submitted to the fate suffered by Damaqua, his advisor, or the wizard.

"Must we wait?" Acrysy asked, eyeing Maggot with a mixture of fear and contempt. "If we split him at noon, he might still be squirming when the dance begins tonight."

"Patience, my young friend." Sebius stepped toward the door, putting his hand on Acrysy's shoulder to send him ahead. "We would not want to ruin anyone's appetite for the feast. Let them eat while they can; save the next spectacle to distract them from their hunger after the bad harvest." He turned his head. "And after that much time, it will be easier to remind everyone that it's the Wyndans we blame and not some poor, maligned, barefoot shepherd boy become a knight."

"Wait," Bran cried, stepping toward the eunuch.

The soldier in the corner thrust the spear at him.

Sebius stopped on the threshold of the door. "What is it, shepherd boy? Have you lost your sheep?"

"Send something for us to eat and drink."

"Drink? Drink, we can give you." He stared out into the hall and up the dark stairs. "All the water you want, before we drown in it. Will that suffice? Romy?"

"Yes, m'lady?" Romy answered beyond the door.

"When you think of it, stick a bucket outside in the rain. A clean bucket, mind, and nothing that's been used for a bedpan. When it's full, bring it down here for the comfort of our guests."

"Yes, m'lady."

"Sebius," Bran said, very softly. "Food."

Sebius released a long, exaggerated sigh. "Romy?"

"Yes, m'lady?"

"This rain so thoroughly soaks the ground that it drives the rats up out of their holes and they frighten the good ladies of the city. When it's convenient for you, take some men into the city and catch some rats. Some big, fat ones, mind. Be careful not to make them angry, or anything like that; then set them loose in the cell here. Alive, mind."

"Yes, m'lord."

Acrysy cackled.

"There you go, Bran," the eunuch said. "If you continue to be so tiresome, I may reconsider my decision and choose not to spare you after all." He wiped a drop of sweat off his forehead with the middle finger of his left hand. "I'm so exhausted by this interview that I may forget to lay the groundwork tonight, and simply relax, and enjoy myself instead. Will you thank me three times for every rat you catch and eat?"

Bran spit on the floor—Maggot wondered how he could with his mouth so dry—once, twice, thrice. "I thank you three times."

"Insults, insults." He took the torch from the holder just outside the open door. "Come, Acrysy."

Maggot jumped the guard in the corner, swinging his bound hands up to knock aside the spear. As his hands slid along the shaft, the guard turned it sideways and drove the butt against Maggot's temple, knocking him to the ground. Maggot heard his laughter, followed by the hard metal clunk of the door bolt.

⇥ Chapter 24 ⇤

Maggot inhaled. The air was heavy with the residue of smoke and oil, the eunuch's perfume, and the meaty stink of the soldiers. Bran was kneeling on the floor beside him.

"Are you hurt?" he asked.

"No," Maggot said. He had managed to scrape the ropes briefly on the blade of the spear, but not enough to slice clean through. "And you?"

"Nothing important, only my pride. When you serve someone loyally, you expect that loyalty returned."

Maggot rolled back to his feet and crawled over to the nub of broken stone to resume his attack on the ropes.

"I misjudged her," said Bran. "Judging men has always been my virtue, one of the reasons I was made knight, then captain. But I misjudged the lot of them. I didn't expect Romy to follow Acrysy's orders over his loyalty to me."

Virtue, loyalty—more unfamiliar words. "Why do they do that, Bran?"

"Do what?"

"Why do your people do what other people tell them? Giants"—
He used the word from Sinnglas's language—"do each as they see fit,
or *vote* for the common good. Even Sinnglas's people reach agreement
or follow different paths."

Bran paced, kicking the door. "The strong lead and the weak must
follow; that is the way of the world. If they do not go willingly, they
must be driven."

"What willingly is there if they are to be beaten or killed? It is not
good, Bran. I do not like the ways of your people. I do not think I want
to stay among you." The rope abraded quickly against the stone, his
wrists pulling apart.

"You have not seen us at our best. Baron Culufre is a good, just
man. He will set things right."

"You said the same thing of the eunuch." The first strand of rope
severed, and the rest fell loose. Tingling pain flooded into Maggot's
fingers. "Here, let me untie your hands."

"Give us a chance—What?"

Maggot rose and went to Bran, and began unknotting his bonds.
"Can you hold your hands a little higher?"

"But how did you get free?" Bran asked, lifting his hands.

"I cut the ropes on the stone, the sharp edges."

"And said nothing?"

"You didn't seem interested."

"Ai! I'm an awful judge of men!"

Maggot's fingers, though numb, worked out the knots by touch.
He started unwinding the rope from Bran's wrists.

"By two gods, that hurts," said Bran. He shook his fingers, slapping his palms against his thighs. "But the hurt itself is a much-
needed balm. When Romy comes back with either our water or our
rats—rats! do you believe that?—we'll jump him. You can stand over
there on the far wall, where he can see you, and I'll hide in the corner
there by the door."

Maggot's hand found the rawhide pouch at his throat. He had been saving it to give to the woman—to Portia—but she wasn't here, and if he didn't get free, he might never see her. He could find another gift to show his interest.

"Perhaps we need not wait so long," he said. "What will happen if I break the wizard's charm? Perhaps the walls will break if the earth shakes again."

"Again? Romy mentioned an earthquake—"

"I had two charms like this one. I broke the other in Damaqua's village when I wanted to take you away from Sinnglas. The earth shook, knocking us all to the ground."

Bran whistled in the dark. Then quietly, "The worst that could happen is nothing."

"And then we could still use your plan," Maggot said.

"Maybe you should save it. We'll have other chances to escape, if we are patient. If our hands weren't tied, we could have taken Sebius hostage and bargained our way out."

"No," Maggot said. His fingers shook as they unknotted the bag and withdrew the teardrop charm. He closed his fist on it, watching it glow through his skin. "I am tired of letting others choose the path I follow."

He held it up, needing to close both hands on it to make it snap. The big, wet pop sounded like a stalactite falling in an underground lake. The glass dissolved, flaring up in a bright green flash, lush like a hillside in spring, illuminating their little cell with a lightning's flash. Maggot saw Bran very clearly, for a split second, his face worried, rubbing feeling into his hands. And then nothing.

Neither man said anything for some time.

Bran cleared his throat. "Did you do it right?"

"I think so. How else should I have done it?"

"You're the wizard."

"I'm not a wizard."

"Well, you have the wizard's charm."

"Wait." Maggot wrinkled his nose. He smelled something new, something fragrant with fresh earth and vegetation. His ears caught a tiny humming sound.

"What?"

"Over here, where the wall leaks," Maggot said. He took one step in that direction, and his feet splashed. When he bent down on his knees to search for the trickle in the wall, he discovered stones jutting inward, out of place. "What's this?"

Bran knelt beside him. "It's buckled from the water. We should get back. If it caves in, the rocks will crush us."

"But it will also give us a way to escape."

"Perhaps." Bran pulled at Maggot's arm, laughing as he dragged him to the far wall. "Come, wizard. When Mother Bwnte does her work, mere mortals step aside."

The tide of water soon stretched all the way across the floor to lap at their bare feet. The trickle turned into a fountain of water, gushing and splashing, rising as high as their ankles.

"How much longer do we have to wait?" Maggot asked.

"You're the wizard," Bran said again.

"I'm not a wizard."

There was a sound of Bran scooping and sipping a handful of water. "Ugh! Too muddy to drink."

"Then don't drink it."

Still locked in the murky darkness, the water soon swirled around their calves. The icy cold numbed Maggot's feet. "How high do you think it will rise?" he asked.

"Reach up and tell me what you feel."

The ceiling was barely a foot above his head. He ran his hands over the surface. "I only feel the stone roof."

"About that high then, I'd guess," Bran said. He turned and pounded on the door. "We'll be treading water soon unless Bwnte gives us a little more help first."

Maggot sloshed over to the collapsing wall. There was no breeze or stirring of the air to show a gap to the outside.

"What are you doing?"

"Perhaps Bwnte waits for us to help ourselves." His fingers probed the wall for purchase in the buckled stones. He tugged, but the stone didn't budge. He braced his shoulder against the wall, grunting as he pulled. Suddenly the stone shifted, pinching his fingers against its neighbor. "Ow!"

"What happened?"

"Nothing," Maggot said, gripping the stone with his free hand and ripping it loose. It splashed into the water as he danced his toes out of the way.

Bran shuffled over to his side. "I guess I'd rather be buried in rubble than drown. Where—ah, here. Do you feel the mortar between the stones?"

"The what?"

"The mortar. The gritty, crumbling stuff. Like sand. Scratch it away and the blocks fall out easier."

Another splash announced his success. The two of them worked side by side, one stone after another falling into the water in slow succession. The water sprayed out of the wall, rising over their thighs. Gravel and then mud began pouring in through the gap. Suddenly, Maggot felt something like rain fall across his back. It splattered in the water all around them.

"The ceiling!" Bran cried. "Get under the doorway fast!"

Maggot never lost his sense of direction underground, having learned a long time ago to keep a mental picture always in his head. He dived for the right spot, through water and mud as high as his thighs, and pressed hard against the wood.

Bran splashed around the wrong wall. "Where is it?"

Before Maggot could answer, a rush of little splashes crescendoed with several big ones. Bran gasped in pain and Maggot jumped for the noise, taking hold of his friend's arm, dragging him back to the doorway.

Thick, muddy water rushed in, swirling past their waists, sludge settling in over their feet.

"This is a stupid way to die," Maggot said.

"You would rather—"

A section of the ceiling fell, slamming into the water, splashing it up to their heads, as the roar of a thousand stones crashed somewhere. The outside wall buckled and folded like a big thunderclap, followed by the rush of the wind, not strong but biting cold and filled with the scent of rain, and sharp air, broken up by the cries of people elsewhere in the castle, and muted light, a dark gray luminance in the air that not even all the clouds in the world could wholly extinguish.

"How are you?" Maggot asked.

Bran grinned foolishly, blood flowing from a long raw scrape on his cheek. "I'm alive," he cried. "And free! Let's run while we can!"

They scrambled up the pile of stones, through a cascade of water, and out of the gaping hole in the castle foundation. Maggot looked up and saw the rain pour off a broken section of the roof and fall straight down where their cell had been. A low spot by the wall had caught all the water running down the hillside too. Bran kicked up water as he ran through the remnants of the pool, heading downhill toward the river.

Maggot hurried after him.

"Where are we going?" he asked. He thought of the hills behind them, the shepherd's path into the wild country.

Bran stopped, turning to grip Maggot's arms. The air was so thick with rain it blurred the features of his face even at that short distance. "Into the city to see the Baron."

"Why? Let us go into the mountains."

"I'll go to the Baron and throw myself on his mercy. It's the Dance of Masks tonight. Between midnight and dawn, he'll take on the guise of Verlogh and dispense justice to all petitioners. I'll attend the dance, and go to him, and ask for his mercy, another chance to serve."

"But why? They mean to kill you. Come with me!"

Bran lifted his face into the rain. "This is the only life I have, friend Claye. If I cannot continue as I am, it has no meaning to me."

"I'll go with you, then," Maggot said.

"You don't need to do that. It would be better for you if you go to the mountains. If you climb between those hills—"

"No, I will go with you and will tell the Baron what I know, what I have seen." If Portia was not here because of Acrysy, he would leave and go back to the place where he had seen her last and find some way to talk to her. "And then I will follow my own path away from your stupid people."

"You've saved my life twice already! I beg you—"

Another man came slogging toward them, up the path that led to the damaged palace. Bran tensed. Maggot prepared to fight, but the stranger leaned into the rain, the hood of his cloak pulled down over his face, and hurried quickly by without a word or glance in their direction.

"We can't stand here," Bran said.

"I'm coming with you," Maggot answered.

Bran nodded and resumed his journey with Maggot beside him. The two men slipped, rose, fell again, sliding down the muddy slope toward the torrenting brown river. Across the water, behind the city wall, the steep-roofed houses and narrow streets looked abandoned. On the nearer bank, boats were pulled up high on the shore and there were no demons to be seen. Downstream, the bridge made a black scar across the gray skin of the day. Little figures rushed across it toward the city, stopping outside a guardhouse built atop the span.

Skidding to a stop, Bran looked up and down the river. "We have to cross. We could use one of those boats. The demons'll be buried in the mud, hiding from the currents and—"

"There's a bridge," Maggot said, pointing.

"It's guarded," Bran said. "They'll recognize us."

"In this rain, I can't tell you from my mother."

Bran lifted his head to the sky and laughed. "Yes, the Empress declares that all bridges must be guarded, so this one, under the Baron's own nose, stays guarded. But bridge guard is a dull duty saved for dullards. The bridge it is, then."

The mud squished in Maggot's toes as they followed the drowned road past some smaller buildings toward the bridge. "And if they do not let us pass?"

"If we fight, you take whoever I don't." He made his left hand into a fist. "Then we run like greycats into the city. Stay close to me."

"Fight, run, stay close."

"But just keep behind me, so that I'm between you and the guards. Don't meet their eyes."

Even on an ugly day like this, the bridge was a thing of amazing beauty. Its curving stone reminded Maggot of a wind-smoothed arch he had seen high in the mountains, only this had eleven broad arches instead and was wide enough for two mammuts to walk across abreast. A stone railing ran along both sides, and it widened slightly in the middle, above the central pier, to form two broad platforms that looked up and down the river.

As they stepped onto the bridge, Maggot heard the river surge and bellow underneath them though the stone stood still. A large pillar marked with carvings occupied the center of the bridge, between the two platforms. But just past this halfway point Bran broke into a jog, his head bent forward, arms folded over his head against the rain. Maggot scrunched down, copying the posture. He ran along behind Bran like a shadow if the guardhouse were the sun.

A soldier appeared in the doorway. "Who goes there?"

Bran slowed but didn't stop. One arm was draped across his face while the other flapped in the general direction of the river. "The new palace!"

"What about it?"

Maggot balled his fists.

"The north wall collapsed," Bran said. "Caved in!"

The soldier stepped out under the eaves to look at the massive shape that crouched on the hillside. "We heard that it was sagging—"

Any other words were lost as Bran kept on running across the bridge and into the city. He took a sharp left at the first street, turned right and went past several side streets along a curving road, then made several more turns in quick succession. Maggot ran at his heels, trying to orient himself to the city the way he would in the forest or the mountains—he thought they were headed somewhere with the golden-domed building and the river to their right, and the castle ahead.

Bran slowed down now, picking his way more carefully through a neighborhood of small houses, mostly constructed of logs, with tiny patches of grass or garden in front. The streets were chewed-up mud and sewage. Every step sucked at their bare feet, and the soupy mess oozed between Maggot's toes. They came to wider, straighter streets that didn't smell as bad, with stone houses, and then to a wider street again, with stone houses rising two and three stories high, where the streets were filled with large stones instead of mud, and lined with trees.

The trees comforted Maggot, who grew tenser the deeper they penetrated this strange maze. His eyes darted constantly around, as they had when he first left his mother's side and ventured into the forest in the daytime. Once or twice, he glimpsed people passing in the distance, along cross streets or at the side doors of houses. The drizzle became a dreary mist.

"It's somewhere around here," Bran murmured.

"What do we seek?" Maggot asked.

"We'll need costumes for the dance. I only know one man big enough to trade places with you, another knight. About your age, too. He might be willing to help me—he wasn't with Acrysy when we were captured. He lives near here. . . ."

The street ended in a large paved square, with a circular pool in the center, a small dun-domed building on one side, and an arched building shading a deep porch where small birds huddled in cages.

"He lives there!" Bran pointed across the square.

The second house in from the corner was a plain two-story stone building with wide steps leading up to a double door. The steps were framed by life-sized statues of collared hunting cats, one sitting upright, the other stretched out reclining.

"Just be careful of his pets," Bran said as he walked toward the steps.

⇥ CHAPTER 25 ⇤

Standing in front of the double doors, Bran loosened his shoulders, rubbed his hands over his arms, kicked his legs loose. "Be ready. Tubat's young and unpredictable."

"Un-pre-what?"

"I don't know in advance what will happen."

"We never do," Maggot answered.

Bran grinned. "We escaped Sebius's palace and crossed the bridge without a fight. Let's praise two gods."

He lifted a large brass knob shaped like the tongue in a lion's mouth and knocked it against the wood. When no one answered, he repeated the action. A moment later, the left-hand door cracked open.

A plain-looking woman peeked out. She had white hair and a face shaped like an onion. She took one second to look at the two men's faces, their clothes and feet.

"I'm sorry, but we're not at home," she said. Then she pulled her head back and slammed the door closed.

Bran was too quick, catching it before it latched. He pushed it open, saying, "It's perfectly all right, m'lady. Tubat is expecting me. It's about the dance tonight."

He slipped inside the door, and Maggot squeezed in behind him. The woman did not appear to believe Bran, but she didn't seem fearful either. Her wrists were crossed firmly at her waist. "I'll inform Tubat that you're here. Which lord sent you, again?"

"Forgive me for not saying so, I beg you three times, please forgive me. Servant Bran, here on behalf of Lord Claye." He bowed before her.

Her eyebrows, plucked into two tidy rows, lifted at the names. She studied Maggot's features. "Lord Claye would do well to provide boots to his servants, so they could remove them and not track mud into other people's houses. Tubat is with a guest, preparing for the masque. He said absolutely no interruptions, so he may choose not to see you."

"I understand. Tell him Bran, his servant, is here, please."

"Whose servant are you—Lord Claye's or Tubat's?" She turned around, her robes rustling along the floor of the narrow hallway. Her voice drifted back toward them. "Do not touch the furniture."

The door at the end of the hall creaked as she opened it and disappeared into another room. Maggot tried to take everything in—the floor laid out in square tiles forming a pattern, the closed doors on either side, the couch.

A voice boomed from the room down the hall. "Bran? That rascal! He serves no one but himself!"

The door swung wide open, and in strode a bare-chested bear of man, as tall as Maggot but wider. He wore a pair of loose pants, the color of chestnuts, and little green slippers on his feet with pointed toes sticking out in the front. A broad mustache drooped over his mouth and bristled along his cheeks, but his chin was naked. He carried a large ceramic cup, nearly a pitcher by the size of it, in one hand, and walked down the hall with his arms wide open. Maggot had the sense of having seen him before.

"Bran!" the man said. "Knew it was you as soon as I heard the name. No one would dare steal your good name, eh?"

The old woman followed him back into the hall and exited silently through one of the side doors. A golden cat with black spots thrust its head into the hall, then padded out after her. It was six feet long without the tail. Two more followed after it. They lingered in the hallway, bumping against each other. Maggot knew the man now from the camp beside the river.

"Greetings, Tubat, greetings," Bran was saying. "May luck and justice shine on our meeting."

Tubat approached his visitors, beaming a broad smile behind his mustache. "Lord Claye, huh? The clay on your feet!" He stopped short. "How are you?"

"Not so good."

He sipped from his cup. "You were never one to let the cold or wet get you down. But I heard you were dead."

"I should have been. The peasants captured me and Wys when they swarmed over the outpost in the middle of the night. Don't know if the guard was sleeping on duty or if they just happened to kill him, but they killed the rest of the men and took Wys and I back to their village for some fun."

Tubat's smile faded a bit as he looked at Bran's clenched hands. "We should have rooted them out of the mountains a long time ago. So I take it Wys didn't have as much fun with them as you did."

"No, I was lucky enough to miss the worst of it. The fire was burning at my feet when my friend here saved me. Walked right into the village, knocked the headman on his head, and cut me loose."

"And they let you walk out, just like that?"

Bran laughed. "Would you stand in his way? Does anyone ever stand in yours?"

Tubat sized Maggot up frankly, seriously, but spoke to Bran. "So Sebius set you both free instead of killing you?"

"She had a change of heart," Bran said without hesitation.

The biggest cat strolled curiously toward Maggot. It wore a bright red collar on its neck.

"Good!" Tubat said. He took another sip. "Name yourself, friend of Bran."

"Maggot." He watched the cat's approach.

"That's an odd name. Well, we're short of good men, good fighting men. Your friend looks young for a braid that long, Bran. Is he a knight, then? A renegade knight?"

"He's a lord of the trolls," Bran said. "He came down out of the mountains."

Tubat stared at Maggot. His mouth tightened slightly and his shoulders tensed; then he burst out laughing. "A troll?" He slapped his thigh loudly. "A troll! He could be one too!"

While he talked, the cat came up to Maggot with its mouth wide open, pink tongue lolling between yellow teeth. It sniffed him, then circled around behind him and rubbed up against his legs, rumbling in its throat. When he ignored it, the cat pressed its mouth against his hand, dragging its sharp teeth against his knuckles. Still Maggot didn't flinch.

Tubat watched all of this while he laughed. "He's got nerve too. A man's got to drink to that!" He slapped his leg again and drained his mug.

The cat leaned forward, stretching out its long front legs, and flopped on Maggot's feet. Its tail lashed up and down.

Bran cleared his throat. "We need your help, Tubat. I have to get into the dance tonight to see the Baron."

Tubat tugged at his mustache, his cheeks still red from laughing. "Didn't Sebius give you writs? Because your friend doesn't even need a costume—he can go as a troll! Hey, Crimey!" he called over his shoulder. "Come here, damn you! I've got a troll in the foyer!"

A second cat bounded down the hall to pounce on the first one's tail. When Maggot glanced at it, the big mug came flying straight at his head. He dodged, but it clipped his ear and shattered on the wall behind him. The cats leapt up and away as Tubat punched Bran in the chest.

"What the—?" Another man—Crimey—called from the doorway, knotting a rope that held his pants up, as the third cat jumped forward and stopped uncertainly.

"We've got ourselves a brace of traitors," Tubat shouted as he attacked Maggot.

Maggot knocked his forearms aside, lunging forward to drive his forehead into Tubat's face. Tubat staggered back, blood flying from his nose and lips, but he didn't fall.

One of the cats growled.

Maggot ignored it, grabbing Tubat's wrist. He yanked it straight and hammered his fist into the elbow. As the knight yelped in unexpected pain, Maggot kicked the legs out from under him and drove him into the floor.

Crimey skidded to a stop, just like the cat had. "The war god's crap." Bran tackled him and put him in a chokehold, bending one of his arms back at an awkward angle.

Tubat groaned and tried to rise, so Maggot grabbed a lock of his hair and slammed his head into the floor. The noise stopped, along with all movement.

One of the cats came over and sniffed at Crimey's face. "Attack," Crimey strained to say. "Kill, ki—"

"Quiet," Bran said, tightening his hold. "I warned Tubat about the cats. Told him they were way too independent, no matter how fast they run. He needs dogs."

Maggot stood up. The biggest cat watched him, laying back its ears and baring its teeth. Then it hissed at him. When Maggot made no move, the cat backed away.

Bran jerked Crimey to his feet and pushed him toward the door at the end of the hall. "Can you bring him along?" he asked Maggot, tipping his head at Tubat's unconscious form.

"If it's not too far." Maggot rolled the big man over on his back, picked up a bare foot—one of the slippers had fallen off—and dragged him down the hallway after Bran. The cats pounced after him, batting at the trailing braid.

Dropping the legs when he'd pulled Tubat through the door, Maggot thrust it closed before the cats could enter.

The high-ceilinged room was unlike anything he'd ever seen. The walls were tinted bright blue. Pillows of all sizes surrounded a large plush rug in the center of the floor. A shiny metal spiderlike object hung from the ceiling, with a flickering candle sticking upright from each foot. A short table, no higher than Maggot's knees, sat to one side with a large pitcher and several cups all like the one Tubat had thrown at Maggot's head. Two racks in the corner held clothes, one with the pattern of a greycat, another with a wolf's gray pelt. Masks of the two animals sat on another, higher table.

While Maggot gaped, Bran ripped a long cord from the curtains that covered the windows and bound Crimey's arms behind his back.

"Traitor," Crimey harangued him. "If you mean to kill me, get it done with now. And may Verlogh's ven—*murphhh, mrrmr!*"

Bran shoved a piece of cloth snatched up from the floor into the man's mouth to stop his talking. "Let the fact that I don't kill you prove that I'm no traitor." He flipped through the clothes on the floor, picking up a piece that had two shell-like circles connected by a web of strings. "There was at least one woman in here. Let's hope she's hiding in a closet somewhere. He's dead, is he?"

Maggot prodded Tubat's body. "No, he still breathes."

Bran touched his forehead, lips, and heart with three fingers. "The luck of the gods is with us then. Let's tie him up, and then block the doors so no one can get inside. Roll him over on his stomach, in case he pukes when he wakes up. They do that sometimes, and it would do us no good to have him die choking on his own vomit."

They made use of every cord, belt, and rope they could find in the room to bind Tubat up tightly and tie Crimey's feet as well as his hands. Tubat woke up gagging before they had fastened the doors. He bucked against his bounds at once. "You stinking peasant shepherd. Your father stuck his pizzle in a sheep and got you! You're a traitor. Sebius told us all about it. You can't get away with this, Bran! I'll kill you!"

"You had your chance," Bran said. "And you failed. I have my chance now, and I refrain. Remember that." He took the double-shelled cloth and shoved it into Tubat's mouth.

The big man spit it out again. "I'll kill you! And I'll kill your friend too!"

"Be silent before I change my mind." Bran held Tubat's head by the braid and thrust the cloth back into his mouth, using its own strings to bind it tightly behind his head.

When he was done, Bran took a deep drink from the pitcher, then offered it to Maggot. One sip burned his mouth and throat, and he recognized the fire water that Sinnglas had taught him to hate and avoid. Though thirsty, he declined the drink. "What do we do now?"

Bran walked over to the costumes. "We dress for the dance."

"I danced with Sinnglas's people," Maggot said.

Bran guzzled another drink from the pitcher. "When the Baron starts receiving petitioners, I'll go to see him. If I don't come back, then leave the party and the city."

They cleaned themselves and dressed in the costumes. The greycat outfit fell to Maggot, but it hung loose around his middle. The long tail was supported by a wire, buoyed into the air, and Maggot kept spinning to see what jumped behind him. Bran's costume fit better, but Maggot didn't know how to properly tie the knots that held it together, and Bran had to talk him through each one. He finally mastered it just as he ran out of knots.

Outside the door, the cats roared and scratched. Tubat and Crimey glared at them from the floor.

Maggot rested, glad to have dry clothes against his skin, while Bran paced around the room, turning pillows over.

"What do you seek?" Maggot asked.

"The paper writs that'll get us entrance into the castle. We might be able to bluff our way in without them, but it'll be harder. They might be in another part of the house."

Maggot helped him turn everything over with no success. Bran bent to ask the two tied-up men for information and thought better of it. Finally bored with looking, Maggot picked up the cat mask to put it on. Inside he noticed a pale leaf. "What's this?"

"That's it!" Bran said, pulling another from the second mask. "Ha ha! We're set." He rushed over to the curtain, pulled it aside, and peeked through the wooden slats of the shutters. The clouds still hung over a greenish sky, but no rain fell and a bit of sunlight stabbed through here and there as it began to set. Maggot heard people outside, walking in the streets, singing and laughing.

"As soon as it's dark we'll go," Bran said. He paced.

Maggot, used to waiting for the darkness, understood Bran's impatience. When it finally arrived, Bran pulled aside the window and pushed open the shutter.

"Wish me luck," he said to Tubat.

The big man screamed into his gag and strained against his bonds, kicking his feet against the pillows that surrounded him.

Bran helped Maggot put the mask over his face and then fastened on his own. He made that same gesture, with three fingers, touching between the wolf's eyes, the tip of its snout, and over his own heart. "The gods have been with us so far, my friend. Let's hope they continue to smile on us."

"And we will smile back at them," Maggot said.

Bran laughed. They climbed out the window into a little yard, pushed the shutter closed again, and let themselves out through the gate. Voices and laughter sounded from the houses, yards, and streets as they walked. Other people in costumes all moved in the same direction, weaving their way among the puddles. Stags, mammuts, and ringtails; greenbirds, redbirds, and jays; panthers, wolves, and hawks—it was as if all the creatures of the forest had turned into people and come down to occupy the city for a single night.

Maggot and Bran flowed with them toward the building that towered over all the other rooftops. They came to an open area before it where hundreds of costumed people milled about like bees at a hive. Small boys with brooms whisked the paving stones dry. Though dark outside, the courtyard of the castle blazoned light through an archway.

The light flickered on water—the castle stood like an island inside a narrow pond. The archway opened on a bridge beside a dagger-toothed lion carved in stone like the statues outside Tubat's house, but much larger than life. It stood as a lion did above its fallen prey, mouth open, roaring at the scavengers—

A striking woman dressed in orange and blue fabric feathered like a sparrowhawk paused at the light-filled gate. Recognition fluttered in the pit of Maggot's stomach.

The guard said something to her; then she passed across the wooden bridge and inside. A female servant followed after her, bearing a large bundle.

The sparrowhawk was Portia, Lady Eleuate, here after all.

⇥ CHAPTER 26 ⇤

M<i>aggot started toward the bridge.</i> He had nothing to give her to show his interest, but he would find something, anything. Words, if that was all he had.

Bran grabbed his arm. "Where are you going?"

"She's here, the woman, the only one!"

"What? Lady Eleuate is here?"

"Yes, her. She is a bird."

He took another step toward the gate, and again Bran's hand held him back. "It'll be better if we wait until the crowds are thicker. Let's not draw attention to ourselves yet."

Maggot pulled his arm free. "Is there any other way out of that house?"

"*Castle.* No, no one can leave except by that gate."

"It's a small cave that has no second hole to squeeze out of," Maggot said. "But I will wait here, by the bridge, watching until we go inside."

"We'll have to avoid those who know Tubat and Crimey well. Nod at anyone who speaks to you, but act as though you are talking to me and move on."

"Nod and move on," Maggot said. His head spun with the things he wanted to tell Portia. "And hope we do not have to fight."

A smile showed under the edge of Bran's mask. "Exactly."

They loitered at the fringe of the crowd. The cat mask covered all of Maggot's face except his mouth, with a flap in back that tucked inside his tunic. It limited his peripheral vision and the movement of his head, but he never let his eyes waver from the bridge. Portia did not come back out.

A horn blasted inside.

"That's the official signal for the feast to begin," Bran said. "The line will move along quickly now as the ordinary guests enter. Let's go."

As they came close, joining a crowd of others, Maggot saw that the lake was lined with stone and rimmed around the edge with a solid parapet. The torchlight mixed with the greenish glow of little demons swimming lazy circles. Long chains connected the wooden bridge to a little building that jutted out from the castle wall. A flag hung from the tooth-shaped roofline displayed a tan lion on a field of green with gold roping all around the edges. The sound of music and people's voices flowed from inside. As the people ahead of him in line pressed forward, Maggot stared over their shoulders into the castle yard, hoping for a glimpse of her.

"Writ please."

Maggot turned blankly toward the soldier—or rather knight, judging by his short braid. Bran elbowed him and pointed to the piece of paper now crumpled in his fist. Maggot passed it over.

"That's all right, Tubat," the knight said, smiling as he smoothed it out. "You're not the only one who's had a bit to drink beforehand. You'll need to leave your swords here. I know you're not one to cause trouble, but . . ."

Maggot started nodding, his head bobbing up and down. Bran handed over their weapons, then shoved him across the bridge and inside.

"Hey, Tubat!" the guard shouted.

Bran tensed, but Maggot turned back. "Yes?" His voice was muffled and changed by the mask.

"You're looking awful thin," the knight said, taking a writ from the next guest. "Better get to the banquet table before it's empty—there's not much there this year!"

Maggot waved to him, then proceeded inside with Bran.

The blue sky and sudden brightness disoriented him, as if the night were made day. After a moment he realized that the blue sky was a roof stretched over an immense courtyard—pieces of cloth in wide strips were run out on posts attached to the castle's stone walls. They spanned hundreds of feet from a low wall to a high one, the whole width of the vast yard. A series of torches, in equally placed holders around the perimeter, gave off more light than the sun on a cloudy day.

Maggot turned in a slow circle. A huge building formed one wall of the courtyard, rising three stories into the air, pierced by many windows and a balustraded balcony. The gatehouse wall formed a second side, with a series of smaller connected buildings on the third, and an arched walkway on the fourth. The space swarmed with costumed people, a more breathtaking sight than the city taken as a whole.

But Portia was nowhere to be seen.

"Stop gawking," Bran said. "If she is here, she's probably cloistered inside with Lady Culufre—"

"Which building?"

"We can't go inside. If she's really here, she'll come out at some point. I'll help you look for her." Bran pointed to a group of women wearing scarlet hoods over their heads, as they walked along a row of tables set out in front of the arches. "The priestesses have consecrated the feast. Let's get something to eat, while we can."

Uncostumed servants passed back and forth bringing platters of fresh food. The largest crowd gathered there, and Maggot found it unnerving to be jostled, grabbed, spoken to, ignored, and pushed aside in bewildering swiftness, each encounter coming quickly before he could respond to the last.

"Relax," Bran whispered at his ear. "Unknot your shoulders. And stop jumping."

"I do not like all these people," Maggot muttered. Someone bumped him, and he jabbed an elbow back. "All this pushing and shoving like wild dogs at a piece of carrion."

"Our apologies for that inadvertent jostle," Bran told the angry man rubbing his ribs. He dragged Maggot away. "Keep your mouth full of food. Nod at anyone who speaks to you. If we have to we'll move off."

Maggot had never seen so much food nor smelled such a variety of it: a whole roast bison, to judge from its shape, with a fussy man to carve it; other meats, carved and served at other tables; piles of vegetables, skewered on little sticks and baked; bowls of roasted garlic soaked in oils; green and orange melons, cut in thick sweet strips that made Maggot's mouth water.

All this and more was served onto a wooden platter that Bran had handed to Maggot. They reached an end table where a servant ladled a sweet plum water into ceramic cups for them. Maggot swallowed his in one gulp and held his cup out for more, but Bran pushed him on.

"Don't drink it that fast," Bran said. "We need to keep some wits about us yet. And keep your head down."

"But I don't see her."

"What kind of bird was she?"

Maggot didn't know the word for *sparrowhawk* in Bran's tongue or Sinnglas's—the trolls had no name for it either, since it wasn't nocturnal—so he held his hand in front of his face. "One about this tall," he said, flustered and feeling a little light-headed. "Smells good."

"I'll be sure to keep my nose open."

They paced and ate and drank and waited. The waiting came hardest because it was not the calm waiting Maggot knew when hunting or stalking. This waiting took place amid a riot of distractions. Men played stringed instruments and blew on reeds, making sounds like birds or flowing water, only more entrancing. People clapped along. In the central space, groups formed patterns to the rhythm of the music, opening and closing like the buds of flowers. A man tossed balls in circles through the air, then flaming torches. Another walked on legs as long as a mammut was tall.

Maggot turned his head at every hint of blue or orange, but he didn't see her again. The more people drank the louder they clamored, until the din made him ache. The more he saw, the less human, the more grotesque, the people became. Those dressed as deer, who should have been graceful and fleet, stumbled and staggered under their false horns as if they'd been arrow struck. A man dressed as a stately mammut hopped about like a rabbit squealing. He and Bran stayed constantly on the edges, in the dark, where men and women ducked into niches in the wall or behind columns, bending their faces to one another. A rabbit reached between a bull's legs, parted the gray folds of her skirt, and moaned as she shoved him inside her. But nowhere in the chaos of noise and color did Maggot see his sparrowhawk.

"Do you see him?" Bran asked.

"Who?" Maggot said, and followed Bran's nod.

Someone dressed as a fox—sleek, slender, and deadly—stalked the two of them.

"It is wrong," Maggot said. "A fox would never dare to hunt either a greycat or a wolf."

"It may be wrong for other reasons," Bran muttered as he moved away. "I'm going to try to lose him."

Wolves and tawny panthers roamed in packs, and a group of the former had gathered by the kegs of drink, where they began to howl, a pitiful sound.

"Stay with me," Maggot said. "There are too many wolves about, and I might mistake someone else for you."

"You can distinguish me from them easily enough," Bran replied, smiling under the lip of his mask. Cupping his hands to his mouth, he howled. It set the hackles up on Maggot's neck.

The wolves lifted their heads and called out the names of Crimey and Tubat.

"That was a mistake," Bran said. "Everyone recognizes Tubat for his size." He answered the others with some quick clowning, then ducked behind some of the serving tables and, with Maggot at his heels, retreated to some shadows cast by a jutting buttress in a stone tower.

"I don't see her anywhere," Maggot said as they lingered in the shadows.

"She may not be here," Bran replied. He rubbed his neck. "We can't continue this dodge much longer. The Baron should hear petitions soon, though."

The noise and bustle had reached a new peak when everything fell silent: the musicians first, and the uncostumed servants, then the crowd. A great shushing was followed by a hush.

Bran pointed up.

Maggot didn't need to follow Bran's outstretched arm—the tug in his chest had already pulled his attention to the balcony of the big building, where a woman and a man dressed as lioness and lion looked over the crowd. They wore golden masks that blazed in the torchlight. Green and blue gemstones caught the light and glittered. Polished ivory dagger teeth gleamed at their jaws. Other people milled in the room behind them. Maggot glimpsed blue, perhaps orange. The tug was Portia.

"Who's that?" he asked.

"The Baroness and Baron."

"No, those women behind them." If that's where Portia was, he'd find a way to reach her.

"The dove on the left is the Baron's lover," Bran answered, leaning his head from side to side to see them. "The bird on the right is the Baroness's lover. They bring them out for show every year at the dance, trying to outdo one another. The Baron is bored with his, or was."

A slight wind lifted the tented roof in the silence and snapped it back down, producing a collective "Ah!" that rose like a supplication into the night.

The Baron waved to the crowd, and they all cheered, some clapping their hands, others snapping their fingers. The Baroness stood formally, right hand at her waist, left arm extended, then motioned for them to continue. Cheers followed the pair as they withdrew inside and closed the curtains. The musicians commenced a slower, grander piece of music.

Bran squeezed Maggot's elbow. "That's the sign that the open court should soon begin. I'm going over to the main gate, to see how they're letting people enter. Stay right here and I'll be back in a moment."

Maggot watched him go, scanning the crowd around him for any sign of Portia. He did not, in the general noise, with the limited vision caused by his mask, notice the person sneaking up behind him until she spoke.

"Alone, at last."

He spun. It was her. The shape of her mouth held a tight smile beneath the sharp curve of the beak. Words twirled in his head like leaves spiraling in the wind.

"Uh," he said.

She laughed at him. "So now it's my turn to surprise you. It is you, isn't it? No one else could move like that. One would almost swear that you are a greycat, the way you glide from place to place."

He found it very hard to breathe.

"Come on, say something. I know you're not mute. I've seen you talking all night long to Bran. He's unmistakable in that horrible ill-fitting wolf's costume."

He wanted to tell her that what he felt for her was so vast it reduced all the mountains of the world to a single pebble small enough to swallow, that he would cast the world into the sun and let it burn if she requested it, that he would descend the deepest cave and return with everlasting darkness for her if she desired that comfort.

He sniffled, tried to wipe his nose, and bumped his mask off center. "You smell good."

Her eyes twinkled like the sapphires on her mask. "And you no longer stink like a wild beast, the way you did when first we met."

With his heart pounding in his ears, he pushed back his mask, took her shoulders in his hands, and pressed his mouth against hers, the way he'd seen others do. Her golden beak was sharpened to a point that raked across his jaw, drawing blood.

She pulled away and he let go. He feared, for a heartbeat, that he'd done something wrong, but she smiled as she wiped her lips lightly with the back of her hand.

"Well," she said. "That's another small improvement over our first encounter. Speak quickly, and I may let this affront pass unnoticed."

Language fell away from him like bark off a dead tree. The mask, loose on his head, slipped back down over his face. "I do not know how to say what I want to say."

"Oh, I think you've said it pretty clearly. Twice now. But come, let's do this properly." She straightened herself. "Name yourself, sir, then name your favor."

"Maggot," he blurted. Then, remembering, "Claye."

"Mhaghat?" she said. "A mysterious name, for a mysterious man. And Claye, as clay is simple, although I would not call you a simpleton. Not quite. My name is Portia. What can I do for you, sir?"

"Come," he said, holding out his hand for hers. *Come stay with me forever*, is what he wanted to say. "Be with me."

She slapped his knuckles. "I think not. You'll have to show better manners—and more imagination—than that."

He pulled his hand back. "Ever since I saw you, nothing mattered more to me than pleasing you."

The smile faded from her eyes, the amusement from her voice. "Did it now? And the best you could do to show it was wave your tail in my face?"

He dropped his head. "When I saw that you hunted a lion, I brought it to you," he said softly. "I can do no more until I know what else you want."

"Ah, you are much too serious for me," she answered. "And I came to the dance seeking amusement and diversion." She waved to someone behind him, and Maggot saw her servant hurry away.

"I—" he said.

"I cast divination bones a thousand times," she said quickly, "after that first day when I saw you in my tent, and a thousand times I asked them the same question: would I see you again? A thousand times the answer was yes. And so I've contrived ever since to return to that valley and search for you, but war and all the plots of men confounded me. And here you are, where I never once expected you."

"So you *will* go with me?"

She closed her feathered wings about her and lifted her beak at the balcony above. "Did you see the Baroness?"

"Yes," Maggot said, not turning to look away lest she disappear again.

"The Empress in her wisdom has decided that this province must be unified under a single title. I am the vessel into which it will be poured. In time, I shall be the one to stand at that ledge, and welcome the people of the city into my home. My consort will roam the length of the land, gathering riches to distribute."

Maggot put his hand to chest. "Your consort? That is your mate? I could be him."

She moved her head slowly from side to side. "That is for the Empress to decide, and she has chosen already for me the Baroness's son."

Blood from the cut on his cheek dripped onto his hand, leaving a crimson streak across his palm. "You cannot choose for yourself?"

"I cannot."

He reached out to touch her. "That is wrong. You should be able to choose your own way."

"It is how it is. Be glad you're not Acrysy. He has fewer choices, less freedom. It has twisted him." The servant returned with the bundle Maggot had seen her carry in. "Here. I brought this as a gift for the Baron. I was going to present it to him during the reception. Better that I return it to you."

She reached up, removing his mask. She handed it to her servant and took the bundle in exchange. It was the lion's skin, cured and lined with pine-green silk. The eyes had been replaced with amber gems, and the gold clasp at the neck was adorned by a single shining emerald. She draped it over his shoulders, fastened the clasp, then lifted the hollowed skull and fitted it over his head like a helmet. The great teeth curved down, framing either side of his face.

"It suits you well," she said, her voice as soft as the touch of her fingertips as they lingered on his chin.

Maggot slowly raised his hand, gently pushed back her mask, and bent to kiss her again. This time neither one of them stopped for a long time, not until he was breathless and pulled away because he wanted it to continue forever or end at once.

Her eyes were still closed, her lips parted, when the catcalls of the crowd fell on them. She blushed and tugged the sparrowhawk's fiercer visage over her face.

"Come with me," he pleaded.

"I cannot."

"Will I see you again?"

She took a step backward, away from him. "Ask the divination bones yourself."

Like so many other things, he did not even know what they were.

He started to follow her when he heard another commotion, men shouting at one another, and then, rising above it, Bran's voice— Maggot twisted at the sound. When he turned back, his sparrowhawk had flown.

Looking one way and another, seeing no sign of her, he heard Bran's angry voice again, and throwing his hands in the air in despair, he turned to help his friend.

He knocked men and women aside in his rush through the crowd until he reached an open space outside the castle's door. Bran's arms were pinioned by two guards. His mask was off, and so was the fox's, standing in front of him.

Acrysy. He held Bran by the throat.

⟞ CHAPTER 27 ⟝

Maggot *rushed toward Acrysy* as fast as wildfire sweeping down a hillside, grabbed the scruff of his neck, and shook him like grasses in a flame.

"Demons!" one of the knights exclaimed, letting go of Bran to draw his sword. Maggot picked Acrysy up and threw him at the man, and both went down in a heap. Bran twisted, drawing the other knight's sword and shoving him down all in one smooth motion. He looked at Maggot's robe and blinked.

Then he shouted, "Let's run!"

"Yes, yes, yes!" Maggot wanted to run, just as he had the first time he'd fled Portia. If he ran far enough or fast enough, he might outrun the pain that stabbed at his heart.

Bran swung his sword to scatter the birds and beasts before them. They had rounded the castle wall on their way to the gatehouse bridge when Bran stutter-stepped to a stop and Maggot ran into him.

Tubat and Crimey, dressed in armor with weapons drawn, were

held at bay by the bridge guards. Tubat's cry of "He's inside, I tell you—" changed suddenly to "There he is!"

When the guards turned to look, Tubat charged past them.

Tubat swung his weapon and Bran counterattacked. They came together in a single clash of iron, and then fell back a step like two bucks after butting horns.

"We should have cut your braid off long ago," Tubat said. His face was bruised, his lips swollen.

Bran laughed at him. "Remember the time when Lord Terrere's men attacked us in the middle of the night and you pissed yourself like a baby?"

Tubat roared and swung his sword again, but Bran deflected the blow and countered with a strike at Tubat's neck. The big man parried, and the sword skipped off his armored shoulder.

Crimey and the bridge guards spread out at Tubat's rear, while Acrysy and his two men circled behind Bran and Maggot. Maggot dashed between the men, but toward the wall and not the bridge. Using his momentum, he ran up the stones and jumped for the bracket that held the oil-soaked flaming torch. He caught the metal holder just like he would a branch, hung there while he removed the blazing brand, then dropped to the ground.

Blood streamed down Bran's left arm, but he attacked the bigger man relentlessly, with one two-handed strike after another. Then Maggot had no chance to notice anything as he thrust the torch at the men attacking Bran's back. When Crimey rallied them, Maggot used his long arm and quick wrist to dash the flames in the other man's face. He screamed, and flailed backward, dropping his sword. Maggot snatched it up and bellowed troll-like in his rage, torch in one hand and sword in the other.

The attackers all paused at the sound of this, and Tubat's shout of triumph dropped into this silence like a stone. Maggot turned. Bran lay on the ground, disarmed, stunned perhaps, and Tubat had his sword drawn back to strike.

Maggot leapt, hurling the torch at Tubat's chest. The big knight howled in shock, knocking it away in a shower of sparks, and Maggot attacked, striking hard and fast.

Tubat reeled, backstepping, but parrying so hard the steel vibrated in Maggot's hand. Then he dodged a second blow and lunged forward, swinging his sword at Maggot's head. Maggot twisted away, but the blade clipped the lion's skull and staggered him. When Tubat reversed the arc of his weapon to strike again, Maggot tackled him. The knight bounced off the flagstones, grunting under Maggot's weight. His hand rebounded off the pavement, and his sword flew loose.

Maggot still held onto his weapon.

Despite the knight's fists fastened on his costume, Maggot shifted his feet to the ground and levered himself into a crouch. Then, grabbing the knight's braid, he flipped his head against the ground. Blood splattered, and possibly teeth.

Tubat pawed at him feebly as Maggot used the braid to jerk the knight to his knees. He pulled back his sword to slice through his enemy's neck.

And stopped before he swung.

There was an unexpected silence all around him except for the burned man, Crimey, screaming somewhere beyond the wall of masks. Maggot looked up.

A golden lion stepped out of the crowd: Baron Culufre, not ten feet away. He wore a shirt of golden scales beneath a long robe of lion's fur lined with emerald green. His mask of burnished gold outshone the sun, ivory teeth polished to unblemished white. His arms crossed his chest. Thick gold bands shackled his wrists.

A group of armed men, knights, formed a semicircle behind the Baron—Sebius was there, as was Acrysy and his men, but they seemed entirely superfluous, like young lions left outside the pride. A sword was belted at the Baron's side. He stood like a man used to wielding it.

"Please continue," Culufre said. His mellifluous voice sounded like it came more from the sky than from any man. "You may kill him if you like."

Maggot straightened, tossing down the limp head as he would an apple core or empty shell. The fire of his anger had burned clean away, the fuel that fed it exhausted, and he felt no more. He dropped the sword and let it clatter on the stones. "There is more to the world than stupid killing."

The Baron tilted his head back and laughed. When he stopped to speak again, his voice was as solid as stone. "You know, don't you, that only the consort of the Baroness may wear the Baron's sigil?"

He meant the dagger-toothed lion.

It hurt Maggot to wear it, because it reminded him of Portia. He unfastened the gold chain at his neck and slipped the mantle from his shoulders. He extended his hand, offering it to Culufre. "It was given to me, but it was intended for you. Let it go where it belongs."

The Baron lifted a hand to his chin, as if considering the offer, then made the smallest motion with but one finger. A man hurried forward to take the lion's cape. With his hand resting once more below his mouth, Culufre said, "Name yourself not, but request a favor and I shall grant it."

There was a small, excited buzz among the gathered crowd.

Maggot did not know what to ask for.

"If you request to leave here safely," the Baron suggested, "I shall have you escorted to the edge of my lady's realm. Or anywhere else within the empire that you may wish to go."

Maggot considered this. "I came here with my friend, Bran, because he wished to speak to you. I ask only that you listen to him."

The Baron rolled his tongue around his mouth as if savoring the taste of this. "Come then, Bran. I've seen you. Your friend has just traded his life to let you speak."

The two knights holding Bran thrust him forward. As soon as they let go, he dropped to his knees at the Baron's feet and touched his forehead to the ground.

"Rise," Culufre said. "I expect no knight of mine to come to me bent and bare-necked."

Bran remained where he was, face down. "I no longer wear the braid. Naked the peasants placed me in the flames to kill me, and naked I was carried out again, a new man. I ask to come again into your service, as a lowly shepherd if it suits you, fit only to work among untutored boys until I prove myself worthy of your trust."

"I advise against it," Sebius said, his high voice wavering. "This man is a traitor. He betrayed us once, and meant to betray us here tonight."

"I think not," Culufre answered. "Captain Bran was alleged a traitor only because he could not make a young woman love a foolish boy several years her junior." Acrysy started to protest, but the Baron swung his hand up in a slapping gesture. The woman in the dove costume standing behind him made a small movement with her hand, as if stroking his shoulder from a distance, and then he said, more softly, "Silence, boy."

"If you will but listen," Sebius said, "you will find that your progeny, the only son of your dear lady, and heir through her to your titles—most glorious and munificent Baron, Lord Culufre, Lion of the Eastern Mountains, Emerald of the Empire, dear brother—has a valid point."

"Enough. You, Sebius, heard this man speak. This is not Captain Bran, the knight who once served us, but a peasant with shorn head who seeks to serve us now." He paused, a smile spreading slowly across his exposed mouth. "A shepherd in wolf's clothing, if you will."

A light laughter rippled through the crowd, like the patter of raindrops on leaves.

"My brother—"

"He will be entered into the household staff, where he can be watched constantly by those most loyal to me for any sign of treason. In time, if he proves himself, we may request of the Empress the opportunity for him to become a eunuch. He was trained once by one that is well regarded. This is my judgment, may Verlogh take vengeance on me alone if it proves wrong."

At these words, Sebius dropped his head. "Yes, my lord."

"Rise, Bran. And welcome into my service."

Bran climbed to his feet, keeping his head bowed. "My lord is both merciful and just."

"However could I be both?" Culufre asked. "It is better by far that I am strong. Do not lie to me again if you wish to rise in my service." He hesitated, staring at Maggot with a puzzled expression.

Maggot suddenly felt someone moving toward him, as if a long tether rounding his chest, years slack except for the slightest tugs, were now drawn perfectly tight.

He turned his head expecting—hoping—to see Portia.

The crowd parted at the passage of a lioness, as glorious and extravagant in her costume as the Baron, flanked by women as the Baron was by knights. The Baroness.

The lioness's golden, silver-whiskered visage concealed her face, but her chin trembled. A small, blue velvet bag hung from a chain about her neck. She clutched it tightly in one white-knuckled fist and pointed her other shaking hand at Maggot.

"It's him," she said, her voice quaking.

Culufre stepped quickly to her side, took her left hand, and stroked it gently. "There, my dear, my sweet, Elysse. What is it that makes you overwrought?"

"It's *him*." Her eyes stayed fixed on Maggot's face. "After all these years. His appearance is exactly like his father's."

Maggot leaned back, trying to break the pull of that invisible tether.

"Really?" Culufre was saying. "I rather thought, just a moment ago, that he favored you."

"This is no jape, my lord consort. I was bonded to the nursemaid and my baby while I was pregnant, and I have always felt the tug of that lost boy."

His voice went soft. "And we severed that bond to save your life when child and nursemaid perished in the fire—"

She yanked her hand away from him. Slipping the tiny velvet bag off her neck, she thrust it out blindly. "Fetch me my wizard. He can tell me the truth."

Several women departed, returning to the castle.

At this distance, the velvet had no scent for Maggot, but he did not like the smell of things. His teeth were on edge.

"Elysse," Culufre said soothingly.

She elevated her chin toward the prize at the end of her arm. "This contains the cord that bound him to me and a piece of the meat that fed him in the womb—the wizard may use it to prove that this is my son." Her eyes blazed at Maggot, and her voice dropped very low. "I always knew that you still lived."

"My mother was a troll," Maggot told her.

Someone in the crowd stifled a snicker.

"Don't speak such wicked things," the Baroness said.

"She was a very good mother." Maggot turned his head, scanning the crowd of dumb, bedraggled creatures. His sparrowhawk was not among them. He looked at his own greycat costume, pulling it off to pile at his feet. "She fed me and kept me warm, and would be ashamed at all this stupidness."

The women returned with a clean-shaven man whose blue-black robes were embroidered with stars in silver thread. Maggot saw his head surrounded by a sandy light flecked with streaks of umber, just as Banya's had been.

He faltered at the sight of Maggot. "M'lady summoned me."

A small group had followed the wizard from the castle. Portia was among them, her mask settled firmly over her face, her winged robes folded closed about her. At the sight of her, the other faces that encircled Maggot—Bran's patient relief, Tubat's dazed and bloody anger, the wizard's anxious lean forward—all faded like the stars at dawn.

Before the Baroness could answer the wizard, Culufre raised his hand. When he spoke, a strain ran through his beautifully timbred voice like a crack in a tree. "Consider the wisdom of this, Elysse. If the answer is no, it will be no forever."

She took a short step back.

Culufre wheeled toward Maggot. "Stay. Stay and serve me, as your friend Bran does. We will give you a place in the castle, the use of all the wealth that you desire."

Maggot laughed at him—a deep, resonant belly rumble—and at that sound the tug in his chest vanished. "You offer me a small thing. The mountain ranges are the walls of my castle, and all the riches of the trees and rivers are mine. You offer me an acorn when I already have an oak."

"Stay," the Baroness echoed, pale fingers at her throat.

But Maggot watched Portia, waiting for her to step forward, to speak, to show any indication that she had changed her decision toward him.

"You gave your first gift to Bran," Culufre said. "Now I give you a second. There will not be a third. What offer would you like? Request any favor and I shall grant it." His sword rattled in its scabbard as he placed his palm upon the pommel.

Portia glided backward, her head bowed, arms crossing her chest to grip her feathered shoulders.

"It is not yours to give," Maggot answered. "I would have this be a place where people choose their own paths, and not take those forced upon them. And it will never be."

He turned away. The people in their masks and the soldiers and servants parted before him, as Lady Culufre's plaintive cry rose behind.

"My poor baby, oh my poor, lost baby."

He left the false day of the castle and crossed the bridge into a comforting, uncertain darkness where all trails were his to choose.

✦ ACKNOWLEDGMENTS ✦

I *don't know about other writers,* but getting my first novel published feels like the work of a community because I simply could not have done it alone. I have many people to thank. Gordon Van Gelder, editor of *Fantasy & Science Fiction* (www.fsfmag.com), and John O'Neill, editor of *Black Gate* (www.blackgate.com), published sections of this novel in their magazines. Members of the Online Writing Workshop for Science Fiction, Fantasy, and Horror (http://sff .onlinewritingworkshop.com), the Sock Monkey Parade, and the 2003 Blue Heaven novel writing retreat gave me critiques that made this a much better book. Julia Hessler, S. K. S. Perry, Lisa Deguchi, and Catherine M. Morrison provided essential encouragement and support during different drafts. Marsha Sisolak caught more errors in more versions than anyone else. Deanna Hoak, my copyeditor, corrected many of the errors that remained. Robert Sinclair contributed useful insights into large primate behaviors early on. John Joseph Adams read new additions critically at the very end. Emily Buckell persuaded me that

The Prodigal Troll was, indeed, the right title. Paul and Leann Ulrich graciously contributed a weekend retreat where I could make my final revisions uninterrupted. Thank you, all.

Anyone up for the next book?

Charles Coleman Finlay's short stories have appeared frequently in the *Magazine of Fantasy & Science Fiction* since 2001. In 2003, he was a finalist for the Hugo, Nebula, Sidewise, and John W. Campbell Awards. His stories have been reprinted in the *Year's Best Science Fiction*, the *Year's Best Fantasy*, and the *Mammoth Book of Best New Horror*, and *Wild Things*, his first short fiction collection, will be released later this year. He lives in Columbus, Ohio, with his two children. You can visit his Web site at www.ccfinlay.com.